LOLCRAFT

LOLCRAFT

A COMPENDIUM OF ELDRITCH HUMOR

MICHAEL CIESLAK

Dragon's Roost Press

Printed in the United States of America

Ingram ISBN: 978-1-956824-42-1

Print ISBN 978-1-956824-05-6

Digital ISBN 978-1-956824-06-3

Dragon's Roost Press

207 Gardendale

Ferndale, MI 48220

thedragonsroost.biz

CONTENTS

Introduction   xi

LOVECRAFT IT OR LIST IT   1
Sarah Hans

KING C   17
Nathan Carson

REPORT TO THE CEG AND EXECUTIVE
BOARD V1.0   21
J. Edwin Buja

TARTS, PIE, TEA   33
John Possidente

THE CHATEAU OVER INNSMOUTH   41
John Kiste

THE READING   53
James Dorr

HERE THERE BE (HARDLY ANY) MONSTERS   61
Nathan Waddell

DEAR XUTUIX?!   71
J.D. Harlock

HOW THE OLD ONES SAVED CHRISTMAS   77
Richard S. Crawford

BOKRUG AND THE BOY   93
Liam Hogan

TEN THOUSAND YEARS IN SPACE WITH SANTA   101
Jason P. Burnham

NOT ON MY WATCH   103
Henry Herz

IN THE GRIP OF COSMIC CONCUPISCENCE   121
Jonathan Louis Duckworth and Eric Raglin

HASHTAG TPE   131
Dawn Vogel

OVER THE SIDE   143
Sharon Diane King

CONSIDER THE SHOGGOTH   145
Nick Bowen

ARKHAM BOARD OF HEALTH FEEDBACK ON
MISKATONIC UNIVERSITY'S DRAFT PLAN FOR
A SAFE CAMPUS REOPENING   161
Ron Fein

BHEGNA CTHELLHA'S GUIDELINES ON
PANDEMIC ETIQUETTE WHILST DINING OUT   163
Brandon Ketchum

A SERIES OF NOISE COMPLAINTS, FILED BY
YOG-SOTHOTH, OUTER GOD, AGAINST HIS
NEIGHBOR   169
Nicholas Jay

WHAT ARE THE ODDS   183
Mia Dalia

LOVECRAFT VS. THE BIG-MOUTH MUSKY OF
LAKE MISKATONIC   199
Lena Ng

THE LADY WITH THE LOOK   203
Shaenon K. Garrity

FAMILY VALUES   219
Phillip T. Stephens

WANTED AD   231
Elizabeth Davis

THE KING IN GRAY   237
Alice Loweecey

THE HAPPIEST PLACE ON EARTH   255
Fraser Sherman

ELDRITCH ABOMINATIONS IN MODERN-DAY
AMERICA: A DOCUMENTARY   261
Lucas Franki

BELL BIV DERAILED   275
B. Zelkovich

HE LISTENS   281
Justin Short

THE WORLD ENDS AT THE WORLD'S END   295
Larry Hinkle

NEW YOU   305
Meg Candelaria

WHAT HORROR   315
Rick Danforth

CUT-RATE COUPLES WEEKEND AT THE WITCH
HOUSE INNE AND TAVERN (9 REVIEWS)   329
Stewart C Baker

MY AUNTS AND THE CORNWALL HORROR   339
K.G. Anderson

BLOOD MOON BARGAINS   355
Kyer Kneifel

A MUNDANE ENCOUNTER WITH A CIVILIZED
GOD   365
Samuel Marzioli

Acknowledgments   373
About the Authors   377
Dragon's Roost Press   389
Last Day Dog Rescue   391

INTRODUCTION

Six years ago we channeled our love of the Cthulhu Mythos into our second published anthology: *Eldritch Embraces: Putting the Love Back in Lovecraft.* Since then, despite building a catalog of 25 titles (with more coming soon), people have been clamoring for more. Who are we to deny what the public wants?

We decided that this time we were going to look for stories that blend the weird humor of the Lovecraftian Mythos with humor. We've collected 36 short stories, almost 100,000 words of fiction that will terrify and amuse you at the same time.

It's been said the horror and humor are two sides of the same coin. Both build tension and expectation which is then released in an explosive way — either a laugh of a scream. There is an entire sub-genre of comedic horror which features some of the classic, most re-watchable films.

Besides, after the last couple of years, don't you deserve some nice stress relieving laughter?

All right, this one may be a bit more of a stretch. Stories featuring Cthulhu and his friends (which sounds like it should have been a cartoon in the 80s) tend towards the nihilistic everybody-dies-or-goes-mad end of the spectrum. But, as noted above, when the world is falling apart, you need a little humor. Besides, we've already done Mythos and Romance—Humor doesn't seem all that weird (pardon the pun) compared to that.

We weren't sure what we would get when we put out the call for submissions. What we got was an avalanche of amazing, humorous stories. We laughed, we shuddered, in a couple of cases we got up and turned the lights on. It was a difficult task, but we managed to whittle the stories down to the 36 collected here. We hope you enjoy them as much as we did.

Remember, a portion of the proceeds of each sale of this anthology benefits the Last Day Dog Rescue Organization. Check the back matter for more details on this wonderful organization.

LOVECRAFT IT OR LIST IT

SARAH HANS

Vinni swept her hair out of her eyes, lifted her chin, softened her expression, and swept through the front door in her customary manner. The camera and boom operators swung expertly out of her way as she moved, performing a dance they had executed a hundred times before. The house she entered was unremarkable, and she had a few seconds to wonder whether this was her opinion of the house because she had seen so many similar unremarkable houses or whether it was because she'd seen so many remarkable ones. Then her producer, Brick, whispered the name on her birth certificate—*Lavinia*—and made a rolling gesture with his hands. Her eyes focused again on the bland white walls, the terribly ordinary family photos, and the furniture so modern and sleek it was only notable for its lack of character.

"This house feels…" she groped for the word Brick had suggested before filming began. She'd used "ethereal" last week for a house draped in sparkling, gooey webs and "unearthly" the week before in a home where the walls were infested with tiny, buzzing interplanar mites. Her mind was a blank where the word to describe this house was supposed to be.

Brick mouthed something that looked like "sailboat." Vinni frowned at him and did her best with, "strange and sini—"

She was cut off by a sound, earth-trembling and ear-splitting, like a scream and a roar and a trainwreck all rolled into one. Vinni's hands clapped over her ears and she hit the floor, remembering in an instant of visceral clarity the Whipple house and the terrors that had driven her from it. Her heart pounded, and she struggled to hold her bladder. She tried to crawl back out the front door, but the floor was bucking and trembling so violently she could barely crawl a few inches across the foyer.

When the thunderous roar finally stopped, a human scream sounded thin and tinny by comparison. The boom operator, Wyatt, had ripped his headphones from his head and was now clutching and scratching at his ears like a mental patient in a black and white movie having a nervous breakdown. Bellowing, he ran for the front door, and Vinni barely managed to scoot out of the way of his stomping boots.

The sound of his scream faded as he ran away from the house. Vinni pulled herself to her feet, smoothing her skirt with trembling fingers, and moved for the door. She loved this job, but she'd walk off the production if there was a chance she might return to the madness that sent her to the hospital for weeks after the Whipple house.

Brick, catching his breath, turned to the cameraman with eyes wide. "DeAndre, did you get all that?"

DeAndre looked down at his camera, as if he'd forgotten he held it, and frowned. "I guess so."

"Great," Brick said, pumping his fist in a victory gesture. Vinni bit back a sharp retort. Brick was about as stereotypical as they came for a television show producer: a middle-aged white guy with aspirations of wealth and fame. His conservative haircut, polo shirt, and designer jeans screamed "wannabe." Even his name, Brick Johnson, made it sound like he was pressed from a mold in a factory that made mediocre, entitled white men. Vinni missed the show's original producer, Abby Prinn, who had been more of a creative, free-spirited type. Abby had retired after the first few seasons were so successful, and was resting on her laurels on a beach somewhere. Just then, Vinni wished to join her.

Outside, there were sounds of a struggle as the medical team tackled Wyatt and tried to get him into the trailer. DeAndre touched Vinni's elbow solicitously, asking without words whether she was alright. She sighed, and they exchanged a long, weary look, full of resignation. *Here we go again.*

The stench hit them, then. Brick started gagging. Vinni opened her mouth to ask if DeAndre was okay, and found herself choking on a powerful miasma, a stink like rotten eggs and decaying roadkill and a burning sensation at the back of her throat. It reminded her of the time a shoggoth had crawled into the dumpster outside her college dorm, gorged itself on trash, and died choking on a snack cake wrapper, discovered days later when the wretched stink of its decaying corpse had infested the whole campus.

Tears sprang to her eyes again and she rushed to the door and out into the yard, followed closely by her cameraman and producer. The reek seemed to follow them. Vinni was standing in the street before she found relief.

She sucked in a few deep breaths of clean air and turned to Brick, gasping beside her. "What the hell, Brick?"

He shrugged and grinned. "I told you this house was special. Our ratings are gonna be sky-high." He clapped his hands together gleefully.

Sunand, the show's real estate agent, strolled over to Vinni, smiling broadly. Tall, lantern-jawed, with striking amber eyes and velvety brown skin, Sunand moved with the easy confidence of a man who has never met a challenge his good looks and charisma couldn't overcome. He wore a gray suit tailored so impeccably Vinni could see his muscles moving under the fabric and a pair of Italian loafers that probably cost more than this house. Vinni was usually torn between wanting to lick

Sunand's entire body and also punch him in his smug face. It was very confusing.

"Looks like you already lost your boom operator," he drawled in a baritone both sexy and infuriating. "Maybe it's time to go ahead and admit defeat on this one."

Vinni scowled at him. Her entire life, she'd been a laid-back person, the kind who found little value in competition, but her simultaneous attraction and repulsion to her competitor made her deeply competitive where Sunand was concerned. This was just another house, she told herself, only...smellier. She'd just need a lot of potpourri.

"Never," she told Sunand.

His dark eyes twinkled, and she knew the challenge had been accepted.

The homeowners, Charles and Miranda Ward, reminded Vinni painfully of her grandparents. They had bought their house as a starter home when they were young, expecting to upgrade as they had children and needed more space. But that, of course, was a plan for the World Before, and things hadn't worked out the way they planned, just as they hadn't for anyone else. When the Drowned Gods emerged from the ocean and the Elder Things descended from the stars, half the world's property became unlivable. In the World After, the Wards had one child remaining, Dexter, an adult who still lived with them in his tiny childhood bedroom. Vinni flinched at this information, hoping she wouldn't have to meet whatever now passed for their son.

"I still work at the factory where I've been for 30 years," Charles explained to Vinni and Sunand at a sunny cafe down the street from their house. "I'm hoping to retire soon."

"I spend my days taking Dexter back and forth to the beach. We'd like a house with a pool, so we could make those trips less frequently," Miranda added.

Vinni scribbled a note to herself on her notepad that she would need to find a way to add a pool to the existing house.

"What about something closer to the beach?" Sunand asked.

Miranda shuddered. "No, that won't work. I want a buffer between us and the deep dwellers."

"A first-floor master bedroom would be great, too," Charles said. "We're not as young as we once were."

Vinni added this to the list and held back a frustrated sigh. She hoped their budget for renovations would be massive, if they wanted so many structural changes. Her chances of winning this episode were already dwindling. Could her renovations compete with the lure of the new home Sunand would undoubtedly find for them? Lately her luck with renovations hadn't been good. The corruptions and infections in the homes where they worked were more entrenched than they once were, and thus more expensive to banish, which ate up the renovation budget before she'd even gotten to do any of her design.

"Ranch homes are popular for retirees," Sunand said, nodding. "But of course they're in high demand. It really depends on your budget."

Charles shifted in his seat. "Whatever equity we can get out of the house."

Sunand's eyebrows rose and Vinni suppressed a shriek of triumph. Without a bigger budget, there was no way Sunand could find them what they wanted. But then the realtor smirked. "And what's your budget for the renovations to your existing home?"

Charles turned to Vinni with a rueful expression. "Ten thousand dollars, and not a penny more."

Vinni plastered on her most encouraging smile automatically. "We can do a lot with that amount." Internally, she screamed. That amount would barely afford her the experts she needed to get rid of the roaring and the smell. A pool and a first-floor master suite would be out of the question.

The director sucked in a breath to call "cut," but Miranda reached across the table and took Vinni's hand. "We've watched every episode of the show, and we saw what happened in the Whipple house, Miss Lovecraft. If anyone can help us, we know it's you."

Vinni smiled uncomfortably, aware the cameras were capturing her every twitch and blink, and gave Miranda's fingers a comforting squeeze. She unfocused her eyes and let her lips curve in her famously sage and mysterious smile, and said nothing.

The director finally said, "Cut!" and Vinni pulled away. "I'll do my best for you," she promised the Wards, and hurried to her feet and out of the cafe into the fresh air.

What she didn't say, because she couldn't (not without being sued to within an inch of her life), was that they shouldn't have confidence in her, because she was little more than a television personality. She couldn't say that she'd spent weeks in the hospital recovering after the madness induced by the Whipple House. The heavy lifting in that house had been done by real experts, and only creative editing and a walk-through performed weeks later had given the appearance that Vinni had participated in the cleansing and renovating of the home that had, ironically, become their most-watched and highly-rated episode.

She hated taking credit for work she hadn't done. And she hated, even more, the blow to her confidence the Whipple house had dealt her. It had been an entire year ago, and she still hadn't recovered her spiritual and design confidence, much less the style and panache she'd once possessed that had helped make the show so successful. Brick was getting short with her and pushing her into more and more dangerous situations in an effort to raise their flagging ratings. She saw pity and annoyance on the faces of the crew. She had the feeling in her gut that she would be replaced when her contract was up in a few weeks, and she wasn't sure how she felt about that.

This was the only thing Vinni knew how to do. She'd been born into the World After, and recruited by the network fresh out of design school. She had loved helping people recover their homes, one house at a time, giving hope and inspiration to what remained of the nation, and the crew was like family to her, without any blood relations to speak of. She wasn't sure what she would do without the show. What skills did she have to offer, if she couldn't decontaminate and redecorate homes blighted by unthinkable cosmic horrors?

She walked alone back to the house and visited Wyatt in the medical trailer. He was passed out on the gurney, the sleep of the sedated. The medic was cleaning crusted blood from around his ears.

"How's he doing?" Vinni whispered.

The medic whispered back, "Busted eardrums."

Vinni hissed in sympathy. A part of her wished it was her on the gurney, about to get medical leave from the show. "Will he recover?"

The medic shrugged. "Maybe. Some people heal up just fine. Others end up deaf. Just depends on his body."

"What about…?" Vinni pointed at the ceiling with one hand and the floor with the other. This had become the universally accepted gesture for the gods who ruled the oceans and the sky. It was safer than naming them, or even mentioning them aloud by euphemism.

The medic shook her head. "He's told me many times he'd never even consider it."

Vinni found the prospect of dealing with the Unnamed Gods equally unappealing, but she'd also never been desperate enough to consider it. "But now he might lose his hearing, and he's a boom operator. That's his whole career."

"He told me once his brother called for *their* help, and now he's more fish than man. Wyatt will never go for it."

Vinni cringed but nodded, and tip-toed out of the medical trailer to make her way to her own trailer. Brick caught her crossing the street. "Lavinia! I want to shoot some more footage inside the house."

"When?"

"Ten minutes."

Annoyance made her nerves buzz. She'd been hoping for a nap, or at least some quiet time where she could get her thoughts together. "Brick, come on. We already shot the intro footage."

"Just in the foyer. I want to get further into the house, and I want Sunand there to punch it up."

"I have a headache from the first time we went in there. You seriously want to go back into that smell? And after what happened to Wyatt?"

"The Wards say it usually only happens a couple of times a day, so we should have a window if we go *now*. Take an aspirin and get into the makeup chair." He marched away before Vinni could argue any further.

She did as she was told, though the makeup artist took about 15 minutes to cover the dark circles under Vinni's eyes, a challenging task on someone so pale. When she appeared on set, she had wrapped herself in one of the diaphanous shawls inherited from her grandmother's hope chest. Vinni liked to wear Gran's garments on the show. They lent an air of authenticity to the whole business, and there was something deeply comforting about being cocooned in soft wool stitched together by someone who had once adored her, even if she had walked into the ocean and left Vinni an orphan.

DeAndre, Brick, and Sunand were waiting on the front porch. Brick fitted microphones onto their clothes clumsily and Vinni missed Wyatt. "I guess Wyatt's eardrums burst," she shared with the guys as they readied themselves.

"Jesus," DeAndre whispered, glaring at Brick.

"Thanks for sharing," Brick snapped.

Anger flared hot in Vinni's chest. "I think your crew deserves to know the risk they're taking."

"You never cared about the risk before," Sunand said. His skin had taken on an ashen hue. "What's different?"

Brick stared daggers at her and Vinni shook her head, her heart thumping. "Every house reminds me of the Whipple House. Every house makes me wish I'd spoken up when I saw the warning signs. So I'm not going to be silent anymore, and if that means you replace me with someone more tractable, then so be it."

"Replace you?" Sunand echoed. "Who said anything about replacing you?" He glanced at Brick, tawny eyes wide. "Brick?"

"We're going to run out of light," Brick growled. "Let's get inside the house." He gestured for DeAndre to begin filming.

DeAndre hefted the camera to his shoulder and the familiar red light came on. The foursome moved into the house. It still smelled faintly of rotten eggs, but time and open windows had cleared most of the stench. Sunand stood close to Vinni, and her lungs were tight. He'd seemed genuinely surprised at the suggestion Vinni might be forced off the show. Now he seemed to hover near her as they made their way through the house. His usual verbal jabs were absent from their banter as they commented upon tiny bedrooms and a single tiny bathroom, an outdated kitchen, and a living room crowded with too much furniture. Was he protecting her? Did he...did he care about her?

Vinni's heart thumped at the possibility.

When they had finished an uneventful tour of the second floor, Vinni turned to Brick. "Can I go lie down now?"

Brick smirked. "Almost done. Just one floor left."

A feeling of cold dread spread outward from Vinni's chest, making her shiver. Memories of huge, fuzzy, mustard-yellow mushrooms sprouting in a dank cellar flashed across her mind. "No, please, Brick. You know I don't do basements anymore."

"You do whatever I tell you. It's in your contract." Brick practically ran down the stairs to the first floor and to the basement door, opening it with a triumphant flourish.

Vinni's pulse pounded and her vision narrowed. She attempted a prayer, but the words eluded her. Gentle pressure on her elbow made her turn to Sunand, who said nothing, but met her eyes with his dark brown gaze, steady and reassuring. He was with her, and would help her get through this, his eyes told her. She also felt certain that if she refused to go, he would back her up in that choice, as well.

But she also knew refusal would cost her the job she loved. *Did* she love it anymore, though? There was a time when she was young and naive and felt like helping other people was worth the small salary, endless hours, and risky escapades. But since the Whipple House, she wasn't sure how many more weird, impossible, dangerous, madness-inducing homes she could take without her mind breaking.

There was only one way to find out whether this was a job she even wanted to keep doing, and that was to do it. Vinni took a deep breath, forced her anxiety into a mental lockbox as her therapist had taught her to do, and followed Brick down the basement stairs.

The smell worsened as they descended. It reminded Vinni of the sharp tang of manure. She squinted against the miasma as she picked her way carefully down the stairs in near-darkness, tears tracing their way down her cheeks. A soft sound like the burbling of a hungry stomach surrounded them. Every instinct she had told her to run, but she forced herself to descend, step by step, into what felt like the belly of a monstrous evil, ignoring her galloping pulse and sweating palms.

Brick pulled the string to the single dangling light bulb in the middle of the space. Dimly illuminated, the basement was surprisingly large—the size of the footprint of the entire house—and nearly empty. There were a few labeled boxes of holiday decorations in one corner, the usual mechanical appliances chugging away, and a lot of cobwebs. Clearly this part of the house had been abandoned, and as she gagged against the stench, Vinni understood why.

DeAndre swung into position. Sunand said, in a tight voice, "Well, here's your master suite."

"Not exactly on the first floor," Vinni said, swallowing hard and gagging for a few seconds.

"True."

They both looked at Brick, who made the rolling gesture.

"I can understand why they don't use this part of this house," Vinni said. "Now that I can smell it."

"It's like a farm," Sunand added.

"A corrupted farm where the animals are diseased. I wonder if it's a sewage leak." Vinni glanced at the floor, hoping for a solution to this dilemma that wouldn't involve a team of exorcists. The floor, however, appeared to be clean except for a thick layer of gray dust she could swirl about with the toes of her boots. "Maybe the sewer line is dumping all its odors in here. Like at the Madgen house?"

Sunand nodded. "I remember that. Season...2? Just required a good plumber. But, I dunno, that wasn't nearly this severe."

Vinni's shoulders sagged and her eyes traced the foundation wall, looking for signs of moisture or cracks, mold or seepage, anything that might explain the horrible odor and the impossibly loud roar.

There was a sound, then, sort of a wet *splort*. It sounded strangely familiar, and made Vinni think of her grandfather, before he'd gone to live with the deep dwellers. Vinni and Sunand exchanged a look.

"Oh!" Vinni shouted, realization making her grin.

"Lavinia," Brick said in a warning tone.

Without answering, Vinni walked to the wall and began following it, tracing it around the room until she found the place where the brick had broken away, behind the staircase, hidden in shadow. Brick handed her a flashlight and, still scrunching up her nose against the stench, she held it up to illuminate the source of the problem that had slowly worked its way into the foundation over years of neglect: A massive, fleshy sphincter about six feet up on the wall.

The sphincter—it looked almost like a puckered, toothless purple mouth, but it definitely wasn't a mouth—flexed repulsively. While Vinni and her companions stared, it issued a soft, squeaky fart.

Brick asked, "Is that what I think it is?"

DeAndre was the one who answered. "Only if you think it's a giant asshole."

"Brick," Sunand gasped. "Is it like looking into a mirror?"

Vinni and DeAndre chortled. "Very funny," Brick said. "How are you going to get rid of it?"

"I dunno, maybe offer it a job on a more prestigious show, and it'll leave on its own," Vinni muttered.

It was Sunand's turn to laugh.

"It's huge," DeAndre observed, gesturing at the sphincter as large as a man's head. "It belongs to something enormous. Something we probably don't want to piss off."

Vinni remembered her grandparents, before the ocean's call took them, and how her grandmother had responded to her grandfather's tendency to pass gas wherever and whenever. Smiling, she strolled over to the corner with the boxes and pulled out a dusty broom. She brandished it.

"No way," Sunand said, stepping back from the monstrous anus. "Vinni, that's a bad idea."

"Yeah, I dunno, maybe we should wait for the professionals," Brick said, taking a few steps backward toward the stairs.

"DeAndre, are you still filming?" Vinni asked.

DeAndre gestured to the red light.

Vinni grinned and handed the flashlight to Sunand. She changed her grip so she held the broomstick like a baseball bat. "This is for you, Gran," she told the camera. The men all shouted for her to stop, but instead she took a swing at the anus of a living god. Whether it was from the stars or the sea, it didn't matter, she reasoned. Nobody likes having their asshole whacked.

The broomstick landed with a fleshy *thwack* and the sphincter puckered tightly in response. Vinni drew back the broomstick to hit a second time, but she didn't get a chance. The ground shook so hard they all collapsed to the basement floor, a cloud of dust rising around them. Vinni's eyes burned and she coughed and the floor tilted, making her slide. She contacted something warm and fleshy and thought, for an instant of terror, that she had slid into the giant anus somehow. But when she put out her hands, she contacted the smooth, soft fabric of an expensive designer shirt, and she closed her fingers around the fabric reflexively like a baby monkey.

A pair of hands gripped hers and pulled her to her feet. She opened her eyes just a crack. The flashlight rolled on the floor, the light it produced diffuse in the dust cloud. DeAndre and Brick were nowhere to be seen, their footsteps thudding on the basement stairs. The quaking had stopped, and she gradually found her footing, a sailor on a shifting boat deck that had finally found calm seas.

Sunand looked down at her. "You okay? Did you hurt anything?"

"Maybe my elbow." Now that she wasn't rolling around in a panic, her right elbow smarted like it had been cracked hard against the cement floor, though she didn't remember when that had happened.

"We should get you upstairs to medical," he said, one hand on the small of her back, propelling her toward the stairs.

"Wait." Vinni turned and grabbed the flashlight, shining it around the basement. There were cracks in the floor and walls now, evidence of something massive shifting beneath and around the foundation. But the hole in the wall where the sphincter had blinked at them was now empty darkness. She stepped over to it and shone the flashlight beam inside. The beam disappeared into a tunnel tall and wide enough for an entire marching band to fit, single-file. It was going to take a lot of dirt to fill in the hollow space. Vinni tried not to think about what creatures—or fungus—could emerge from the depths of the earth through the burrow, or how much exactly it was going to cost the homeowners to have it filled in. "It's gone," she whispered.

"Of course it's gone." Sunand stood beside her, staring into the darkness. "You smacked it with a broom." He chuckled. "That was maybe the bravest, stupidest thing I've ever seen."

Vinni laughed. "Just maybe? Stick with me, kid. You ain't seen nothing, yet."

"Oh yeah?" He turned to her, his expression soft.

She looked up at him. The stink was gone, and was replaced by the warm, inviting, sandalwood scent of Sunand's cologne. "Yeah."

"You know, whether Brick tries to replace you or not, I think I have an idea for a new show. One where we work a little more closely together." He leaned toward her, his breath soft against her lips when he spoke.

"I'll let my agent know," she said, smiling, and returned his kiss.

Three months later, DeAndre swung the camera around to get Vinni and Sunand in frame. They both wore jeans and plaid shirts with tool belts strapped to their waists. Sunand balanced a sledgehammer on his shoulder and Vinni held a nail gun. DeAndre slowly panned around, making room in the shot for the show's new logo. "Looking great, guys."

"Are we done?" Vinni asked. "We need to get started on the actual reno work."

DeAndre grinned. "Yeah, I think we're good."

"Thanks, DeAndre," Sunand said, turning back to the kitchen. "So, what do you think?"

Vinni put on the safety glasses and gloves she'd left on the counter. She reached up and ran one finger across the glowing fuschia liquid oozing from the ceiling and down the kitchen walls. She lifted it to her nose. "It doesn't smell like blood, but it's not strawberry jam, either. Who knows what's going on in that attic. We should go in prepared."

"Exorcists?" Sunand asked.

Vinni grinned. "Nah."

Sunand grinned, too. "Broomstick?"

She winked. "And maybe the nail gun, just to be safe."

"Ooh." Sunand pulled her into his embrace. "Baby, talk construction to me."

Vinni laughed. From the next room, she heard DeAndre yell, "Just once I need to get that banter on camera, you know."

"No way," Sunand shouted back. He buried his face in Vinni's neck. "We're the producers, and we say the talent should get to keep their private lives private."

"We're just so cute," Vinni said, pressing her lips to his jaw. Now that his look was less realtor and more demolitionist, he had a divine beard. She just couldn't stop kissing and nuzzling it.

The glowing liquid on the wall bubbled in response to their passion. Vinni rolled her eyes.

Here we go again.

KING C

NATHAN CARSON

For best results, please read in Elvis voice. I always do.

I guess I've known about C since I was real young. Plush toys. Cartoons on the boob tube. Those ski masks with the yarn tentacles that say, "I gave up on sex with other people years ago." But it would be a lie to say I had an ounce of faith before I met Dolphin.

She used to come hear me sing at casinos on the strip. She said I did Glenn and Mr. Mojo Rising better than anyone. And Dolphin did *me* better than *everyone*. I couldn't help falling in love. She was always on my mind. I was hooked on her and she was high on Mythos. Pretty soon I started to see the lights in the water, which was a good trick since we lived in Vegas.

Pappy told me about that magician who made the Statue of Liberty disappear. How he sat in front of the screen and watched it go poof with a steaming Swanson dinner in his lap.

Dolphin and thousands like her had a pledge drive going to raise the big C right out of his slumber, into the homes of reality streamers everywhere. The crowd funding popped off because half the donors believed in him, and the other half—the ones with Miskatonic U bumper stickers on their Priuses—thought it was funny. They wouldn't have been laughing if they knew what was coming.

Dolphin moved into my penthouse. I was wrapped around her finger. We knew this event was our big shot at those fifteen minutes that only come once in a lifetime. Or is it four times an hour? I forget. The problem was that everyone wanted that spotlight to shine on *them*. We needed an edge.

Dolphin showed me the ads. Cosmetic surgery was no big thing on the strip. But a faceful of tentacles? Dolphin said I'd give the best mustache rides in Nevada, and I aimed to prove her right. In fact, I have, quite a few times. Just not with her.

We shared a taxi to the clinic. Held hands and kissed, ready to take our love and faith to the next level.

We walked down the aisle to separate operating tables. "It's now or never," she said.

I went under the knife with a burning love in my heart. But Dolphin was a hard-headed woman.

When they unwrapped my face, she was standing beside me, pretty as can be. Only she still looked like her. And I looked like a seafood platter. I guess Dolphin got cold feet. When she saw me, she got all shook up. "Don't be cruel," I begged her. But she was just another devil in disguise. By the time the staples came out of my face, she'd already packed up her things from our heartbreak hotel and hopped an Amtrak for California.

That didn't pan out well, since the Del Yuge put the golden state underwater. When the cameras rolled and the chants were phrased, C didn't show up for his call. Well, a lot of us like to think that maybe he turned over in his sleep. One helluva bloop echoed out of Point Nemo, returning to sender. Sea level rose like an overnight sensation.

Maybe a couple hundred of us had the surgery, and made the cut—hand-selected by producers who practically drooled over our extreme makeovers. After the show was over, the sun still shined, the world kept turning. If you think getting a job is hard for someone with facial tattoos, well let me tell you what a bitch this was.

Lucky for me, only a couple dozen of the faithful had musical talent. And we all know that Mythos Rock is always a pretty limp imitation of the real thing. The only guys that really made a go of it stuck to death metal. That gave me a monopoly of sorts on the blue-haired buffet crowd.

My agent helped me distill the mash-up. The music of The King and the majesty of C. It was too dumb not to work. Just when tickets on the Carnival Cruise Subs started selling out, Disney California opened up like some bonafide trip to Atlantis. Well, let's just say I haven't collected a funemployment check for a few years.

Sometimes when I'm singing "Suspicious Minds" I'll look out the bay windows thinking maybe I'll catch a glimpse of her body drifting in that seaweed that sways all dreamlike in the fronds of palm trees lining the ocean floor. The rusting graveyard car lots, and the sunken stadiums remind me that the end is nearer than we think.

Here's the thing. C's been stuck on the porcelain throne of R'Lyeh pushing out a peanut butter and banana sandwich the size of Memphis for eons now. All things must pass, but some things pass slower than others. No disrespect intended, of course. I personally worked my way through *The Wheel of Time* on the shitter, so I have some concept of Cosmic Magnitudes.

Maybe C's gonna sleep for ten thousand years. Or maybe the big hunk o' love's planning his oft-prophesied 2068 Comeback. All I know is that somewhere in that Pacific apocalypse is my Dolphin, singing the unchained melody that I hear on the crashing waves in my squid-faced jailhouse rock and roll dreams.

Uh, thankyouverymuch.

REPORT TO THE CEG AND EXECUTIVE BOARD V1.0

J. EDWIN BUJA

1.1   Preamble

Our Lord and Master, Chief Executive God (CEG), and Exalted Sires of the Board, whose names we are not worthy to speak and upon whose countenances we may never gaze lest we be reduced to gibbering imbeciles (i.e. Engineers), please hear our words.

We of Documentation wish to humbly clarify some points raised during the recent Glorious Return of our Masters, the Elder Gods™ v1.0. In this document, it will be made evidently clear that We of Documentation in no way contributed to the errors committed during the sacred Ritual of Summoning, that is, the utter destruction of Pluto, the flattening of Neptune, and the plunging of Las Vegas into the Sun. We were, however, with all humility, instrumental in the successful completion of said rituals[1] to the benefit of all godkind.

We of Documentation have absolutely no doubt it was a complete lack of control and discipline by the previous leadership of the corporation, added to the intimidation tactics employed by several of the sub-teams, that created the horror and uncertainty leading up to your Glorious Arrival. These deficiencies in leadership have, indeed, been at the source of previous failures. [Reference Appendix A: *General History of Previous Failed Attempts to Breach the Dimensional and Spatial Barriers, Volumes 1 though 4* (Documentation Department, Ottawa, 2000 to 2018).

1.2 The Project Plan and the Engineers

The wretched Gateway Team project plan used in this cycle of renewal was created through a deadly mixture of arrogance and annoying stupidity. The first hint of impending doom should have been recognized when the Project Manager (More about him in section 1.3) consented to use the plan as written by the illiterates of the Engineering Department. It was their choice that it be implemented without proper, conscientious, and vital vetting by We of Documentation. The very idea that anything written by an Engineer could be presented to anyone outside of the confines of their department is ridiculous in the extreme. To think that it would be anything other than a repulsive soup of bad grammar, misspelling, overuse of acronyms, and puerile attempts at full sentences is to seriously overestimate the ability of those creatures.

In addition to the problems outlined in the paragraph above, one must consider the propensity of the Engineers to:

1. arrive late to meetings, if at all. One would assume that a team that relies on exact measurements and code would be attuned to the necessity of following schedules. Furthermore, their tardiness, and refusal to adhere to strict and necessary timelines, threw off the timing of the sacred ritual.
2. be unruly and unprofessional. It was only at the insistence of the Project Manager, after much input from We of Documentation, that these animals began to understand the seriousness of the work they had been assigned to perform.
3. appear completely uninterested in anything lesser beings have to say. While We of Documentation do not profess to know everything, the very nature of our work ensures that we know a lot about most things. Our input, however unwelcome, should not be dismissed out of hand (or, in light of the current situation, out of tentacle. More on that later.).

Any single one of these factors would disrupt the smooth and accurate performance of the wholly welcome Ritual of Summoning. Taken as a whole, one arrives at the perfect formula for a disaster of biblical (Necronomical?) proportions until We of Documentation intervened. [Reference Appendix B: Minutes of the Final Meeting of the Gateway Team (Deceased)]

1.3   The Project Manager

We of Documentation tried our best to warn the Project Manager, the former and unlamented Malcolm Tidyman. Being of a lazy persuasion, Tidyman was always ready to pass off work to his subordinates. His primary concern, after assuring himself that he would collect any bonuses available to management, was that he be able to sign off on projects with as minimal involvement as humanly or otherwise possible. In this particular case, however, Tidyman was bullied (we can use no other word) by the Engineers, who sought all the glory, and, worst of all from a standpoint of quality control and accuracy, and Marketing (Details in Section 1.4). Despite our valiant efforts, he succumbed to outside pressure.

Subservience to you, our Masters, the Elder Gods™ v1.0, demands the utmost diligence and supreme sacrifice (pun not intended), he was forced to authorize the release of an inferior product. We of Documentation attempted to make our voices heard, but they were drowned out by the drunken revelling of, need we say it, the Engineers.[2]

Though it is well-known and feared, by all your most loyal subjects and acolytes, that failure will be met with the direst of consequences, We of Documentation would like to put in a good word for the Project Manager. Despite his many failings, lack of initiative, and worship of gods other than you, Tidyman is but a tool of greater outside forces. We of Documentation can handle these forces. [Reference Appendix G: Source Materials Beneficial to We of Documentation (Access Restricted)]

Deserving as he may be of an eternity as an extremely sensitive bloated mass whose sole purpose is to be an incubator for all of your hideous progeny, it seems a bit unfair. Yes, it is fair and right that he suffers the insertion of your ten thousand massive and barbed penises and the chafing that accompanies them. In addition, it seems reasonable, in our most humble opinion, that the burning as a result of the ejaculation of your unimaginably vile and acidic semen is simply part of the job. Perhaps, if We of Documentation may be so bold, if there was a time limit imposed on his punishment, perhaps only ten thousand years[3], it would be an example of the mercy of the Elder Gods™ v1.0. [Reference Appendix C: Definition of "mercy" in *The Concise Oxford Dictionary of Current English, 12th Edition* (Oxford University Press, Toronto, 2011)]

1.4   The Interference of the Vice President of Sales and Marketing, and Quality Control

The failure of the initial project as per the Engineers' flawed project plan was due, ultimately, to the interference of the Vice President of Sales and Marketing, Brenden T. Ogden. This person, though well-versed in the intricacies of marketing, advertising, and sucking up to shareholders, is, like most members of any Executive, thoroughly incapable of doing, or even understanding, the job performed by the company's skilled professionals. He, more than anyone, however, does have the most experience with pumping out noxious and disgusting excrement. He, therefore, would be the perfect candidate for the task of rectal management and cleaning of the one billion incontinent and dripping anuses of That Which Shall Not Be Smelt. [Reference Appendix D: *Management's Inability to Grasp Even the Fundamentals of a Worker's Job: A Handbook for Anyone with an Ounce of Common Sense* (Documentation Department, Ottawa, 2000)]

We of Documentation would like to note that the output of the Sales and Marketing department as regards written material is, at best, juvenile deceit, or, at worst, intentional obfuscation and untruths. In all our combined years of experience, We of Documentation have never encountered anything dumbed down to the point of embarrassment like this, except perhaps for the Mad Dribblings of Oswald of Ghent, Abuser of Sheep and Prophet of Your Return.

Said department has on several occasions attempted to co-opt We of Documentation into creating work for them. However, We of Documentation will only go so low before we must cease to compromise our high standards.

The less said about the influence of so-called Quality Control, the better. They were never about quality, only control. Suffice to say the smearing to a noxious paste of all members of that department, and your subsequent use of that paste as sandwich spread, was most gratifying. We of Documentation would like to add that we had no idea that you, our Masters, the Elder Gods™ v1.0, had a liking for sandwiches.[4]

1.5   Deadlines and How to Meet Them

There should be no need whatsoever to outline the importance of deadlines and the consequences of missing them. However, without the concept of time, you, our Masters, the Elder Gods™ v1.0, may not understand, if we may be so bold, that there is a requirement for tasks to be performed within a reasonable period. This was especially true pre-your return.

Though there was but a short window of opportunity for the alignment of the planets as required for your Glorious Return[5], even had We of Documentation been given the disgusting and incoherent project plan, the required time to perform this absolutely vital task thoroughly was no longer available. As you well know and decreed, a delay in this cycle of return would result in the passage of untold billennia (a term coined by a member of We of Documentation to illustrate exactly how long-lived you are) before another window of opportunity would be presented. There is no doubt that, in the event of such a terrible postponement, humankind would have evolved into something entirely different and thus useless to Your Hideousnesses.

For future reference, We of Documentation would like to point out that We of Documentation have never failed to deliver on time, complete with spellcheck.

1.6   The Criminal Misuse of Grammar

In addition to the appalling spelling, utter lack of grammar, refusal to employ the Oxford comma, and inability to string two words together coherently, and despite our strenuous objections, the employment of acronyms, rather than full words, was nothing short of criminal. We must mention specifically, as a rather egregious example, the referral to Dythalla, Lord of the Lizards, as LoL. [Reference Appendix E: William Strunk Jr. and E. B. White, *The Elements of Style Third Edition* (Macmillan Publishing Co., New York, 1979)]

We of Documentation hesitate to point out that one of the conditions of our co-operation with you in your efforts to return was your assurance that, beginning with the moment of this glorious event occurring, an emphasis on the correct and proper use of language would be made a priority. Please, allow us to remind you that, in an act of good faith and subservience, We of Documentation agreed that this condition could be applied to all languages, living, dead, intergalactic, interdimensional, or other, without prejudice.

1.7 The Botched Ritual of Summoning and the Dividends of the Shareholders

The descriptions in the source material [Reference: Annotated Bibliography of Ancient Manuscripts] made it perfectly clear to anyone who can read (thus immediately eliminating the Engineers) that any attempt to open a gateway in the very fabric of time and space to aid in your return had to follow the ritual to the letter. This obviously meant that shortcuts, acronyms, and the willingness of the Board of Directors to relax strict rules as cost-saving measures for the shareholders, would not, as they hoped, proclaim the arrival of the Great Old Ones™ v2.4.3.

No. Despite the pleading of We of Documentation, this irresponsibility on the part of so-called "leaders" instead heralded millennia of chaos. For the possibility of a few extra dividend points, the Executive allowed the incorrect, out-of-date, and no longer supported Great Old Ones™ v1.6 to burst forth upon the world.

As a result of this, several billion of your potential worshippers were reduced to gibbering blobs for use as cattle or eaten outright. This was a criminal waste of readership.

In addition to the aforementioned staggering loss to us,[6] the reduction in loyal and fearful worshippers has endangered the stability of the Ritual of Summoning. Without careful monitoring by experts, all your efforts, and ours, may be undone because of greed, expensive mistresses, larger yachts, and points in the market. Note that none of the stock markets survived the recent changes to reality. We of Documentation are fully prepared to do our duty and perform due diligence to assure your safety. [Reference Appendix H: Further Demands of We of Documentation]

1.8   The Precise Ritual as Performed in the Tenth Floor Bathroom

We of Documentation prepare for any eventuality. Upon realizing that the Ritual of Summoning for the Great Old Ones™ v2.4.3 would likely result in utter chaos and death, we assembled a contingency plan. Not wishing to face the wrath of the wrong gods, not to mention the anger and opprobrium of the Board of Directors, We of Documentation deemed it necessary to call forth a higher power. It should be noted that the Board of Directors, as well as most members of the Executive, and not a few project managers, have a tendency to blame We of Documentation for any mishaps, mistakes, dissatisfaction, or general failure of projects to perform the jobs for which they were designed.

It is the argument of these groups that customers and clients are exposed to documentation which is supposed to show them how the product works. If something goes horribly wrong, especially if it results in death and maiming, it is easiest to blame the documentation. The Engineers and all other "experts" involved in the creation process are thereby absolved of any wrongdoing. From decades of experience dealing with these fools, We of Documentation knew what was coming.

Fortunately for all, We of Documentation had our own capable acolytes performing the precise Ritual of Summoning in the tenth-floor bathroom where, with the sacrifice of a number of virgins from

Support (where they are most numerous), we were able to call forth not some version of the Great Old Ones™, but a representative of you, the Elder Gods™ v1.0. We knew that only you, our new Masters, could set right the calamity brought about by the clearly flawed project plan.

Upon seeing the horrors wrought by the incompetence of the Engineers et al., your representative, whose name We of Documentation would never attempt to write down nor even speak, calmed the wild beasts, ended the devastating storms, and removed the itchy masses from the inner thighs of your loyal subjects. It was too late, however, to save the billions of humans who became little more than a snack for the incorrect Great Old Ones™ who took advantage of the brief sojourn upon the Earth to attempt to sate their foul hunger.

1.9   Promises Made

Regarding the Transformation of Conquered Species, We of Documentation fully acknowledge and support the desire of the Elder Gods™ v1.0 to have all fresh subjects altered to take a form acceptable to the million eyes of our new Masters.

We of Documentation, however, must use this opportunity to remind our exalted Masters of a number of promises and conditions that were set forth in the preparation of the contingency plan that stopped the invasion of the useless, nasty, and altogether disgusting usurper gods.

These promises and conditions include:

- The previously mentioned correct use of all languages, both domestic and alien.
- The return of cursive writing.
- The utter destruction, to the point of erasing all surviving human memory, of emojis.
- The use of the Oxford comma to become absolute law.
- In all areas that use English, American spellings are to be banned. For example, one would sit in the centre of the theatre. Favour, rumour, colour?[7]

While it is not for such lowly beings as members of the former human race to question the wisdom and wishes of the exalted, almighty, all-knowing Elder Gods™ v1.0, We of Documentation wish to present the following point.

Tentacles, as beautiful and wondrous as they are, are not the most conducive limbs for the creation of documentation. Keyboards are easily navigated with such appendages, or even claws, but, in your great and unfathomable knowledge, you must be aware that neither outperform an opposable thumb for grasping writing implements such as pens and pencils. [Reference: Appendix F Henry Gray, *Anatomy, Descriptive and Surgical* (Bounty Books, New York, 1977)]

It is with respect and humility that We of Documentation request the return of our most useful appendages. As an aside, and to show that we are not entirely without gratitude, We of Documentation would like to thank you, our Masters, the Elder Gods™ v1.0, for our new tentacles. They have proven to be useful in certain sexual pursuits, most especially those performed in privacy and solitude.

1.10   Authority to Anticipate and Terminate

Lastly, We of Documentation would appreciate it if the Elder Gods™ v1.0 could be persuaded, for the benefit of all Elder Gods™ v1.0, to grant We of Documentation the authority to eliminate, with extreme prejudice, any and all (especially Engineers) who presume to have the ability or knowledge to create Documentation.

Furthermore, We of Documentation request the power to anticipate and terminate any being, whether human, animal, engineer, or other, that even *thinks* they can do our job.

1.11   Conclusion

We of Documentation do solemnly believe that we have explained our thoughts and needs within this document. Beings as all-powerful as yourselves are not required to be involved with the day-to-day activities of your subjects except where you derive immense pleasure from manipulating and terrorizing us. In recognizing this, We of Documentation pray that you heed our words and grant us our requests, and honor your promises.

We remain,

As ever loyal and at the ready to take down and transcribe your words of wisdom (correctly),

We of Documentation

Have a good and pleasant day.

1.12   Post Scriptum

With regard to our negative experience with this project, the interference of idiots, and the disastrous results heretofore referenced, We of Documentation have prepared a supplementary Contingency Plan should the need arise. As long as our requests are met in a timely and satisfactory manner, We of Documentation do not feel it will be necessary to implement our contingency plan.

In the event that We of Documentation are not satisfied with the outcome of this most respectful and humble negotiation, we feel it is only fair to provide you, our new Masters, the Elder Gods™ v1.0, with the possible ramifications. This is not so much a warning as an appreciation of outcomes.

Through our careful research of certain forbidden ancient manuscripts [Reference Appendix G: Source Materials Beneficial to We of Documentation (Access Restricted) not attached], we have discovered a Ritual of Banishment and Destruction. This ritual, when performed correctly, and by now you know We of Documentation would perform it so, will bring about the restoration of the Earth to its previous glory and eliminate any and all non-native beings to the farthest depths of the unfathomable void. [Reference: Appendix H, Further Demands of We of Documentation]

Sadly, the ritual would not restore the lives of those engineers who were and would be sacrificed for We of Documentation to achieve our most reasonable goals. In any case, even if the ritual did restore them, the engineers would be slaughtered the instant they reappeared. We of Documentation can only put up with so much.

---

1. Rumors to the effect that a member of We of Documentation had enormous gambling debts and, therefore, deliberately redirected the Death Ray of Ethnon the All-Moist away from Ottawa, are entirely unfounded.
2. Suggestions that We of Documentation kept obvious errors in the plan to ourselves with the objective of sabotaging your return are patently false. If these insulting ideas are perpetuated, We of Documentation shall be forced to take drastic action. [Reference Appendix G: *Source Materials Beneficial to We of Documentation* (Access Restricted).
3. Our repeated reference to units of time is an unfortunate holdover from pre-cataclysmic days. We of Documentation recognize that entities such as yourselves have no need for the restrictions imposed by units of time, nor even the requirement of the concept of time. In our own defence, not all of us can be senators, retirees, or corporate retail managers.
4. For your future reference, our department does still retain a high-end panini grill, functional for those with tentacles, and available for your enjoyment at a moment's notice. We of Documentation do realize that future, past, and present are all as one for you.
5. If we may be so bold as to ask a question, please, do not use us as catheters if we are out of line. If you are so all-powerful, why is it necessary for the planets to be aligned before you can return? Would it not be possible for you to rearrange the planets in any way you see fit?
6. Every member of We of Documentation had a novel in the pipeline. Several movie options had already been signed – Scorsese had expressed interest in the work of the head of our team – and North American and European tours had been booked. With the change in the shape and placement of the continents, along with the disappearance of half of Europe, all this planning was for naught.
7. For the time being, We of Documentation retain the use of the cursed American spelling that has been the documentation standard for decades. As much as We of Documentation are rebels, there is only so far we can go before conscience steps in and overrules desire.

TARTS, PIE, TEA

JOHN POSSIDENTE

April Jeune took a shuffling step back and surveyed her work. Amazing what one could do with duct tape and wood glue. The big wicker cage where her beloved owl, the late Henri Featherbrain, had spent his years sleeping was now a modest physical therapy gymnasium for small birds. Specifically, for an injured goldfinch named Captain Peep. In a day or two, when his wing had healed and she could remove the tiny splint, Peep could exercise in there by fluttering the short distance between the two twig perches she'd created. Satisfied, she went to wash up in the kitchen.

One glance through the window above the sink was enough to spoil her mood.

"Son of a beet!"

She caught herself clenching her jaw. Have to stop that. In a minute she'd be grinding her teeth. The dentist had told her many times not to —but dammit, she could see loose dirt over by the rhubarb. It had to be that rotten groundhog again.

April wrapped up in the cardigan she kept by the garden door and doddered out to investigate. Sure enough, three of her cabbages were gone. Just gone. First the holes everywhere, then the lettuces, the carrots, and now this.

This was the last straw. It was time she did something about it.

Her legs might be old, but her eye and her arm were still true. She spent a few minutes rummaging in the shed, then a quick nip into the pantry.

April set herself down gingerly onto the creaking back porch swing. She had her bow in hand. (Sixty-four years ago, she'd come third in her school's archery contest. She still kept the tiny medal, propped up on the narrow shelf above the kitchen sink.)

A baker's dozen of arrows splayed on the seat beside her, and she had a pint bottle of gin clamped between her knees. The doctor had told her to quit that, too, but a woman needs some consolation in her quiet years.

Patience, now.

The groundhog must have been busy destroying someone else's hard work. The afternoon wore on.

While she waited, April sipped, and she catalogued the things she saw needed to be done: weeds under the back gate, the mock orange could stand some pruning, split that overgrown forsythia, and the concrete cover over the old well had broken. Again. She'd have to get that fixed before the snow covered it, but the stupid thing was too heavy for her to shift.

A little more gin, and she grumped at the injustice of that repair falling in her lap. Somehow, the well had ended up in her parcel when they divided the old Gardner farm land. It had never been a working well in any case. Just a hole in the ground, really. A circle of crumbling, ancient brick no higher than her calves. High enough to trip over, but too low to sit on comfortably. Every few years, like clockwork, the lid cracked open—must be frost heave or something.

By rights the useless homeowner's association should have been required to fix the thing, but they'd never. All the HOA busybodies ever did was boss people around and hand out fines for trumped-up "violations".

"Bunch of petty martinet buttinskis, the lot of them."

None of her doctors had told her to stop muttering to herself. Not yet, anyway.

The well also stank, foetid as if something had fallen in and died. Which it probably had. Birds wouldn't light on it, and for April, that was the deciding fact. She wondered how much it would cost to have the damned thing filled in. Too much, undoubtedly.

She was holding up her bottle and wondering why there was so little left in it and whether she should open the other one in the pantry when something fat and brown scurried around the corner of the shed.

To arms! Her first shot went wide, maybe a little high, and right over the plank fence into Duncan's yard. Duncan, who was vice president of the HOA.

April shrugged. No risk of doing any harm there. His wife had taken the noisy brats with her when she left. They wouldn't be out playing. Maybe the arrow'd hit his cat, Thomas Aquinas. Serve him right. Duncan left the nasty thing out, and that's probably what had happened to poor Captain Peep.

"What the hell? You tryin' to kill me now?" Duncan stuck his head up over the fence. Styled hair, rag sweater—and always three days growth on his face. Why wouldn't he either shave or grow a proper beard? "You almost hit my chicken coop! I'm reporting you to Becky again."

"Fuck off, Duncan."

Oops. Language, April. Must be the gin talking. She suppressed a giggle.

"You're lucky I don't call the police." Duncan retreated, probably to phone Becky, HOA president and all-round pain in the under-garments.

A rotund, furry shape waddled beneath the ficus.

April's second arrow cracked a hole right through the sun-faded forehead of a ceramic gnome, where it stuck.

"Balls!"

It was time to go on the offensive. She nocked an arrow and rocked herself back and forth until she managed to dismount from the swing. The empty gin bottle thunked to the wooden floor and rolled over the edge of the porch. Arrows rolled, too. She arrested two by stepping on them.

April tottered down the three steps onto the grass. The sudden sun made her squint. Nice and warm, though. She drew her bow and pointed it skyward, ready to drop the aim and fire. Where was that fat, cabbage-eating bastard? There, by the well.

She loosed the arrow, then aimed.

Oops. Got it backward.

The groundhog, unbothered, scuffled away behind the largest piece of the broken lid. April's arrow ended its ballistic arc by diving point first through the gap and down into the depths of the well. She expected to hear it splinter on a stone at the bottom, but she didn't.

She also expected the sun to keep on shining, but it didn't.

A heavy dusk rushed in from all directions and filled the world.

Oh dear. The doctors had warned her about this. Was she finally having that stroke? April dropped the bow without noticing.

Nameless dread swirled throughout her mind, a relentless driving river. She felt...*wrong*.

Not a stroke, then. It must be a heart attack. All her friends had said you feel like this when you have a heart attack.

The air went cold. She could see her breath, small and feeble like Captain Peep when she'd found him lying on the ground.

Cold? What kind of a death was that?

"Make up your damn mind," she grumbled at her body.

Least expected of all was the undulating black column, thick as a utility pole, that rose up out of the old well like an abbreviated gusher of oil. She'd heard of this, too: hallucinations caused by her brain being deprived of oxygen.

Why couldn't she have a proper, quick death?

"Oh for fuck's sake, get on with it."

The top of the column shaped itself into an ear.

What was this now? An ear, ringed with tiny eyes, and an arrow sticking out like a wayward thatch of hair.

Preposterous. April determined to shoot it (again). She tried to pick up her bow, but her legs wouldn't bend. Well, her mouth still worked.

"You're an ugly one."

The Thing (she wouldn't think of it as The Ear; that would be silly) didn't speak. April *felt* its words rumble, as if the Earth itself were speaking inside her head.

"WHO DISTURBS MY DREAMING?"

Were all hallucinations this pompous?

"Me," she said. April rolled her eyes and tried again to reach the bow, with no greater success. "What are you doing in my garden?"

"I AM THE SOURCE AND THE SEED. ALL LIVING THINGS ARE OF ME AND SERVE ME."

"All living things? Well. Then you ought to be able to get rid of that nuisance of a groundhog."

If a two meter column of tar with an ear full of eyes and an arrow poking out the top can be said to look nonplussed, this one did.

The awkward silence stretched out.

"I HEAR YOUR PLEA, MORTAL. WHAT SACRIFICE DO YOU OFFER?"

She was dying, probably lying on the grass hallucinating while Duncan did fuck all, and this must be what they called lucid dreaming. Why not play along? Might as well have some fun in her final moments.

She shouted, "Hey Duncan. Come over here. I've got a *huge* violation to show you."

In the morning, April's body felt like a sponge that had been soaked in sand slurry. Fog wrapped her mind, her head ached, and no matter how she blinked and rubbed, her eyes refused to focus properly. Might be time to give up the gin after all—or else get fitted for glasses.

She was exquisitely careful removing Captain Peep's bandage and splint. Small favors, her hands weren't trembling any worse than usual. Afterward, poor Peep only sat, gazing forlornly over at the other perch.

She shook her head over breakfast tea, remembering the mad dreams she'd had. Duncan was a piece of work, but she'd had worse neighbors. What nasty little urges curled up in the back of her mind had come up with that horror?

Deep breath and a sigh. Forget all about it. Time to check on the garden. That brought back the memory that her cabbages had been savaged. She needed to buy a groundhog trap. That would do it.

But the groundhog was already dead. April found it lying in front of the old well. Next to it was another, presumably its mate, and three pups. The arrangement was oddly formal. It reminded her of a family portrait. She stood squinting. The sun hurt.

"What fresh hell..."

To the left of the well: a pair of boots. Empty. Very new, probably stylish. (Who knew any more?) Well, not completely empty. Half filled with heavy, clotting blood.

Oh shit. Not a dream, then.

Becky was going to have conniptions.

April didn't imagine asking an ear to murder your neighbor was covered in the HOA bylaws, but she was sure they'd find away to call it a violation and fine her.

She'd just have to hide the evidence.

She got on her long rubber dishwashing gloves, and with with one finger and thumb she picked up the boots, one at a time, and dropped them into the well. Normally, she'd have considered making a stew with the groundhogs, but not this time She hadn't the stomach for it. They went into the hole, too.

The thing below rumbled. She felt its momentary satisfaction, but it was still hungry. Implacably, eternally hungry.

She retreated to her kitchen. The cheerful daisies on the tablecloth looked sickly. Her pottery pigs' usually adorable faces were accusing. Gin in the pantry. Ugh. Too early to drink it straight. Better mix it into the leftover tea.

April sat and sipped and scowled. She knew what that Thing was up to. She asked for one groundhog. It gave her five. It had intentionally over-delivered to create an obligation. Just like when that blonde busybody Elsabeth had moved in next door. April hadn't liked her, right from the start, but just to be neighborly, she'd made a couple of blackberry tarts and left them in a basket on the doorstep.

A few days later, Elsabeth had returned the basket with a whole pie inside. That meant April had had to retaliate by inviting her over for tea. After that, they'd had to pretend to be friends for months. April's scowl deepened at the memory.

Elsabeth had begun hinting around about taking down the fence between their gardens before she'd (finally) been forced to move away. Her son had put her in a "home." April wasn't often glad to have had no children—mostly she just didn't think about it at all—but that day had been an exception.

She knew what the Thing wanted, but how could she? Just thinking about what had happened to Duncan made her nauseous. Or maybe that was the gin and tea. She noticed she'd had a lot of it. Well, that was understandable; she was all nerves this morning.

Three sharp raps at the door brought her out of her panicked (blurry, but still panicked) reverie.

"Miss June?" Rap rap rap. "I know you're in there."

Becky.

April shuffled to the door and spoke through it. "I'm not feeling well. Go away."

Rap rap rap. "None of your fibs. Duncan says you've been shooting at him."

Duncan is no more, April almost said. She heard it in her mind, in sepulchral tones. She giggled, then shushed herself. How could she get rid of Becky?

"I was shooting at a groundhog."

"So you admit it?"

Oops. Damn.

Rap rap rap. "Let me in. I have some papers here for you."

April's thoughts whirled. Papers meant violations, fines. She suddenly saw the trap she was in.

So this was how it had to be. Tarts, pie, tea. Feeding another unwanted friendship. She'd have to lay in a supply of gin, for courage, and a spare pair of dishwashing gloves.

She yelled through the door. "Come around to the back garden, Becky. I have something to show you."

She hummed and wondered what she should ask for this time—and what would happen when she ran out of neighbors.

THE CHATEAU OVER INNSMOUTH

JOHN KISTE

The most dull-witted thing I ever did was taking Carl along with me to Innsmouth. In the first place, the trip had been planned as a way to study my genealogy in the town from which my family tree had sprung—there would be no time to deal with my friend's constant need for attention and entertainment. In the second place, I had shared rooms with him twice in the past, and the experience never ended pleasantly. In the third place, what the hell was I thinking?

The great aunt with whom he lived had been put into nursing care the previous month, and at the last minute I had caved to his insipid whining about being alone for the week. He had helped me during numerous past exploits, terrifying adventures that I won't elaborate upon here, other than to say that we sometimes hunted monsters together. Scoff if you must. Carl's preternatural ability to hand me the proper weapon at the exact moment it was required to save both of our lives had made him invaluable in our line of work. Otherwise, he was as dumb as a pile of Lincoln Logs, but I figured I owed him a trip that would not involve wooden stakes, rings of salt, or wolfsbane.

We left the train at Newburyport, and Carl happily carried all the luggage, scuttling under the weight of my trunk behind me like a hunchbacked lab assistant from a 30's horror movie. A sweaty fellow with a botched Botox lip job ushered us into his rickety gray bus for the final leg of the journey to the Innsmouth coast. Carl could not disguise his disgust for the driver, and I slapped him into his seat to keep him from making some callous, bullying remark. My own brutality turned him sullen, and in retaliation he noted the fishy lips were merely a more pronounced version of my own. I could not deny the allegation, so I cuffed him in his left ear and pushed him against the bus window.

The decrepit vehicle held only one other fare, and I heard him address the driver as Joe. This passenger was clearly traveling home to Innsmouth, for his greasy visage and sunken chin and oddly wrinkled neck impressed on me that he was probably closely related to the ugly busman. Never one to debate issues of lineage or an unhealthy pH in a local gene pool, I settled back and watched glimpses of the ocean across Plum Island roll past outside the window during the few moments Carl kept his unruly tangle of hair out of my view.

The salt marshes grew more and more wild, and an hour on we topped a hill and spied Innsmouth in the far distance attempting a final crumble into the Atlantic. As we bounced along the last desolate stretches before reaching the decaying port town, I saw the passenger nod to Joe, the driver, and that one pulled the bus to the roadside and opened the door. My jaw dropped at this, for the blotchy fellow grabbed his bag and hopped off, though it was still miles to the city limits and no dwelling or structure was anywhere in sight. He trudged off into the fen, and I nudged Carl, who had fallen asleep, and pointed at the departing figure. Carl merely shrugged and pulled his hat back down. I must offer full disclosure to the dear reader that this curious event foreshadows nothing later in the narrative. The strange departure of this odd passenger has nothing more to do with the tale; he will not be met again. It simply demonstrated the incomprehensible behavior of these denizens of Innsmouth and its outskirts.

Joe started the bus again, and we continued our rumbling jaunt. Steeples of ancient churches rose above the other gambrel roofs and cupolas, though one of the spires had partly collapsed. Even from this vantage point the town appeared eerie and unearthly, and did not seem to get as much sunlight as the surrounding bogs and the ocean off to the east. Still, I could see eagerness in Carl's eyes—to him the creepier the better—and I could not bring myself to tell him we would be getting out at one of the very first thoroughfares we encountered. As we came to the northern border and Adams Street, I alerted the driver that we wished to depart. He was as surprised as Carl, but stopped the bus again, and my friend and I gathered our goods and jumped down. Once the uncouth conveyance had rattled away, we began walking west, admiring some of the larger and better kept houses of the town.

Then we walked some more. Again, Carl toted all the luggage, and I was suddenly glad for two reasons that I had allowed him to come. The first was obvious: the domicile to which we were headed sat at the extreme end of a very long and rather steep street. Even I was panting in ten minutes and I carried only a small valise. Carl grunted at my back, but did not once complain or fall behind. The second reason I was glad of his presence was that I had forgotten how the buildings in this hamlet affected one's nerves. Both the fairly well-kept mansions and the deserted ones prickled the hairs of my back. I remembered again a vague feeling from my youth when I had last visited, and the decay had been palpably added to since.

The town had been founded in the mid-1600s and been a strong center of fishing and refining until the plague of 1846. Afterwards, it had decayed exponentially but retained about four hundred residents until the government sent men into the wharf district in 1929 to roust the criminal element, and perhaps other things. Through most of its existence, the Marsh Mansion on Washington Street had been the grandest home, though the family itself had worn the epithet 'bizarre' for a century or more. The Eliots and Gilmans boasted fine manors as well, but my own family's French-style chateau on the highest point after Adams became Southwick Street had at one time rivaled them for splendor. The witch's hat of one tower now came into view, and in a matter of minutes we had forced open the rusted front gate and climbed the fifty steps to the columned porch.

From this marvelous vantage point—one of the town's best—I turned and surveyed the architecture that terraced down to the town square, the weird church outlines, and finally the collapsing wharf district. Beyond, the Atlantic shimmered in the early afternoon sunlight, though I noted again that the actual buildings seemed to float in the shadows of low clouds. Far out in the ocean a long black smudge denoted the infamous Devil Reef, around which had festered a myriad of unwholesome legends. I involuntarily shivered while Carl stared at me in astonishment. Then I found the house key in my vest pocket and opened the heavy door.

To say this dusty and unlighted house had been my family home was a bit of a misnomer. I had not been in it for thirty years, and it had actually been occupied by my uncle by adverse possession (squatter's rights), though my father had a claim to it that he never exercised. I think it legally belonged to me now by dint of all my relatives being dead or mysteriously missing, but I had not been involved with any probate lawyers. Carl and I had been wandering in the Carpathian Mountains for the last two years. I had no intention of moving myself in or of moving possessions out. My plan was to uncover any genealogical materials and documents Uncle might have stashed here, and—ah, a third reason for Carl's presence—maybe trying to get his old jalopy running again. I had been told it was still in the carriage house.

While I wandered the cobwebbed and cavernous rooms, poking into bureaus and desks, Carl headed to that garage to see what he could do with the automobile. I doubted we could drive it on to Arkham, but it might allow us a sightseeing trip through this dreary and unpleasant borough. I came across half a dozen documents that looked relevant to my studies, and because the electricity had been turned off since my uncle's unexplained disappearance, I climbed the four floors to the room I knew had the best light in the whole chateau—the high cupola which enjoyed large windows around its entire circumference. The windows held a film of grime, but I quickly scrubbed it away on the panes that faced the ocean by pulling a large white cloth from a misshapen object atop a tripod. This was my uncle's fine brass telescope, and as soon as the cloth had served its purpose as my rag, I trained the tube on Devil Reef. Bright daylight reflected from the black stone that glittered in spots, but I saw no beauty in the deformed rocks and sheltered caves. In fact, I shivered again involuntarily. Carl would have mocked me.

Then I began to pore over the paperwork. I found the information woefully inadequate for my purposes. There were obtuse hints that somewhere my own family line intersected with another of Innsmouth's premier clans, the Waites, but I found no documentation collaborating such ramblings. And ramblings they were. I recognized my uncle's handwriting on some of the sillier pages, and recalled that he had, supposedly, simply left the house one day on foot and had not been seen again. This seemed to be a pattern amongst my relatives. As I dwelt on this and other half-recollections from childhood, I heard Carl calling from below.

My voice guided him up, and he at once took a stand at the eyepiece of the telescope. "That's one creepy reef," he whistled. Then he turned and began thumbing through the documents without a hint of asking my permission. Finally he looked up and saw me glaring at him. Nothing perturbed him. He laughed and said, "Frankly, if I had to guess, I'd say you were related to Joe, the bus driver. Same wide lips; same watery eyes." Now he saw me scowling with those eyes and added, "No offense."

"None taken," I grunted. "What's up?"

"Oh, I got the car running. I founded some gasoline that miraculously had not sugared. The tires are crap, and only one headlight works, but there we are."

I clapped him on the back with good humor. "Excellent!" I roared. "We better take the town tour in daylight, then, in case that other headlight fails. We can read this stuff by candlelight tonight. It doesn't look promising."

So we descended to the carriage house and aimed the rickety Ford toward the Manuxet River and the Square. At what had once been the village green, we passed the boarded-up churches I had viewed from the chateau porch. Across from them squatted the Congregational Hall, also boarded and ravaged by time and neglect, and on its pediment was a broken and faded sign that read "Esoteric Order of Dagon." I had been told of this defunct cult as a child; I had been threatened with its arcane rituals whenever I misbehaved.

We headed toward the coast before crossing a bridge near the deserted refinery and the rotting fishery. I explained to Carl that the Marshes had gotten access to a vast quantity of weirdly colored gold from either, depending on who told the story, some hidden South Sea islands or from the abyss just beyond the reef. Priceless examples sat on display right now in the museums of surrounding cities. I saw the doubt etched in the lines on his rough forehead. I tried to convince him, but was forced to shout as the bridge crawled over the river right beside the lowest of three waterfalls that extended back to Lafayette Street. The water swirled far below but the roar was deafening.

Then he saw the heaped bodies of Atlantic shad trying to make their way upriver to spawn. It was the last day of April, and the school lay thick in the flowing water, though it would be a rare thing to see one scale the prodigious heights of the trio of cataracts. Most would give up and head for a stream farther north. They amused Carl, however, and he recalled a title of a book he had read long ago. "If they could leap those falls and accomplish their heart's desire," he said, "we'd see the shad roe over Innsmouth."

I did not laugh. No one should ever encourage Carl. I simply said, "Shad roe is actually a delicacy that tastes like sweetmeats. It's a lobe-shaped egg sac."

"Lobe-shaped?" grunted Carl. "Like the ears of these residents." As he spoke we passed a gaggle of the populace, and they all possessed the same semi-disfigurements—bulging eyes, shell-like ears, and thick, flabby lips. Some of their necks appeared sunken and ribbed.

"Well, anyway," I rejoined, "more of a culinary treat than anything the town restaurant ever provided. If they are even still in operation."

We traversed the town square, which was flanked by evil-looking husks of buildings, and made our way to the business district, which boasted one foul lodging spot, the Gilman Inn, and a functioning if decrepit dining establishment just beyond. We parked the car and went inside, quite cognizant of the fact that many faces had turned in our direction.

The manager of the eatery watched us sit at the counter with his own watery eyes, and then, reluctantly I thought, sat one menu between us. I was not disappointed to see the stew we ordered dumped into the pot from a can—I preferred it in this dingy place—but I did wish the can had not been quite so rusty. We had not eaten all day, but even Carl with his cast-iron stomach could tolerate only a few bites of the tinny, runny broth. I laid money on the countertop and asked the man behind it if he had known my uncle who had lived in the chateau at the far end of Southwick Street.

"Old Amos Phillips?" he responded in a guttural type of croaking voice. "Aye. He left town some months ago. I know not where he be now."

"Is there anyone that might?" put in Carl as he swirled his spoon, the disgust evident by the wrinkles on his brow.

The manager leaned on the counter in thought. He seemed to be debating with himself as to whether he should bring up a taboo subject. "I can't say anyone in these parts had much in the way of deal-ings with Amos. He kept himself to himself." After a moment, he added, "You picked a very poor night to come a-looking fer him, though."

Now it was my turn to lean forward. "Oh," I said calmly, "why is that?"

The eyes of the restaurant man bulged a bit more as he answered. "'Tis the feast of Dagon tonight. Tonight, and again on All Hallow's Eve. Many here used to perform rituals to him."

I recalled the broken sign we had read on the green. "So I have heard," I replied. "But surely no more."

The man shook his head, and the wattle of skin on his neck that looked decidedly like a set of gills shivered horribly. "Surely no more," he repeated. I heard the ticking of a clock on the grimy wall beside me. Then he added, "But Dagon still expects them."

My own neck broke out in a sweat. I nudged Carl, nodded to the manager, and exited into the street. More dark-visaged residents now stood about the Gilman House, and every one of them watched us. Trying and failing to ignore the chilling gazes, we started the car and clattered slowly back to the chateau. We spent the remainder of the hours till dusk gathering candles and hurricane lamps and oil so we would be able to work after true darkness fell.

As the last rays of the setting sun tapped the western windows, we heard a roaring noise on the street and both recognized it as the bus we had arrived in. I touched my nine-millimeter Luger inside my jacket and was quite glad it was nestled there. Taking a deep breath and reassuring myself that Carl was behind me, I opened the front door. A dozen unkempt men stood on the porch and trailed down the steps. I saw Joe among them. The man in front shrugged his thin shoulders inside his oversized coat and began to speak in what can only be called an intelligible gurgle.

"Sir," he said, "we are afraid you misunderstood Simeon, at the restaurant. He warned you to go; to leave. We must insist."

I smiled sardonically. "This is my house, Mr. –?"

"Eliot," he answered. "We are not questioning your ownership. And we are not threatening you, whatever you may believe. My companions," he waved behind him, "and myself are the last victims of a rather unfortunate community evolution. But we are not evil men. We do not practice the rites of our ancestors—but that does not stop the ceremony. You have picked the worst possible day to visit Innsmouth, and your lives will not be worth a farthing if you are still in residence come nightfall. Take your uncle's vehicle and depart. Or we can have Joe remove you on his bus. The choice is yours."

I clapped my hand to my breast and again felt the gun beneath. "My *choice*," I emphasized the word, "is to remain here with my associate this evening. Good night!"

Some of the uncouth men grumbled in guttural tones, and the speaker shook his head sadly, but they left without incident. As darkness descended rapidly, Carl and I lit the candles and the hurricane lamps, and climbed once more to the cupola. I began a careful perusal of the documents of my uncle that I had not yet examined, while Carl busied himself studying the rooftops of the town in the dying light through the brass telescope. I had become thoroughly engrossed in a particular section of the Waite family tree, when, a quarter of an hour later, Carl gasped audibly. A stoic fellow like my assistant never gasps. I looked up.

"What is it?" I queried.

"You better look," was all he said.

I rose and put my eye to the eyepiece. Now it was my turn to gasp. Only I didn't. I shrieked. Carl had aimed the scope once more at Devil Reef, and the water between it and the wharf district roiled wildly. The heads and shoulders of a hundred shimmering and slimy creatures bobbed above the churning ocean as they swam madly for shore. Indeed, the first wave of the beings was now exiting the sea and standing upon the piers and the sandbars. The things stood like hunched humans, but even at this distance, it was evident they represented a different species, a fishy or amphibian one. They possessed massy, fringed heads and puffing gills, and their muscled, scaly limbs ended in wide webbed hands and feet. Moreover, as they moved inland, they seemed to be headed precisely in this direction.

"To hell with genealogy!" I shouted. "Grab your stuff."

Carl and I effected an unceremonious exit down the stairs, out the door, and into the Ford. The initial attempt to start it failed, and I saw sweat glimmer on Carl's neck as he tried again. The motor roared to life and we turned south, hoping to skirt through the whole town and reach the road to Arkham before the fish things spotted us. Unfortunately, both the bridge at Hawk Place and the next one over looked dangerously dilapidated, so our course kept guiding us closer to the piers. We finally crossed at the old village green, but this time we saw lights wavering and dancing in the Congregational Hall. The townsfolk that had accosted us might not be participating in the ancient sacrifices, but something was.

We crossed the Federal Street Bridge and saw no men outside the Gilman House, but just beyond, the street pulsated and squirmed. As our one headlight bounced from the heaving mass, we realized we had arrived too late. Dozens of the denizens of Devil Reef hopped and stumbled up the road, and their huge, rheumy eyes had fixed us in their collective glare. They were far more hideous up close, gray and humped and slithering, and they came closer every second. Carl spun the steering wheel in terror, and we turned right onto Bank Street. This was taking us away from the throng of amphibious demons, but to get out of town to the north we would now have to cross one of the spans of which we had been leery. More frightening still, the horde quickened its loping pace behind us, and they did not fall back as we had hoped. Carl pumped the accelerator, but the Ford only coughed at us and actually slowed down.

We turned right again onto Hawk Place at the deserted railway station and decelerated to again survey the bridge. Every I-bar dripped decay and a key eyebolt looked far too rusty to Carl, who had once taken a single course in engineering, and failed it. As the front tires pulled onto the edge of the structure, the whole monstrous skeleton of the bridge groaned in agony. We had no choice; the flopping footfalls were a hundred yards behind. Carl eased the vehicle across, but protruding rebar jutted from the burst concrete of the roadway and punctured both tires on the passenger side. The bridge groaned louder as we ran off its surface and up a grade, but then the entire vehicle body listed to one side and we realized the wheels would get us no farther.

Carl grabbed a heavy tire iron and leapt out his door as I exited mine, but we only had one spare tire. Nor would there be time to change it. The creatures had leapt onto the other end of the structure and would be on us in seconds. I pulled my Luger and aimed at the head of the pack. Then I heard my assistant swearing. He had forgotten to set the parking brake on the Ford. It was suddenly thumping backwards on two good tires, dragging the bare wheels along in a wide arc. As the surface of the bridge filled to capacity with the grunting gray pile of pursuers, the car slammed into the rusty eye-bolt on this end of the suspension. The bridge could take no more abuse. The bolt snapped and the great erection of iron tore loose from that same corner, screeching madly, and hurling the vanguard of the posse of fish men into the rapids below.

They were marvelous swimmers, of course, but they were also far too close to the brink of the first falls. Some made it back to the other bank, but most spilled down the cataract. I could see them swirling in the vortex below the drop, unhurt but unable to claw their way back up to us. In fact, some of them gave up altogether and began munching on the unlucky shad who had battled to top the other two falls. Only one of the gilled things crawled up our side of the bank, and that one was determined to reach us. I shot him three times and watched a thick red-yellow ichor ooze from the wounds, but he was only stopped when Carl beat his head in with the tire iron. Not a pleasant sight.

The creatures still upon the opposite bank watched the scene in impotent fury and began to lope further upriver where they could cross with ease. Carl and I immediately turned and beat our path away from the Manuxet into the morass. As we started trotting rapidly through the dry section of the marsh, we startled a solitary female deer. She stared at us and cocked her tiny head, as though she heard other unearthly sounds afar off. Then she bolted toward a copse of shrub trees a half mile to the west. Carl, panting as he was, could not resist. "Farewell to the sad doe over Innsmouth." I paused to punch him in the belly and refused to acknowledge him during the rest of our escape. We ran and sloshed and shambled to the northwest and by morning the exhausted and bedraggled pair of us had reached the outskirts of Rowley.

We told our incredible story to the authorities there, and more than a few of them believed more than a little of it. They all knew of the eldritch tales told about Innsmouth, and they mumbled promises about finishing what those in charge had started in the late 1920s. They never did, of course. These appropriate steps had before met with but limited success, and politicians and constables in the know pondered just how many of the anthropoid frogs might live in the trench beyond the black reef, and wondered just how far inland they could tramp if sufficiently harassed.

Carl and I returned north, where he stills comments on my slightly bulging eyes whenever he's had a snootful. I personally don't sleep very well these nights. After all, we did bash in the head of one of their kind, and the seacoast here is only two miles distant. I cannot imagine the things could track us this far, but I am not absolutely certain that it is beyond their power. These days I keep Carl and his odd karma close, and a dozen loaded spearguns in the corner closer. And every time I pass a realtor, I go in and inquire about property in the middle of the Sahara.

THE READING

JAMES DORR

I

The poet was nervous. There was no way he could politely get out of it; he had been trapped. He had no excuse. There was no way he could have denied it, he *was* a published poet, and so when the Ladies' Library Culture Committee asked him—in public—to perform a reading at their next meeting, how could he deny them? He had been hooked fairly and, now that the appointed Friday evening was scant hours away, it was time to be reeled in.

The poet had a friend who was wiser, perhaps, than he in the world's ways. His friend's name was Marcella and he went to her.

"Marcella," he said, "I am nervous about tonight. I have agreed to do a reading of some of my work for the Library Committee and you know how I hate that. I don't have the voice for it. I cough and splutter, I even have trouble p-p-p-pronouncing words, especially when I'm nervous like this."

Marcella nodded. It was not the first time they had had this conversation.

The poet went on. "And you know I don't have a car, poets never making much money at their craft, so I will have to take the bus there. You know I hate buses. But, much worse than that, the bus line will have stopped running by the time my reading is finished and I will be forced to walk home, and the hall the reading is to be in is not in a nice neighborhood."

Marcella nodded.

"In fact, the neighborhood I will be walking through is downright perilous after dark, what with junkies and murderers teeming the sidewalks. Well, maybe I exaggerate somewhat there, but you know what I mean, the kind of neighborhood police do not cruise through, as a general practice. The kind most people like me would avoid."

Marcella smiled. "I know," she said. "It is the same hall your last reading was in, the one you did for that university group—oh what was it called? It doesn't matter. But, you must understand, it, like the library, was taxpayer funded and so, naturally, it had a small budget. It could not afford a more upscale hall, one that might be, perhaps, in a better neighborhood. Nevertheless, you came back from *that* one intact."

The poet smiled too. "Yes," he admitted, "although I did take precautions. I did make the long walk back home successfully. Yet the reading itself, I felt, was a disappointment. I fear that this reading may disappoint too."

"But why?" Marcella asked. "You are a good poet. You're well enough known, albeit your subject matter may be a bit…"

"A bit distasteful?" the poet prompted.

"I would say 'unusual,'" Marcella answered. That is, it is in a noble tradition, a literary tradition, that of Poe, of Lovecraft, even of Keats. 'La Belle Dame' and all that. I should revel in it myself, if I could write like you."

The poet sighed. "Let us call it as it is: Horror. I write horror poetry. My muse is a dark one. And the people that I will be reading before, while they may see that word on their programs, they will still expect poems about daisies. Not Keats, but Wordsworth. They will be looking for poems about flowers, about bluebirds and young love and dew on the spring grass…"

"And not corpses beneath it, you mean," Marcella said. "Yes, that is true enough. So it is your job to educate them. Enlarge their perspectives."

"But they will not like me," the poet said. "They will dislike my reading. If I were a *good* reader, deep-voiced, confident, well then I might perhaps win them over, that is if they would stay quiet till the end of it. But they will fidget. They'll cough. They'll murmur. They'll make me more nervous. I'll lose my place. You see, Marcella, that is why I fear this."

Marcella laughed, a gentle, sympathetic laugh. This was not the first time they had had this discussion. "There is an irony in this," she finally said, "that is, of the writer of horror poetry being himself scared. But that is the way of the world, is it not, that life itself is filled with ironies?"

The poet nodded.

"But here is what I think," Marcella said. "Were I in your place, I, too, would be nervous. That is because, up on the platform, the lectern before me, I staring out into the darkened hall over the rows of stone-faced people waiting, I might think, for me to falter—waiting for one reason *not* to enjoy the performance I wish to give—I would feel vulnerable.

"Is that not how you feel?"

"Yes," the poet said.

"Then let me suggest a trick: Were I in your place, what I would do is to imagine the audience naked. You are a poet, an artist, a dreamer. One whose work is *based* on imagination, so it should be easy. Especially for you. And then you must ask yourself what is more vulnerable than one who is naked, bereft of the armor that clothing gives one.? Of all pretense of dignity, of taste. How can the *nude* have taste, or, if they did, how could they express it? What better could they do than listen in rapt silence to your offerings?"

The poet felt dubious about this, but he decided he would give it a try. "Very well," he said, "I will think of them naked. Perhaps it will make my reading more pleasurable, both for them and me, than it was the last time." He picked his bulging briefcase up; he inclined his cheek so Marcella could kiss it—just for luck, mind you. He even eschewed the bus, taking the time to walk to his reading despite the down-at-heels ambience he strode through the closer he came to his destination, the rats and the garbage.

He took inspiration from one glance he had of a crow eating something that looked like an eyeball.

He arrived at the hall and stood on the stage, arranging his papers on the lectern, the lights bright above him. He peered out over the darkened rows of expectant listeners, middle aged ladies for the most part, most going to fat, their still dumpier husbands. Some saggy, some wrinkled. Some sallow-skinned, some bald, the women as well as men, some with their wigs slipping. Some with their teeth out, their legs crooked, their breasts flat.

He imagined them naked.

Appalled—*frightened*—by the thought, he reached, again, into his bulging briefcase and pulled out his Uzi, the one that he had bought the last time to help assure safety on his dark walk home. He held down the trigger, spraying its bullets into the yawning hall, this way and that way, one way or another to make the audience more vulnerable than he.

He began his reading in pin-drop silence, except, perhaps, for the annoying sound of something, somewhere in front of him dripping. But it was an ancient auditorium, its walls thick and quiet, blocking at least the often more abrasive racket from outside traffic.

All in all, all right.

He finished his last poem, then repacked his papers and bowed and departed, taking his other things with him as well. He accomplished the lonely walk home without untoward incident, as had been the case the last time too, as Marcella had reminded him. He had read his work, after at least that first uncertain moment, in confidence and— dare he think it?—even joy. All in all, a good night.

Still, he reflected, it would have been nicer when he was done if at least *someone* had applauded.

II

T he poet knew all too well that tricks would not work, despite his friend's advice. What, he should think of the audience naked? He had tried that once—the memory came back. It had been a disaster.

Yes, he had finished the reading okay, but the audience had not been appreciative. He had sensed that. They had been quiet, attentive perhaps, but, when it was finished, and he had walked his lonely, long way home, it had then occurred to him that not a single one of them, slumped in their seats as they were, had even *acknowledged* him.

No, this time it would have to be different.

He did not like readings. They made him nervous. He was a good poet, but an indifferent speaker, his voice tending toward stutters and whistles, clucks and catches, especially when he was nervous like he was now.

His friend, Marcella, had told him that, on the lighted stage like this, the lectern the only wall between him and his sullen-faced audience, he tended to feel vulnerable. His friend, Marcella, he realized was wise.

She had told him he must face his audience, speak directly to them, using the subjects he knew were unpopular almost as if a shield. That is, they wanted daisies and bluebirds? He must give them their flowers wilted, their birds supine and half-eaten by cats. What he wrote was horror: He must revel in it.

In that way his audience would be enlightened, like it or not. Perhaps not *everyone*, in any crowd there were some who were dull-witted, but someone, somewhere in the dark before him, would hear and respond.

It was, after all, a noble tradition, the one he wrote in, that of Lovecraft and Poe.

He shuffled his papers on the lectern. He cleared his throat. He had had no way of getting out of the reading, despite what had happened at the last one. He had been hooked, fair and square, asked under circumstances such that he could not have refused.

He cleared his throat again: He was *so* nervous.

He started his first poem, a long one, a homage to the author and poet H. P. Lovecraft whose work had inspired him. His voice cracked. It broke. He spat and his lungs wheezed and yet he soldiered on.

He would get through this poem.

Finally completing it, he even received a small spattering of applause. Buoyed by this slightly, he began a second poem, his voice no better.

He croaked—he felt like a frog. Words buzzed and hummed and quacked. Whistled and growled and popped.

Some of the sounds even seemed familiar, as if themselves utterances not quite in English, but—

A sudden, sulfurous cloud rose from the platform floor, masking the spotlight above his lectern. Just for a moment.

The poet stopped in mid-word.

The fog, the cloud, the *miasma* parted, revealing an odious, scaled, tentacled figure, oozing slime over the stage-apron's hardwood. Its cephalopod head rose to tower above the poet, drooling filth down on him. Foul-smelling. Sickening.

The audience was silent—paralyzed in its seats. In an ironic reversal, however, the poet was less afraid. A lifetime spent studying his genre's masters, he knew what this *thing* was.

"C-Cthulhu!" he stammered.

The monster bowed its horrible countenance. It opened its fearsome maw, revealing—the poet dared not look too closely inside!

"Yes, it is I," the monster thundered, belching a new cloud of jaundiced, unwholesome stench. "I have answered your summons, Poet, made directly to me in the Ancient Language. I—"

"Now wait a minute," the poet said. His friend, Marcella, had told him once that, when one was nervous, one might try transferring one's fear to a different emotion, such as anger.

The poet was angry.

"Now just wait a minute," the poet said again. "It so happens I did my dissertation in college on H. P. Lovecraft and, while I'll admit my reading voice tends toward some gosh-awful sounds sometimes, I can tell you for a fact that what I was uttering was no 'summons to you in the Ancient Language.' Sure, maybe parts sounded a *little* bit like that. If you push things enough, I suppose anything sounds like anything else. But even if I was summoning you through some convoluted twist of reasoning, you didn't give me time to finish—"

"So?" the monster said.

The poet stamped his foot. "So it isn't *fair!*"

The monster shrugged, what would have been a shrug if it had had shoulders, and smacked its hungry lips. What might have been lips, though in some ways they came off as being more beak-like, albeit with teeth as well. It roared its answer:

"So who says Cthulhu is fair?"

III

C thulhu oozed on a stage in front of a darkened room, filled with petrified rows of frightened-faced people. Before it stood a lectern on which were what humans called "poems." It sensed, somewhere in the recesses of its mind, that it was expected to read these

Cthulhu was nervous.

HERE THERE BE (HARDLY ANY) MONSTERS

NATHAN WADDELL

X yrgXgryX roared, and the universe contracted. Not all the way, but a little bit. Perhaps if XyrgXgryX had roared in anger, the universe would have shrunk back down all the way to a singularity. But XyrgXgryX roared in pain, and so the universe just sort of tentatively shrunk for a second or two, and then went back to expanding. XyrgXgryX went back to roaring, and cosmic goo spewed forth from his carapace. A globscenity of corrupted, jellified plasma poured out of him where he had been pierced. He tried to strike back at his eternal enemy, at the Incorruptible Mind, but it was too late. XyrgXgryX died. It was the first time XyrgXgryX died. It was the infinitth time he died.

H atching is but the first task, and the easiest. The start of a new psycle, another turn of the Eclipsular Wheel. YrgXgrY bursts forth, fury and gaping hunger driving him to accomplish the second task. For he never hatched alone. He was but one of a multitude, which must be made into a singletude. A sindividual. An individual. Whatever! Only one allowed! Which was him. He gave himself one single femtosecond to lick his fteeth in anticipation, deciding which of his mouths he should use for the frenzy, when he was ingested by a sibling. A gribling! She used her tertiary masticator on him, a grievous insult. As he was swallowed, YrgXgrY roared, and somewhere a pulsar very nearly stopped spinning. Well, it thought quite hard about it, definitely.

The Eclipsular Wheel turns on, infernal. Eternal. RgXgR hatches anew, rebirthing into stunning violence. There will be no artistry this time, no curating of fteeth and maw, no hesitation. Just devouring. RgXgR devoured, and devoured, and devoured until the second task was complete. The lone survivor, he surveyed the carnage. He spat out a bit of the gribling that ended his previous psycle so ingloriously, using her masticating mandible as a ftoothpick. Something like a burp came out of his stomick. Satisfied, RgXgR prepared for the next task.

RgXgR pupates. He putresces. Using the raw material of his ingested griblings, he builds a corporeality for himself. Where he is going is harsh and hostile, and he knows he will need both armor and arms. He manifests quite a few arms for himself, tentacles with spikes and suckers, sensacles to see and craste and glim, and nonsensacles with weaponized illogic. A slightly different array than his last few incarnations- it was always necessary to tweak and refine. The Incorruptible Minds were formidable and the hurdle he must clear to realize his inexorable destiny, his feight.

Just thinking about the Minds ignited the fury engine in his core that drove him. How many lives had he lost, how much time wasted? He reveled in his dark ruminations, and the tuminations that followed. It was good to dwell in murky hatred. For this next task was just a tad tricky. It would be a lot easier if he was still XyrgXgryX. But RgXgR would have to be sufficient. He was nothing if not adaptable to the most infernal conditions. His very existence *was* an infernal condition!

He would need to shrink. But don't think of it as a lessening, a diminution! Not so. More of a compression, an optimizing of density and intensity. If he concentrates, he can concentrate himself. Like so: R$_G$X$_G$R.

Maybe a little more: ^{R_GX_GR}.

Almost.

$_{RgXgR}$.

Yes.

In order to pierce the interstices between voids, he must make of his essence a spear tip. A pierceation. $_{RgXgR}$ must be sharp enough to poke a hole into the next universe. But $_{RgXgR}$ was frustratingly round and blunt. What if he- $_{RgXg}$R. Oops, too much. Yrxtz. He'd never had this much trouble before. He screamed in rage and frustration. On a small planet in an unremarkable galaxy, a prototree dropped a protopinecone. A protosquirrel ate it.

Enough of this. $_{RgXgR}$ knew what to do. All things can be done by brute force and chthonic hate. And by diving really fast at the barrier between dimensions, like so:

R

    g

        X

           g

           R

Almost there. Push! Harder! Do it! Scream curse rage! Just. Push. Through.

                R

                  g

                    X

                      gR

Ha! Triumph! Planck space shuddered and resisted, but could not deny RgXgR his task. He was through! RgXgR welcomed the crushing pressure and absolute darkness. Laws of physics were always a refreshing change of pace. And he could always rewrite those that got on his nerves- most of them, to be honest- once he was finished with his ultimate task. Which was to establish an empire of corruption. Should that be Empire of Corruption? Laws of grammar were even more annoying than Laws of Physics. Whatever.

In previous attempts he had chosen a different entry vector, establishing first a presence on a world of lesser minds. Desecrating such worlds presented no challenge, and no reward. No, it was this little ball of water and rock with its immune inhabitants that were the key. If he could obscenify such virtuous beings, the entire universe would be his to reshape. Speaking of which, better decompress. There. RgXgR was himself again. He was about to let loose a victorious roar, but then he remembered how more than a few previous incarnations had ended, and decided to roar inside his hearts instead.

For this part of his Imperative was the most dangerous, the most challenging. In fact he had never progressed past this phase in all his preincarnations. The Incorruptible Minds, his implacable enemy, perfectly evolved foils to his corrosive corruption, stopped him every time. Every time! Just thinking of them made his newfound corporeality feel very exposed. Vulnerable, even, if such a thing were possible. One reason for seeking out this crushing depth and darkness. RgXgR backed into a cave ~~to hide~~ where ~~it was nice and cozy~~ he could best plan his strategy and tactics for the coming conquest.

There were some lifeforms in the cave already, which RgXgR ingested for fuel and mass. He scalibrated his sensacles and sent them forth. Immediately he sensed something was very different than last time. Was this right? He shook his sensacle and crasted again. The Minds . . . where were they? Their presence was but an echo, their detestable song nearly silenced. At first RgXgR felt elation. His hated enemy, hurting and ravaged! This would make everything so much easier. Using the chromatophore biotechnology he had absorbed from the previous inhabitants of this cavern, RgXgR altered the way the outer surface of his exoskeleton absorbed and reflected radiation in such a way that he turned a very pretty pink.

Just as quickly, however, he turned a much less soothing greenish-brown color. Suspicion and anger overcame him as a new notion erupted in one of his tentacular glial clusters, and quickly dispersed throughout his neuronal network of arms and appendages: the only thing capable of decimating the Minds was him, or one of his kind! Which of his misbegotten griblings was responsible? He would rend and rip the offender. Only he was allowed to avenge his... but . . . wait. It was impossible. Wasn't it? His kind reveled in the impossible, of course, but even so, he was nothing if not thorough with his tasks and was almost certain he had left no gribling uneaten.

He drew his eyestalks and all extendacles into himself. A moment of scentering, calm. Shhh. Count to $\sqrt{2}^* \oplus$.

Better.

Now he could take another crasting in scerenity and interpret the results free of misconception. This universe operated on very strict rules- cause *had* to come before effect, which, eww, and he would definitely change that when he had a chance- but useful for etheorizing a timeline of events he did not actually experience himself.

Hmm, the images he was receiving from the ether were nonsensical, illogical, and even so he still had a hard time processing what he was crasting. Tiny minds? Little parasites on mindless bioshells floating atop the unvoid? RgXgR left his shelter, it was safe enough after all with so few Minds to worry about now, and floated upwards. One of his sensacles told him that there was a hive of these anomalous minds above him. He would investigate, and then almost certainly ingestivate. Unless... an alliance could be made with these strange beings who obviously hated the Minds as much as he did? No! Globscentiy to even entertain such a thought. He could suffer no friendship, nor allow any usurper. Also, he was getting hungry.

RgXgR activated his chromatophores, taking care to blend in with the greater variety of light wavelengths bouncing around near the top of the void. He could see the little bioshell above him, though it was practically featureless from this angle. He would need to find a better vantage point. He grabbed the bioshell with some of his arms, then rescalibrated all the suckers on one of his sensacles into eyes and sent them scouting up into the unvoid. Such a strange state of being, neither void nor soothing skrush. What manner of creature would choose to live in such an environment?

One way to find out, he supposed. He plucked a tiny creature from the bioshell and dove a fathom or two to examine it. Gross! So squirmy. And it's mind…yrxtz! If RgXgR wasn't careful this little mind would corrupt *him*. That would be embarrassing… RgXgR learned its language, probed its memories. He could see now how these little beings had managed to nearly rid this world of the Incorruptible Minds. Such wanton slaughter. It was a little unsettling, really. Kind of disturbing.

 Oh- the ugly little thing stopped struggling. Probably driven even more ins- no, it was dead. What? Such fragility was shocking in such a maligonized organism.

RgXgR popped the thing in his tertiary masticator. Didn't want to upset his primary stomick if it didn't agree with him. Hmm, not bad! Was that a hint of umami? He would have guessed it would be bitter and disgusting. For the infinitth time he wondered what the Incor- ruptible Minds tasted like. The fact that he still didn't know after this many turns of the Eclipsular Wheel really chafed his fteeth. And now these tiny little pukethings would steal that pleasure from him? Absog- lutely not!

He surfaced again, this time making no attempt to camouflage himself. He wrapped the 'whaling ship' in his myriad appendages, causing a commotion on the deck. He plucked a couple 'whalers' from the ship and lazily dropped them into his tertiary masticator- they were too stupid to know how badly he was insulting them! He would insult each and every one of them before he was done. He would grind them with his fteeth, and excreech them at the bottom of the void. He would-

Pain! Chaos! Shock! Ouch! RgXgR no RgXg was hurt, badly. Incomprehensibly, these tiny gnats had somehow injured him. Him! He was maimed, mangled and mutilated. A 'harpoon' made of 'iron'. The pain was immeasurable. Thrashing, RgXg fled, seeking the safety of the cavern at the bottom of the ocean.

Safely ensconced, RgXg took stock. He was badly hurt. His favorite sensacle was gone. Maybe he shouldn't have packed it with so many eyes and loaded it with so many of his glial neurons. And it was the only way he could craste the presence of Incorruptible Minds. RgXg would have to go into vibernation. A period of dormancy, equivalent to a turn of the Eclipsular Wheel, or a mere century or two as these pukethings reckon time, would be ample time to repair and regrow. He could seek vengeance when he awoke. The Minds would undoubtedly be extinct at the rate the pukethings were extinguishing them, but perhaps that was a good thing after all. RgXg had a new task, the eradication of these contemptible soft-bodied horrors. Yes.

RgXg slept.

R gXg0 awoke. Stretched. It felt nice. So relaxed. He thought about snoozing for another decade or so, but he did have to excreech quite badly. He yawned and finally got up to do his business. Only then did he notice that something was amiss. For yrxtz' sake! His sensacle hadn't grown back properly at all. RgXg0 examined himself. Deformity and decay. Normally good things. But not this time. What went wrong? He queried his fribosomes. Ah. It seems the alien digestible in the pukethings had interfered with his interferons. Yrxtz! Well, he already planned to make them pay, now he would make them pay even . . . painer! He shivered in anticipation, chromatophores fluorescing in sympathetic animation.

Even without his best sensacle, RgXg0 could tell things had changed a lot while he vibernated. The ocean now had a distinctive taste that it lacked before. Quite a nice mélange of pollutants, in fact. He made a glial note to find the recipe. But for now he had a task, and he would do it. He launched himself upwards to the unvoid, tentacles and other protuberances trailing behind him, a streamlined horrpedo.

Even hampered as he was, it didn't take RgXg0 long to find his prey. The 'ships' were no longer made of 'wood' so maybe it was just as well he hadn't relied on his sensacles, which he probably would have had scalibrated to look for the wrong biosignature. These new ships were made of unalive stuff, similar to the harpoon that had caused such pain and havoc. All the more reason to devour! But caution was in order, as well. Here was one such ship already. Stealth mode activated.

RgXg0 approached, invisible, silent, weightless. A true terror of the deep. Inspiring and impressive, to be honest. He kind of wished he still had some griblings so they could admire him. But no matter. The ship floated passively, totally unaware of the ignominious and gloriously nightmaric fate that was about to strike from below. RgXg0 almost gave himself away by giggling. He clamped that noise down, and extended his stretchiest, stickiest tentacle. Slowly, carefully, he caressed the side of the boat. It was full of little pukethings! Juveniles even! Yum!! He reached over the side and

gXg0 was pulled suddenly and violently downward. What was happening? Such pain, how? gXg rolled, he spun, he struck out blindly. Something was devouring him. A Mind! Here? Impossible! Wasn't it? There was so little of Xg left now, and that was barely enough to form thoughts, let alone suss out how this could be happening. X struggled, but V knew he was lost. With his last conscious avolition, he roared in pain. In response, a couple of bubbles whipped up from the struggle popped. One was a pretty decent size, even.

On board the whale-watching boat *Kaikoura*, a child pointed to starboard, shouting "Look! There's a whale! And he's eating a squid or something!"

The tourists rushed to that side of the boat, furiously snapping pictures, oohing and ahhing. It had been a great day for whale watching, they had seen four or five sperm whales already. They watched as the whale dove, its tail breaking free of the water majestically, incorruptibly, as members of its species had since time immemorial.

Madison the tour guide looked over the side of the *Kaikoura* and called out to its captain, Dave, "Dude, I think something ripped your 'Save The Whales' banner off. There's like, a bunch of slime all over. It's gross."

Dave rushed over. "Not my whale banner! That was vintage."

"It was old, you mean. Kind of ratty."

"But I got it on eBay. It was originally on the *Rainbow Warrior*."

"Probably a fake. Anyways you can always get a new banner. Something more modern, don't you think? I mean the whales are doing good now."

"I guess." Dave muttered a curse word, but nothing in the cosmos took note at all.

DEAR XUTUIX?!

J.D. HARLOCK

*"Dear *¥+¥!*(Xutuix?!)*

We really appreciated the time it must've taken you to send us your experimental essay (short story?), but I'm afraid that on this occasion we're going to have to reject it. We don't usually respond to submissions, but luckily this time, we decided that underrepresented writers (you mentioned you were a resident alien?) should get some sort of feedback on how to improve their writing moving forward, and hopefully, one day, attains the heights that'll allow their work in our pages.

Now we here at The Endless Fantasias of Arcane Lores *try to make sure that our feedback mostly zeroes in on what works about a piece, and I have to say you've got something unique and very, very interesting going on here. I don't think I've ever read a piece about a day in the life of "€£¥*" (CeYx? Ceux? Am I using the term right?) as a grak-splor-g rustler on "&*&*$%^" and I'm not sure I ever will again. We don't usually recommend that writers send in their first drafts or works-in-progress or preliminary notes, but we think you should really capitalize on this underrepresented perspective and maybe work on some of the other minor stuff that's holding your writing back, like spelling, grammar, and punctu-*

ation. I really, really think if you really invest the time into at least one of these things, there'll really be a noticeable improvement in the quality of your work and you can really start tapping into that (potential) potential that I'm certain you probably have.

I completely understand that this may be frustrating to hear at this stage of your writing divertissement, but I think you can take comfort in the point of view that this is only one award-winning editor's opinion. Other editors at smaller small press magazines may disagree, and I would recommend you take their feedback almost as seriously as mine. I'm afraid that art just hasn't been decolonized yet in the old U.S. of A., and we're unfortunately still working off arcane (love using this word) frameworks that only emphasize western storytelling values like story, plot, and character. I'm sure where you're from, there's a whole other dimension of art that we can't wait to explore someday, and you can rest assured that we took that into full consideration when judging your piece.

And I guess that's all we have to say!

We apologize we took so long to get back to you. The piece took some time to parse through. Quite some time, actually, but we're really glad that we were able to somehow get back to you on this. We know you opted-in for our premium deluxe fast response option with premier responses from every single one of our twelve volunteer editors, but for some reason, we couldn't process your payment. The app glitched and said it couldn't recognize your currency (something about it not existing), but there's no need to worry, we've messaged tech support, and they'll get your money to us in no time!

~~Thank you for your (INSERT COMPLIMENT) work~~

We ~~appreciated~~ acknowledge your piece, and ~~we welcome you to submit again~~ hope you find a ~~better home~~ outlet for it.

~~If you have any questions, feel free to ask....~~

Actually....

You know what?

Since the other editors aren't going to even bother to look over this one, I'm going to be a bit blunter than I usually am about these things.

So...

Are you trolling us?

That's what I thought at first. But who would spend this kind of money to hear back from a bunch of Eng lit majors who started a blog for ten dollars? Honestly, we didn't put up all these payment options expecting someone to buy the full, FULL package, but it's really hard out there for a revolutionary intersectional small press these days.

I really, really appreciate that you thought we were worth it, though, so, for once in my career, I'm going to give it to you straight:

    What the fuck was that?!

    I mean, what the fuck?!

    This was just wrong.

    Why would you, in your right mind, think this was worthy of our time?! My time!

Where do I even begin?

Would you even understand if I did?

Can you?

I don't know.

Maybe there's a language barrier here? Or a cultural difference? I don't fucking know.

I just know that you don't send a story about the mating rituals of "interplanetary time dilators" on the Carputhian beat in the mean streets of Galaxar! Whatever the fuck that means because I don't fucking know!

Do you?

Do you know what the fuck any of this means?

Well, I don't think so.

Here, let me prove it to you.

Tell me, what is a €£¥*?

Or a grak-splor-g?!

Or grak-splor-g rustling!

And how do you pronounce "&*&*\$%^?", if you can call this (or really any of these) sounds real words?! If you can all any of these symbols sounds!

I mean, you can't even pronounce them in English!

And it doesn't end there.

None of this, I repeat NONE OF THIS, is realistic or even makes the tiniest chromosome of sense!

Why do the €£¥*\$ have ejaculatory suction proboscises instead of faces? And if they have ejaculatory suction proboscises for faces, where do their six million transdimensional eyes fit?! Inside of them?! And if they have ejaculatory suction proboscises with six million transdimensional eyes inside of them, why have them cry from their rectal orifices!

Explain! Explain!

I mean, come on!

It doesn't even factor into the story!

I think...

Anyways, I'm almost certain that some other publisher out there would ~~love to~~ have received this.

~~Respectfully,~~

Acknowledging-ly,

The Editor(s)"

On finishing the letter, *¥+¥!* found it harder to breathe–through all the ejaculation. Having taken time off his pressing work as an interplanetary time dilator to try and make it as a writer on his favorite planet Earth–away from all that Carputhian beat on the mean streets of Galaxar–this hit them particularly hard. But, unable to find the mating call to express their unbridled anguish, they turned their ejaculatory suction proboscis away in shame, for their six million transdimensional eyes could not bear to look at the rejection letter any longer.

A *grak-splor-g* mooed far off in the distance as the €£¥* rectal orifices began to liquidate.

HOW THE OLD ONES SAVED CHRISTMAS

RICHARD S. CRAWFORD

Dedication: For my wife, Jennifer

Now...

S anta looked... different than Jimmy was expecting.

Jimmy was hiding behind the sofa. It was where he hid whenever anything scary happened, like when the monsters showed up on *Doctor Who* or when kissing happened in one of the movies his parents watched. But this time wasn't scary. This time he was hiding because he didn't want to be seen when Santa arrived.

He'd seen Santa at the mall, of course, though he was still unsure whether that was the *real* Santa or just one of his helpers. But he knew what Santa looked like: a big, fat guy with a long white beard, and wearing a red suit.

But when Santa appeared in the living room, he didn't look like Santa at all. He was tall, for one thing, so tall that he had to stoop to avoid hitting the ceiling. And instead of being dressed in red, he was all dressed in yellow. He wore a long yellow cloak that reached down to the ground, and a pale yellow shroud hid his face entirely.

"Santa?" little Jimmy said.

"Uh oh," Santa replied. He looked down on the child, but Jimmy could not see any sign of his face. "You weren't shuposhed to shee me." His voice slurred, like Daddy's did when he'd had too much eggnog. He lifted up his hand, and sparks began to shoot from it. "What ish the polishy in thish shituation?"

"What?"

"Do I deshtroy you now, or wait until you have resheived your giftsh?"

NEITHER, boomed a voice. It seemed to come from all of space and time at once, more of a feeling than a voice, but it was mostly focused on the chimney. THE CHILD MUST LIVE.

"I do not understhand, Nodensh."

DESTROYING THE CHILD WOULD BE AGAINST THE SPIRIT OF CHRISTMAS.

"Ish thish true?" the tall figure asked Jimmy.

Jimmy nodded enthusiastically.

The figure lowered its hand, and the sparks disappeared. "Chrishtmash is very confushing," it said.

But before that...

Doctor Evergeen sipped his peppermint tea and made another note on his clipboard. This was such a sad state of affairs. He almost could not bring himself to lift his candy cane pen.

"How is he, Doctor Evergreen?" It was the nurse, Jenny Cupcake.

Doctor Evergreen sighed. "It's worse than before. He's started screaming in his sleep. I'm afraid he'll never recover his sanity."

Jenny's face screwed up, and Doctor Evergreen thought she might break into sobs. "It's so sad," she said, her voice tremulous. "Poor Santa."

"Indeed. And I'm afraid he is unable to perform his duties. We may have to cancel Christmas this year."

The two of them watched Santa. The Big Guy was strapped to a gurney, writhing and wriggling. He burbled and gibbered, but nothing came forth from his mouth but utter nonsense. Doctor Evergreen had tried to make sense of the words, but so far he'd been unsuccessful.

"What did he see?" Jenny Cupcake asked. "What happened?"

Doctor Evergreen shook his head. "He talked about a giant monster in the Atlantic Ocean. A moving mountain miles tall. Utter nonsense."

Jenny turned pale. "Did... Did he mention any names?"

"No. Only nonsense words that I could not make out. Why, what do you know?"

"Nothing. There are things that elves aren't supposed to know. You told me that yourself. But I have an idea. I'll be right back."

When she returned a few minutes later, she carried with her a small black book which had the eldritch word "Eibon" inscribed on its leather cover. "There's a chant in here that just might work. If we can bind the proper being, we might have a replacement Santa for this year."

"What are you talking about?"

"We can summon and bind an Old One. Only they have the power needed to go all over the world and visit each home during the night. Some ancient writings suggest that Santa himself is an avatar of Nodens, guardian of the Dreamlands."

Doctor Evergreen shook his head, afraid that little Jenny Cupcake's mind had gone, just like Santa's. Was there an epidemic of insanity affecting the entirety of Christmas Village?

"Sector 7-G is abandoned, right?"

"Has been since 1922."

"Great! I'll perform the ritual there. Just wait for me here and keep an eye on Santa." She scurried out of the lab, her jinglebells ringing merrily as she did so.

Doctor Evergreen looked back at Santa, who writhed and gibbered on the gurney. "I hope she knows what she's doing."

Not now, but not quite back then either...

The smoke alarm did not go off, nor had it gone off for centuries, not since Hastur had cursed it, and it probably should have given the amount of smoke in Hastur's kitchenette right now.

BEHOLD, said Nodens. THE COOKIES ARE DONE.

Hastur waved away the smoke, and it vanished into the void. "I do not undershtand thish," he said. "Why musht we bake theshe cookiesh?"

I AM EXPERIMENTING WITH HUMAN HOLIDAYS, Nodens replied. THIS ONE IS CHRISTMAS. IT IS VERY IMPORTANT TO MANY HUMANS, AND I MAY INCORPORATE IT INTO THE DREAMLAND MYTHOS.

With one tentacle-like finger Hastur poked desultorily at the cookies that had just come out of the oven. They were black, and shaped like... well, they were shaped like shoggoths. Formless, with protuberances that defied imagination. "They are burned."

THEY WILL SUFFICE. TASTE ONE.

Hastur did, and spat the cookie out after one bite. "They are burned," he repeated.

HM. Nodens picked up the recipe and examined it closely. THE RECIPE STATES THAT THEY MUST BE BAKED AT 350 DEGREES BUT IT DID NOT SPECIFY FAHRENHEIT OR KELVIN SO I ASSUMED CELSIUS.

"That asshumption may have been incorrect," Hastur said.

Just then the phone rang.

I THOUGHT YOU CURSED THAT.

"I did. It musht have reshurrected itshelf."

The phone rang again. Twice more.

The answering machine wasn't going to pick it up.

"Damn," Hastur muttered. He picked up the receiver. "Yesh?"

There was no voice on the other end. But there was a sensation, a feeling that Hastur hadn't felt for some time. He recognized the sensation, and he hated it. He slammed the receiver down as quickly as he could, but the sensation remained. He sighed then turned to Nodens. "It appearsh we have been shummoned."

SUMMONED? Nodens said, aghast. BY WHOM?

"I do not know. I rarely know until I arrive at the deshtination."

Nodens looked thoughtful. BY 'WE' YOU REALLY MEAN YOU YOURSELF HAVE BEEN SUMMONED, CORRECT? I AM NOT TO BE INVOLVED?

Hastur hesitated. He did not wish to lie to his friend, but he also did not wish to act alone on whatever task he was being summoned for. "Yesh," he said at length.

YES WHAT?

"Yesh, you have been shummoned with me."

Nodens cursed, damning a civilization that had only just emerged on the faraway Leng Plateau. BUT I HAVE WORK TO DO. A RECIPE FOR GINGERBREAD AWAITS.

"Neverthelessh we are shummoned. Come with me." Before Nodens could object, Hastur wrapped his tentacled arm around the other being's wrist, dragging him through the Void to Earth itself, where the call had come from.

. . .

A wee bit later...

Jenny Cupcake trembled at the sight of the two smoke-enshrouded beings before her. The first was obviously Hastur, though he seemed to have traded his yellow shroud and robes for a trench-coat and hoodie. The other she didn't recognize; it looked like a large human male, though it had pale blue skin and seemed to have kelp for a beard.

Honestly, she hadn't expected the summoning spell to work. The ancient copy of *The Book of Eibon* that Miss Candy Cane had given her before their breakup was so dusty and worn that the spells therein were half-illegible. But here they stood, two beings from beyond the depths of time and space.

"I—I only meant to summon Hastur," she stammered.

The bearded human thing turned to Hastur. BUT YOU SAID... it began in a voice that reverberated through the huge chamber of the abandoned workhouse.

But Hastur shook his enscarfed head. "Hussh," he slurred, like Santa on one of his benders. Then he turned to Jenny and bent forward so that she could see her reflection in his sunglasses. "Why have you shummoned ush, tiny human?"

Jenny stood up straight, stretching to her full height, all two-foot-five of it. "I'm not a human," she said proudly. "I'm a Christmas elf."

"Oh," Hastur said.

The two of them stared at each other in silence for a moment, neither of them moving. The other Old One twisted his beard in agitation.

Finally, Hastur said, "Sho, why have you shummoned ush?"

Jenny found herself surprisingly unafraid in the presence of the Old Ones, now that the shock of their sudden appearance had passed. "Well," she said, "it's about Santa."

"Shatan?"

"No, Santa. You know, Santa Claus? He brings toys to all the children on Christmas Eve?"

I AM FAMILIAR WITH THE ENTITY, the other Old One said. HE AND I HAVE SHARED MEAD IN THE HALLS OF THE DREAMLANDS.

"I am not," said Hastur. "Ish he an Old One? A deity?"

"No," said Jenny, "he's none of those things! He's just the spirit of Christmas personified. You know, cookies and milk and ho-ho-ho."

Hastur shook his head.

Jenny sighed, exasperated. "The point is, I need someone to take over for him. I summoned you, and you are bound by the ancient rituals outlined in the *Book of Eibon*. So you have to go out and deliver toys to all the good girls and boys throughout the world."

"How ish that posshible?" asked Hastur. "I cannot travel through the ether fasht enough to do thish."

I WILL LET YOU BORROW MY SLEIGH, said the other Old One.

Hastur sighed, and the scarf around his face wrinkled, and Jenny thought the being looked very annoyed. "Very well," he said. "But I musht know... What happened to thish being known as Shanta?"

"He... He saw... something. Over the Atlantic Ocean."

"What did he shee?"

"No one knows. But for sure it was something bad."

"Very well. I am, ash you shay, bound by the ancient ritesh of the *Book of Eibon*. Therefore I will deliver theesh toysh for Chrishtmash."

"Oh, thank you, Hastur!" cried Jenny. She rushed up to give Hastur a friendly holiday hug, but he stepped back from her. She stopped, realizing for the first time that Hastur was easily five feet taller than her, and she would only have been able to hug his leg. That, and the fact that touching his tattered trenchcoat might drive her just as insane as Santa was.

I WILL ACCOMPANY YOU ON THIS JOURNEY, said the other Old One. WE WILL USE MY SLEIGH.

"Is it... Is it pulled by reindeer?" Jenny asked.

NO. IT IS DRIVEN BY EVIL DOLPHINS. BUT RELAX, SHORT ONE. I HAVE TAMED THEM.

"Oh," said Jenny, feeling faint. "I'll go get Santa's sack of toys, and then you can be on your way."

Back to now...

Hastur looked down on the city below them, and was intrigued.
BEHOLD, said Nodens. THE CITY OF BOSTON.

"How many children are in this shity?"

HUNDREDS OF THOUSANDS OF THEM.

Hastur's shoulders slumped. "How doesh Shanta do thish all in one night?"

HE EMPLOYS AN INTERDIMENSIONAL PORTAL SYSTEM CREATED BY A TEAM OF QUANTUM ENGINEERING ELVES. ALSO HE DRINKS MUCH COFFEE. DO YOU DOUBT YOUR ABILITY TO COMPLETE THE TASK? ARE YOU NOT ENJOYING YOURSELF?

"I find, to my shurprishe, that I *am* enjoying thish tashk. However, there ish so much to do, and sho many children." He sighed. "Come. Let ush deliver shome preshents."

Millions of children. Billions of presents. So many cities. And that was over what the humans called the North American continent alone.

It was over the Equator and the Atlantic Ocean when Nodens brought the dolphin-driven sleigh to a shuddering halt. BEHOLD, he said. A DISTURBANCE IN THE WATER.

Hastur looked down to the water. He sighed. "I believe I know what hash happened. We musht inveshtigate. Can your shleigh go underwater?"

MY SLEIGH IS PULLED BY EVIL DOLPHINS. IT CAN GO ANYWHERE.

With no more preamble than that, Nodens brought about the sleigh, and dove downward toward the ocean.

The source of the disturbance was a gigantic creature, miles high, sulking on the bottom of the ocean and nursing a scar on its belly.

"Cthulhu," Hastur said. "I sshould have known you were behind thish."

Cthulhu looked up at Hastur and grinned. "Behind what?"

HE MEANS THAT YOU HAVE FORCED SANTA CLAUS TO GO INSANE THUS FORCING HASTUR TO DELIVER TOYS IN HIS PLACE.

"Now, would I do something like that?"

"Yesh, you would."

Cthulhu chuckled. "Now, *why* would I want to do that?"

Hastur was brought up short by the question. Why, indeed, would Cthulhu drive Santa insane? Hastur had no doubt that Cthulhu had revealed himself to the human. But why?

THE STARS, Nodens said. THEY HAVE CHANGED POSITION!

Hastur looked up at the sky, then back at Cthulhu. "What'sh going on?"

Cthulhu smirked through the tentacles that sprouted from his chin. "Whatever do you mean?"

HE CHANGED THE STARS. I DON'T KNOW HOW, BUT HE DID.

"But that'sh imposshible!"

"It's a Christmas miracle," said Cthulhu.

"A what?"

I DO NOT THINK HE DID IT HIMSELF.

"It's true. Every year at this time, the stars align in just the right way to allow that crazy old man from the North Pole to fly through the world and deliver all those gifts in one night. And every year he defeats me as I attempt to rise. Not this year, though. This year I had help."

I BET I KNOW WHO IT WAS.

"It wash Yog-Shothoth, washn't it?" asked Hastur. "You conshpired with him to drive Shanta Claush inshane."

"And so what if I did?"

WE'LL FIND A WAY TO STOP YOU. WE'LL RESTORE SANTA CLAUS TO SANITY AND BRING CHRISTMAS BACK TO THE WORLD.

"Oh, but you can't! It is too late! I have already begun to rise, and soon all mortals in the world shall tremble in fear before me!"

Hastur rolled his eyes. He'd heard this speech from Cthulhu before, and it hadn't been impressive then. But this time, things looked more serious.

"But Hastur," Cthulhu went on, "surely you realize that you, too, will benefit from my rise to the mortal dimensions? All Old Ones and Great Old Ones and Elder Ones and... Well, all of us will return to our dominion. Mankind rules now where we ruled eons in the past. Our time has finally come!"

Hastur did not like this idea. He knew what would happen if the Old Ones were to arise. There would be bloodshed all over the Earth. And not just of humans. Human beings had developed impressive weapons of war over the millennia, and if they felt their world was being invaded, they wouldn't hesitate to use them. And Hastur doubted that even Cthulhu could remain unscathed after a nuclear blast.

More importantly, though, there would be upheaval not just on Earth, but throughout the Cosmos, and that included his home on the tiny planet that orbited Aldebaran. Currently the place was abandoned, except for Hastur's own apartment, but an upheaval in the Cosmos would mean that his apartment complex would be invaded by Mi-Go, Elder Things, Shantaks, and worse. All he wanted was to be left alone, to live in isolation in his tiny place. And Cthulhu's rise would bring an end to that.

He had to stop Cthulhu from coming. But how?

"Come, Nodensh," he said. "We musht find a way to shtop thish."

"It's too late!" cried Cthulhu. "Do whatever you can, but the souls of mankind shall all soon be mine!"

Hastur shook his head. "Back to my apartment," he told Nodens. "Now."

BUT WHY DO YOU WISH TO STOP THE RETURN OF THE OLD ONES? asked Nodens. SURELY YOU WOULD LIKE TO WALK THE EARTH, DRIVING MANKIND INSANE.

"Why do you *want* Cthulhu to rishe?" Hastur replied. "After all, if mankind ish driven inshane, then the Dreamlandsh will fall to ruinsh and you will have no more realm to reign over."

Nodens opened his mouth to reply, then closed it again. YES, he said at length. YOU ARE CORRECT. SO HOW DO WE STOP THIS?

"How wash he shtopped before? In the year the humansh call 1928?"

I BELIEVE A STEAMBOAT WAS INVOLVED.

Hastur nodded, remembering; a human steamboat, piloted by an insane crew, had rammed into Cthulhu, injuring him and sending him back to R'lyeh.. "Yesh, that ish correct. But we have no shteamboat at our dishposhal thish time."

NO. BUT WE DO HAVE ACCESS TO A SLEIGH. AND NINE TINY REINDEER.

"Nine?"

YOU FORGET RUDOLPH.

"Then we musht return to the North Pole."

LET US GO, THEN.

J enny Cupcake shook her head sadly as she looked down at Santa. He had not stopped gibbering, nor had he shown any sign of sleep, despite the massive sedatives that Doctor Evergreen had given him.

"Do you suppose we'll have to find a new Santa?" she asked.

Doctor Evergreen shrugged. "Let's hope not. Finding a new one is always so difficult. I don't want to contemplate finding a new one at this point."

"But we might have to, if Hastur doesn't come through and help us."

"Yes, I know. And this year... Well, this year we may just have to cancel Christmas."

THERE IS NO NEED FOR THAT, came a voice from behind them. NOT YET.

"Indeed," slurred another voice. "We have determined a way to shave Chrishtmash."

Jenny Cupcake spun around. The two entities that she had summoned had returned. Hastur had a Christmas wreath around his neck, and the other —Nodens —had woven a strand of Christmas lights into his beard.

"I— I—" she stammered. The two beings stood at least eight feet tall, yet, impossibly and improbably, did not have to bend over to fit in Doctor Evergreen's workshop, nor did the workshop have to expand in size. The sight of it was terrible to comprehend, and Jenny Cupcake started to understand how Santa must have been feeling.

Doctor Evergreen, however, seemed unfazed. "And what is your plan?"

WE NEED ACCESS TO SANTA'S SLEIGH.

"Yesh. And hish reindeer. And toysh."

"But why?" asked Jenny Cupcake. "You have your own sleigh."

MINE IS PRICELESS AND ANCIENT.

"So is Santa's."

LISTEN, TINY MORTAL, WHO SUMMONED WHOM HERE?

"Oh for God's sake," Doctor Evergreen said, "just give him the keys to Santa's sleigh."

Santa's coat hung on a hook on the wall near the writhing fat man. Without taking her eyes off Nodens and Hastur, Jenny Cupcake went over to it and took a set of keys from it. She tossed the keys over to Hastur, who missed them entirely, forcing him to bend over and scoop them up, cursing.

THANK YOU, said Nodens. WE'LL TAKE IT FROM HERE.

And with that, the two beings were gone.

"What are they going to do?" Jenny Cupcake asked Doctor Evergreen.

"They're taking the sleigh and the reindeer," Doctor Evergreen replied.

"I hope it's nothing too dangerous."

"I don't care how dangerous it is," Doctor Evergreen said darkly. "Just so long as the toys get delivered in the end."

· · ·

H O HO HO cried Nodens.

"What wash that?"

THAT IS THE SOUND THAT SANTA MAKES WHEN HE IS DELIVERING TOYS.

"Oh." Hastur pondered for a moment. "Pleashe do not make that shound again."

VERY WELL.

They had flown over the frozen tundra of the North Pole, down the East Coast, and out over the Atlantic Ocean.

Cthulhu was not where he was supposed to be. Nor could they see the risen city of R'lyeh.

WHERE IS CTHULHU? asked Nodens.

"I do not know." Hastur did not like this development at all. Had Cthulhu been driven back to the deep by some other force? Had he moved on to another dimension? Or had he traveled elsewhere on Earth, taking his city with him?

LET US TURN BACK. PERHAPS CTHULHU'S RISING IS FOR THE BEST AFTER ALL.

"No. I'll be damned if I allow Shantaksh to live in my shity in Aldebaran."

WHAT DO YOU HAVE AGAINST SHANTAKS? I HAD NOT TAKEN YOU FOR A RACIST.

"I wash being figurative. I wish for no one to join me in Aldebaran. It ish my private reshidencshe."

BEHOLD, Nodens said, apparently ignoring Hastur's comment, I SEE CTHULHU CROSSING INTO CARIBBEAN WATERS!

Hastur took an eldritch breath, and squared his tenctacular shoulders. "Thish ish it," he said. "Prepare for ramming shpeed!"

HO HO HO!

Cthulhu turned when he heard Nodens's shout. He saw the sleigh and reindeer hurtling toward him and cried out. "NOOOOO!"

It was Rudolph that crashed into the ancient eldritch being first, his bright red nose flaring bright against the darkened sky. Then the rest of the reindeer —Dasher, Dancer, Prancer, Vixen, Comet, Cupid, Dunder and Blixem —crashed into Cthulhu.

JUMP! Nodens cried.

Hastur had just had the same idea. He cursed himself for not having brought a backup sleigh to get Nodens back to his home among the Dreamlands. But he did not want to be caught among the wreckage of Santa's sleigh, so he jumped out of it and landed in the warm waters of the Caribbean.

As Santa's sleigh plowed into Cthulhu's massive, blubbery body, a huge fireball lit up: probably the propane tanks or whatever fuel that powered the sleigh. Hastur felt the shockwave and heat of the explosion, could smell burning Cthulhu-flesh hanging in the air around them. Cthulhu sank back into the ocean, crying out all the while, until he was submerged completely, defeated once again.

MY SLEIGH, Nodens wailed. I DO NOT HAVE MY SLEIGH. IT IS AT THE NORTH POLE.

"Yesh, I'm afraid it is."

WE MUST RETURN THERE TO RETRIEVE IT.

"I am afraid we cannot. The dimensional breach created by the elf'sh shummoning shpell hash disshipated. There is no way back. But come. We can return to my apartment. The gingerbread men await."

Hastur opened a rift between the Caribbean and Aldebaran and returned to his apartment along with Nodens. It was the end of a long night. Hopefully he would never have to do this again.

· · ·

L OOK! Nodens cried as they appeared in Hastur's apartment.

Hastur looked, seeing the damage that had been done. Walls had been broken, windows smashed. The Christmas tree —an eldritch thing, damned and slender and laden with tiny stars —still loomed in the corner, but was pressed up against the ceiling.

In the center of it all, Nodens's sleigh. And two squeaking evil dolphins.

All tied in a silver bow.

SANTA HAS RETURNED MY SLEIGH!

"Yesh," Hastur replied, dismayed at the wreckage. "Yesh he hash."

He peered out the window. He would not see Santa's sleigh, nor the bright red light of Rudolph's nose, of course, but he did hear a voice emanating from the heavens:

"Happy Christmas to all! And to all *Cthulhu fhtagn!*"

BOKRUG AND THE BOY

LIAM HOGAN

"You know we don't care?"

"Yes. You've said."

It wasn't much of a beach. Estuary mud, littered with debris from both river and sea. A hulking, concrete sewage outlet, that only discharged at the minimum recommended distance from land when measured at high tide. Betwixt and between, neither ocean nor shore, even the seabirds avoided the area, as Samuel Pelsey trudged through the boot-sucking sludge, half-heartedly poking a stick into it.

No more than a giant step behind, the Great Old One lurked. Against the grey sky, reflected by the grey sea (or was it the other way around?), foregrounded by grey mud. The eldritch horror's powerful limbs and webbed feet were better suited to the conditions than an eight-year-old's short legs and hand-me-down, but still-oversized Wellingtons, one of which had long ago sprung a leak, the cracked and weathered seals not up to the pull of the thick mud, rank water oozing in with every second step and soaking his doubled up socks. His jeans were turning the same dismal grey, caked layers that would only flake off when next he went to put them on, there being little point in being washed until the "holiday" was over.

The horror, which went by the name of *Bokrug*, (but not to many, not in these unenlightened times,) had first observed this dirty-straw-haired youngster as he'd stood, hands in tight fists, backed up against the rough, slime-covered sewage outlet, facing down a motley crew of older, local kids. Something in Samuel's stance, in his refusal to cry and run away as the taunts and handfuls of mud flew in, had snagged the water god's attention. Finally, the gang had tired of their sport, perhaps assuming their victim was mentally incapable of the response they sought. And so they'd wandered off, hurling the casual "loser!" and "dumb kid" in their wake.

The horror had taken a short step forward, into the space the bullies had vacated, and the boy's wounded gaze snapped to it.

"Your turn," Samuel said, with more defiance than either hate, or fear. "Go on. Do your worst."

Bokrug's worst was very, very bad indeed. Apocalyptically bad. The total destruction, overnight, of a thriving city, of a prosperous kingdom, bad. Only psychotic heads of cults who, deep in their soiled, shrivelled hearts, believed more in themselves than in legends of River Gods, ever asked Bokrug to do their worst. And the horror sometimes gave the fools the merest taste of what they were capable of, just for the remote pleasure of watching those so-called 'priests' claw out their own eyes, and other organs.

But this kid?

"That would mean we'd noticed you," the horror replied, after a lengthy pause. "Would mean you were worth noticing."

The boy nodded, just the once, and then shrugged, drifting towards the water line, following the receding tide.

"I'm Samuel," he offered over his rounded shoulder.

"We don't care," the horror replied, which is why the boy didn't get to hear the horror's true name, and reality didn't shred itself around the unspeakable syllables, as those unwise priests had once done, their eyes swelling and their bodies hunched, the *snap!* as bones broke and reformed to become frog-like, to better serve Bokrug's unfathomable will.

After a while, the horror, not having anything better to do this side of this century, had slithered in the boy's footsteps, sniffing the pools of grey water that filled them. The horror's own feet were fleshy and three pronged, ending in sharply curved talons capable of ripping through the hull of even metal boats. The pools Bokrug left behind spanned six or so of the boy's smaller impressions, but because they were shallow, the horror could still see where Samuel had stepped, the combined footprints even more bizarre than theirs alone. If Bokrug was careful enough, it looked like an extended arrow, the dotted shaft pointing back the way they had come.

The boy didn't appear to pay Bokrug much attention as he worked his way down the gentle slope, and then up again, hours later, chased by the turn of the tide. Samuel's pockets didn't have much space for finds, but then, he didn't make many. Plastic bottle tops and rusty drinks cans; these were not treasures that he could make use of, that would fill the void of time, and so on he probed, the hiss of the waves and the oh-so-soft tread of Bokrug for company.

At the end of the long day, as a baleful sun touched the horizon and a chill air lifted a foul miasma into the air, Samuel had nodded from the top of the low rise behind which sheltered a caravan park, hell on Earth. "See you tomorrow," he'd said.

Had it been obviously a question, had it been said in a way that could be thought presumptuous, had one of the thousand and one insults and put downs and vile curses escaped Bokrug's rubbery lips... but Samuel hadn't even waited for a reply, trudging towards the distant lights of *Sandpiper: Holiday Homes and Caravan Park*.

And so Bokrug had hunkered down, staring out to the darkening sea with myriad eyes as night settled around them.

. . .

"You're not my first, you know."

"No?"

"I've had monsters before."

Bokrug tilted their head, ran a bifurcated tongue over serrated teeth, the noise like chalk on a blackboard. "We don't—" they started to repeat once more, but let the truncated phrase drift on the stiffening breeze.

"They come at night," Samuel went on, ignoring the interrupted interruption, or maybe just completing it mentally on the eldritch horror's behalf.

Bokrug wasn't foolish enough to dismiss such comments as *merely* a creature of the child's mind, of the dream realm, and even if they had, would that make them any less potent? Maybe such visions explained why the boy accepted their ominous presence, their dreadful existence, without doing all that pointless screaming and running away that those who normally stumbled across them did.

"Not for a while, though," the boy added, as an afterthought.

"No."

"I'm a big kid," Samuel said, from beneath Bokrug's looming shadow, the skies today a lighter shade of grey. "Can't go running to my parents' bed, whenever I get scared."

"I suppose not."

The boy squinted up at the monstrous form, at the jagged spines that ran along Bokrug's elongated arms and down the broad back. "I'd get into trouble if I even mention them. Or *you.*"

Bokrug wonders, idly, if they would be doing the boy a favour by devouring his absentee parents. Parents who sent their young kid off for the long summer day, without food or drink or even a few coins for entertainment, while they did whatever it was adult holiday makers did when kid unencumbered. It would be easily done; the horror's wide jaw unhinged, so that they could swallow prey larger than they were. A whole, rust-flaking static caravan, at a stretch. But such *direct* action wasn't really Bokrug's style, unbecoming of a god. Perhaps they would wait a thousand years instead, before destroying every one of their descendants. Revenge was a dish served so frigid that few could even remember what their ancestor's transgression had once been.

Though that probably wouldn't help the boy much, especially as their descendants included his descendants... This was why Bokrug avoided the pitiful affairs of humankind. *It's complicated,* kind of summed them up.

Still. The horror wanted to do something. Some small act, not to show that they cared—for had they not said that they did not?—but just to nudge the balance of the universe an insignificant smidgen in Samuel's forlorn direction.

Though perhaps just being there was enough? The boy seemed to think so, as another day came to a close and he repeated his backward "see you tomorrow."

As dusk descended once more, Bokrug shaped the dream creatures they had glimpsed in the boy's thoughts from the estuary mud. It would take the merest breath, the slightest touch, just their *will*, to bring the blighted fiends to awful life. Perhaps then the boy's parents wouldn't be so ready to dismiss his nocturnal fears. Perhaps those fears, rendered in effluent tainted mud, would do the irksome chore of punishing Mr and Mrs Pelsey for their contemptuous ignorance.

But would they stop there? Doubtful. And even if they did, would Samuel truly be better off an orphan? The kid was lonely enough already.

It was, indeed, *complicated.*

They watched, as the tide washed the creations away, wiping the slate, if not clean, then at least uniformly filthy, resetting it for tomorrow. In the distance a one-eyed lighthouse turned and blinked, turned and blinked, slow and sorrowful, as the lights on passing container ships drifted across the horizon.

Bokrug sat and watched and pondered, as high above the moon tugged the water back and forth. It would be fuller, tomorrow. Already it glittered on the wet mud and shallows, pointing the way with its own arrow, tempting the horror to go on their way, to leave this doleful place, Samuel included, far behind. They had not, after all, made any promises.

Had they?

S amuel was not alone when he returned the following morning. Though nor, as Bokrug batted irritation aside, could he be truly said to be with anyone either. It was the same group of older boys as last time, hounding his footsteps. The same torments, a little slicker perhaps, a little more personal, their edge honed by a day's absence.

Once again, Samuel backed up across the mud to the concrete sewer pipe, and once again, the boys followed, their prey cornered, helpless, alone.

Bokrug watched, unmoved and unmoving, until the serpent like, half-buried tail gave the tiniest twitch.

For a moment, the boys stopped, sensing something they didn't understand, couldn't compute, a ripple that wasn't repeated.

It didn't need to be.

The mud remembered. That's what mud *is*, the vague persistence of the land the river that had bore it had passed through. Memories, of fields, yes, but also of long gone villages, and burial mounds, and of things much more ancient.

The shapes Bokrug had formed might have been smoothed and flattened by time and tide, but the same mud lay beneath the boys' feet. That tremor was all it took to summon back Samuel's nightmare creatures. And Bokrug needed to do nothing except stand by, as pustulant arms, and wicked claws, and tentacular tentacles, reach up through the soft mud to wrap around the older boys' feet, slithering up their bony ankles and slapping against their pale calves and gripping them *tight,* as they belatedly realise their terrible plight.

Needed to do nothing at all, to let those dream realm abominations drag Samuel's tormentors down, to smother them, to tear them apart, to show them the *real* meaning of—

"*No.*"

Bokrug looked over in surprise. The boy wasn't watching the plight of his foes, the green fog that swirled around their imprisoned feet, eating away at their trainers and sandals, but was staring right at Bokrug instead.

"Not with *my* monsters, if you don't mind," Samuel said, before dropping his gaze. "Let them go."

And Bokrug, who hadn't been asked to do something in nearly two thousand years, ("do your worst" having already been discounted) and hadn't been *told* to do something for far, far longer, let the boys go.

"They're bullies and louts, but they don't deserve that, *and* they're not worth it—barely worth noticing, in fact."

"Are you *sure?*" Bokrug asked.

"Positive."

The boys, released from the mud, made desperately for higher, firmer, safer ground, stumbling and falling as often as not in their haste. By the time they got to the low ridge overlooking the estuary, they were six grey golems, their limbs shaking with unquenchable fear. Just one of them stopped to glance back, whether in fear for Samuel or in fear *of* Samuel, it was strangely hard to tell. Bokrug's shadow darkened the mud between the waste pipe and the shore, and seemed to stretch towards the trembling watcher. The kid shuddered, mouth wide open, and stumbled on.

Samuel, after a moment's pause, carefully and steadily waded through the churned up mud, following in the gang's footsteps, picking up the loose change the boys had shed as they'd struggled to escape the unseen but very much sensed threat.

U p on the pier, adults shifted out of Bokrug and the boy's way. They'd claim, if pressed, that it was because the boy's legs, and hands, were covered in foul-smelling mud, which was true enough. They'd claim, if asked, that the boy was alone, which was not.

They certainly wouldn't be able to explain the very large candyfloss, hovering in the air above the boy's more normal-sized one like a pink cloud, any more than the shop that had sold them both could explain why it only charged for the one, and how come the girl who normally operated the machine with practised apathy had been unable to stop twirling the long stick in the drum around and around until it felt like her arms were about to drop off, until the machine finally ran out of sugar.

Bokrug looked out to sea. Away from the unfrequented and unpopular estuary the view was more like you might expect a seaside town to offer, gulls riding the wind, a few brave souls splashing in the always cold waters, even a sparkle of sunlight as the day brightened.

The river god preferred lakes. Placid ones, where a sudden ripple could send the right sort of dire warning. And there were other eldritch beasts of the oceans, hidden in darker depths. Even on the wooden planks suspended above the waters, Bokrug felt a little like an uninvited, unwanted guest.

But... but they had been invited. They were, implausibly, *wanted*. They licked at the sugary, light as air confection with a tongue that could oh so easily rasp the living flesh from bone, and sighed contentedly. Bokrug could almost imagine getting used to this. Perhaps. Given another thousand years?

TEN THOUSAND YEARS IN SPACE WITH SANTA

JASON P. BURNHAM

Gather 'round children, for your insider information on the *real* Santa. How do I know about old Saint Nick? When you spend ten thousand years with something, its legitimacy becomes evident—undeniable one might argue.

One thing the stories and portrayals get wrong is Santa's appearance. A big, bearded guy in a red and white suit? Santa is more of an amorphous blob, conjured from the space in between atoms, from the fabric of the universe itself. The only time he's red is when he's redshifted as he moves rapidly away from Earth to another planet he terrorizes. For some reason, Earth is the only planet that doesn't fear him. You have only yourselves to blame for not listening to us elves.

The stories also paint him as jolly. Wrong-o. What's jolly about someone that spies on children throughout solar transit? If you were to use the word 'creepy' to describe him, you'd be getting closer.

But Santa is real kids—you were right! He gives out presents, but not the neatly-wrapped ones under your Christmas tree (those are from your parents). Santa's presents are a lot less... tangible.

Being made from the space between atoms means that Santa's gifts are grisly daydreams, ones your parents will probably never admit to. What do these look like? Here's an example: your parent gets close to a balcony while they're holding you and, even though they love you dearly, for a minute they picture what would happen if you flew over the side and smashed into a million pieces as they breathlessly forecast the ways they'd have to justify it as an accident to your other parent. Or the police. You'll have these daydreams too, someday. Maybe it won't be with your kid too close to a ledge. Maybe a murderous instinct will flame through your body over a perceived slight and you'll envision flaying alive the person who's (minorly) wronged you.

So. Amid all this grotesquerie, how did Santa become inextricably linked with presents?

Santa may be a cosmic horror, but the universe still has to be balanced lest it spiral out of control and swallow itself. For each terror Santa plants, a good deed must arise, i.e., you get presents. The rituals aren't exactly the same on every planet—this just so happens to be what worked out on Earth. Santa doesn't agree with the calculus in principle, but the daydreams he delivers occasionally turn into reality and Santa's bloodlust is sated.

I know it's hard to believe. But I've been traveling with this abomination through space for ten thousand years. You should take my word for it. Unless you'd like to replace me in Santa's workshop and see the horrors for yourself? I leave the choice to you. Sweet dreams, kids!

NOT ON MY WATCH

HENRY HERZ

F or the final assignment of my paranormal reporting career with Agence France-Presse, I transferred from DC to France. Three months in, and browsing the newspaper, I noted the date – October 27, 1987. At sixty-five, I'd managed to stay in shape, but gray hairs lightened my close-cut dark auburn locks. I was ready to retire next year, having seen more than my share of weird.

Some might claim bravery and cleverness for surviving encounters with vampires, zombies, and werewolves. But I'd reached this age due to spectacular good luck and strict adherence to Tacitus's adage, "He that fights and runs away, may turn and fight another day." That and wearing comfortable sneakers.

I sat up at a missing person's notice. *Another? That's three since I've been here.* Any big city's bound to have a few. What got my nape hairs standing was that the missing were all last seen at Hôtel Hydra. The oddly designed hotel stood on an exclusive island in Paris's Seine River. Location, location, location.

As I finished my croissant, I noticed an announcement for TerrorCon, a horror convention scheduled for Halloween... at Hôtel Hydra. *I should probably attend. Maybe I can uncover something. Dagnabbit.* Fate had conspired against my weekend plans to putter around the village, enjoying *vin* and *brie*.

F riday, I took the *Métro* under the River Seine to Île de Cité. Cigarette smoke wafted through the subway car. I schlepped my suitcase up to street level and strode past the 13th-century Cathédrale Notre-Dame. Crossing the bridge to Île Saint-Louis, I reached Hôtel Hydra.

The structure's design made Gaudi's Sagrada Familia seem conventional. Its five-story exterior walls outlined an irregular five-pointed star. A subtle outward cant of the surfaces lent the building a threatening aspect.

None of the walls' straight lines aligned vertically or horizontally. No two of the dark trapezoidal windows possessed the same dimensions or angles. The disharmonious geometry evoked unease and dizziness.

Unbroken by mortar lines, the smooth facade created the illusion of being carved from a single cyclopean stone block. I approached within arm's length. The walls had a soapy, greenish-black hue, with iridescent flecks and striations that made it hard to focus the eyes. I touched the surface, yanking back my hand. The smooth stone felt unexpectedly chilly and unpleasant.

I entered the building. Its interior was, if possible, more bizarre than the exterior. While the outside might have been designed by an intoxicated M.C. Escher, the inside seemed to have been laid out by a demented H.R. Giger. The interior featured only disorienting curves – not just arched ceilings, but concave walls, bending hallways, and even sinuous door lintels. Ebony paneling exhibited bas reliefs of menacing eels, deep sea fish, and octopuses. No colors brightened the grayscale foyer. I felt as if trapped at the bottom of the ocean. My chest tightened.

Locating the TerrorCon registration desk proved difficult due to the curving hallways, sloping floors, and lack of a traditional floor plan.

No two areas were shaped alike. Even the same hallway looked different when walked in the reverse direction.

After finally collecting my badge and convention booklet, I headed straight to my room. Well, not really straight. After repeatedly getting lost in the dimly lit labyrinthian hallways, I found my room and locked myself in. That night, I slept like the dead.

The next morning, I dressed in jeans, white button-down, and sport coat. I slung my camera's strap over my shoulder.

TerrorCon attendees buzzed with excitement that the Con was being held *here*. I wandered down a curving hallway to the enormous dealers' room. Vendor booths formed islands around which currents of fans swirled. Sellers hawked horror-related wares, from cheap trinkets to collectible comics to valuable items like original movie props.

I felt inexplicably drawn to a booth displaying antique leather-bound books. One practically hummed under my touch. The title read, *Codex Monstra et Carmina*. It smelled like a dusty attic.

I leafed through the yellowed vellum pages. Despite the codex's age, the colors of illuminated manuscript remained vibrant. Latin text surrounded illustrations of creatures, many of which I'd never seen, despite my considerable exposure to the abnormal.

"*Combien?*" How much? I asked the gray-haired vendor.

He stared intently with his deep brown eyes for several seconds as if assessing me. At last, he nodded and smiled. "Sixty-five hundred francs."

You knew I was American from my lousy French accent. At the current exchange rate, that was a bit over a thousand bucks. I'd never spent that much on a book... or a suit, for that matter. But there was something irresistible about it, and somehow I had the feeling he was grossly undercharging me. I handed him my credit card without blinking.

By mid-day, I was thirsty and exhausted. Amid the low rumble of hundreds of French conversations rose the thin voice of the last person I would have expected.

"Charles? Charles Colbert?"

I turned to face a slender man wrapped head to toe in white gauze, leaving only his beady blue eyes and mouth uncovered.

Sure enough, it was Randy Upfield, a longtime AFP co-worker and general pain in the tuchus. I forced a thin smile. "Hello, Randy. What brings you here from DC?"

"Well, I've long been fascinated by the paranormal," he simpered. "Paris is a lovely city, and I was due for a vacation." He spread his bandaged arms wide. "TerrorCon was too good to pass up. Want to hear a French joke?"

I grimaced. "Not really."

He forged ahead. "Why do the French only eat one egg? Because one egg is an *oeuf*."

I tipped my hat. "Clever as ever, Randy." *Which is to say, still dimwitted.* "That's a terrific mummy costume, but did you consider *all* the, um, logistical details?"

His brow furrowed.

I lowered my voice and pointed at his wrapping. "Doesn't that involve a lot of effort when you need to use the men's room?" I almost laughed aloud when his eyes widened. He hadn't thought that far ahead.

"Randy, I must be going, but I can't tell you what a delightful surprise this is." I couldn't tell him because it wasn't delightful.

He nodded, shambling off in character.

I slipped into the hallway, nearly colliding in my haste with a sturdy young man cosplaying a Knight Templar. The blond, brown-eyed fellow wore a white tabard with large red cross, a chainmail coif, and a brown leather belt from which hung a safety-tagged sword.

My stomach's growling and my feet are killing me. Maybe he knows where the green room is. "*Où est la chambre verte?*"

"I'll take you there," he offered.

Is my accent that bad? "Thanks. I'm Charles." I extended my hand.

He shook it enthusiastically, taking in my attire. "I'm Jean-René Legazon. Please call me JR. Are you the famous reporter, Charles Colbert?"

"Infamous, more like," I replied, tickled he'd heard of me.

"Nonsense. I've long admired your work. I'm also an investigator of sorts." He turned left at a three-way intersection, the vertically undulating floor disorienting. When he noticed my book, JR halted, wide-eyed. "The *Codex Monstra et Carmina? Mon Dieu.* We must speak." His pace quickened.

At the green room, the monitor waved in my guide, but I had to flash my AFP credentials to gain access.

JR gave me a moment to grab a *pain aux raisins* and fill a paper cup from an engraved coffee urn. We sat at a round cloth-covered table in an unoccupied corner of the room. Before I could take a sip, he asked, "Are you here about the missing people?"

I sat up, arching my eyebrows.

JR nodded. "I thought so. May I ask what you've uncovered?"

"In the last three months, there have been three missing persons last seen at this hotel."

"*Oui.* The full tally is twenty-four over the last two years."

"Twenty-four!" I choked on my pastry. "Do the cops have any leads?"

He smirked. "The *Préfecture de Police* may be headquartered nearby on Île de la Cité, but they've come up empty. They don't believe in the supernatural."

I leaned in. "But you?"

"*Oui.* Just like you, I delve into the bizarre. Believe me when I say it's of the utmost importance that there not be a twenty-fifth victim."

"I take it you mean it's more critical than the life of a single victim."

JR lowered his voice. "The entire city's at risk. Have you heard of the Old Gods?"

I shook my head.

He leaned closer. "Dagon and Hydra are gargantuan Old Gods entombed deep beneath this hotel… dead but still dreaming. This hotel was designed as a horrific focusing lens for dark energy. Servants of Dagon kidnap and sacrifice innocents. The numbers five and twenty-five are of arcane significance to them. Blood from a twenty-fifth victim will complete a twenty-five-month murderous ritual to awaken their dark gods." JR bunched his fists. "Not on my watch."

My stomach twisted.

JR shifted his chair closer and continued in a whisper. "On the north-western tip of Île de la Cité stands the Mémorial du Templier Jacques de Molay. He was the last grand master of the Knights Templar. In the fourteenth century, they actively opposed the Old Gods. But Dagon corrupted the mind of Philip IV. The king ordered false confessions tortured out of five leaders of the Order. When de Molay and de Charney publicly recanted their forced lies, King Philip ordered them burned alive in front of Notre-Dame. The others were sentenced to life imprisonment in Chinon fortress, ending the public activities of the Order."

"Public?"

JR nodded. "One Templar leader, Geoffroi de Gonneville, managed to escape prison with help of loyal Knights. He established an under-ground movement that continues to this day."

My eyes flicked to his costume.

"*Oui.* The codex you have was once owned by the Templars. May I look at it?"

I'd been around the block enough times to know when someone's being honest. "Sure, but please be careful."

"*Merci.*" JR glanced around the room before gently opening the ancient tome.

My stomach knotted at the vividly disturbing illustrations on the brittle vellum pages – a huge one-eyed multicolored toad with a sharp proboscis, mouth tentacles, and crab claws; a nightmare monster mashup with elements of a whale, fish, and octopus; and something that resembled a thick-bodied sea cucumber with triple-taloned legs and five eyes.

My pastry was only half-finished, but my appetite departed.

"Ah, found it." JR pointed. "This is a Deep One. They worship Dagon and Hydra."

The Deep One looked like a disturbingly humanoid fish-frog. Shiny gray-green covered its warped body, except for a white abdomen and scaly back ridges. The fish-like head, supported by a thick gilled neck, featured dead bulbous eyes. Long gangly limbs ended in webbed clawed paws. It was altogether repulsive.

JR flipped the page. "Here's a Deep One hybrid."

I flinched. Imagine a man, but with scabrous folds lining both sides of his neck. His narrow balding head sported a downturned thick-lipped mouth, small ears, and watery-blue bulging eyes.

"It's even more repulsive than a Deep One."

"*Oui.* Hybrids are the damned spawn of Deep One-human matings."

What human would have sex with a frog-face? What would have seemed fantasy to most, I knew from painful experience could be dangerously real. The stakes were too high to ignore. "How can I help?"

JR's shoulders relaxed as I marked the Deep One page with the faded red silk ribbon bookmark and closed the codex, my arm protectively encircling it. "Our best bet is to search for hybrids." He flipped through a convention schedule, then glanced at his wristwatch, incongruous with his medieval attire. "We're in luck. A Cthulhu cosplay contest started ten minutes ago. Cthulhu's an Old God," he added in response to my blank stare. "Perhaps a hybrid will attend."

Rows of folding chairs dominated conference room 7AB. On a low stage at the far end, a contestant dressed as a giant multicolored demon toad waved at the enthusiastically applauding audience. We stepped inside the doorway.

Starting at the first row, I scanned the audience. A third of the way back, I spotted a mummy. *Randy*. Behind him sat what looked like three Deep Ones and a hybrid. I pulled JR out of the room and into the hallway, leading him to a vending machine about ten yards from the doorway. My heart pounded so hard it was a struggle to keep my voice low. "I saw a hybrid and *three* Deep Ones."

JR smiled like a patient parent. "Those must have been cosplayers. Real Deep Ones smell like three-day-old fish. Their stink would've cleared the room. But the hybrid could be real. If it is, the other three are likely humans of the Esoteric Order of Dagon. It's from that accursed cult that Deep Ones choose their mates. We should follow them."

The costume contest ended to thunderous applause fifteen minutes later. Audience members filed out. I zoomed in with my camera for a closer look, pretending to take pictures of the cosplayers.

JR pretended to mull a vending machine purchase.

I whispered, "The hybrid and three Deep One cosplayers are conversing in the hall, watching the doorway."

Staying in character, JR kept his eyes on the vending machine, but he scowled. "They're choosing their next victim."

I enlarged my camera's field of view. "There's Randy."

"Who?"

"Oh, just a co-worker..." Cold seized my spine. "... that our four fishy friends are now trailing.."

"*Merde.*"

We followed our targets, keeping back twenty yards.

Randy meandered through the oddly configured floor plan. The hallways held increasingly fewer attendees, so we slowed to widen the gap between us and the four cultists. I felt a growing sense of dread.

The cultists trailed Randy around a non-ninety-degree bend.

Twenty seconds later, JR and I reached the corner. I risked a quick peek. No one but Randy and the cultists walked in the undulating hallway. I dropped to the floor, scooting forward so that only my face was exposed beyond the corner. A large carved black marble frog statue at the corner provided additional cover, should the cultists glance backward.

JR stood behind me, completely out of the cultists' sight.

Randy strode with urgency toward the door at the hallway's end, which a zoom of my camera revealed to be a men's room.

The hybrid and two of the cosplayers followed Randy into the restroom. The other cosplayer stationed himself outside the door.

Five minutes later, the hybrid left the bathroom followed by two cosplayers carrying a bulky man-sized duffel bag between them.

They've got Randy. So that's how they kidnap people.

The hybrid tossed a glance down the hallway to ensure they were alone before reaching up to press the eye of a baleful anglerfish carved into the wood panel to the left of the restroom door. A five-foot high by two-foot wide section glided open. They slipped into the darkness. The secret panel shut with the finality of death.

"*Sacre bleu*! We must save your friend… and Paris." JR reached into his left sleeve and withdrew a switchblade. He handed me the knife. "Just in case."

The hotel's insidious aura of despair bore down on me. "Damnit, JR. I'm a journalist, not a knight. We should call the cops."

JR frowned. "Charles, you of all people should know they won't believe us. And I'm not familiar with this section of the hotel. So, even if the police did come, I'm not sure how long it would take me to lead them here."

I sighed. "I can't believe I'm risking my life to save that schmuck."

JR tilted his head. "Schmuck?"

"You know. Doofus. Dummy."

"Ah, *oui*. But even schmucks don't deserve to have their blood drained." JR strode toward the secret panel without hesitation, though I followed with enough trepidation for us both. He drew his sword, indicating with his free hand the carved anglerfish, which I reluctantly pushed. When the panel slid open, JR advanced.

We found ourselves on a hewn stone landing at the top of a narrow spiral staircase. JR removed his chainmail coif and set it on the floor. "We must be absolutely silent."

We plunged into the bowels of the Deep Ones' lair. Diseased phosphorescent fungi, detestable parodies of toadstools, clung to the damp walls. The putrid smell of decaying fish viscera worsened as we descended, as if we'd been swallowed by a gargantuan shark. Many people had questioned my sanity over the last dozen years, but now I agreed with them. My breathing accelerated.

We reached the bottom. "Exactly 250 steps," I whispered. The high-ceilinged hallway exhibited the disorienting curves and height variations of the hotel far above us. We paused outside the entrance to a twenty-foot long high-roofed cavern with three roughly carved exits. *Which way?*

As JR and I exchanged a glance, the faint echo of chanting in a strange tongue emanated from the left-hand opening. JR pointed his sword in that direction, and we continued toward the discordant voices, gliding through a dank maze of empty passageways and small caves.

Every ten feet or so, JR scraped glowing mushrooms off the wall at ground level. *Clever.* This series of non-illuminated "dashes" would serve as a bread crumb trail for our escape.

After minutes of tiptoeing our way through the subterranean maze, we approached a yawning opening. It radiated palpable menace. We peeked into a large grotto before retreating a safe distance. The nearly insufferable fetor of rotting fish made me gag, but we were concerned with far graver things to pay it any mind.

The clammy scene reminded me of Dante's *Inferno.* Long sharp stalactites hung from the ceiling like Leviathan teeth. This temple for the worship of unspeakably noisome gods emanated the ultimate quintessence of inhuman evil. Trembling, it took every bit of courage for me not to flee.

A raised rectangular dais extended from the far wall. Sprouting from the dais like a stone tumor was a thick fluted pillar supported a seven-foot long oval bowl. *An altar.* A fungal yellow slime hung from the altar's rim like putrid congealed jelly. Worst of all, a human shape, bound and gagged, lay face-up on the altar. White gauze wrapped the figure like a mummy. *Randy.* Two torch stands shaped like writhing eels flanked the dais.

Disturbing chiseled half-ichthyic, half-batrachian monsters and hieroglyphics befouled the greenish black stone walls. Lurid flickering torchlight animated the malign bas reliefs. The blasphemous carvings danced about two hulking Deep Ones sculpted high on the far wall. *Dagon and Hydra.* Sunless water lapped the edges of a five-foot oval pool in the center of the room.

The occupants were no less unsettling than the architecture. I counted five hybrids and fifteen human cultists wearing regular street clothing. I caught my first sight of Deep Ones, four of them, naked and putrescent. May I someday forget their hideous appearance.

Though I crouched in concealment, the bestial jabbering, panting, and guttural croaking of the participants in this depraved ceremony assaulted my ears until I thought I would go mad. Without warning, the feral baying shifted to a baleful language, "Ph'nglui mglw'nafh Dagon Seine wgah'nagl fhtagn."

We stole another look from the rear of the grotto.

A fifth Deep One, larger and more odious than its comrades, rose from the pool. His arrival prompted sepulchral adorations from the others. He wore priestly garb and clutched a black jagged-edged dagger in a webbed hand. Malevolent sigils glowed a sickly yellow along the high collar of his blood-red robe.

"Iä Dagon cf'ayak'vulgtmm, vugtlagln vulgtmm."

My last vestige of self-control nearly broke, but JR's unwavering courage stiffened my resolve. "They're speaking R'lyehian, the Old Gods' language," he whispered in my ear. "At the end of their ritual, the priest will slice your friend's neck." He continued as my stomach knotted. "The blood will drain down a channel within the altar column to where Dagon and Hydra lie dreaming. The priest's spell, powered by the twenty-fifth human sacrifice, will unshackle what should stay entombed forever beneath the Seine. They will rise and lay waste to Paris. We must stop them… at any cost."

My fists clenched. *So much for a quiet retirement in France.* I was neither brave nor much of a cusser, but a surge of anger banished my fear and loosed a stream of mental curses. Taking deep breaths, I slowly unclenched my hands.

While JR's weapons suggested combat training, I knew myself to be far more adept at fleeing. Leveraging our respective strengths, I hurriedly devised a plan. "If I can lure them all off, you can rescue Randy. Give me your tabard. Normal clothing will increase your chances of being mistaken for a human cultist."

JR set his sword belt on the floor. Removal of the tabard revealed a military style tactical vest and small backpack.

"Whoa. That's not gonna blend in." I set down the codex and JR's knife, yanking off my sport coat. "Here. Cover your vest." While JR slipped his knife back in its wrist sheath and donned my jacket, I threw on the tabard. *Might as well make myself a glaringly obvious target.*

JR dipped his chin. "It suits you, *Sir* Charles."

I scowled, feeling ridiculous. Still, a cross had saved my tuchus more than once. "I'll interrupt their ritual and run like the dickens for the stairs. While they chase me, slip in, cut Randy loose and hide. Once the commotion settles, lead him back to the hotel. It's a crappy plan, but it's all we have."

He handed me the sword belt. "I can't very well wear this either if I'm to blend in. Just be careful you don't put your eye out."

"Very funny." I strapped on the belt. "Wait. What if you have to fight your way out?"

JR simply offered a grim smile. "May the Lord guard your steps." He backed away from the temple grotto to find deeper concealment.

I sighed before advancing to the opening where I'd be in clear view. Venting my anger at the fish-faced priest, I shouted an improvised insult. "You fish-faced son of a tadpole."

My blood froze at the utter silence that filled the cavern following my interruption. The incongruous moment of tranquility felt more terrifying than their degenerate prayers.

Twenty-five pairs of eyes locked on me. *Taunt him a second time.* "You are one ugly son of a salmon."

The priest's eyes glittered with malevolence. He pointed a clawed finger at me. "Y'ai 'ng'ngah, Dagon h'ee."

I high-tailed it back toward the stairwell, following JR's bread crumb trail. Too soon, odd moist slapping sounds, not quite like footsteps, echoed behind me. My heart pounded. When the detestable odor of dead fish intensified, I glanced over my shoulder.

A Deep Once closed in, far outpacing his human minions with long frog-like bounds through the high-ceilinged hallways.

There's no way I can outrun it, I realized with dread. Halting abruptly, I yanked the sword out of its sheath and turned – just as the Deep One slammed into me mid-hop. The impact knocked me to the ground, the Deep One impaled atop me. Viscous green ichor stained my tabard.

Gagging at the putrescent gore, I rolled onto my right side. No longer trapped under the Deep One's weight, I withdrew my blade from its bloated belly. Intensifying slapping sounds reached my ears as I scrambled to my feet. *Another one?* Snatching up the codex, I fled again, though my breath nearly ceased to come. As I exited another cavern, my foot caught on the raised passageway threshold, sending me sailing headfirst into the narrow way. My sword tumbled twenty feet down the hallway. The codex landed on the floor near my face, falling open to the bookmarked page. *This is it*, I thought. *I don't have time to retrieve my sword.*

The codex's Latin words glowed red. *Huh?* I didn't comprehend Latin, but in utmost desperation, I spoke the words.

A deafening boom made my ears ring. I sat up to view the cavern behind me.

Even my darkest nightmares couldn't have prepared me for the gut-churning sight. The codex's spell had imploded two Deep Ones into steaming piles of green entrails. Five hybrids, being only half Deep One, suffered half the damage. Which is to say their mangled prostrate bodies twitched, sightless eyes staring at the ceiling.

I gagged.

The human members of the Esoteric Order of Dagon remained... unaffected by the incantation, except for having been knocked off their feet.

Through years of impersonation in the pursuit of journalism, I'd developed a convincing poker face. Scooping up the codex and scrambling to my feet, I strode to the cavern entrance. Like an avenging angel, I cried, "Leave now if you want to live." Most of them fled. I'd like to credit my bluffing skill, but more likely, they found the sight of their quivering or disemboweled leaders even more persuasive.

That left the four bravest, who advanced toward me with murderous intent.

Crap. I sprinted back to my sword, the cultists hot on my heels. The narrow passageway prevented me from slashing, but it also meant my unarmed assailants could only attack two abreast. I jabbed repeatedly, forcing them to keep their distance. My arm ached and my throat tightened. *I can't keep this up much longer. When I become exhausted they'll swamp me.*

Bam. Bam. Bam. Bam!

The four men tumbled to the ground, shot through the chest.

JR lowered his Beretta M9. He angled his head to the Deep Ones' remains. "I didn't think you knew how to use the codex."

I shrugged. "I didn't. But I definitely got my money's worth." My breath caught. "Where's Randy?"

"Back in the temple." He turned to retrace his steps. "Let's go get him."

I sheathed the sword and followed. "Why'd you leave Randy alone?"

"Because not only was he tied up, he was unconscious. They must have used a powerful sedative on him. I'm in pretty good shape, but I can't fight my way through cultists while hauling him up 250 steps. So, I hid him until we could return."

We entered the temple, heading for the dais. A Deep One lay on one side of the pool, green ichor still draining from a slit throat. The priest lay on the dais with JR's knife handle protruding from one eye.

JR must have noticed my stare. "These two stayed behind while the others chased you."

Note to self: never piss off JR.

He yanked out his blade, wiping off the viscous blood onto the Deep One's robe. JR clambered to the far side of the dais, stooping to remove Randy's gag and cut his bindings.

I tapped Randy's cheek with my palm, but he remained unresponsive.

JR removed a timer attached to three sticks of dynamite from his small backpack.

My eyes widened.

"My Templar duty has taught me it's best to be over-prepared. They can always summon another priest, but if we destroy the temple above Dagon and Hydra, their gods can't be revived." He set the timer and placed the bomb within the altar basin. "Time to go. Help me carry him."

"Sure, but let me borrow your backpack." I stuffed the codex inside, and we schlepped Randy back to the stairwell. Roughly half way up, footsteps echoed ominously behind us.

"Set him down," JR ordered. He removed two grenades from his vest, pulled the pins, and sent them tumbling down the stairwell. "Move."

Blam. Blam.

"That should take care of our pursuers."

My lungs ached. My arms felt like they were going to drop off. *I'm too old for this crap.*

Several minutes later, after struggling up the stairs, we reached the landing and set Randy down. I collapsed beside him.

A thunderous WHOMP reverberated up the staircase.

JR crossed himself. "And that should take care of their altar." He took off my jacket and passed it to me.

"Hey, you got green stains on my jacket," I complained in jest.

"Ha." He pointed at the tabard. "And you returned the favor."

I grinned. "Bill me for it. Better yet, bill Randy."

JR shook my hand. "*Merci*, Charles. I couldn't have done this without you."

"And you saved my life, JR. Thank you." I handed him the backpack. "Keep the codex. I imagine a Knight Templar will need it. This was *definitely* my last story as a journalist."

He bowed, struck speechless by the invaluable gift.

"You know what the worst part of this was, JR? Other than the stench, facing otherworldly horrors, and nearly dying, that is?"

"What?"

"Randy'll never believe that we saved his life."

JR nodded. "No good deed goes unpunished, *mon ami.*"

I smirked. "Too true. Well, let's get Randy some medical attention and then find the hotel bar. First round's on me."

Author Notes

Dagon, Hydra, Deep Ones, hybrids, and human members of The Esoteric Order of Dagon were created by H.P. Lovecraft, and appeared in the stories *Dagon* (1919) and *The Shadow over Innsmouth* (1931). The character name Jean-René Legazon is a French wink at the Lovecraft character from *The Call of Cthulhu* (1928), detective John Raymond Legrasse. "Gazon" is French for "grass".

The French geography and Knights Templar history are accurate except, of course, for Dagon and de Gonneville's escape.

"Taunt them a second time," is a wink at *Monty Python and the Holy Grail.*

IN THE GRIP OF COSMIC CONCUPISCENCE

JONATHAN LOUIS DUCKWORTH AND ERIC RAGLIN

Ambrose Hargrave
Attorney at Law
1438 Caldwell Street
Arkham, Massachusetts 01960

October 9th, 2021

Dear Mr. Sawyer,

I have initiated this correspondence on behalf of your wife, Mrs. Violet Sawyer, who I have taken on as a client. Mrs. Sawyer wishes to initiate divorce proceedings in light of irreconcilable conflicts within your marriage. Due to the sensitive, unsavory nature of these conflicts, she is reluctant to disclose the details in a public court of law. It is her preference that we negotiate the terms of separation and equitable division of marital property privately. If you are amenable to these terms, please sign and return the attached documents within seven business days.

On a more personal note, my client has asked me to relay her continuing concern for your wellbeing. She does not wish for this separation to further jeopardize your sanity and sexual health.

Sincerely yours,

Ambrose Hargrave, Esq.

Lawrence Howard Sawyer III
786 Whateley Lane,
Arkham, Massachusetts 01960

October 11th, 2021

Dear Mr. Hargrave,

Are you a religious man, or are you worldly? Can you even comprehend the precarity of your position in the cosmos, or do you suppose that because you write me from the apparent solidity and prosperity of your walnut-paneled office and from the resplendent surface of your coco-colo desk that you are master of your own destiny, that you can even begin to fathom the exquisite depravity to which I have been witness? I ask if you are worldly, but I should just as well not ask, for you wouldn't reckon *which world* I refer to.

My wife believes I am in danger, as if her ignorance of the sublime and terrible concupiscence interlaced with the background radiation of the universe's ill-starred conception is any insulation from its sanity-blasting ubiquity and enormity. If I am in danger—and I may well be—then we all are. Should my wife desire a spell of separation, I am not against such an accord, however I object in the most strenuous terms to her insipid idea that I should forsake the artifacts whose discovery have been my life's work to this point. What she so crudely and foolishly calls "pornography" is something quite beyond her ken. She should leave me to my great and important work. Furthermore, tell Violet that the coffee maker is mine, purchased with my own money, and I expect it returned to me, posthaste.

Sincerely,

-Lawrence Howard Sawyer III.

Violet Sawyer
PO Box 1130
Arkham, Massachusetts 01960

October 16th, 2021

Lawrence,

By the time this letter arrives, your pornography collection will be gone. I hoped you would give it up voluntarily, but your last correspondence suggested you'd much sooner jump into the sun. As such, I took it upon myself to act in your best interest.

My heist was simple. All I had to do was wait for you to leave for your Saturday grocery run. (You really should eat more, by the way. You're as thin as my patience). I unlocked the door with the spare key under the pot of dying petunias (water them!) and headed to your study. It took five trips to get your entire collection loaded into my car, but I was gone before you got back.

Looking through your collection now, I can say beyond a shadow of a doubt that you're a sick man, Lawrence. And I don't just mean that as an insult; you're psychologically unwell. While I once felt anger catching you with an ancient toad-leather tome in one hand and your cock in the other, I now feel only pity. You can't see that your supposed pursuit of "forbidden knowledge" is just a spiral toward ruin.

I'm sure you think my actions are unfair. But consider this analogy. Imagine you're a heroin addict. Would you give up your supply if asked politely? No. But if you're likely to overdose, is it acceptable for me to confiscate the poison? Of course. The same logic applies to your pornography.

As I write this in my new home (don't ask for the address), I'm flipping through your volumes of depravity. Each yellowed page feels like another nail in the coffin of our marriage. Each Ancient Sumerian inscription, another rose petal withered. And each illustration of tentacled smut, another reason to burn your collection. But I haven't yet. Destroying it would feel like destroying *us*. And while I may have accepted the reality of our legal separation, our emotional separation has been much harder to process.

All this to say, I know you'll be mad at what I've done. You'll tell your lawyer I'm a thief and demand that he take me to court. I implore you to save yourself the embarrassment, wait out the withdrawal symptoms, and see the potential for a fresh start. A fresh start for *both* of us in our new separate lives.

With tough love,

Violet

P.S. — I left your precious coffee maker on the kitchen counter.

INCIDENT REPORT

CASE NO. 5623

REPORTING OFFICER: BURGESS, J.

DATE: 10/19/21

INCIDENT: AT 07:25, SUSPECT, L.H. SAWYER, TRESPASSED UPON THE PREMISES OF THE HARGRAVE & FEINMANN LAW OFFICE AT 1438 CALDWELL AVE, AND CAUSED PROPERTY DAMAGE AS WELL AS ASSAULTED THREE EMPLOYEES, INCLUDING AMBROSE HARGRAVE. SUSPECT IS ALSO CHARGED WITH INDECENT EXPOSURE AND RESISTING ARREST.

DETAILS OF EVENT:

AT 07:25, SUSPECT WAS SPOTTED SHOUTING IN THE PARKING LOT AND BEHAVING ERRATICALLY. AT 07:35, COMPLAINANT, AMBROSE HARGRAVE, APPROACHED THE SUSPECT AND, ACCORDING TO MR. HARGRAVE, REQUESTED THAT HE LEAVE. THE SUSPECT THEN STRUCK MR. HARGRAVE ACROSS THE HEAD WITH A KEURIG-BRAND COFFEE MAKER HE HAD ON HIS PERSON (SUBMITTED FOR EVIDENCE) AND PROCEEDED TO RUN INTO THE OFFICE, STILL SHOUTING A STREAM OF INCOMPREHENSIBLE OBSCENITIES AND WORDS IN AN UNKNOWN LANGUAGE. WITNESSES AND VICTIMS REPORT A CERTAIN PHRASE, "IA! SHUB-NIGGURATH!" WAS REPEATED FREQUENTLY, AND THAT APART FROM VISIBLE SIGNS OF STRESS AND POOR HYGIENE, AN UNIDENTIFIED GREEN LIQUID SUBSTANCE WAS LEAKING FROM HIS LEFT PANT LEG. NO SUCH SUBSTANCE HAS BEEN FOUND EITHER ON THE PREMISES OR ON THE PERSON OF THE SUSPECT, SO THESE CLAIMS ARE UNVERIFIED. FOR APPROXIMATELY TEN MINUTES THE SUSPECT CAUSED PROP-ERTY DAMAGE INCLUDING: TWO SHATTERED WINDOWS, ONE BROKEN STAPLER, ONE DESTROYED LAPTOP, TWO SHATTERED COFFEE MUGS, AND ALSO URINATED ON A WHITEBOARD. EMPLOYEES CLAIM THAT AFTER STORMING THE BREAK ROOM, THE SUSPECT REMOVED HIS SHIRT AND DOUSED HIS CHEST WITH NON-DAIRY CREAMER, WHICH HE THEN RUBBED ONTO HIS NIPPLES IN A "SENSUAL FASHION," ACCORDING TO ONE WITNESS.

OFFICERS ARRIVED AND ATTEMPTED TO DE-ESCALATE BY FIRING THEIR TASERS AT THE SUSPECT. THE SUSPECT COLLAPSED AND WAS THEN TAKEN INTO CUSTODY.

THE VICTIMS AND WITNESSES CLAIM THE SUSPECT IS INVOLVED IN ONGOING DIVORCE PROCEEDINGS WITH ONE OF MR. HARGRAVE'S CLIENTS. MORE INVESTIGATION INTO THE SUSPECT'S MOTIVES MAY BE NECESSARY.

Violet Sawyer

PO Box 1130
Arkham, Massachusetts 01960

October 24th, 2021

Lawrence,

Forgive my schadenfreude, but when I heard you'd taken up residence at the Arkham Penitentiary, I laughed. Even without reading the news article, I could've guessed your charges—minus the public urination and indecent exposure. You're predictable, Lawrence. All addicts are.

But I've come to understand your addiction better since our separation. Truth be told, we probably have more in common now than we did when we were married. Not that I want to get back together. No, that ship has sailed straight off the edge of the world. What I mean to say is that I understand what drew you to this pornography, though it feels inaccurate—disrespectful, even—to call it simple "pornography."

Take *Shagging Shoggoths*, for instance. I opened the tome yesterday morning to read before work, and the next time I looked up, the sun had gone down. My boss had called me ten times, and though my phone had been on full volume, I hadn't noticed it ringing. The final voicemail informed me that I'd been fired, but I didn't care. No work meant more time for *Shagging Shoggoths*. Even mentioning the book gets me hot in the cheeks.

I'm sure my mention of the tome causes you great pain, deprived as you are behind bars without the pleasure of a squamous literary lover. I do not pity you enough to return your collection—*my* collection—but I will grant you one small bit of relief. Inside this envelope is twenty dollars, enough to purchase a decent supply of prison coffee. At least you won't go through two withdrawals at once.

Kind regards,

Violet

/D GREAT OLD ONES

https://www.duggit.com/d/greatoldones/comments/shag
ging_shoggoths_here_in_arkham!!!/

Shagging Shoggoths HERE IN ARKHAM!!! Posted by u/iaallday 2
hours ago

Ia! Ia! Cthulhu fhtagn!

True believers and connoisseurs of cosmic concupiscence, it has
come to my attention that one of the most exquisite and rare of
ancient texts, *Shagging Shoggoths*, is in my hometown. All this
time, while I've been combing the nighted trenches of the
Darkweb to find any online retailer or collector who might have it,
it's been under my nose. Apparently some local weirdo—not
weird like us, I mean he's a Republican, but I guess he's also a
weirdo like us in other ways—had a copy of *Shagging Shoggoths*
all this time. He just got arrested for going absolutely coo coo for
Cocoa Puffs at a law office, and get this, now his wife has the
book. Apparently they're getting divorced. I know, I know, you're
gonna say I'm full of shit, but it's true—my brother's friend's
roommate said he used to do lawn work for this couple, and that
he always saw the dude jacking it in his study (guess he didn't
even bother to close his blinds) to a book that looks just like
Shagging Shoggoths, in the original pink assflesh binding, no
less!

Hard to believe it's right here in Arkham of all places!

So what do you guys think? Should I get it? I don't have any
money, but I know how to pick a lock and I already found where
the wife is staying with her relatives, some crappy little house in
some crappy little seashore town between Innsmouth and
Newburyport. Maybe some other believers in the Mass area can
help a believer out? We can share the book, all for the greater
glory of our exiled masters.

gumballwhisper9 1h

Whoa! Wish I could help you out, brother. Share scans if you get it?

iaallday 1h

Pfft. You casual. As if you could scan such rare majesty. Might as well ask for a PDF of the Nec.

shubsshrub 52m

Wait, why are you surprised it's in Arkham? Don't you guys have like five copies of the Nec just floating around in your Little Free Libraries?

iaallday 49m

Let me be excited! >:(

painlord 50m

Where my N****raths at?

shubsshrub 45m

Can the mods PLEASE get rid of this guy? Starting to think the report button's for show.

diegobowwow 48m

I live in Newburyport and I'm down. DM me. Maybe I can even bring some friends if you need extra muscle.

iaallday 45m

Awesome! Appreciate it, brother!

shubsshrub 25m

      Planning a break-in on Duggit? You Eastern time zone people are wild.

Violet Sawyer
PO Box 1130
Arkham, Massachusetts 01960

October 31st, 2021

Lawrence,

I know it's hard to keep up with the outside world from prison, but I'm certain that even you, inside that cramped, miserable cell, sense the world is being reborn. Next time you're in the prison yard, look to the sky, sick and wrong and glorious with yellow light. It's been like that for days now, and if you squint at it just right, you can see the cracks between constellations. They're growing, slow but sure, and whichever timeless god creeps through will come for us. Maybe not tomorrow, maybe not next week, but inevitably.

It's all my fault. And perhaps yours, too, though I can't prove it. Did you send those devotees of the eldritch erotic to steal back your collection? Somehow they found out I was living at my sister's house. No use hiding it from you now.

When I heard those would-be thieves lockpicking the front door, I set down *Shagging Shoggoths* and my Hitachi, then crept to the living room. The intruders cursed and fumbled with the lock for several minutes, utterly unequipped for a break-in. More of them peeked through windows and paced the house's perimeter. I could have used that time to awaken my sister and call the police, but there was a more pressing concern. If the thieves planned to take *Shagging Shoggoths* from me, I would at least finish the tome first.

Surely you've seen—or at least glimpsed and recoiled from—the final incantation. Its ancient words shift like a black ocean. The page is fragile and thin, but stare at it long enough and you sink into its loathsome, impossible depths. Deeper, beyond the world of light, to darkened realms brackish with the semen of Old Ones and swarming with their tentacled servants. The longer you let yourself sink, the higher these beings rise. Even now they're ascending toward me, toward dry land, toward humanity's supreme domination. They're howling into the farthest reaches of space, calling forth their ever-more-ancient brethren. Land, sea, or sky, there is no exit for us. We await our terminal erotic destiny.

When I opened my eyes, the thieves were gone. My sister's house was gone. Salt water lapped at my ankles—rising, rising—and a moonless black enveloped me. My body ached with pleasure and ruin. My mind spun with the beautiful, cruel knowledge of our fate.

You won't hear from me again, Lawrence. All I can say is savor the end. It's coming sooner than you think.

Violet

HASHTAG TPE

DAWN VOGEL

The Miskatonic University campus tour guides had a running betting pool: who would be the first to garner a TPE—or total prospect enrollment. They went so far as building up a hashtag (tpe) for that mythical day, but getting an entire group of unruly high schoolers to complete the tour and sign their letters of intent was really nothing more than a fantasy.

Anthea Morrison had the lowest odds out of the whole bunch. Her first three campus tours had instead been "TPKs"—*none* of the touring seniors having made it through the whole tour. The normal attrition rate was around 25 percent, and the other student guides had started a side pool for how long it would be until the dean called Anthea in for dismissal from the guide program if not the university altogether. At least, that's what Naomi Carter claimed. None of the other students would confirm it, but Anthea saw the way they looked at her when they thought she wasn't looking. Pity from some, wonder at how she'd even made it into MiskU from others.

It wasn't that anyone expected her to keep all of the prospects interested. MiskU wasn't for everyone, after all. But Anthea was on a mission now. She wanted to prove all the other student tour guides wrong and be the first to bring back a TPE.

A stack of files lurked in her inbox. She pulled them out with some trepidation, noticing that three of the five had gold stars affixed to the front—high-priority students. In a way, that might make today's tour easier. Many of the high-priority students *wanted* to sign their MiskU enrollment intent letter the day they toured, so they were less likely to run screaming. But it also meant that any of those three who didn't complete the tour or sign at the end would reflect even more poorly on her record.

Anthea flipped through the files to get a sense of the students. *Tabitha Flynn, pre-med. Shiloh Cavanah, archaeology. Zeb Rutherford, folklore. Philip Darby, languages. Belladonna Whateley, library studies.*

The last one gave her pause both for the name and the intended major. Everyone in the area knew about the Whateley family. They'd been in the Miskatonic Valley for generations. And library studies meant taking the tour to the library, which was low on her list of places that led to a successful tour. Even regular MiskU students got lost in the book stacks on a weekly basis. She'd have to keep a close eye on her charges when they checked it out.

At admissions, a group of students and parents lingered in the lobby. Anthea gave them all a once-over. The two guys were as average white boy as average white boys could be while the girls appeared anything but. One of the girls looked Chinese, and Anthea pegged her as Tabitha but immediately chided herself for assuming the Chinese girl was the pre-med student. The second girl had ebony skin in dramatic contrast to the third girl, an albino.

Anthea put on her best chipper smile, hoping it would come through her voice as well. "Hi, everyone! I'm Anthea Morrison, and I'll be your tour guide this afternoon. I'll show you around the campus, and we'll make sure to stop off at all of the locations important to your prospective majors, and then we'll meet back up with your parents here so that you can sign your letters of intent if you so choose. I've got nametags for everyone—" She named each of the students, and they came forward to claim their nametags. She still couldn't differentiate between the boys aside from them wearing nametags now. The Chinese girl turned out to be Shiloh, while the black girl was Tabitha, and the albino girl was Belladonna Whateley.

The woman beside the albino girl narrowed her eyes at Anthea. "I'm gonna go on the tour too."

Anthea forced her smile to broaden. "I'm sorry, ma'am, but we've found that the prospective students get a better sense of the school if they tour it without their family members. I understand that the admissions staff have some excellent refreshments for you here while you wait."

"I ain't drinkin' their Kool-Aid," Mrs. Whateley grumbled.

Ignoring her, Anthea smiled at the prospective students. "Shall we?"

The five high schoolers trailed behind Anthea, the guys bringing up the rear with Belladonna in front of them and Tabitha and Shiloh walking to either side of Anthea.

"So what do you major in?" Shiloh asked.

"Ancient history," Anthea replied. "There's a little bit of overlap with archaeology actually. Mostly on the anthropology side of things."

Shiloh nodded. "Do the ancient history students get to go on digs as well?"

"Ah, not really," Anthea said. "We're more inclined to see what the archaeology students have found and see if that fits into what we're researching."

"I am looking forward to the digs," Shiloh said, nodding for emphasis. "So many secrets hidden below the dirt."

"That there are," Anthea said, turning to walk backwards and face all of the students. "So how much do you all know about the history of Miskatonic University?"

"Founded forever ago and always dedicated to cutting-edge research and innovation while still honoring the past," Belladonna replied, her voice completely without inflection.

Anthea nodded. "Got it in one. Many of the buildings on this part of the campus are the original university buildings. They've been updated on the inside, but this part of campus looks just like it would have 'forever ago,' like Belladonna said. Conveniently, we've got one stop to make for those of you who plan to major in folklore, languages, and archaeology." Anthea gestured at one of the old stone buildings, which looked like it was held together solely by the ivy that covered it on all sides. Only a few of the windows had been cleared, and even they looked as though the ivy might overtake them as the campus slept. "This is also where most of my ancient history classes are held. It's sort of a catch-all for a lot of the history- and language-based majors."

Leading the group up the steps, Anthea continued. "There's a beginning-level Latin class that we can pop into for a moment if you'd like. Just about everyone takes at least a year of Latin because it's applicable to so many different subjects."

The door to the Latin classroom was open, and from within, they could hear the intonations of the class reciting what Anthea could identify as a verb declension. But she wasn't sure what verb it was, which puzzled her. She'd aced both semesters of Latin.

Peeking into the room, it became clear why the verb sounded so unfamiliar. This was the section of Latin for religious studies students, and based on the arrangement of the desks around the pentacle in the center of the floor, it looked like this was an exorcism not a verb declension.

Anthea scanned the room for the professor and realized the professor was the subject of the exorcism. He looked confused and a little terrified, and Anthea turned to herd the prospective students away from the open doorway. "You know what, wrong classroom."

"No, that's definitely Latin," Philip said, peering over Anthea's shoulder. "Fifth-century text, I'm pretty sure."

Cold sweat broke out all over Anthea's skin. This was how campus tours went sideways. If one of the prospective students decided to go into the classroom and somehow got involved with the exorcism, either they or another student wouldn't finish the tour. Through clenched teeth, Anthea said, "Well recognized. But it looks like they've got it all under control, so let's not get in their way. Oh hey, Belladonna, could you open that door?"

Belladonna looked between Anthea and the door and finally let out an exasperated sigh. "What, you mean with my hands?"

"Uh, yeah," Anthea said. "That's usually how doors work."

Belladonna shrugged but did as Anthea had requested.

The scene inside the other classroom was much more sedate with one student reading from a standard Latin textbook rather than an ancient tome. The professor nodded at Anthea, her eyes sparkling. As the student completed his reading, the professor said, "Class, it looks like we've got some prospective MiskU students in our midst. What do you say we give them a warm welcome in Latin?"

"Salvete omnes vos esse," the class intoned as one.

"Et salvete omnes vos esse," Anthea replied. "Thanks, Doctor Moore. We'll get out of your hair now." Anthea herded the touring students back into the hallway and closed the door to Doctor Moore's classroom.

Across the hall, the doorway to the religious studies Latin class was strobing between black and blood red, and a low-pitched squeal emanated from the room.

"Right," Anthea said. "Unfortunately, there aren't any folklore classes we can drop in on this afternoon, and I understand that most of the archaeology students are either in the field or the lab today. So let's head downstairs to see the labs."

"I think something's gone wrong with their ritual," Philip said, peering into the scintillating doorway.

"Well, we've got campus security for just that reason. So we don't need to worry about it," Anthea said.

"Yeah, but I might know how to fix it."

"As admirable as that is, seriously, you don't need to get involved." Anthea gestured to a phone receiver a few feet down the hallway. "You can make a report over there if it'll make you feel better."

Philip sighed but nodded, approaching the phone.

Anthea turned to herd the other students toward the stairs to the labs. "Ironically, our archaeology labs are all subterranean. So we're pulling things out of the dirt only to put them back underground."

Shiloh chuckled softly. "Very good."

"Hey, isn't he supposed to come with us?" Belladonna asked, pointing back the way they had come.

Anthea looked back just in time to see Philip leaping through the doorway into the Latin for Religious Studies classroom. *Dammit. No TPE today. At least he's not high priority.* Smiling at the group, she said, "Okay, well, hopefully he'll catch up to us downstairs."

As the high schoolers headed into the stairwell, Anthea glanced back toward the classroom. The doorway was now pitch black, and either fog or smoke had begun to roll out from it. She scribbled the classroom number on the palm of her hand in the hopes that she could send someone back to at least collect whatever was left of Philip Darby.

The hallway leading to the archaeology labs had long had wiring issues, and the lights flickered as they walked. "Most of what we'll see down here is what a lot of people consider the boring parts of archaeology. All of the artifacts that come in have to be cleaned, weighed, photographed, and cataloged. But there are some students who prefer that to field work, so there are two primary foci you can take with an archaeology major—field or lab studies." Anthea paused and knocked on one of the lab doors. The cataloging room seemed the safest bet to take her remaining four students into.

When no response came, Anthea tried the knob. The door opened with an eerie creak and revealed a room containing a dozen vacant computer stations.

"Where is everyone?" Zeb asked, wrinkling his nose at the empty room.

"This way," Shiloh said, pointing toward an open doorway to one side of the lab. The other students nudged past Anthea to follow Shiloh, and Anthea followed in their wake, unconsciously crossing her fingers.

"You know that doesn't work," Zeb said, glancing at Anthea's hands.

"Has that ever been proven?" Anthea shot back. She wondered, not for the first time, if it was too late in the year to get assigned to a different work study program.

Shiloh crouched on the floor near one of the lab tables. "Something fell and shattered," she said, reaching for a fragment of what looked like pottery.

"No, don't!" Anthea shouted. The students looked at her, and she said, much more calmly, "Proper lab protocol says that you should wear goggles and gloves at all times in the archaeology lab." She pointed toward a sign on the wall that said just that.

Shiloh rose and nodded. "Of course. Where would I find the proper safety equipment?"

Anthea pretended to look around the lab and shrugged. "You know what, I'm not really sure. But it looks like this area may have been evacuated. We might want to consider doing the same."

The students other than Shiloh shuffled out of the room, but Shiloh took her time looking around. "This looks like a good lab. I think—" Her voice cut off as her shoe brushed a fragment of the artifact, and she vanished.

"Okay, everyone watch where you step," Anthea said, her voice an octave higher than normal. "Don't touch anything, and just tiptoe until you're clear of this room." She scanned the floor before each step as she hurried toward the computer room and back into the hallway.

"Hey, is it cool if I just head back to admissions?" Zeb asked, his face now white as a sheet.

"You know what, that sounds like a great idea all around," Anthea replied. "Let's all go back to admissions."

Both Tabitha and Belladonna crossed their arms over their respective chests and shook their heads.

"I'm here to see the library," Belladonna said.

"And I the med school," Tabitha said.

"And I'm not going back to admissions until I've done so." Belladonna stamped her foot for emphasis like a spoiled three-year-old.

Anthea took a deep breath and let it out slowly. "Okay, alright. Let's walk Zeb back to the admissions building, and then we'll continue on the rest of the tour."

Zeb rolled his eyes. "Oh, come on. I'm not a baby. I can find my way back there on my own."

The lights in the hallway flickered out, leaving them in pitch darkness. Even the emergency exit lights seemed to have been snuffed out. All around, the sounds of shuffling feet echoed as if the entire hallway was filled with students.

When the lights flickered back on, Zeb was gone.

I've still got 40 percent. Anthea breathed deeply, trying to maintain her composure. She looked between Tabitha and Anthea and pulled a quarter from her pocket. "Heads we hit the med school next, tails we go see the library next."

The girls nodded, and Anthea flipped the coin. She slapped it down on her wrist and lifted her hand, and it showed heads. *Great.* "Alright, the West Building it is."

Tabitha and Belladonna both stuck close to Anthea as they made their way between the buildings. Overhead, the previously sunny day had turned overcast, the clouds with a weird purple tint to them.

"You often get weird weather like this here?" Tabitha asked.

"Mostly on Thursdays," Anthea said. "Or if the meteorology students are conducting experiments."

A bolt of lightning shot out from the clouds and struck the West Building ahead of them.

"Aw, crap," Anthea said. "Or if some med student thinks he's the next Victor Frankenstein." She turned to Tabitha. "So there it is, the West Building. I'm gonna guess it's about to go into containment, which means no one in or out until it's dealt with."

Tabitha sighed. "But I want to specialize in containment! This would be a fantastic opportunity for me to see exactly what that entails."

An iron portcullis slid down in front of the main entrance to the West Building, and Anthea pointed at it. "Sorry, Tabitha. We can't get in."

Tabitha pointed toward a unit of campus security officers jogging toward the building. "Are they going in?"

"Probably not. They're probably going to maintain a perimeter until they get word of what's actually happened." Anthea sighed. "I mean, it's like in the archaeology lab. There are a lot of rules, and you have to learn them and follow them if you want to be a student as MiskU. Rule one: if there's trouble, run the opposite direction. That's how you survive."

Tabitha grinned. "My rule one is to help. If it makes you feel better, I'll head to admissions as soon as I'm done and sign my letter."

"I appreciate that," Anthea said. "But I'd really feel better about this if you'd come with us to the library."

"Noted and rejected," Tabitha said. "You don't have to worry about me. I signed the waiver."

"C'mon," Belladonna said, tugging at Anthea's arm with fingers so cold she could feel them through her hoodie. "Let her go play hero if that's what she wants to do."

"Alright," Anthea said with a deep sigh. "Just remember. Running away from the problem is still an option. There are trained professionals here. You've got to survive if you ever want to become one of them."

Belladonna skipped away in the direction of the library while Anthea followed at a slower pace. She was well on her way to having no students with her when she got back to admissions. Even if Tabitha did survive to sign her letter of intent, Anthea was beginning to think that getting a TPE was just a dream, and the only thing that kept her going was the possibility that Naomi Carter would remain just as stymied as Anthea was in her pursuit of the lofty goal. Maybe it was time to drop the competitive streak and get a job in food services. At least the students there just got glassy-eyed and numb. That seemed easier.

"Hurry up, slowpoke," Belladonna called back, mirth evident in her voice for the first time since the tour had begun. She stopped and turned to look at Anthea. "You look miserable. Is it really that bad here?"

Anthea shook her head. "It's not all bad. There's good stuff too. I'm just doing a difficult job, and I'm not very good at it."

Belladonna frowned. "You're doing a fine job. We've seen a bunch of buildings, and now we're going to the library. Do you know how long I've waited to get into the library?"

"But the goal of my job is to get students to sign their letters of intent. Instead, I keep losing students." Anthea shrugged. "It's hard for them to enroll if they're not here."

"What makes you think they aren't here?" Belladonna asked.

Anthea looked at the girl, frowning. "What makes you think they are?"

"Philip and Zeb made it back to admissions. Shiloh teleported straight there from the lab. Tabitha will probably be fine since she's with campus security. They'll likely even walk her back to admissions afterward."

"Okay, wait. How do you know that Philip and Zeb and Shiloh all made it back to admissions?"

"Telepathy, duh."

Anthea sighed. "My current run of luck tells me you're full of it."

"Nah. My mom's side has loads of psychic abilities. 'til her at least. Don't sweat it, okay? I get that you want to be good at your job, but maybe you just haven't met the right students until today. MiskU isn't for everyone, right?"

Anthea chuckled. "That's true." She sighed. "So you're dead set on the library?"

Belladonna shrugged. "I could wait a few more months if it helps. I'm going to enroll regardless. I just really want to see the library."

"Somehow, I think you'd do better there than a lot of people, Belladonna," Anthea said. "But your intuition's got me really curious. Tell you what. We'll go back to admissions and see who's there. And then if you still want to, I'll take you by the library."

"Can you come up with an excuse why my mom can't come with us?"

"It's restricted to current and future MiskU students? No general public allowed?"

"That'll work," Belladonna said, spitting into her palm and offering it to Anthea. "Deal."

Wincing, Anthea spit into her own palm and shook with Belladonna. "Deal."

. . .

Back at the admissions office, everything was as Belladonna had promised. Philip had helped stop the exorcism gone wrong and came back to admissions to sign his letter of intent. Shiloh had in fact teleported to the place she most wanted to be—the admissions office with pen in hand. Zeb had taken advantage of the blackout to duck the remainder of the tour, and he'd already enrolled for an independent study on the effects of crossed fingers on reality. And Tabitha had come back from the West Building to verify that it had indeed been a Victor Frankenstein–wannabe gone wrong but that the lightning bolt hadn't been enough to awaken his creature. So that crisis, too, had been averted. And she'd made good contacts with the containment force that she hoped to work with, and they had, just as Belladonna had suggested, accompanied her back to the admissions building.

Belladonna Whateley smiled at Anthea as she signed her letter. "You wanna get a picture of all five of us signing?" She frowned. "You're thinking something about a hashtag *T-P-E*?"

Anthea whipped out her phone. "Belladonna, you're kinda creepy, and I'd rather you not try to read my thoughts. But yeah. Hashtag *T-P-E*."

OVER THE SIDE

SHARON DIANE KING

"It's got to go."

"You know as well as I do, son. Not an option."

The pair stood on the pitching deck, peering at the dark, slimy, tentacled Thing inside the cage. Not all of it was actually in there, a few indescribably loathsome parts having already oozed out from between the bars. Still, a comfortingly thick mass of the nameless sludge-like horror remained contained, if only for the moment.

"I'm serious, Dad. It has to go. *Now*. Tonight!"

"Nope."

"*Dad*. It ate two of my wives!"

"Good. You know you were only supposed to bring one along anyway."

"It tried to eat my last one, just last night!"

"Is she all right?"

"Mostly. One of her boobs is bigger than the other."

A pause.

A single slippery peduncle from the unspeakable abomination slithered out from the cage, slicking briefly against the elder man's foot. He kicked it back.

"I just don't see why we have to keep it, Dad. We don't even have a pair of them!"

"You WANT another one of these on board with us?"

"You're the one trying to follow the letter. We don't have two, I say we can ditch it."

A sigh.

"I'm just not sure."

"Okay, all right, I wasn't going to tell you this, but it attacked me too, last night!"

"Are YOU all right?"

"Mostly. One of my balls hangs lower than the other."

A silence.

"I'm sorry, son. I just can't do it. Maybe we'll see dry land soon. We'll let it go."

"Can't come soon enough for me. I'm so sick of being sick it's making me sick."

The deck heaved again, as if trying to shrug something off.

"You and your brothers come up with a name for this craft we're on?"

"The Arkham, we thought. Not sure why, but it has a nice ring."

"Hm. Too long. Maybe just the first half?"

"Sure. That'd work."

And the pair gazed out at the fathomless waters.

CONSIDER THE SHOGGOTH

NICK BOWEN

E ditor's Note:

As the tabloid news cycle has finally turned its gaze from the tragic and unconventional demise of our former Miskatonic professor, Dr. Charles Webberly: Professor of Sociology, which occurred on campus a mere three months ago, we have chosen to publish a heavily redacted print of his final essay through the university's small press, "Consider the Shoggoth," a work previously rejected by all scholarly publications. The original article will remain in the Miskatonic Reference Library for Webberly scholars or aficionados to peruse.

I prefer to remember my dear colleague as a dour yet generous man who was willing to grant time to any professor, student, or bystander to elaborate on his dissertation over "Ceremony and Custom in Small Town America". For those curious about the late Webberly's work, I recommend seeking out his contributions to the *American Encyclopedia of Local Celebrations*.

On behalf of the great man's dignity, I do implore one to keep some of the more esoteric aspects of this article out of the publications of academic journals or public knowledge. Indeed, despite what I regarded as a close friendship to Webberly, he never once mentioned this work nor his apparent trip to Kingsport for "field research". The very fact I cannot find a circuit by the name of the "Necrocominist" suggests the seed of this project may have been the work of disturbed parody; though grossly out of the late Webberly's character, is not totally implausible. Much tiring discourse has fixated on the fact that the original work and accompanying notes were found in a journal bound in what later examination revealed to be human flesh. Perhaps the hours transcribing this essay from its "sensationalized" source has numbed any mystique. Understandably, the primary source has been stored in the rare text archives only to be accessed by scholars with the highest orders of permissions, although for what purposes I can hardly imagine.

Consider the Shoggoth

By Dr. Charles E. Webberly

Thursday

On the banks of the sad, gray waters of Kingsport Bay, I enjoy a cold beer from the local tavern's patio. Inside the walls of the bar hang ancient, discoloured buoys stinking of the sea, which in turn stinks of runoff sewage. Every detail from the cross-stitched nets draped from the ceilings to the peeling floor planks suggests the building is a trap set to snap. Wet boot prints stain the ground, and never seem to rinse away the record of thousands of fishermen, who have slopped down these harrowed halls, a century's worth of drunken detritus embedded into the building's soul.

The figure across the table from me wipes her mouth with the plastic off-coloured tablecloth, slurps a bioluminescent liquid that I conjecture could be either pickle brine or mucus, and belches before "digging in" to a "Seafood Surprise." I stir my own dish: cod congealed into a muddy ragu, with slightly less enthusiasm.

This fine diner is none other than Kingsport's own Delila Travers a.k.a. Madame Claw by festival folk. For the past forty years she has run the Kingsport Historical Society, a quaint assortment of antiques and placards scattered around a tiny lighthouse.

June marks a special time of year for Delila along with the rest of the town as they set up for their annual Cuttle-Fest. For three hundred and thirty-three years, Kingsport shuts down the town square for a weekend to include all the tired standards of local revelry: a modest parade, contests, a depressingly regressive beauty pageant, a competitive sailboat race, and a Faire tent that promises both Caligula levels of drunken hedonism by night and clean family fun by day, complete with petting zoo. From what I can discern, three major events separate Cuttle-Fest from any other small-town carnival: the opening "Summoning of the Sea-Gods" which commences the festivities, "Prime Slaughter" the major culinary experience, and the penultimate event "R'lyeh Waga'thn 'Shoggoth 'nwen " or what non-residents recognize as "The Tidal Offering." the official termination of the celebration.

Delila describes the duties of "Madame Claw" with a Deacon's gravitas rolled into the cheekiness of a department store Santa Claus. It is an honor she was bequeathed by the last Madame Claw, chosen only a year before her death, when Delila was a teenager.

Adorned in hollowed out lobster shells, fresh seaweed, and dried barnacles, Delila goes on in vivid depth about the creation of her costume but gives few details about the actual purpose of Madame Claw in Cuttle-Fest. Traditionally, the sea-mistress creates an annual ceremonial garb, left to her own creative liberties, barring two requirements: 1) a majority of the materials come from the shoreline and 2) she must wear the ceremonial headdress. Delila shows me a picture on her phone of her suit from last year's ceremonies, a meager dress of kelp and seashells, crowned by an impressive miter shaped like an enormous squid's head. I would like to tell her the hat does not so much resemble a crown befitting a queen; rather, it appears she is being consumed by said cephalopod. I am, however, not well-versed enough in local custom to know if this comment would be taken in bad taste.

Through the darkening street corner, I carry my odorous, damp doggy bag. Delila, worried I would not finish my "grub," insists I box it up for late night feasting. Everyone has been welcoming and polite, yet I still feel they are watching me. For all their talk of the tourist industry, I have yet to run into anyone else from out of town. I quell these questions and settle into a cot at a nearby inn. Tomorrow, at the crack of dawn: The Summoning.

Friday

The Summoning, for all its pomp and circumstance, does little to live up to its name. It is precisely the antiquated image you conjure when you think of hokey backwater traditions. From what I can tell all that is "summoned" is a sinking feeling of disappointment for the remainder of this visit.

Seemingly the entire town was out on the pier this morning dressed in their Sunday finest. I arrived in my typical attire to be met by the fierce gazes of men and women in suits and plain, ankle length dresses. My poor fashion statement did not last long, for soon Madame Claw took to the stage. I must admit her wardrobe overshadowed my own indiscretion.

Dead seaweed dried like a broom's head cloaked her withered legs in a ragged skirt. Green straps of kelp glued themselves to her body like long flatworms to a freckled trunk. Atop her hair: the squid head with its dull, confused eyes that peered over the crowd.

Today—faced with the reality and the prospect of three days (!) of this mind numbing, behavior—makes me glum. The overcast weather only lessens my excitement regarding Cuttle-Fest. After a recitation in the High R'ylen these people are frenzied, droplets of sea water are flung into the audience as a young boy with a graying mop of hair blows a rusted instrument.

Here is where tradition turns to true farce. Over the deck clambers a dozen strange, masked creatures. Their appearance recalls cartoon mascots that are almost impossible to describe. One wears a muted, purple octopus bobblehead, too large and too heavy for the bearer who walks with tentative shakes. A man with three flat mouths of dead fish and one crimson eye drawn into the center of his forehead follows along. A malformed colourless creature lopes behind the others, its strides the careful maneuvers of masterful stilt-work. Like an animated aquarium, the school of "sea-gods" trounces through the crowd to the local high school band's paean, saltwater taffy flying from their tentacles, flippers, pinchers, and other appendages to a giddy mass of children, who scramble over each other seeking tributes.

The library is closed which means the local folklore is under lock and key. I don't know if my fascination on the topic can sustain me enough to keep me here longer than my appointed time. The garish costumes and enthusiasm with which the locals participate in this affair only distance me further. I am reminded that I am an outsider, an observer of a ritual I have no part in.

No one wants to converse on matters of origin or symbology. Mostly they cheerily tell me to stick around for The Offering on Sunday, marking the first day of the year when the shoggoths are ripe for slaughter.

"What is a shoggoth?" I hear a few of you non-cryptos ask. And despite a few scant references in antiquated readings of New England history I, myself, could do little to describe them until today.

Inside the food tent I come face to face with a huge glass tank filled with hundreds of the creatures. Around the shoggoth tank, townspeople munch on more standard sea-food cuisine ranging from dried krill chips to clam chowder to deep fried puffin. I cannot fathom how one could feast in the presence of such hideousness. Instead of interviewing fairgoers, which was my initial purpose, I linger in the shoggoths' surveillance. My gaze cannot help but divert itself from the voracious feeders, thoughtlessly devouring the gifts of the deep, and revel in this anthropomorphic curiosity.

If symmetry is God then the shoggoth is godless, for there is no rhyme or reason to its freakish formation. A biological impossibility, an existential anomaly, a flagrant symptom of a cruel and unfathomable universe. Sightless eye-things waver over me through the thick glass, their orifices opening and closing mutely. I cannot comprehend the life of a shoggoth, much less could a shoggoth conceive of my own existence. And yet here we are, inches apart, sectioned off from the other by a sheet of glass that resembles a portal to an alternate dimension, both utterly inconceivable to the other. How does one butter up this unfathomable beast and eat it with corn and coleslaw? The act feels somehow more alien than the creature itself.

I do not recall how long I spent in front of the shoggoth tank pondering this endlessly fascinating creature. The feelings of repulsion fade away and are replaced by an admiration, a respect for its unnatural formation. A few men dressed in black robes and bearing strange tattoos, beckon to me as if they wish to clarify, to explain, yet I pay them no heed. To me the universe exists unto me and the shoggoth in its totality.

Later that afternoon, my watch is interrupted when the town elders, led by Madame Claw herself, enter the eating tent. The costumes are somehow even less inspired, their bearers' half undressed, masks tucked under their armpits, makeup smeared, cords and barbs and festoons now hanging loose from briny suits. These do not look so much like gods as they do like mockeries, farces. Ugly attempts at slander to the Old Ones, whom this world is but a fleck in the eye of eternity.

What is more offensive, the elders chose four of the fattest shoggoths (the size of beagles!) to slaughter for their commencement feast. Shoggoths are the most popular delicacy of the festival and are sampled first by the "Sea Gods". This loathsome custom leaves a bitter taste in my mouth.

I, dear reader, witness the entire process from the choosing of the sacrificial shoggoths to the tactless execution to the—pains me as it does—consummation of the sacred meal.

Do they not hear the beasts squeal as the ax severes their thoraxes? The pain and anguish at which these cries roar through my nervous system make me feel as if I too have been put to the blade.

As they lather hot sauce and ketchup upon the noble beasts' flesh and then cram it between stale pieces of bread, I automatically avert my gaze. Against the pleas of many in the village I cannot remain here in the tent. Instead, I take to my room feeling sick.

After a few hours of contemplation and rereading my writing, I see my reactions may have been dramatic; however, a deeper theme elucidates.

How is it that we, humankind, can believe ourselves so self-righteous, so ignorant in our deluded predestination, we cannot perceive any creature more deserving of this world than our own? The shoggoth does not wage petty war, it does not hate or conquer or covet or kill. I believe in Darwinism, I acknowledge the food chain, and I enjoy a barbeque sandwich sprinkled with extra bacon bits. The belief that animals are too sacred to consume is plain idiocy to me and I have been accused of "insensitivity" or "offensiveness" when I share my culinary beliefs. To put it plainly, I believe nothing is off the table when it comes to what should be on our plates.

Though there is something about the shoggoth, something beyond beauty, beyond mystique.

When I remember the faces of the elders as they slurped down more shoggoth flesh, I do not see the faces of men who were dining in bliss, but starved vultures desecrating a sacrament. For while Cuttle-Fest's charter decrees that shoggoth is the main dish on the menu, what it does not divulge is that the shoggoths are not unaware of this pact. The shoggoth is not an insentient being to be pulverized and chowdered. That the shoggoth willingly feeds itself to others is against base instinct itself. The dining dynamic is so grossly wrong, so terribly backwards, akin to a single krill swallowing an entire whale. The very act of this abomination will be our deserved end.

In short, I do not relish tomorrow's events.

Saturday

My stomach churns as my eyes open to a "shog-dog" topped with relish in my hand. The fairgoers cast concerned looks as I let the precious meat slip from my grasp. Their judgment does not upset me. I wish to return to my latest nightmare.

Dreams of Kingsport's Cuttle-Fest wracked my weary mind. If that was not enough to disturb one, this festival was desolate, devoid of all townsfolk and covered in floodwaters. In my periscopic vision, I floated through the empty festival, popcorn and cotton candy suspended, lights humming dimly amidst the still tents. I was deep beneath the sea where the sunlight could not cast its rays. Massive foliage glowing irradiant, in noxious colours, lit the scenery. Without a diver's suit or any apparent hope of reaching the surface, I should have been terrified; instead, I was filled with a warm familiarity.

Did I say this was a nightmare? I do apologize, I do not recognize now why I described it so. In the bottom of the deepest oceans, there lies a fairground much like this one, except peaceful, dead. Echoes of a great civilization now lost to time.

A shoggoth does not perceive temporal landscapes, yet another advantage over simian lifeforms. It is not foolish enough to process experience in consecutive causal moments. It lives in the before and in the after; it does not demand justification and motive to conceive of the darkness. There is pathos in its black oculus.

A man offers me another shog-dog and I recoil. How dare he offer me this divine beast's beef?

"I guess you ain't much of a relish man huh?"

Such flagrant insipidity. I leave the man gawping while I seethe in an anger I barely articulate.

Then I catch myself. I realize I have no idea what time it is, much less how I ended up in such close proximity to the shoggoth tanks. The haunting dream is more readily recalled than any recollection of the walk to this place. Inside the tanks, the shoggoths (the size of fattened sows) hover like bloated corpses in a bog. In the mass of dusky shells and wormy segments, I can feel their attention on me. Even if it cannot be perceived, they are watching my every movement. Wicked beasts.

I ask the man what he is talking about in a restrained voice, careful to disguise my fury. He reports with an aggravating cordiality that I can barely stand that I had reached out to him prior to the festival via Cuttle-Fest's website for an interview.

The character before me is none other than Cuttle-Fest royalty, Armun Grunch. Descended from six generations of fishermen, Grunch broke the mold by working for a canning factory on the town's outskirts. Despite his shirking of familial responsibilities like Madame Claw, he does not squirm from Cuttle-Fest duties. One of the festival's board leaders, a position he gained from 1) nepotism and 2) a lucrative income, he has been honored with the privilege of running the local celebrations for thirty-three years. As a local historian, a Kingsport alumnus, and a manager, I must have believed he would have been a good source for the project at the time. My vision, however, has grown so much greater than I first anticipated, and this talk seems beneath the lofty aims my words seek. I dispense with the niceties quickly and turn on my recorder. Although a somnambulist, I maintain a reliable sense of professionalism; my recorder travels with me everywhere.

Scholarly obligation compels me to take out my device and ask a few regular questions. I leave this transcription in its full recording for the reader to make their own judgments.

> Grunch: So, what's on your mind? I'm basically Cuttle-Royalty—any question is on the table. Speaking of tables, have you checked out this food tent yet? You try the mussels or the prawns? Sir, let me tell you about the shoggoth. Words can't describe—
>
> Webberly: No.
>
> Grunch: I'm sorry?
>
> Webberly: What you described. I reject it. You are not "Cuttle-Royalty" or any form of royalty for that matter. Not a drop of royal blood flows through your mortal veins.

Grunch: What the hell are you talking about? Don't tell me you're one of those squid loving PETA freaks. We used to get a couple of them every few years.

Webberly: And how do you define a freak, Armun? Is it an unadulterated love of the vastness of nature? The impossible deluge of existence? The staggeringly inexpressible truth we are but gnats in an expanding, emptying darkness?

Grunch: Umm… Are you okay?

Webberly: The shoggoth, Grunch. The shoggoth. You have not considered the shoggoth.

Grunch: What are you talking about? All our shoggoth are organic and fresh from the sea. If you're upset about their tanks, you gotta understand they are only in there for less than a week. For such long lived creatures, it's but a blip. Plus, they're good eating. (pause) Ain't this for a cooking magazine or something?

Webberly: Do you not hear the screams?

Grunch: What screams? Shoggoths can't scream. They got no vocal cords to my knowledge.

Webberly: I'm not talking about shoggoths.

Grunch: I apologize, sir. I just don't think I follow.

Webberly: Your feeble brain would melt if it could comprehend.

Grunch: Is that a threat?

Webberly: The saddest part is that you do not know. You're merely following a pale imitation of those before you. None of this is your fault.

Grunch: Are you crying? You need a minute, sir?

You understand, dear reader, how anyone would be malcontent after such utter disrespect. There was great temptation to rip my press pass up in his moronic face and tell him what I truly feel about his festival. But I cannot leave. I know this. I cannot leave these blossoming, glorious shoggoths to such fates.

I listen to this afternoon's recording again and I am flummoxed by the audacity of this yokel, who professes himself as "royalty." Permit yourself, a frenzied laugh into the void for his insolence. I do not care for his kind. He is not my king.

The shoggoths whisper to me in my sleep, secrets I dare not repeat.

Sunday

Heaps of empty carapaces and pinchers, antennae and limbs, the vision entails a mass grave after a horrific war. I have failed in my summoning. Last night, while I brooded in the hotel bathtub, the Great Feast occurred. My brethren, the shoggoth, have been unjustly devoured and their remnants have not even been given proper respect. Instead, they have been placed in a pile to be pushed into the sea as a commencement for the final event, "The Tidal Offering," which appears to be some way for the townies to get rid of all the "trash" they have accumulated over the weekend of festivities.

But you and I know there was another name for this ritual once. "R'lyeh Waga'thn 'Shoggoth 'nwen", it was called in a tongue lovelier than even sirens themselves could dare articulate.

In the fog encrusted morning light, I watch over the dead while hungover ingrates wait for sailors to return from their race, so they can regale them as "heroes".

I creep over to the empty food tent away from the coastline. Too captivated by the local theatrics, no one cares when I break away.

Inside the tanks, too small, too cruel, the remaining shoggoths watch me in vacant anticipation. I feel a pang of guilt. There were so many inside the tank when the fair began and now few remain. I wonder if they hate me but know that they do not bother with nonsensical emotions. To be eaten, to be consumed, that is the fuel the universe runs upon. Life for life. The only law that stands up any way you twist it.

The glass is easy enough to break, a plank of wood does the trick, and though my hands bleed, I feel no pain—only a rush of joy and adrenaline. The young shoggoths (today, the size of prehistoric tigers!), majestic and lethal, shuffle out of their prison. I count twelve among them. Twelve. I feel my innards squirm with envy as their orifices suckle the pavement hungrily. They glide across the ground like figure skaters on ice leaving slick moisture in their path. I trail behind them in tentative awe, following like a starstruck acolyte. Today, I am blessed among the disciples, the prophets, the martyrs.

When they feed, it is not a bloodbath or a hunt- it is an engulfment. I watch in fascination as men and women with their children stampede from the tent, their shrieks the most melodic sound I have heard in all my life. My feet are careful to creep behind the beasts, who make no noise except the snorts of their tendrils snuffling for cuisine. A faint stain is all that remains of any who cross their wake. The ooze steams in the summer heat and creates a pungent odor of a candy aisle inside a slaughterhouse. No one comes to aid of the ensnared because the killing is too quick. All that one can do is run and pray they are faster than their fellow festival goers. The early drinkers are the first to go, stumbling into the shoggoths, too inebriated to realize their mistake. Poor souls will never recognize the honor in their demise. At least the ones who are caught are able to recognize the vast purpose they serve. In terror there is awe.

Most of the town, however, is not here in the fairgrounds. Like lemmings, they gather upon the rocky shores near Kingsport harbor for "The Tidal Offering," the climatic ending of Cuttle-Fest. Here, Grunch and Madame Claw and all their inbred charlatans shall finally know how one makes a true sacrifice.

But the shoggoths do not cooperate. Beings of greater purpose, they never make it to the shoreline. They suddenly rush off, splitting into every direction as if they have no interest in the beach or their home, the ocean. Instead, they scatter into opposite trajectories. I am at a loss on who to follow. I blunder over to an injured shoggoth. I theorize its wince-induced gait comes from being partially eaten during the festivities, a chunk hangs loosely where it was dismembered for steak with a hatchet. Truth be told, it is not the one I wish to pursue. Instead, I want to gallop amongst the leaders of the shoggoth pack, but they are too swift for me. I amble behind the quivering heap, wondering if I can safely prod it towards its destiny.

The shoggoth, enigma that it is, does not receive my call. The communication I believed we had falls short and I shadow the creature in a ridiculous jog that is more appropriate for exercisers at an outlet mall and not a disciple of darkness. The sluggish ooze bubbles lazily across main street like a lazy river of toxins and eye spots. The other shoggoths have since disappeared into the wilderness that stretches along the highway.

I cannot help but admire the shoggoth form—a brilliant glaze of slime and pustule, a glob of innumerable eyes and orifices, the embodiment of hunger and urge. No creature on earth compares in its exquisiteness. Scholars make empty comparisons to the cephalopods or the crustaceans, to the amoeba, obscure sub species of fungi and protozoa. Words truly fail in an encounter with such. Scant references to the Old Ones and the kin have come before, but none have ever begun to do justice to the sagacious bodice of a shoggoth. Even malformed and weak, the shoggoth drifts in liquid ballet. It gobbles another family of surprised fairgoers, who are gathered around a shooting gallery. The son impotently fires a bullet as he is consumed.

As fortune would have it, the Dark Ones smile madly on their fallible son. For my labor I am granted a boon. While I nervously ponder whether a truck traveling at 60 miles an hour could inflict any damage upon a cavalier shoggoth, the parade float plows down the road. The grill wears the countenance of an Octo-God, its bulged eyes and hideous bulbous nose are suctioned to the green cab. It stirs me. Madame Claw and her posse sit in the bed of the truck, still damp from their sacrilege, costumes half discarded, drinking beer and smoking cigarettes with smug glee. Whatever "magic" occurred in the bay will not prepare them for what is to come. In spite of a gruesome injury, which has left one of its tentacles flapping flaccidly, the shoggoth enfolds their vehicle like an enormous sugar glider around a rotted fruit. As they are devoured, the faire royalty barely have time to process the monstrous texture, much less scream. Only one form takes longer than the others to evaporate—Madame Claw, who observes me with a glimmer in her eye. Envy, pure envy. What she has mocked in garish dress up and pseudo-trinkets over decades, I have destroyed in a few hours. But malice leaves her expression. Eyes wide and mouth curved, I cannot read her final thoughts before the shoggoth encompasses her.

I snap Grunch's neck and shove his oafish carcass off the wheel. His blundering obliviousness juxtaposes Madame Claw's serenity almost too perfectly. I take off with the shoggoth snorting and gobbling and feasting in the bed of the float. Now, I have victory, now I can find a home for my child. Along the road we can stop to eat- any curious bystanders or solicitors or hecklers or thieves or killers that can be baited. A shoggoth in the bed of the "Octo-God" float is just the security system I will need to escape Kingsport with my life intact.

From the rearview mirror, Kingsport shrivels in the distance and so too does my madness. By the time I pass through Arkham, I am in a state of anxiety. What the hell am I supposed to do with a live shoggoth at the university? When will the survivors report my deeds? How does one keep an interdimensional phantasmal nightmare a secret?

But eventually, I let a breath pass. I am, after all, my father's son, and he did not dream this universe without some cruel sense of cunning and virtuoso. Without words, without fear, I know what I must do. Start with the recruitment of university students, aides, who will satiate the blood requirement until I can figure out another solution.

I dread what I must now inflict upon my lone shoggoth, my responsibility. I pray our brethren have made their way across the States and beyond. I cannot fathom what will come of my actions, but I do know it has awakened the eyes of other things. They survey me in shadowy corners when they think I cannot see.

And for the shoggoth? It watches me sadly invoking a deep sense of guilt, sitting in an antique aquarium in my university office where exotic animals, now extinct, once entertained semi-serious, decrepit scholars. Do not repeat to me the irony- how this magnificent creature has gone from a journey from one tank filled with brethren to a solitary confinement much smaller, with less regular nourishment. Eventually, I promise, there will be no confinement. If it can wait- if in a shoggoths' being there is patience, it will reap rewards unimagined. I chronicle in my notes and study until my head hits the desk in exhaustion. The world is an illusion, a dream and when the Great Old Ones awake, they alone will judge me for my deeds.

For now, I hear the footsteps of another hapless intern for "work study," eager for a high-grade point average and an academic reference. I hide my notes beneath my desk and slither to the Hunger's gate. For in all my great steps to liberation I have not forgotten the primary tenet:

Consider the shoggoth.

E ditor's Endnote:
This article, bound in a book of human flesh along with the suicide note found nailed into his chest, illuminates little motivation. Through autopsy the book was revealed to be pieces of Webberly's own dermis, while the remaining corpse attracted inappropriately overblown media coverage for being "shed like a snakeskin" or in a more respectful and accurate terminology, "molted".

The aforementioned cage was never located in his office and this "shoggoth" has never been reported by the remaining university students who frequented his office. "Shoggoth" is an obscure term, of which little has been written, with the exception of fringe folklorists, whose controversial works are better left out of the dialogue.

I must admit even I cannot help but feel an air of superstition. Although a monster, Webberly, my beloved friend, is dead. Faculty and student disappearances have continued to increase at a troubling rate. I write this now from the safety of the café away from the tiny study and that hideous book. I watch the quiet mass with a paranoid suspicion my friend likely possessed in his final days.

The phantom of the suicide note hovers over this unfortunate case. While I am hesitant to disclose my friend's final private words, they have already gained an infamous misnomer through news leaks and have stirred the imaginations of conspiracy theorists everywhere. I do not know what offering these morbid details will provide other than the truth.

The note embedded to dear Webberly's sternum, reads the following:

"Consumeris quo tu es"

Many of the journalists have carelessly interpreted this as the common idiom, "You are what you eat".

I am loath to suggest that these "professionals", however widely regarded, have not had the rigorous Classical training of academics such as myself and poor old Webberly.

The phrase in Archaic Latin, if I may correctly assert, must be translated as:

"You are eaten by what you are".

Perhaps I will take a sabbatical to clear my mind of this lurid affair and leave this university town until events settle. There is unrelated research on the ecological trenches located in the deep mountain ranges of unexplored Antarctic territory that may prove intriguing. Whatever ill fantasy brought the demise of my friend in the coastal town of Kingsport, pray it does not befall our own selves.

ARKHAM BOARD OF HEALTH FEEDBACK ON MISKATONIC UNIVERSITY'S DRAFT PLAN FOR A SAFE CAMPUS REOPENING

RON FEIN

To the Dean and Board of Trustees:

Thank you for submitting Miskatonic University's proposed pandemic safety plan. We have a few brief comments and questions.

Social distancing in classrooms

You write that "through queer and monstrous perversions of geometrical laws, students will be seated at blasphemous angles outside the curves of our dimensions, thus remaining safely six feet apart." Please clarify whether safe distancing could be achieved without resort to "loathsome horrors beyond human conception."

Food services

We agree that students need not wear masks during meals. However, please revise the final plan to say "while eating," rather than "while slobbering and ravening with delight."

Data reporting

You propose to report how many students become "squamous," "ichthyic," or "batrachian." Please instead report how many students display fever or respiratory distress. Also, clarify why you have included a 15-page contingency plan for a potential outbreak of "waxy membranous wings."

Student arrival and isolation

To comply with Massachusetts travel orders, you propose to "quarantine all out-of-state students deep within the hellish stygian abyss, for a fortnight of indescribable fungoid terrors." Please note that students from the other New England states are exempt from quarantine.

Library services

You note that all of your library's holdings have been digitized for online reading, including certain "foul, repellent, and irrudinous tomes that bespeak eldritch accursed rites and which, once made public, may unleash nameless aeon-dead horrors." The board is extremely concerned that "irrudinous" is not a word.

Mental health impacts

You note that you expect increased incidences of stress, anxiety, and "abysms of shrieking and immemorial lunacy." What about the students?

If you would like to speak further in person, you will find me crouching and gibbering in the darkness.

Sincerely,

Herbert West

Health Inspector

BHEGNA CTHELLHA'S GUIDELINES ON PANDEMIC ETIQUETTE WHILST DINING OUT

BRANDON KETCHUM

The interdimensional pandemic, and subsequent quarantine procedures enacted by the Great Old Ones, have severely hampered billions of Cthulhic lives, and upset billions of Cthulhic routines. The service and entertainment industries have been especially stricken. Now, with the loosening of restaurant restrictions to allow outer realms dining, it is essential to address the Dos and Don'ts whilst dining out. The following guidelines are appropriate for every Cthulhic being, regardless of dimension, natural philosophy, or tentacular makeup. Much of this advice is applicable to a host of other existential situations beyond dining out and should be applied as is proper.

BEFORE THE MEAL

1: Choose an appropriate hood for proper maw coverage. The hood should fit snugly upon the cranium and encircle each tentacle without tightening so much as to chafe. Sperm whale skin is the preferred material for safe pandemic hoods.

or

human hide, with the proper attendant rituals, will suffice in a pinch.

2: Avoid crowded portal stations. This may occur in an outer realm where there is great demand for seating and beings have backed up along the sidewalk. If possible, call ahead for reservations to anticipate this possibility.

or

have a nearby outer realm in mind as an alternative if one's first choice falls through. The portal station may not allow for safe social distancing (sanity support cultists do not count, as the pandemic melts their immune systems within moments of contraction. Carriers lose their sanity instantaneously, and so can easily be avoided). The sacrificial slabs may not be properly distanced either, as discussed below.

3: Be prepared for inclement weather. In case of cosmic storms or interdimensional lightning, either be aware of one's surroundings and note possible shelter (such as building awnings, covered doorways, and bone pyramids).

or

ready an appropriate disapparating spell to phase home, or to another dimension, instantaneously. Always remember that, though one's dining experience may be ruined, one is inevitably responsible for the bill. Return after the storm, or the following century, to settle up.

4: Investigate sacrificial slab distancing. If there is not sufficient distance between slabs, the chance of spreading the pandemic increases exponentially. Remember that tentacular length cannot be counted upon for safe social distancing—like snowflakes, all Cthulhic beings' tentacles are different, and of different lengths. This is as relevant to spacing between slabs as in regular crowd situations. If packed too close together in the dining area, one may as well be dining in the inner realms! Sacrificial slabs should be forty-two cubits apart.

or

the restaurant may chain thirteen cultists head to foot between each slab. Even at their shortest, adult cultists are at least three and a third cubits long, so thirteen will offer more than enough safe distance.

DURING THE MEAL

5: Do not send or accept tablet-to-tablet runic messages at the sacrificial slab. Whilst this is considered gauche under normal circumstances, touching a tablet without afterward disinfecting one's tentacles creates a multitude of deadly health hazards during the pandemic.

6: Likewise, keep tentacles off the sacrificial slab. This has always been a major faux pas, and, similar to tablet use, threatens one's health and that of any other Cthulhic beings one comes into contact with. Tentacles can brush against the hood, which may be holding infectious spore matter, and tentacles must carry food under the hood and into the maw. Tentacles are one's greatest vulnerability dining out in a pandemic. Do not compound the danger by resting them on the sacrificial slab.

7: Do not speak with a full maw. These traditional guidelines should really go without saying, although they must be given added emphasis during the pandemic. The outside of the hood is already a germy breeding ground; no need to dirty the inside of the hood as well.

8: Never cough into the napkin, even if hooded while coughing. The napkin may not be properly cleaned or sanitized. Miniscule flesh particles from past sacrifices can still pass through. Granted, it is unlikely that the coughing will generate enough impetus to pierce both hood and napkin, better safe than sorry is a laudable mantra.

AFTER THE MEAL

9: Tentacular hygiene is a priority. Diners should already be attending to this in their private existences, though it is increasingly important after dining in the outer realms. Be sure to thoroughly scrub all tentacles in warm blood for the time it takes to sing the lyrics to "Ph'nglui Mglw'nafh Cthulhu" three times.

or

tentacle sanitizer may be used as a substitute. In this instance, be sure to thoroughly coat all tentacles in temperature-controlled plasma and rub them together until the plasma is absorbed into the scales. Tentacle sanitizer is considered more hygienic than merely washing with blood. The high cost of sanitizer, which has to be separated industrially en masse from human blood, is worth the price.

10: Finally, tipping has gone from flat science to art form. Whereas there are long-standing traditional formulae for tips, adjustable to the quality of service, now one must factor in the astronomical health risks undertaken by one's server. One should add a least one cultist to the tip.

or

three brains in a jar

or

five elder signs.

Also, consider the venue. If dining in a lowbrow establishment with minimal menu prices, the tip should be proportionally larger, as your server is risking more for less pay. Double the above-mentioned tip additions in this case. Adjust accordingly for other types of dining establishments.

. . .

I n conclusion, the Great Old Ones' decision to ease quarantine restrictions is a welcome change to what has become a listless and stale existence. Even so, one must be wary of not just one's own health, but the health of all Cthulhic beings, whilst dining out. The guidelines of etiquette I have presented should be followed to the letter, without fail. Otherwise, one's Chtulhic soul may be lost in the balance. Remember, whilst the pandemic is a threat to one's existence, provoking the Great Old Ones will certainly end it.

A SERIES OF NOISE COMPLAINTS, FILED BY YOG-SOTHOTH, OUTER GOD, AGAINST HIS NEIGHBOR

NICHOLAS JAY

L YCEUM on Grand, Luxury Live-Work Apartments
Incident Report 1352

Date: September 7, 2021

Subject: Noise complaint

Summary: Plaintiff alleged Respondent has repeatedly violated quiet hours, interrupting his work. Due to Plaintiff's special circumstances, Leasing Office interceded on his behalf, providing enclosed message directly to Respondent. NOTE: NOT STANDARD PRACTICE. Neighbors are encouraged to settle disputes amongst themselves before filing a complaint or requesting Leasing Office assistance.

-A.G.

Dear Neighbor,

While we have not met face-to-faces, it has been a pleasure to make your acquaintance since you moved into the apartment next door a few months ago. In that short time, I've become intimately familiar with your quirks and misadventures. Your short-tempered dealings with your "crazy" cat, for example, or your tendency to wet yourself when surprised or enraged. Not to mention, of course, the smoldering resentment you harbor toward your son and his teenagerly lack of motivation.

I apologize for prying, but ascertaining these insights into your character was unavoidable, as I will explain forthwith. You could be forgiven for thinking I discovered them through my achronological surveillance of the universe. Such is my specialty, after all. But ask yourself: why would I, Yog-Sothoth, the All-in-One, exercise the infinite and consequential power at my disposal for trifles such as these?

No, the answer is much simpler. I learned all about you through your voice—that powerful, deliciously hideous instrument which every morning seeps through the brittle wall that separates your bedroom from my interplanar workshop.

Allow me an aside to describe its exquisite properties. It is at once shrill and sonorous, not unlike a horde of prepubescent byakhee, or (for a more mortal example) a roller derby coach barking abuse at her quarries through a megaphone. Moreover, every word crackles with a rage rivaling the primordial fury of lesser demons. The wall between us does nothing to muffle the sound, yet still I find myself shambling to the barrier, pasting my many eyes to the drywall in the hopes of absorbing your voice's delightfully poisonous vibrations straight into my sclera.

I digress. Despite the pleasures your impassioned arias bring me, I must ask you to tone it down. The "noise complaint" mechanism proffered by the Leasing Office seems the most suitable medium for this request, but please know that "complaint" is far too strong a word. I am not "complaining" as other, more impotent beings might whine about noise disrupting trivial pastimes like "sleep" or "sex" or "movie night."

Rather, I must ask you to consider lowering your spine-tingling voice for one simple reason: it entices me too much. It renders me incapable of focusing on anything else. It tempts me especially when raised in anger toward your son, when you berate him for missing track practice or "failing out of eleventh grade." If I were of weaker constitution, I would surrender to your voice without hesitation; however, my cosmic needle and I are engaged in a project of great ambition that will transform this disgustingly drab and orderly universe (I shudder as I scrawl) into something marvelously chaotic.

Such needlework requires great precision and concentration, which I am repeatedly denied, often to disastrous effect. Thanks to you, this week alone I have inadvertently birthed a sinkhole near Sochi, a tsunami off the coast of the Philippines, and a gravitational anomaly that inverted all the arches in Arches National Park. While I do not mind a few episodes of errant destruction, drawing too much attention to my project would cause its premature collapse.

To avoid provoking more incidents (for now), I must ask that you abide by the Leasing Office's arbitrary regulation of "quiet hours," which last from 11:00 p.m. until 8 a.m.

Based on my careful and purely clinical observations, your voice is most active, angry, and alluring around 6:00 in the morning, when you are trying in vain to inspire your son to do "something other than smoke pot all day." This occurs two full hours before this quiet period concludes. If you could delay your extremely pleasurable diatribes for two more hours, that would enable me to safely tie off any last stitches I've made in the universe and turn my attention to other things.

Again, I cannot stress enough how much it pains me to ask you to lower your voice. Certainly let me know if there is anything I have done to infringe on your right to unimpeded enjoyment of your home. However, in doing so, please refrain from knocking on my workshop door—I will not answer, for the prospect of ensnaring you on sight and hurtling you into the void between worlds will be too tempting to bear. Instead, you can file a complaint with the Leasing Office, as I have.

Thank you for your consideration of my needs.

Respectfully yours,

Yog-Sothoth, Outer God, The Lurker at the Threshold, The One-in-All, &c.

. . .

L YCEUM on Grand, Luxury Live-Work Apartments
   Incident Report 1352-A

Date: September 13, 2021

Subject: Noise complaint (follow-up)

Summary: Addendum filed on referenced report. Plaintiff alleged Respondent continues to violate LYCEUM on Grand's quiet hours policy and seeks redress for disturbances caused. Leasing Office once again assisted Plaintiff by delivering message contents. Leasing Office issued a warning to Plaintiff as well, notifying him of the misappropriation of staff time his complaints have caused.

~A.G.

Dear Neighbor,

Greetings once again from the other side of our shared wall. It appears you have neither heeded nor acknowledged my request to respect "quiet hours." Quite the contrary, in fact. Since my last communiqué, the frequency of your exquisite tirades has only increased.

While this has continued to scratch an itch so dormant within me that even I and my myriad eyes were blind to it, it has yielded yet more devastation thanks to your remarkably chaotic timing. Just yesterday, my limbs twitched violently when you lambasted your son for his "utter and complete lack of a future," which opened a rift that transported the pyramids of Palenque all the way to Yuggoth. (On the bright side, the Mi-go love them.)

Perhaps I have not fully expressed how much your voice stirs me. When you scream at your son—things like "do your homework!" or "get off the couch, you lazy piece of shit!"—it produces within me a transcendent euphoria. Imagine a lovesick puppy, stroked by thousands of disembodied hands repeatedly and all at once. Multiply that sensation times ten and that's what it feels like. It soothes me. It *nourishes* me.

Alas, it also distracts me, breaking the focus my visionary project requires. And we—myself, yes, but also your puny but persistent world —cannot afford to be distracted.

Therefore, I must ask you *again* to please keep your voice down, if only during "quiet hours." Sleep means naught to me, so I can make accommodations to continue my work while you rest your fragile shell and feeble brain at night. I am certain both grow weary after a long day of your son testing the limits of your patience.

I am deeply sorry to bother you with another official missive; if I had any confidence that you would survive an encounter with me in the flesh, I would facilitate a direct meeting. Thankfully, the Leasing Office has magnanimously offered to pass along my concerns. I hope that the rather dry format of my complaints does not offend you or prevent you from taking them as seriously as I intend them. I would regret having to resort to more drastic measures.

Respectfully yours,

Yog-Sothoth, Outer God

LYCEUM on Grand, Luxury Live-Work Apartments
Incident Report 1352-B

Date: September 16, 2021

Subject: Noise complaint (follow-up)

Summary: Second addendum filed on referenced Incident Report for noise-related dispute. Request to elevate this ongoing incident to upper management. Plaintiff's communications are becoming more aggressive. Leasing Office staff knocked on Plaintiff's door with the intention to address both the Plaintiff's concerns and his misconduct. Plaintiff did not answer.

~A.G.

Dear Jennifer, The Banshee Beyond the Wall,

Oh, how you test me.

Your commitment to the demise of my project is nothing short of admirable. Despite my well-argued need to consider the fate of others before your own, your unpredictable outbursts have only become more frequent and fervent. Must you always express your emotions with such sound and fury? What mortal being benefits from you screaming obscenities at your stupid cat, or from your primal shriek at the sight of a cockroach skittering across your floor? Your son must grow weary of your perpetual anguish.

Under any other circumstances, I would admire the utter vehemence you wield and would delight in hearing it manifest in your signature squawk. But you have distracted me with your temptations for far too long. Do you not watch any news? Sicily buried underneath shale and lava, blizzards in Puerto Vallarta—all thanks to your fanatical explosions making my cosmic needle flinch.

Think of the tremendous suffering you have caused! It is far from bothersome to me, of course, but don't *you* care?

Despite my penchant for assisting (and in many cases, accelerating) the universe's natural entropy, I am revered among the Outer Gods as methodical. Rarely do I abandon projects or forsake tasks; if I temporarily set them aside, I always return to them eventually. After all, I literally have all the time in the world.

So you can imagine how dire it is that I have, for the first time, considered ending a project prematurely. I have tried to persevere despite your blatant disregard for my needs. I have, to my great chagrin, considered more grisly ways of dealing with you, even though I swore off direct meddling with humans ever since Dunwich. Yet still I find myself slithering toward the precipice of abandoning my project altogether, simply because you cannot or will not keep your goose-pimpling klaxon of a voice within a reasonable volume. To think a simple, human voice could wield such hypnotic power over Yog-Sothoth, the omniscient Key and Gate.

Based on your unchanging behavior, it seems you neither know nor care about the great and satisfying pain you bring me, nor are you moved by the disasters your outbursts have wrought on your fellow humans.

Thus, I am compelled to touch on the only remaining subject I am aware of that could pique your attention: your torturous relationship with your son. At this point, I have been privy to so much of your delicious invective that your relationship has become amusingly predictable. Every day occurs as follows:

He disappoints you over something trivial. You excoriate him. He breaks things. The argument escalates to a fever pitch. He flees, slamming the door behind him. You loudly bemoan his idiocy to a friend on the phone. Later, he returns, but neither of you apologize, stifled by the uneasy silence. Then you sleep, wake up at six in the morning, and continue where you left off.

Let me ask you something. The intense resentment you display toward him…it isn't really about him, is it?

Surely he could perform better in school or on the track team, and surely those little shortcomings bother you. But I hypothesize that those don't rankle you nearly as much as your own failure to mold him as you see fit. That failure, as agonizing and conspicuous as a stye on your eyelid, is what truly vexes you.

Perhaps you consider yourself to be his only role model, the sole entity responsible for his growth and development. Thus, any misstep on his part reflects poorly upon you and your success as a mother raising him on your own. And because there seems to be no end to his string of disappointments, the image you've sought after your whole life of being a perfect, functional family is at risk of slipping from your clutches. So you resort to harsh discipline to keep him in line. You wield shame like a cattle prod, hoping it will zap him out of the stupor of ennui you believe clouds his judgment.

Maybe, you conjecture, if you wriggle into his psyche and pinch each rebellious or apathetic wrinkle in his brain until the only neuronic pathway left is that which is morally good and right and productive, then he will miraculously become a straight-A student, upstanding gentleman, and virile father of four grandchildren who you can also bend to your will as matriarch of this wholesome, virtuous family.

Let me be the first to say I get it. I really do. Being a parent is hard, especially when you feel you have nothing in common with your children. Some say my son is a nasty creature himself.

But while I admire your surgical approach to your son's development, I anticipate your approach may backfire. Your experiment is a tricky one, with many confounding variables that could pervert your desired results in unforeseen ways. For example, instead of channeling your son's free will into the right pathway, there is a considerable chance that the blockages you create in his brain could coagulate and swell into a cerebral aneurysm of potentially ruinous proportions. We wouldn't want that, would we?

If your harsh discipline is not producing the desired effect on his behavior, perhaps another approach will work? One that relies on— oh, how difficult it is to write this word—*kindness*? Empathy? These are not capabilities I possess but, as I understand it, humans often have to learn these to survive in a number of social arenas. "Work" or "the gym" or "middle school," to name a few. If they've worked for others, they just might work for you as well.

And then I could *finally* make some uninterrupted progress on my project, free from wanton attraction to your horrifically beautiful voice. Oh, how I would miss it.

My own priorities aside, do remember I'm thinking of your family's well-being, especially that of your son. Try a different tack, for a change. You might find it brings you some relief.

Respectfully yours,

Yog-Sothoth, Outer God

L YCEUM on Grand, Luxury Live-Work Apartments
Incident Report 1352-C

Date: September 30, 2021

Subject: Noise complaint (follow-up)

Summary: Third addendum filed on Incident Report 1352 for similar reasons (see previous reports for more information). After discussing Plaintiff's special circumstances directly with Plaintiff, Leasing Office staff will be extremely happy to provide courier services for the duration of this ongoing dispute.

NOTE TO MGMT: Do yourselves a favor and just deliver the letters. Do not knock on Plaintiff's door.

This will be my last day. Apologies for the short notice, but I must go. Far away from here. Take my little shell-body and lock it in a room filled with light, keep the lights on at all times.

-A.G.

Dear Jennifer,

I hope this letter finds you well, though I suspect it does not, based on what I have heard through the wall lately.

First, let me offer my condolences. I have heard it said by your kind that the loss of a loved one leaves behind a deep, incurable wound from which you can never recover. You can only manage the pain.

I sympathize with this, though I do not think in terms of wounds, only voids. To imagine a void I could not close is...tantamount to heresy. When I try to fathom it, my myriad eyes quiver with hysterical incomprehension. If this revolting reaction I'm experiencing is anything close to resembling your current emotional state, please know I am deeply sorry.

But the sorrow I feel must be a fraction of yours. I can tell as much from your voice. Your breathtaking, boundless anger seems to have vanished along with your son. No longer do you chide or castigate. Now you simply cry, round full moans that punctuate the silence. No words...you seem to have lost your taste or capacity for those.

I cannot blame you, given that you must feel there's no one there to listen.

I suspect I could have done more to offer my support. Practically, I'm not sure what shape that support could have taken, given the horror I inspire in humans, but certainly my multiple letters did not help matters.

As recompense, please allow me to make you an unorthodox and potentially perilous offer. Undoubtedly you regret how you left things with Trevor. Let us say, hypothetically, you had the opportunity to speak to him once more, to resolve things. Would you take it?

Before you balk and claim the impossibility of this scenario, let me remind you of my numerous talents. I am the One-in-All, the All-Encompassing. As such, I hold dominion over the union of time, space, and all that which is material. I exist neither inside this union nor outside it, but *beyond* it, unhindered by such flimsy barriers as "chronology" or "spatio-temporal integrity," as you humans are.

Allow me to indulge in metaphor. Think of yourselves as trains on tracks. You and every other creature in the known planes constantly move forward toward some imperceptible goal along ley lines traversing a wasteland of cosmic debris. You shuffle along your restrictive tracks, not only incapable of braking or changing course, but also disinterested in it.

I can squirm above, below, and through this debris, opening portals between points to show you things you wouldn't ordinarily see. In this way, you could lay eyes on Trevor once again.

Now, before you ask about the prospect of reversing Trevor's ruptured aneurysm and bringing him "back to life," let me issue a disclaimer. While it is true that the distinction between past, present, and future is essentially meaningless for *me*, humans have yet to comprehend the true nature of time and thus can only conceive of themselves and the world around them as what-was, what-is, and what-will-be. (Of course, my project strives to change all that, but that's neither here nor there.)

Regardless of its place in time, Trevor's death—his crossing of the threshold—is permanent. That event exists as a focal point in the intricate latticework of your ley lines. It is an eyelet through which your life-threads pass, both together for a moment. To disentangle them would mean your own undoing.

In short, I cannot bring him back. However, I can offer you contact. Be advised this is quite dangerous and could produce extreme cognitive dissonance. After all, humans tend to stubbornly resist any change to their worldview, especially when they're not prepared. Yet for those who look for answers, the ones with shattered hearts who *yearn* for them, well...more possibilities are within reach.

It is this yearning which prompted me to write you once more. When you were on the phone earlier today, I overheard you mention you need what humans call "closure." It is an intriguing concept, to be sure, one that I routinely face. If you decide to pursue this "closure," especially if it requires speaking with Trevor, I will voluntarily extend my aid, though with the following warning attached:

The universe is full of holes. Some open on their own, while some are opened by others. Sewing up all of them is a futile task, even for me. Closure, as I understand it, is something you will chase until the end of your days, when you have far surpassed the end of your ley line and crossed the threshold yourself.

With that warning given, if you take interest in my offer, please do not hesitate to let me know. Simply knock on my door to signal that you are ready.

Respectfully yours,

Yog-Sothoth

L YCEUM on Grand, Luxury Live-Work Apartments
Incident Report 1352-D

Date: October 15, 2021

Subject: Noise complaint (closed case)

Summary: Fourth and final addendum filed on Incident Report 1352. Case has now been closed, as Respondent has moved out. At Plaintiff's request, Leasing Office staff have made copies of this notice and sent it to Respondent's forwarding address on file. Any further amendments to this report can be taken up directly with management. Special circumstances still apply for any interactions with Plaintiff; please consult lease agreement for unit 2214.

~H.F.

Dear Jennifer,

Today was beset by an eerie stillness. Your voice, which had graced my ~~interplanar workshop~~ apartment and thwarted my progress for months, was silent.

Of course, this did not come as a shock to the All-in-One. I had been expecting your departure from this place in the wake of your son's death. I have already admitted in a previous missive to scrutinizing your life-thread, as well as Trevor's. While I suspected your soul would continue creeping forward along your predetermined ley line following his demise, I had wondered if you would muster enough willpower to accept my offer.

Do not trouble your little heart; I am not offended. After all, we do not really know each other. Though I feel I know *you*, thanks to your awesomely hideous voice, it is clear you are not familiar with me or my capabilities. Had you heard of me, surely you would have taken advantage of the immense power I offered you to gain that elusive closure you craved.

Perhaps my warning was sufficient to dissuade you. Or perhaps you simply took exception to unsolicited advice from a stranger. Honestly, it niggles at me that I do not *know* the reason. In all my other dealings with humans, I could always deduce the reason! What is it about you that baffles me so?

Though all of my attempts to contact you have been met with impenetrable silence, I will leave my offer open should you ever have need of reaching through the void to see Trevor one last time. It is the least I can do after all you both have suffered.

In the meantime, I thought it might interest you to know I have officially paused my project. The destructive episodes in Russia and Utah and the Yucatan and many more, all caused by my erratic behavior over the past month, render the entire thing a risky pursuit at the moment.

Moreover, I feel a cloud of existential ennui hovering over me as of late. I have always pined for the transformation of the known universe, origami-like, into something beautifully grotesque, something befitting my multiplicitous, synchronic nature. But now I can't help but ask: why? In service of whom? Me? What satisfaction could a project of this magnitude bring me if it means thousands upon thousands of people longing for one last goodbye or one more opportunity to set things right would be untimely ripped from all they know and hurled into the void by the careless appendage of a dispassionate deity whose needle happened to tear through the fragile fabric of the universe and sundered the ground beneath their feet?

Hopefully you understand, based on these troubling thoughts, why it's imperative that I retreat for the moment to reassess.

As such, I will have a lot of time on my hands, so to speak. I may not be the most approachable entity in the known planes, but please remember my willingness to help soothe and relieve your pain.

If you need me, please contact the Leasing Office, who have marvelously agreed to continue serving as liaison for our correspondence. I would be delighted to stay in touch. My offer does not expire, and I will always be here to listen.

Respectfully yours,

Yog

WHAT ARE THE ODDS

MIA DALIA

The arm of the slot machine looks like a tentacle. Because, of course, it would. That's what I get for going to a themed casino. I'm not even a casino person — I don't have a gambling bone in my body, but Aunt Ruthie is, and this is her birthday and this...this is the art of compromise at its finest. The Old Ones is Las Vegas' latest attraction – a horror-themed casino with a distinct Lovecraftian angle to it - and a visit to it is my horror-loving self's gift to my gambling-loving aunt. Something for everyone, right?

I get to walk around, check out the stunning scenery (open-gawk style) and check out the stunning waitresses (clandestinely and discreetly) while sipping on some strangely colored concoctions the ingredients of which I don't dare to question, while Aunt Ruthie gambles her blessed betting heart out.

This place is a trip. It's a spectacle. It's so over the top, it makes Dubai seem modest by comparison. But credit where credit's due, the designers mostly did appear to stop right before hitting the gaudy threshold and never dropped the ball on their theme. For a horror junkie, this is a feast for your eyes and senses, a one-of-a-kind bonanza of epic proportions.

The creatures are fully articulated animatronics, the special effects are movie-grade CGI quality. I've been to more haunted attractions than I can count, and *this* is a place they've all aspired to be, I bet. This is awesome. Monstrously awesome.

From iridescent ichor oozing walls to the otherworldly glowing suns on the ceiling and whatever the sinister mist that's twisting around my feet is - this place is magnificent. The technicolor nightmare you wish you had after binging on cosmic horror and old B-movies.

Everyone's in costumes. Everyone who works here, anyway, and a lot of visitors too. I thought about dressing up, but it just isn't my style. I'm also in-between gigs right now, and money is tight. Instead, I settled for my Miskatonic University Dropout black t-shirt, freshly laundered for the occasion.

I've never been the best-dressed guy at any party, but at times I've been the most amusingly attired, which is a close second as far as I'm concerned.

I make my drink last a long time, idly contemplating its strange greenish tint. I've budgeted this evening just right to make Aunt Ruthie feel special and still leave me in ramen and bananas for the rest of the month.

Gig work is like that. Especially, when the gigs don't pay that much individually. Still. At least, when I do work, I work at something I love - I draw. One day someone somewhere will discover me and my web comic and then the fame and fortune will pour in. You hear the story so many times, you start believing it. Because it's just too bleak otherwise, isn't it?

. . .

I got fired from my last gig. The editor said I wasn't good at taking direction. I refrained from saying his directions sucked. Ok, I suggested it, but I didn't say it out loud. I'm not an idiot, I know it's a small world, and everyone knows everyone, and everyone talks. He could have been more gracious, though. I was there for a while, and during that time, I've acquiesced to a series of his increasingly unreasonable demands prior to the said firing. I met deadlines. I wore shirts with buttons and combed my hair. Fuck that guy. I don't want to think about that guy.

Except, of course, here I am thinking about him because I just saw him. Of all the places, of all the days, he's here. Sweaty and socially awkward as ever, looking like he's had one too many, Jerry is leaning on the bar trying to chat up the bartender. The bartender, even with her terrifying creature-makeup, is so far out of Jerry's league, it begs the question of just how overserved Jerry is at the moment to think that this might ever work.

Oh well, at least he's too drunk to notice me. I walk away in the other direction as quickly and inconspicuously possible, trying to shake off the unpleasantness of the ugly past rearing its head into an otherwise perfectly pleasant present. What are the odds? Seriously?

Every time, with every gig, you go in thinking…Is this it? The big break? The one that'll make all the crap that came before worth it? And no, it never is. That one certainly wasn't. All I got was some money, another credit on my already unwieldy long resume, and another pummeling to the ego.

Wow, that waitress is hot. Or is it a server? I can't follow the linguistic trends - I'm at a point where I'd rather pretend I have a terrible memory than chance misgendering someone or offending them with my antiquated vernacular.

But I mean, she's smoking hot. How does someone even look that good while wearing a costume like that? That's a skill. She must have had to audition or something. I gotta stop looking. I'm not a creep. I'm sure she gets a lot of those in her line of work. I try to be a good guy, a stand-up guy, the class act my Aunt Ruthie raised.

Vegas is insane. It's all flash and flashing lights and bright hyperactive neon energy. New York may be the city that never sleeps, but Vegas is a city that can't sleep for the fear of disappearing. The same way the sharks can't stop swimming, or they'll die. Vegas is a seizure-inducing dream that must continue to self-perpetuate or blink out into oblivion.

If someone ripped through the fabric of existence to burst into a darker dimension populated with ancient deities lying dormant and dreaming their deadly dreams, it would be here. And no one would notice, either. Or they would - and build a casino around it.

Aunt Ruthie isn't choosy; she'll gamble anywhere. She has, too. To think, she was a mild-mannered librarian for 45 years prior to retirement. Never gambled a day in her life until she turned seventy, now she can't stop. You can't argue with it, she followed all the rules her entire life – worked hard, raised a wayward nephew after his junkie mom ODed one too many times, paid all her dues, paid off a small comfortable house and a large jalopy of a car - Aunt Ruthie earned the right to do whatever she wants in her old age.

I never thought it would be gambling, but what do I know. I'm no good with character development; it's why my graphic novel has stalled. Well, that and the ebb and flow of funds.

Aunt Ruthie believes in me wholeheartedly. Her faith in my abilities nurtures my ego the way her cookies nourish my spirit. She's only read the tamest of my comics over the years. I never chanced showing her the darker ones.

Then again, maybe after this trip, I might. She'll be pre-conditioned for it by then.

. . .

She loves slot machines, that woman. I've told her time and again that the newer models are all digital and programmed, but she still treats them like they are the old-style ones where chance and perseverance actually matter. Maybe it's something she'd tried once long ago, something that left her with fond memories.

I once went as far as watch an entire one of those infotainment mini-documentaries about slot machines with her. Found it on YouTube especially for her. The glasses-wearing smart-sounding - or maybe it was just the British accent - dude explained in a very accessible language, with graphics to boot, all about the evolution of slot machines and the way chance has been all bred out of the equation. Aunt Ruthie indulged me, watched it with me, smiled and then went right back to her gambling ways.

At any rate, when I last saw her, Aunt Ruthie was pulling on that tentacled arm like it belonged to The Old One, freshly awoken and ravenous, and she was the only thing standing between it and the world.

I wonder what such Eldritch horror would make of Aunt Ruthie, a five-foot-nothing old lady with a stiff spine and a stiffer grey chiffon hairdo, as prim and proper as ever in her sensible shoes, neat as a pin dress and a comfortable matching cardigan. Aunt Ruthie wears the largest-framed glasses you'll ever see worn unironically and a stern expression that decades of dealing with the public have bestowed upon her face.

When I was younger, I remember being afraid of her. Then I came to love her, and the fear turned into respect. Now that I'm a foot taller and, at least technically, an adult, the love and respect remain. We never discuss her gambling because she never goes overboard. Discipline in all things is her motto. I wish it was better instilled in me, but no. I must have inherited some of my mother's addictive personality. I tend to indulge.

Having just the one drink right now…it's tough. I'm glad I don't feel the urge to gamble, at least. There would go my ramen money.

I circle back to Aunt Ruthie to see how she's doing. She seems happy. Her drink is the most unnatural shade of purple I've ever seen. I ask her what's in it and she tells me she has no idea.

"Try it if you want," she says, not taking her eyes off the glowing screen in front of her.

I do. It tastes…purple. That's the best I can describe it. Something's missing, too.

"You like?"

"Not so much."

"Well, you wouldn't. It's virgin."

"What? Why?" Aunt Ruthie is strict and disciplined, but she's no teetotaler. Her book club has been known to imbibe, so has her knitting circle.

"Gotta stay sharp," she smiles at me, tapping her head with her pointy finger. "Gotta beat the odds."

I groan inwardly but don't correct her. It is, after all, her birthday.

"Now that you're here, would you mind keeping the machine warm, while I go to the ladies'?"

"You want me to play it?"

"No, Samuel, I want you to cuddle it." She pushed her glasses back up with her finger. "Of course, I want you to play it," she explains patiently. "I've been priming it for a win for a while now and I don't want to miss the opportunity."

"Sure, Aunt Ruthie."

"You're a good boy." She smiles warmly at me and grabs her enormous bag. That bag is like something out of *Around the Word in Eighty Days*.

On any given occasion, you can find all manner of random and practical things in it, from band-aids to batteries and more. I could swear the bag is getting larger as Aunt Ruthie is getting smaller. One day soon they'll equalize in size. My aunt has had that bag ever since I can remember. Or maybe they are successive reincarnations of the same bag. I couldn't tell you.

I sit down. The stool in front of the machine is warm, so is the tentacle when I reach for it. That's as expected. The sliminess, though, completely takes me by surprise. I gotta say, the attention to detail here really is most impressive.

"Here goes nothing," I say under my breath and pull the tentacle-lever.

"Why so cynical?"

"What?" I look around. There's no one behind me. "Who said that?"

"Me. I said that. Hello. Right in front of you. You're looking at me."

You know that thing in the movies when the character is stumped and so they just sit there looking side to side and blinking like an idiot? Well, I think I'm doing that thing right now. Apparently, that's a real thing people do. My fingers are clamped down on the lever.

"If we're going to hold hands, I might as well introduce myself." A procession of impossible vowels and fricative consonants assails my ears. "But you can call me Manny."

"Manny?" I repeat dumbfounded.

"Yes. And you are Samuel?"

"What? How do you know?"

"Why, I read your mind, of course."

"WHAT?"

"Oh, relax, would you? Your Aunt just said your name like a minute ago."

"Ah, right…yes, well, she's the only one who calls me that."

"What do you prefer?"

"Sam."

"Sam, it is, then. Nice to meet you" The tentacle goes up and down in an approximation of a handshake and I finally drop my fingers from it.

"So, come here often?"

I check myself. This is, apparently, actually happening. A sentient slot machine named Manny is making conversation with me. It's awesome when you think about it, how far animatronic technology has come.

I relate this to the machine. To Manny.

He rearranges his electronic displays into something like a smile. It's 40% friendly and 60% menacing. Or maybe I'm misreading the graphics.

I decide to go with it wherever it takes me. At the very least, it's infinitely more entertaining than gambling.

"So, is this like the latest in marketing? The plan to make the slot machines well and truly irresistible at last?"

"Oh, I wish." Manny sounds wistful. "But this is actually just a short-term assignment for me. At least, I hope it'll prove to be short-termed."

"An assignment?"

"Well, ok, it's more of a punishment. But really…I mean, you ever disagree with *your* boss?"

"Funny you should ask. I just did and now I have no boss."

"You killed him?" Manny sounds impressed.

"Er…no. He fired me."

"That so and so."

"So and so? That's quaint."

"I'm supposed to watch my language when conversing with potential clients. It's one of the things that came up in my review."

"Clients?"

"Oh, we don't have to go into that now." Manny waves his tentacle dismissively. "So, you don't have a boss anymore. You are a free man."

"In a manner of speaking."

The symbols on the front of the machine rearrange themselves into a question mark.

"Well, you know that thing they say about freedom being just another word for nothing left to lose," I elaborate.

"Oh, I assure you, Sam, you have plenty to lose still."

"That's pretty menacing."

"Is it? Sorry. Crap, I'll tone it down. Your Auntie seems like a nice lady."

"She's the best. It's her birthday. You could let her win, you know. She'd love it."

"Statistically speaking, Sam, people are the happiest right before they think they might win. The moment four out of five cherries, or bloody hearts as we have it here, line up is the peak of gambler's happiness."

"Well, I guess you're the expert."

"I am."

"Been at it for a while?"

"Too long. I honestly thought this would be easier. I mean, if someone like me can't hit their target goal at a casino…well, then maybe my boss is right."

"Why? What'd he say to you?"

"He said I don't do enough to represent the company's values. Not getting enough new clients."

"And your business is…?"

"Greed. Same as everyone. We live in the world dedicated to the exigencies of Mammon and I am but one of his servants."

"Mammon sounds harsh. What's his deal?"

"Seriously, Sam?"

"Seriously. Why? Is he someone I should know?"

Manny sighs as deeply as his slick shiny metal confines allow.

"Mammon. Prince of Greed, Greedy One, the Golden Demon, the Treasurer of Hell, Avaricious Wolf, Lord of the Gambles, Master of the Gambling Houses, Ace of Poker, Creator of Alchemy."

I nod.

"Nothing?"

"Sorry."

"He's the guy who forged Hellboy's Right Hand of Doom?"

"Oh. Oh, right. Ok, yeah, thought he sounded familiar."

"You need to broaden your frame of references, Sam."

"I know, I know, should have stayed in college and all that."

"I mean, professionally speaking, I'm going to say yes, just because college debt is a huge business for us, but, personally, it's just like… read a book, you know."

"I read books." I know I sound defensive.

"You read books with pictures and not even thoroughly enough to get the references from those."

Ok, he got me there.

"So, Mammon, that's your boss?"

"That's my boss."

"And you pissed him off and he stuck you into this machine?"

"Well, I'd say that's a grotesque oversimplification of things, Sam." Manny sounds kinda huffy. I backpedal.

"Ok, well, sorry. So…um…how do you get out?"

"Got to meet my quota. And the overdues."

"Are you close?"

Manny sighs very deeply, a sigh that seems to rattle all the change within his machine body.

"Sorry, buddy. What seems to be the hold-up, you think?"

"I just get distracted. It's so distracting up here. All the bright lights and all the shows. And I mean, I kind of thought things would just take care of themselves, you know. I followed your politics, I watched your reality television and the marketing trends…everyone seems to be well on track for the master's kingdom without any additional help. I thought if I just sit back and let things proceed naturally, I'd be golden, and no one would ever know the difference. But no, someone told on me. Dereliction of duties. And now here we are."

"Sorry, buddy," I say again. My sympathies are genuine.

"Thanks, Sam. And see, the thing is I don't know that they are wrong either. They might be right, actually. I might just not be built for this. I mean, if a demon can't meet his soul-quota in a Vegas casino…" The digital display changes into something like an exasperated eye roll. "My mother was an artist. I always had a certain talent for watercolors. I wish I could just re-specialize."

"Oh. Is that an option?"

"No, Sam. I'm a freaking demon. I can't just go into watercolors. I serve at the pleasure of his Dark Highness, The Prince of Greed."

"But if he were to let you go…?"

"I can't possibly speculate on that now. Sure, I'd love to do art for our propaganda department, pick up right where cubists left off, but it's more like a dream."

An uncomfortable thought occurs to me.

"Manny...were you going to try to get my Auntie's soul?"

"Um, I mean, I thought about it, but she just seemed like such a nice old lady..."

"Seriously, dude?"

"No, I mean, she seemed like a tough old nut you wouldn't want to mess with, and I don't really rock the hard sell."

"What about *my* soul?"

"I don't know. I mean, you seem nice. Why? Is that something you might be interested in?" His voice, normally gravelly and sibilant, picks up a lighter hopeful tone.

"Nah, I don't really want to mess with that."

"Fair enough," he sighs again, disappointed.

"I might know a guy, though."

"Oh yeah?" There's that hope again in his voice. It sounds like driving at high speed through a pebble road, all those pings off your car.

"Yeah, saw my old boss here earlier. The guy's greed personified. He fired me strategically instead of just laying me off so that I couldn't collect unemployment."

"He sounds like a right..."

"So and so?" I smile.

"I was going to say cretin."

"Nice."

"Maybe even dipshit?"

"Very nice, Manny." I high-five his tentacle. It is a singularly strange sensation.

"Can you get him over here, Sam?"

"I can try."

I should go find Aunt Ruthie; she's been gone an awfully long time. I'm sure she's fine, which is more than I can say for some poor sap she's probably reading the riot act to for lewd behavior or some such infraction. Aunt Ruthie has never shied away from confrontation, especially if it's a name of upholding good manners and good values. I've once seen her chastise a wrestler-size dude with face tattoos for littering. He picked up his cigarette butt too, afterwards. You do not mess with my aunt.

I should find her and then find Jerry.

Wait, I can't leave. I told her I'd stay. I relay my dilemma to Manny.

"No problem," he says and rearranges his display into Out of Order with charming alacrity. "You go do you, Sam."

I find Aunt Ruthie chatting up the same bartender Jerry was creeping on earlier. This looks like a much more enjoyable sort of chat. At least, the bartender seems amused. She whips up some crazy concoction while chatting, I can't even begin to describe the colors of the drink, but she finishes it with a nice umbrella floatie just like how Aunt Ruthie likes.

I gallantly escort my aunt back to her seat, after assuring her the machine is staying warm and eagerly awaiting her return.

. . .

Jerry proves tougher to find. At last, I spy his tubby form, curled up into himself on one fabulously decorated doomsday divans, sleeping off either his booze, his embarrassment, or both. I bet the cretin, the dipshit, the so and so, never even gave me a second thought after firing me. He's crossed my mind plenty, though. I have a plan of making him into a petty tyrant in my graphic novel, whenever that gets going again.

"Jerry. Hey, hi. Are you ok there?" I lightly shake his shoulder. He stirs just enough to open one eye and fail to recognize me.

"I'd like to go upstairs now," he slurs at me, mistaking me for the help. Or maybe that's just all he ever saw me as. He smells like a distillery, sweat, and trying too hard. The latter is a scent I permanently associate with the Axe brand.

I help him up, trying not to cringe, and do my best one-man impression of the Weekend at Bernie's with Jerry as Bernie. It takes a while to get going – Jerry has never been exactly svelte and now the alcohol has rendered him deadweight-heavy – but I'm strong when motivated.

By the time we finally make it back to Manny, I'm exhausted. We approach the machine from the back, just as Manny suggested. Usually, slot machines are stacked back-to-back but not these. These are too elaborately designed and thus are proudly standalone creatures.

Aunt Ruthie doesn't notice, she appears completely absorbed. I'd wager her latest drink, the one with the tiny umbrella in it, wasn't mixed virgin.

I prop Jerry against the machine, tap my fingers against the slick design of it as if to let Manny know, and leave. Back to the other side, the one with the birthday girl. I put my hand on her shoulder and kiss her cheek to let her know I'm there.

. . .

And then, Aunt Ruthie wins. The cute, thematically appropriate morbid designs on the front display line up, a song rings out, and the coins begin to pour out.

Aunt Ruthie screams in delight and then tries to catch them with her bucket. I help. She tells me that I'm her good luck charm. A bunch of looky-loos gather around to gawk at someone's good fortune and hope it rubs off on them.

In all the commotion, no one seems to notice the discreet chewing and slurping sounds emanating from the back of the machine. I hear it but only because I expected to. When I look back there a short while later, there's nothing left but a couple of dirty napkins, a belt buckle, and a puddle of blood that is rapidly disappearing somewhere underneath the machine. There's more slurping and then all is quiet.

I look away. Look at Aunt Ruthie, who is positively glowing with happiness. I bet Manny's wrong. I bet she's happier now than she'd been with all her almost and near wins.

The display arranges itself into something like a wink which is only mildly menacing and slightly sinister. I fist-bump the tentacle and whisper-wish Manny luck with his future art career.

We finally get all the shiny freshly won coins together - had to get an extra bucket – and head over to exchange them.

Later, as Aunt Ruthie treats me to an epic three-course meal with her winnings in the thematically connected attached restaurant, she tells me that this has been the best birthday celebration ever, and I agree with perfect sincerity. And I do my best to ignore the spectacularly menacing-looking tentacled cyclopean beast of a jukebox winking at me as if trying to get my attention.

LOVECRAFT VS. THE BIG-MOUTH MUSKY OF LAKE MISKATONIC

LENA NG

C all me Ishmael. I, Plymouth Huxley Lovecraft, whose name has never been Ishmael, am a descendent cousin thrice-removed to the terribly pretentious over-writer HP Lovecraft. I, rather than labouring under the fumes of imagination fueled by absinthe as a nervous, nail-chewing author, instead has taken a day off from his tax-battling life of an accountant to hunt the immense, silver-bodied fish of the Lake Miskatonic. From disturbing dreams I awoke, fishy smells lingering from fragmented glimpses of frothing, thrashing tentacles, surrounded by a temple of big-mouthed, fresh-water dwelling, scaly, swishy, fishy creatures of the unfathomable deep.

These muskies, monster-mouthed progenies of Pisces in the fresh-water realm, have haunted me since the infernal Day of the Seven Lines. One particular walleyed, ugly musky taunted me with his insolent snatching of the bait, the tempting, wriggling meat of night-crawler, and I have since burned with desire for vengeance.

Instead of the dark oily body, its flesh was pale as that of a great white whale, the battle with which lasted through seven snapped lines until it had last, with a flip its tail, choked down the bait, hook and all, and escaped. I had regaled my neighbors and drinking buddies for years hence, artfully ignoring their rolling eyes. More than a tall tale, it was only a slightly embellished yarn of epic proportions. We had done combat under the setting sun, we battled with lure and line until with a sharp yank the master fish of all fish eluded me. I have the scars to this day.

For years I had nursed these wounds. Now under foreboding signs—a change in the tax laws, a reduction of child-care credits, a tightening of loophole 7.5.9—the time was nigh again to catch this infernal, elusive fish of hulking magnitude.

I packed my gear: my hand-carved fishing pole, engraved with protective charms; my lures made from the feathers of a monkey and tipped with poison-dipped barbs; my beer cooler filled with enchanted-yet-fortifying libations.

As I transported these tools to the car, still under the darkness of night, I noticed an unnatural alignment of the stars. According to known mathematics, the celestial bodies should travel in foreseeable formations. But the stars of *Neptunus*, *Anchovious*, and *Barnacleby* did loop-de-loops in the sky. The constellation of Pisces seemed to mock me.

Besides the bizarre positioning of the stars, other premonitions disturbed me. A burning of my bagel, a twitch of my eye, a bizarre burble deep in my gut. The smoke in the exhaust, the bump on my back, midlife and stuck in a rut.

My ancient vehicle, a twenty-three-year-old *Fordus horribulus*, puttered its way to Lake Miskatonic, dragging behind my dinghy. Along the ancient, forbidden road of 1666, the Highway of The Beast, I formulated my plan: to capture the evil, elusive fish, to mount it upon my wall, and to have it croon songs in the style of a kitschy, novelty singing bass, trapping it forever in this dimension.

At the water's edge, I slung out my weapons into the boat: my fishing pole, the F-890, turbo-charged, titanium-ground, fish master catcher; seductive lures of lakewater temptation; bottomless beer cooler of malt and barley libations. I rowed to the middle of the lake of my doom.

With the rising of the sun, I kissed my lure, clapped my hands together, and wiggled my middle fingers, for blessing from the cosmic gods of the catch. I flung out my line…

…and waited…

…and waited…

…and waited some more, the libations fueling my patience.

Finally, with beer-laden breath, I shrieked the command, "Come forth, ye soggy bastard of the sea," accompanied by the violent shaking of my fists.

Then, from the depths of the mystical lake, came a frothing, a foaming, a boiling over of massive hyperbole. Fins bigger than sails, large as an irradiated submarine with gaping mouth eclipsing the sun, this monstrous musky would bring about mankind's total annihilation. Such creatures should never swim the seas.

It looked upon me with a red, gimlet eye, recognizing my countenance from our previous encounters, my walleyed nemesis of oceanic battles of history. Through flick of fin and splash of tail, it sped towards me, slicing through the heaving waters. My dinghy was tossed about as a rubber duck circling around a colossal drain, threatening to capsize.

As I took the last fortifying libation, beneath this dust-laden amber growler, there lay the *Fisherman's Necromicon*. Blessed by the *Deus Ex-Machina*, the God of Unprepared Protagonists, who had previously protected me from the trash pandas of the apocalypse, Garbagezilla, and a brutal gang of feral felines, this book from seemingly nowhere appeared. As told from its pages, the conditions of the fishpocalypse must be met for the demons of the deep to emerge triumphant from the freshwater sea, for mankind to be dethroned and the muskies to rule the earth.

- An unnatural alignment of the stars
- Ominous portents of tax-changing laws
- Revenge under alcohol-fueled influence

Only a powerful spell could save me. Quickly, I flipped through *Fisherman's Necromicon*. A huge wave sloshed over the dinghy. I choked as I expelled the spell and the incantation remained incomplete. Armed with weapons of line and lure, bait and beer, I cast the unbreakable line and flung the book into the musky's gibbering jaws. A blasting bellow sounded overhead with a spewing of silvery scales. The monstrous musky and I pushed and pulled against the line. As the position of power jostled between us, I wondered who was catching whom. Who would be at last mounted upon the wall? With a twist of its head, the monstrous Miskatonic musky took to the depths, burbling its curses until I was flung forsooth into the sky and landed with seizing heart into the whirlpool blackness of the waters.

A fishy smell pervaded my sleep, a terrible odour of musky malice. I awoke upon a wooden mount, lying horizontally against a wall, restraints holding me fast. A tinny tune rang out. As an electric jolt surged through my body, I opened my mouth and a melody poured forth, like that of a novelty bass.

THE LADY WITH THE LOOK

SHAENON K. GARRITY

with apologies to Edith Wharton

To say that Boston welcomed the Baroness di Levanzo would be gross exaggeration. It examined her through lorgnettes, clucked its many tongues, and finally allowed that she would make a colorful addition to Society. "Colorful" was not a compliment. True, she was rich; and true, she was titled; and true, she was attractive, though not beautiful. Rather, she had a sensual undertow that announced her as a separate species from the debutantes dropping curtseys before Lowells and Cabots.

Perhaps it was her eyes, which were too large for her face, or her coral smile. Or perhaps it was the musk of rumor that swirled about her and the entire coterie of di Levanzos who descended on Boston that year. The family all but owned the fishing islets around Sicily, reported the tenured gossips of Brattle Street. The pecrage had been acquired via marital alliance with a crumbling English line, and the current Baroness was lately of India, where her branch of the family had engaged in unknown business under the Raj. There they were rumored to have "gone native," an idea which inspired no end of speculation. It was almost as exciting as if the Baroness had been divorced.

With such a cloud of foreignness surrounding her, it was a wonder the Baroness was invited to any respectable parties. But she happened to arrive just as Society was starved for entertainment. It was the dull damp season between winter opera and spring boating, when Boston becomes too grim even for Puritans. Nobility from hot and distant climes seemed a pleasant novelty. And so the Baroness di Levanzo's letterbox began to fill with expensively unassuming invitations.

One of those invitations was to the engagement luncheon of Lillian Otis and Crispin Horne.

She arrived very late, well past fashion and into rudeness. Crispin, an indulgence of brandy in one hand, was watching with measured affection as across the room his fiancée made an hour's work of a sliver of toast. Lillian was a woman assembled with Shaker practicality; she required little and was deceptively sturdy. Then the door flew open, as in a gust of Mediterranean wind, and di Levanzos flooded in. On closer examination there were only five: two matrons, two young men, and the Baroness herself. But they seemed to fill the room.

The Baroness had the strange eyes of which Crispin had heard, and roiling hair of which he had not, and she was not beautiful. Swigging the rest of his brandy, he tried to focus on the relations in her orbit. They moved in a swirl of reds and golds and peacock blues. The two older women dripped with jewelry, culminating in a large and curiously carved stone, set with gold, adorning the forehead of each. They plowed through the drawing room like ships laden with silks and cedars of Lebanon.

"My aunts," said a voice in Crispin's ear. "They love an entrance."

How she had slid to his side, glittering, he couldn't imagine. It wasn't to talk to him, he realized after a dizzying instant; it was to get at the sideboard. She helped herself to a glass of port, which she inhaled with visible pleasure before swallowing.

"They're certainly dressed for it. I notice you don't wear—" Crispin gestured at his forehead, feeling foolish.

But the Baroness laughed. "No, only married women have those." Her accent was impossible to pin down. It seemed a perfumed blend of all the world's warm places.

"Who are the men?" he asked, grasping for an excuse to keep her talking.

"Cousins. The family felt they needed a change of company, so I brought them along."

"And what brings you to Boston?"

"Marriage, what else?" The Baroness rolled *marriage* over her tongue in a way that entirely changed the definition of the word. "Our village has a shortage of eligible bachelors."

"Your cousins must have enjoyed that situation."

"Hm?" She glanced at the boys. "Yes, in fact, rather too much. It's best they grow out of it. At any rate, I'm afraid I'm looking for the same thing as every tender youth here."

"Well, I'm not looking. There's my fiancée." Crispin felt a strong need to mention his fiancée.

"Ah!" Defying anatomical possibility, her eyes grew larger. "You must be Mr. Horne."

"You can call me Crispin."

"Then you must call me Genevra." She smiled, more distantly this time. "A pleasure to meet you, Crispin"—his name unfolded as enticingly as *marriage*—"but I should circulate, don't you think? I know how much value your people place on propriety."

"You missed lunch, but there's lobster salad if you're hungry." Another stupid thing to say.

"Boston lobster. A blue-blooded fish for a blue-blooded people."

Crispin was pleasantly startled. "Most people don't know lobsters have blue blood. Or care, I suppose."

"Oh, I take biology seriously. And seafood, so I believe I will try that salad." And she was gone, trailing incense.

"What brought her here, anyway?" said Lillian, later that afternoon. The guests had cleared out and the older relations had retired to the back rooms, leaving Crispin and Lillian alone together. They weren't very good at it. Lillian played to best effect in groups, and Crispin never knew what to do with his hands around women. He'd always imagined it would come easily with the right person, that when the time came he'd experience a natural—no, a heavenly and timeless fusion of souls. Now, two months from his wedding, he'd had to discard this as adolescent fantasy, along with the idea that he would ever be any good at tennis.

But Lillian was making an effort at conversation, and he tried to meet her courage. "Who?"

"Who else? By next season every girl in Boston will either be wearing those Indian fabrics or burning her in effigy."

"Oh, her." Crispin glanced at his fiancée, but she had turned to open the drapes. "She told me she came to Boston to find a husband."

"The poor thing," said Lillian. Crispin was inclined to agree. The Baroness might be many things in Society, if she played by the rules, but matrimonial material she could never be. A woman like that, keeping house for some lean-faced Harvard man and his lean-faced children...

"She seems amiable," he said. It was normally the highest compliment he could give, but it dropped tasteless from his tongue. "Did I ever tell you I started out at Harvard studying biology?"

Lillian turned. "What does that have to do with the Baroness?"

"Nothing. Of course after a semester I got it out of my system. It made much more sense to go into law and enter Uncle's firm. Science was a youthful passion, that's all."

"One needs passions," said Lillian, "in youth." She turned back to the window, but not before Crispin glimpsed a dying ember in her cheeks. What girlhood love was she remembering: art, sports, a longed-for adventure, a romance with some honest but poor boy whose name, found nowhere in the logs of the *Mayflower* or *Arabella*, Crispin would never know? For a moment Crispin felt closer to his wife-to-be than he ever had.

B ut she did not turn from the window, and the moment passed.

W ith the engagement party completed to satisfaction, the wedding preparations accelerated. At last there came a week when Lillian went off to be formally congratulated by her New York relations (Late Colonial, park view, large but not ostentatious), leaving Crispin's schedule temporarily free of suit-fittings and teas with eroded senior Otises.

It was the chance for an afternoon of quiet amusement—but as Crispin considered his options, he realized his premarital status placed him in social limbo. The usual bachelor pursuits would draw disapproving clucks from Society, but so would his appearance, *sans* fiancée, at any event for couples. He shuddered at the thought of forcing upon some innocent hostess the puzzle of filling the chair across from him. At last Crispin, his old interest in science fresh in his mind, settled on a presentation on ichthyology at Harvard. It wasn't the type of thing at which a Horne would ordinarily be seen, but it would raise no eyebrows. Whether Crispin was influenced by the possibility that someone else might attend—someone who took biology and seafood seriously—was a question he dared not ask himself.

The Baroness was already there when he entered the lecture hall, flanked by two girls who, though they struck Crispin as plain and even a bit mannish, identified themselves by their flamboyant dress as yet more members of her family.

The lecturer, lately returned from the research ship *Albatross*, did not disappoint. He described wonders trawled from the Atlantic, which he displayed in jars: shapes snakelike and toadlike, bull-headed and woman-lipped. A single net might dredge two or three species previously unknown to man. "And at present we have barely plunged below the pelagic levels. When science allows us to touch the ocean floor, the true deep, who knows what wonders we'll find?"

The Baroness chuckled. Several heads turned.

Crispin found himself looking at the two girls. Something about them bothered him. When he realized what it was, he trembled with a shameful thrill, though he could hardly explain why. It was like his first time tasting an oyster.

Afterwards, Crispin caught up with the Baroness in the damp spring night outside.

"The girls with you tonight," he said. "They're the men from the engagement party, aren't they? Your cousins."

The Baroness glanced back at the lecture hall, where her companions were still mingling with the crowd. "As I said, they needed a change of company."

"What are they really?" he said. "Men or women?"

"That's a limiting sort of question. Not very scientific. What did you think of the lecture?"

No more information about the cousins was forthcoming, Crispin sensed. He dredged up a few points from the lecture that had stuck in his mind, and within moments was engrossed in conversation. The Baroness did indeed take biology seriously. Her knowledge of natural science, and especially the genera of oceanic life, seemed bottomless.

Only when the two di Levanzo girls trotted up was Crispin shaken back to the peculiarity of the evening. Up close, they were without question the same two young men from the engagement party, only...altered. Their frames were thinner, their features softer. A few lines of grammar-school Shakespeare rose to mind: *a sea-change / Into something rich and strange...*

"By the way," he said to the Baroness before they parted, "what made you laugh at the lecture?"

"Oh, something the man said. It was..." She searched for a word. "It was sweet."

C rispin barely noticed Lillian's return. He felt more distant from her than ever, now that he had a secret. Of course he had many secrets from her, but they were the ordinary kind; one didn't talk about one's youthful indiscretions, nor did one ask, and thereby was marital peace obtained. But here was something new. Within the di Levanzo family was scandal beyond scandal, the open flaunting of Uranian practices of some sort. (Private practice of such things would, of course, have been acceptable.) But even in the sobering light of day, Crispin did not believe that was what he had witnessed. It was something else, something beyond the most stunning breach of etiquette.

Lillian noticed her fiancé's distance, tried and failed to re-engage, and returned to wedding preparations and learning to shoot duck. She had resigned herself to the realities of married life.

One evening, on the way to dinner with his parents and Lillian, two threads knotted in Crispin's mind, and again he felt a shiver of unthinkable discovery. Boston was shrouded in night when he finally arrived, panting, at the Baroness's door.

"*Serranidae!*" he shouted. "I studied it, years ago!"

The Baroness, standing in the doorway, cocked an eyebrow.

"It's a family of fishes! A...wait..." Crispin pawed through a library book. "*A family of fishes within the clade Perciformes, including the sea basses and groupers as well as smaller tropical marine species. A notable feature of this family is hermaphroditism, with many species exhibiting the ability to change sex in response to the environment. In some species, if a population suffers from an overabundance of females, one individual may change to male to fill the reproductive need, while in others a male may change to female.*"

He glanced up. "The first type is known as protogyny and the second as protandry, but, well... I'm right, aren't I? Your family is the same. Oh, please say something."

"Do you make a habit," said the Baroness, "of calling at a single woman's quarters without notice?"

But she let him in. The apartment was small—Crispin wondered if she dared live alone—but lushly furnished. It was like stepping into an illustration from the *Arabian Nights*.

"Why all this curiosity about my cousins?" said the Baroness. "It's a bit forward."

"How could I not be curious? How is it possible?"

"It's there in your book. Life is capable of amazing transformations."

"But human life?" Questions fogged Crispin's mind. "Does anyone else know?"

"Here in Boston, you mean? Anyone who's noticed has been far too polite to mention it."

"Is all your family like this? That is...hermaphroditic?"

"That's *more* than a bit forward. Tea?"

Crispin perched on the edge of a velvet-cushioned curule. "I assure you, I mean no ill will. I'm not...repulsed."

"If you find me repulsive," said the Baroness, "it's no concern of mine. You're a married man."

"Only engaged," said Crispin without thinking. Tea sloshed into his saucer.

The Baroness's wry smile faded. "My family has known the sea for a long time. The very deep sea. How to put this? I understand you

Boston families, though American, take peculiar pride in intermarriage with European aristocrats. My people have a similar relationship with the aristocracy of the Deep."

"Blue-blooded lobsters?" said Crispin, trying to joke.

"Older than lobsters. Some branches of the family still worship them as gods, others treat them as, let's say, wealthy and occasionally indulgent old relations...but we've known them for a long time. It's from them we inherit certain traits of the sea. Proof of blood, you might say."

"I can hardly believe you're sharing this with me."

"I enjoy our conversations, Crispin. Too much." She stood. "But surely you have somewhere to be?"

"My parents!" Crispin bolted from his seat. "And Lillian! In the excitement I completely forgot."

He was gone for all of five minutes. The Baroness answered his knock. "You left your book," she said, holding it out.

"I love you," he said.

The Baroness shut the door.

C rispin called again two days later. One of the aunts answered. "Genevra is unavailable."

"Wait!" Crispin floundered. "She told me everything. About—" It was so difficult to put delicately. "About the family's ancestry."

"My niece is free to say what she likes."

"Aren't you afraid I could tell people? Or do you think no one would believe such a bizarre story?"

The aunt laughed. The gold encircling the gem on her forehead gleamed. Crispin found himself distracted by the carvings on the gem, its whorls and furrows. "Do you think such things are so uncommon? Genevra must have told you why we came here."

"She's here to find a husband."

"All the more reason for a committed man to stop sniffing around." The aunt shot him a sharp gaze. Like the Baroness, she had very large eyes. "This city has its own history with the Deep Ones. Genevra is looking for a suitable husband, a man with some of the old blood."

"Is that why she won't see me? I'm not good enough for your family of…of sea monsters?" The idea of sea monsters was less ridiculous, to his mind, than the idea of anyone being too well-bred for a Horne. The Hornes had produced three presidents of Harvard and not a single president of Yale, a perfect record.

"She's looking for a lifelong bond, not a spring romance. And we live long lives, my boy." Perhaps it wasn't a gem. It had an organic look, like a piece of coral or a walnut shell. It dawned on Crispin that this was true of much of the di Levanzo clothing; what he had at first glance assumed to be Indian or Mediterranean patterns followed an inhuman geometry. "Go home to your wife."

"My fiancée," said Crispin as the door shut in his face again.

The rehearsal for the wedding dinner went so smoothly that the groom's disinterest barely mattered. Only Lillian broke from etiquette enough to look displeased.

Crispin had visited the Baroness's apartment again and received no answer. The two cousins, now pink and feminine as two peonies, had passed him on his way home. He had written letters but sent none. Nothing he wrote captured his conviction that here was his only chance to feel deeply, that in this woman he might experience that fusion of which he had once, hopelessly, dreamed.

After dinner he walked Lillian home, as courtesy and the watchful eyes of Society required. At her parents' door, Lillian turned. "I'll say this only once, Crispin. Resolve this."

"Resolve what?"

"Don't humiliate me by making me say it." Lillian took a measured breath. "Let me be clear. I don't care how you get her out of your system. But we marry in a week. If the matter isn't behind you by then, the wedding is off."

"Call off the wedding? With the uproar it would cause?"

"This is your life, Crispin." She reached out to touch his shoulder, held back. "Isn't it more important even than propriety?"

As he walked back along the wine-dark street, Crispin felt swell within himself an overwhelming regard for his fiancée. He had never imagined her capable of such courage. To risk the shame of a broken engagement! She was right. Lillian deserved a man with an undivided heart, and if he could not offer that he had no right to marry her.

Somehow he was not surprised to find the Baroness in the Public Gardens. It was fate, or perhaps the salt tang in the air had drawn him.

"I've been trying to avoid you," she said.

"Is it because you dislike me?"

"No." Her overlarge eyes shone. "Quite the opposite."

Crispin's blood surged. The words poured out of him—he, who never ordered coffee or tipped his hat to a porter without sober consideration. "Then for God's sake have me, because I'm yours. What does blood matter?" Outrageous words. "Even if I'm not...compatible with your family, there must be a way for us to be one."

"But you are, Crispin," said the Baroness. "That's not the trouble at all."

"What?"

"You have some of the old blood. The scent of the Deep Ones is unmistakable, however diluted. It seems almost common among Bostonians."

Crispin put the shock of the idea aside. "But if that's true, then what's the problem?"

In the mist the Baroness should have looked more ethereal than ever, but at that moment she was just a woman, not beautiful. "I thought it was clear. You're engaged. I can't have a casual romance, you see. Not at this time. I need a husband."

"Then I'll marry you," said Crispin.

"Should I find one, we'll return to the di Levanzo estate in Sicily. The family is well-established there, with preparations for children."

"I'll marry you."

"If not, I move on to another port. Southward, perhaps."

"Did you hear me propose to you?"

"Yes. Did you hear me say I don't intend to stay in Boston? You have a life, a marriage planned. Can you honestly say you would leave all that?"

"I can say that together we might experience such a union as no one here can comprehend. Do you feel the same?"

She smiled then, and all her answer was in her smile. "Walk me home."

There were no aunts at her apartment that night.

The wedding of Lillian Otis and Crispin Horne was credited with full marks by all of Society. Tasteful and elegant, it focused on feeding and watering the worthies on its fastidiously curated guest list. Everyone praised the lobster and the port. The bride's beaded gown and jacket shone softly in the candlelight at dinner, and the groom's white tie was pure as morning in Eden.

Crispin's heart rose each time he looked at his bride. All, at last, was as it should be. His passion for the Baroness had passed like a fever, and now he entered marriage with a cool brow. And if purging his heart of her had required extreme—and, he reflected with a shy inward smile, exhausting—measures, well, it was worth it for his Lillian.

He had sent the Baroness a letter, kindly phrased, apologizing for promises made in a moment of foolishness and swearing to protect her reputation. She would understand, in the end. Anyone could see that marriage between a di Levanzo and a Bostonian was impossible.

It did not surprise him that the Baroness chose not to attend the wedding. But when time passed with no word from her, he began to worry. Was she taking this too hard? Society gossip had her going about town as usual, although there were rumors the di Levanzos were packing to move.

His concern grew, spread, and metastasized into fresh passion. The souvenirs from the Hornes' modest honeymoon in Newport were still piled in the front hall when Crispin found himself thinking, again, only of the Baroness. But it was worse this time; infinitely worse. He craved her. Each morning, the pain of waking up apart from her cut deeper into his marrow. He stopped eating. Clumps of hair appeared on his pillow.

Lillian deployed her best bedside manner, feeding him broth and setting him out in the afternoon sun. Nothing helped. After a fitful week, he dragged himself to the law office. His colleagues stared at his sunken eyes and trembling hands. He could barely remember their names. On his desk he found an unmarked envelope. Inside was the briefest of notes.

My dearest Crispin,

We are married already. I thought you understood.

C rispin gasped with the urge to run to her. He forced it down. Before the Baroness, if he could bear another hour without her, there was someone he had to see.

The lecturer in ichthyology was pleased, if baffled, to receive a guest of Crispin's pedigree so late in the evening. "You were at my lecture, weren't you? Very gratified, if you don't mind my saying so."

"I have a question," said Crispin, slumping against the doorframe.

"Are you feeling all right, sir? You look..." Unable to end the sentence tactfully, he trailed off.

"Have you come across a fish that creates...a bond during mating? Tying the male to the female?"

The lecturer brightened. "It's funny you should ask. I just received the most remarkable specimen from a fellow researcher."

From the clutter of jars on his desk he scavenged one and held it to the light. The creature inside was small, but Crispin staggered back in horror. It seemed to be all teeth. Behind the gaping jaw he made out only swollen protuberances and a pair of too-large eyes.

"From the order *Lophiiformes*," said the lecturer. "Popularly known as the anglerfish—you see the protrusion above the eyes? These are deep-water fish, the very deepest. When she was alive, that protrusion was luminescent and could be used to lure prey."

"It's a female?"

"Until recently, we thought there were no males. Every specimen we recovered was female. Then we looked closer. See the fleshy bit dangling there?"

Reluctantly, Crispin leaned in close enough to observe a sickly tentacle.

"That's the male."

The lecturer continued into the silence. "When anglerfish mate, they become fused. The male, as you can see, atrophies into little more than a set of gonads. An ingenious way to keep him around to, ahem, do his duty, as it were."

"Impossible..."

"Very possible, sir. We don't yet understand the mechanics, but it seems triggered by contact between substances in their bodies." A fluttering laugh. "You could say they have chemistry."

"Can he escape?"

"You mean disconnect? No, he lives off her blood. But what an odd way to put it, sir."

"My god..." said Crispin. "What am I becoming?"

"Mr. Horne?"

Crispin clawed at the door with a hand like an autumn leaf and staggered into the night.

The Baroness opened the door wide. "My husband."

Crispin's breath rattled in his chest. "Will it hurt?"

"Very much the contrary." Her large eyes glowed. "I'm sorry for our small misunderstanding. It's all behind us now."

She extended a hand. Crispin toppled forward into the warm moist deeps.

By the time the police launched a search for Crispin Horne, chuckling up their sleeves, the Baroness was long gone. Some of the gossips of Brattle Street placed her on a train to New Orleans, others on a steamship to Italy. No one had seen Mr. Horne with her, but it was hardly difficult to guess what had happened. And so soon after his marriage! Crispin Horne's elopement with the Baroness di Levanzo would provide Society with conversation enough to warm the city through a Massachusetts winter.

There was one point on which all gossip agreed. Wherever the Baroness had last been spotted, she had been wearing one of those gaudy gems on her forehead, curiously carved.

B oston pursed its many lips, poured another cup of tea, and swore off the whole business.

FAMILY VALUES

PHILLIP T. STEPHENS

Worst Christmas ever?

Not for my family. Not until my sister Bethany opened her hog maw of a mouth, her jowls flapping against her jaw, and said: "I don't know who's the worst liar. My stoner dad or devil worshipping brother."

She'd heaped half of mother's potato kugel onto her plate. A 12-inch stuff-your-face dinner plate with Jesus' face shining from the center—glow-in-the- dark with a televangelist's personal prayers and blessing. She bought it for fifty dollars on iLuvJesus.com with my parents' credit card ($20 a dozen on Amazon). She eased the kugel plate onto the table next to her plate of kosher lamb stew, which spilled onto her columella salad plate, which nudged her bowl of Molokhia soup past the edge of the table.

That's when she said it.

"I don't know who's the worst liar. My stoner dad or devil worshipping brother."

Mother wiped her fingers on her napkin. A dozen wipes, each more exaggerated than the previous.

My father stirred his soup. "Speaking of liars, this soup is plain old spinach."

He referred to the Christmas menu my mother printed to certify the Biblical accuracy of every dish. Trumpet blowing angels—angels tied at the ankles by green and red ribbons—framed the offerings, which included Molokhia soup, made from "authentic Egyptian herbs."

Father was miserable after mother pulled his graying hair into a pony-tail and tied it with a holly berry ribbon. His tangled mane resembled a briar patch, but only from the ear line. His hairline signaled retreat when I was in fifth grade, and it retreats another half inch each year.

Mother tapped her spoon on her soup bowl. "It is spinach soup."

"Then why're you calling it Molokhia soup?" He pronounced it 'mola cola.' "What the hell is Molokhia, anyway?"

My sister rallied to mother's defense: "Something they don't sell at the Plano Safeway."

A wall-sized portrait of Jesus praying over bread framed my father's split ends and shoulder length beard. A dove fluttering in a beam of light bathed Jesus' silky brown hair, transmitting an inspiring message. Surrender to God's will.

And don't foget to buy volumizing shampoo.

Bethany's spinach outburst and my mother's portrait of Jesus will surprise no one who's spent fifteen minutes in Plano, the whitest suburb in Texas. Molokhia, by the way, is an Egyptian herb, a staple consumed by Jesus' followers in Jesus' time. God's anointed vegetable —or so say my mother's Bible brandishing friends whose latest obsession is authentic Jesus food.

(I should add that my mother's church friends also invoked a "spinach dispensation" so they wouldn't have to shop for the real herbs at an Egyptian or Middle Eastern market in Dallas. "Those people," to quote my mother, "are terrorists.")

Jesus said, "It's what's in your hearts that matters." Or something close. And what's in their hearts is authentic food from Jesus' time as long as it's saturated with pesticides and pumped full of chemicals to look fresh in their grocery aisles.

However, my sister's counterattack allowed my mother to focus her attention on me. She pressed her cross to her chest with one hand, and with the other hand she jabbed a finger in my direction. "Let me tell you, young man, your devil can't deliver you from your family's judgment."

My father buried his forehead in his forearm. "Jesus H. Christ, Marnie."

Mother's finger parried with the air, knocking aside the devil's darts.

My fault.

If only I'd left my stupid jacket at home.

O nly it isn't a stupid jacket.

My girlfriend Sharon, my ex-girlfriend Sharon, would've disagreed. "This is, without question, the most dimwitted purchase you ever made." She didn't wait for me to zip it and show how well it fit. Or for me to show her the cool club pins I bought to wear with it.

Or show her the spells.

I looked stylish in the mirror with my gray and black varsity jacket, with my crimson varsity letter and pewter society pins.

I told myself to keep cool. Pick my fights. Then I said, "Stupider than your engagement ring?"

She was the only girl friend my mother liked.

You might think me certifiable to choose a jacket over a girlfriend. But Sharon wanted to marry "the man I could be." Trust me, those words signify road hazards on the highway to happiness.

I left out the most important detail. My varsity jacket was a Miska-tonic University varsity jacket. *With hood*. Miskatonic, the center of higher learning in H. P. Lovecraft lore. Not only did I buy the jacket, I sprang for six additional club pins at ten dollars a pin, including Medieval Metaphysics, the Alchemical Choral Society, Conjuring Club, and Rune Finders.

I dropped $460 for the complete package on eBay and the owner tossed in four pages of bonus spells. Hand written on ruled notebook paper.

I'm not even a Lovecraft fan. While my high school friends read "Color Out of Space," and "Mountains of Madness," I smoked weed and watched *Re-Animator*. And all three sequels.

I bought the jacket as a gag. I imagined standing in line for coffee at Starbucks. A hottie would tap my shoulder. "Where's your college? Michigan?" she'd ask, and I'd say, "Massachusetts." The nerd barista behind the counter would raise a thumb to signal they got the joke.

M y mistake wasn't buying the jacket.

I loved that jacket. Especially the spells. I'd read them when I was pissed off at my boss, a friend, the world. I didn't care that they were stupid spells scribbled on notebook paper. It certainly didn't matter that the words meant nothing, culled from the web by a fan boy who never got laid because he was too busy reading Lovecraft stories, and Lovecraft knock-offs.

Just between us, however, when I browsed those spells, and imagined reading them aloud, I felt better.

My mistake wasn't buying the jacket but wearing it to my parents' house for Christmas.

. . .

T hat and spending $460 on eBay.

T wo months after Sharon bailed I found the jacket brand new for seventy-five dollars at the Lovecraft Society site.

"M iskatech? Where's that?"

I hadn't seen my mother in a year and the first thing she said was, "Miskatech? Where's that?"

She wore a green sweater with a dove pin and a crucifix heavy enough to give her whiplash. Her green sweater proclaimed—in candy cane red—Romans 8:28, "All things work together for those who love the Lord," written by the Apostle Paul while he counted the days until his execution.

Merry Christmas.

A carol played in the background. Not a generic carol either. "The Coventry Carol," a joy-filled ditty about a mother singing a lullaby to her baby. Spoiler alert. The baby is one of the children Herod slaughtered in his campaign to eliminate baby Jesus.

"No idea, Mom. I bought it at Good Will."

I usually keep the jacket on a coat hook next to my front door, a hook where I planned to leave it during my trip to Dallas. Until I reached for my keys. When my fingers touched the fob, thunder rattled my windows and the rain battered my roof like mallets on a steel drum.

My only thought was, keep your head dry. So I grabbed the jacket with the hood.

.   .   .

How wrong was my jacket for this family gathering?

Consider this: The other houses on my parent's street blind drivers with LED projected lights, LED lights in trees, LED lights lining their driveways and windows, electric Santas with red-nosed reindeer, and inflatable lighted snowmen.

My parents' house?

Wax candles smudge the windows. Crosses dangle from the wreaths. A life-sized nativity scene features Jesus standing in his manger to bless the shepherds and wise men. His neon halo glows through the night. Giant white Jesus hangs from their door, his arms open in welcome.

Their neighbors play "White Christmas," and "Winter Wonderland" through their outdoor speakers. One or two play Manheim Steamroller holiday covers. My parents' house broadcasts "Angels from the Realms of Glory," and "As with Gladness Men of Old"

In the carol "As with Gladness," Christians climb a staircase to heaven. The steps narrow, and backsliders slip into darkness as the verses progress.

Their living room stereo plays esoteric, if not cryptic, carols. "The Endris Night" where baby Jesus tells everyone he's the greatest baby God gave earth in the history of babies. "Adam Lay Ebounden" thanks Adam for falling into sin so God could give us Jesus. And, of course, my favorite dead baby ditty "The Coventry Carol."

My sister Bethany Elisha wears a homemade house coat decorated with angels. Cute angels with tiny wings, baby faces and rosy cheeks. Did I say house coat? I should have said house boat. Size 18XXXXXL.

My parents (i.e., my mother) named Bethany "Alora" (which means "vision") because in the 1990s my mother ran around the house lighting incense, ringing bells and sleeping over crystal pyramids. Dad was happier then because Mom shared the pot in his night stand rather than flushing it down the toilet.

Bethany flushed her birth name Alora when Mega-evangelist Brother Ballard swooped into Plano and swept her into the fold. Mom joined a month later and donated the earnings from the family business. Bethany Elisha means "singing salvation of God." A micro fact she shares at every opportunity.

If I were my father, I'd have hopped in the Volkswagen minivan, popped a Grateful Dead tape into the dash deck and bailed for San Francisco. Instead he took a real job at a Walmart warehouse, which allowed him to fall underneath a passing forklift and qualify for disability.

Once Jesus repossessed the house, my father built his fortress in the living room where he plays the Grateful Dead through earbuds tucked behind sound blocking ear muffs. He trolls alt-right websites for conspiracy theories and every few hours sneaks into the backyard to torch a roach.

M other herded us to the dinner table for the "ritual of praise and hands." Dinner featured plates stacked on plates which pushed aside even more plates of festive, authentic New Testament delicacies. The Baby Jesus lay in his manger underneath them, hand stitched into the authentic nativity tablecloth. Gaps between plates exposed the infant messiah's eye, ear, nostril, or toe.

We stood in a circle, hands clasped and stomachs growling while my mother thanked Jesus for our food, my safe arrival, for giving me that great job I haven't foreseen yet, for finding a husband for my sister, and for curing my father's drug addiction even though he hasn't accepted it yet.

My father pressed a joint between my fingers and said, "Amen." Then he whispered, "Let the debacle commence."

My sister passed the lamb stew with apricots, pears and mint. (The menu informed us this was the meal Jesus and his family shared during their Christmas celebrations.) My mother—who never abandons a personal question polite folks avoid—chose (for the first time) not to ask how my job was going, if I was seeing anyone new, or if I'd considered reattaching my foreskin to become a better Christian.

Instead she asked, "Where's this Miskahotech University again?"

I ladled the stew onto my plate, trying to avoid the apricots, which I detest, and the mint, to which I've been allergic since I was six. "It isn't real, mom. Think of it as a Harry Potter joke."

Her fork tumbled from her fingers, bounced from her plate rim and poked tablecloth Jesus in the eye. "You mean devil worship?"

My father grabbed his personal spice dispenser and sprinkled "parsley" on his meal. "What's the problem, Marnie? You wanted Chris to be more religious."

I passed the lamb tureen to my sister. "Magic school. A fictional magic school."

Bethany poked the vegetable tine into my face. "If you weren't a back-slider, you'd know there's no difference. Witches use magic to worship the devil. Real witches."

If only I had answered, "Michigan."

My mother slapped her napkin against the table. "You have the nerve to bring devil worship into my house?"

My father grabbed the few hairs that sprouted above his brow. "My house, Marnie. You haven't brought money to the game since you found the Lord and quit our weed business. Our profitable weed business. The profits which you donated to that Christer grifter."

Mother's voice fell several octaves. Into the deep freeze section below the bass clef. The deep freeze inside the walk-in freezer inside the subzero arctic lab.

"I never touched marijuana in my life."

M emory serves self-interest. Mother's hippie friends dropped by every afternoon when I was in elementary school. While mother fished her stash from her fringe tassel tote bag, her friends slipped money under the place mats. Once they dispensed with old business, mother lit incense, opened the patchouli oil, and everyone got baked.

But me.

Which brings us to the moment this story began. The moment before the cavalry arrived. The *diabolus ex machina.*

Bethany filled a plate with potato kugel and placed it next to her plate of kosher lamb stew which spilled onto her columella salad plate which nudged her bowl of Molokhia soup past the edge of the table.

"I don't know who's the worst liar. My stoner dad or devil worshipping brother."

I pushed my chair back and leaned forward until our faces were inches from nostril lock. "Oh really? Well how about this?" I pulled the spells from my pocket.

Even though I had no clue what the words meant, I'd read the incantation so often I'd memorized it. "Yogsothoth, alsalaf Hastur, alsalaf Cthulu, wulidat min dubab la maenaa lah, taqadam. Tastahlik lahum. Ashabha 'iilaa aljahim. Ghanaw ealaa eizamihim. takhudh hayati wadafe."[1]

My mother slammed her fist on the table. "Don't you dare speak heathen in this house, young man." Or she would have said it, but as her lips formed the word "man," a mist gathered above the lamb tureen. Formless at first. Then taking the shape of an orb covered with even more orbs. Pulsing eyeballs, oozing pustules, and windows revealing hellish dimensions where creatures screamed in pain.

It drifted across the table and latched onto mother's head. Tendrils spread from its belly and wrenched her body into the chaos.

Bethany collapsed into her chair, which splintered under her weight. She wriggled her massive limbs to right herself and scramble away, but the creature vanished from my mother's empty chair and rematerialized above Bethany's jiggling, scrambling mass. The tendrils forced open her mouth, dived inside, and diced her internal organs.

My father clutched his chest, not from horror but to recover from laughing. "Thank you, Jesus. Or thank you, son. I thought I'd never unload those two soul-sucking, bank account vacuuming leeches."

The orb materialized above him. His blood plunged from his face to his turkey neck, backed up like water at a clog, then burst through and flooded his lungs. "I don't deserve this shit," he gurgled. The creature absorbed him. Three new orbs, resembling blisters, bubbled on the surface. My family's pleading faces pressed against the translucent walls.

I kicked my chair backward and dashed toward the front door, expecting the creature to devour me. Instead it spiraled inward into a pulsing point in space and vanished. Only trace particles of ectoplasm and the slightest whiff of ozone remained.

I dropped my spells in the stew. Apricot and mint gravy soaked the pages and soaked them into the slime. I burst through the front door and rushed from the house. Whatever came next, cops or ghouls, I wanted as much distance as possible.

Fire erupted from heaven. A ring of sulfurous flame rose from the lawn. An angel descended, the shadows of judgment shrouding her face. Her sword cast a light that sliced through the night with a bright white arc.

The gravity of her presence pulled me to my knees. My hands clasped, as though in prayer. "This is the part where I killed my parents, so you kill me. Right?"

She kneeled in front of me, laid her fingers across my shoulders. "Nonsense. You did God a service. Your family were assholes. Your sister ate more than a third world country, and your mother would pass judgment on Christ Almighty." The warmth of her touch permeated my body, filled me with a sense of Divine glory.

"So, I'm off the hook?"

Her smile dissolved, her new expression as stern as my third-grade teacher's. (Battle-ax Brasswell, who could terrify thirty hyperactive nine-year-olds with a single glare.)

"When you contract with an old one, you pay with your life. It's the bargain that seals the deal."

I should've known there'd be a catch.

Her sword bisected the heavens when she raised it over her head. She swept her arms downward and severed me from skull to pelvis. The claws of hell shoved aside the dirt and dragged me with them into a pit of perpetual pain.

Y ou know what sucks?

My last thought before hell's claws wrenched me into brimstone:

I should have bought the Bob Dobbs *World's Best Salesman* Jacket. It was only a hundred dollars and came with a free Slack Sales Kit.

---

1. Yogsothoth, progenitor of Hastur, progenitor of Cthulu, born of the nameless mist, come forth. Consume them. Drag them to hell. Gnaw on their bones. I pay with my life.

WANTED AD

ELIZABETH DAVIS

Wanted: Yithian For Human Mindswap Partner

It would not be an exaggeration to say I first fell in love when I read "A Shadow Out Of Time," the first story in which Lovecraft mentioned your great race. With his descriptions of your magnificent library city—Pnakotus —I could not help but look around my own city of Springfield, OH with a new disdain. While he reviled your bodies, I felt nothing but wonder.

After that moment, after that story, I tracked down all I could find of your great race: a copy of *The Dark of the Moon: Poems of Fantasy and the Macabre* just for the "Dreams of the Yith." (This was shortly before *The Yith Cycle* was published, much to my chagrin). I even read through all the stories of the Yekalians (first introduced in "Challenge From Beyond"). I must admit I am still confused on whether they are cousins, an earlier state of your race, or merely an example convergent evolution. But these shadows weren't enough.

I next spent a summer between college semesters wandering the Great Sandy Desert of Australia, starting from Wolfe Creek Crater and ranging far out in the red dunes with just a backpack. After days of traveling, I stumbled upon the remains of your great city, explored the sun-hot black stone, weeping over the loss of what I couldn't see. I suspect that I am one of the few of my own mortal race to walk in those broken boulevards, and shelter under those tumbled towers. None of your metallic books survived—damn those flying polyps! I imagine I will remain one of the few to travel down those streets, thanks to the disbelief found among my supposed human kin, especially those aboriginals who found me and doused me with water, which woke me up in the bed of their truck when I passed out from sorrow and maybe just a bit of dehydration in your city. How I left that city and was buried myself in the dunes to be found is still a mystery. (Please allow me to interrupt my narrative to ask that any human hosts currently possessed by your kind to consider research into the rock art of Australia. I still have the contact information they gave me for coordinator of the Wiluraara Creative programs in that area.)

But feeling the rock and mapping the grounds was not enough for me for I was no more but an illiterate tomb robber. I had to understand what I saw, to make sense of the maps that I looked over every night, until the paper grew frail and my mind could repeat the lines with my eyes closed. No, I needed to track down the Pnakotic Manuscripts.

I tried the safest route of exploring the land of dreams, braving those wild seas and suffocating mold forests to reach the city of Ulthar. I walked carefully, making sure not trip over the cats sunning themselves on every surface, before approaching that Temple, the gargantuan temple of the Elder Ones. I beseeched my case to the masked priests, watching their impassive faces for any sign of pity or compassion, I begged on those cold stone stairs for long nights, driving my body haggard from my restless dreams. Eventually, they remitted, opening those pearlescent brass doors, and letting me into the library. Three watched me, guided me, lifted down the chained scroll for me to read. But alas! I did not know your mother tongue, not even in the world of dreams. (Upon reflection of writing this account, that should have been a rather obvious pitfall, but one that I somehow failed to consider before I undertook this grand adventure.)

So, after a week spent in dreamless sleep, and a pot of coffee, I revised my plans. I would have to undertake two terrible expeditions. The first one would be to find and infiltrate the Pnakotic Brotherhood, a secretive cult with a dark and bloody past, and the only known owners of the Manuscripts. The second would be to learn Greek. Of the first endeavor, I can only admit to is meetings in the YMCA, a rather overly elaborate tattoo, a wardrobe filled with robes covered with various stains, a fire in the old Masonic theatre, a break-in at the Cincinnati Natural History Museum, and a whole slew of noise complaints from the neighbors. Not to mention someone of unknown origins leaving up balloons of a drawn and quartered winged pig, or the acquisition of an exotic animal handling license for what may or may not be Nightgaunts. For the second: making the years spent studying Greek into an exciting narrative is beyond my skills of a writer. (I do however, have the dubious honor of managing to lure all three of my thesis judges to sleep during my presentation.) But what I will say, is that I obtained several nights reading the Greek Translation: the Pnakotica. I studied those first five chapters well, having no cares about Chaugnar Faugn, Yibb-Tstil, Xiurhn, or Rhan-Tegoth. Instead I memorized your history, like I memorized the map of your shattered city.

By now, you are probably asking why. Why have I given you this account of my love? In order to show my love, my dedication, and my willingness to learn - all aspects that make me a perfect candidate for your mind-swap program.

I have more than mere love to recommend me for a candidate. Greek is not the only language I've studied. Starting from Spanish in High School and most recently starting a course in Japanese from a language learning program, I am conversational in over fifteen languages. This will be helpful in comforting other transported minds from all over space and time since I will be able to quickly learn their language, along with a wide base for further learning the languages that filled your libraries.

I 've also read quite extensively in psychology and counseling, in order to help comfort others who would be occupying your bodies. I understand others may be confused and frightened by these circumstances and while I can never understand why one would not glory to be among your kind and your great knowledge, I will do my best to comfort them, so that we may learn and maybe even add to your great collection of knowledge together.

I have not abandoned my physical body in pursuit of the mental, I assure you. My body is fit and able to succeed in any task you give it. Part of my exercise routine is dressing in a wire cone made from an old petticoat, so that I may be able to move gracefully and not cause undue accidents when in your body. (This has also given me a reputation with the neighbors for eccentricity which would only work to your advantage - you do not have to worry about drawing undue attention if you fail to adhere to the norms of society around me.) I further have trained my body in dance class, which also includes training in castanets. (Castanets are probably the closest object I could find to simulate your language in - this practice will be helpful in learning how to use my given body more easily.) I can also shout "Exterminate!" in a perfect monotone.

I work a local job as a code monkey - one that you can quit easily if you wish in order to pursue your research. I have abundant savings for your use. I have subscriptions to numerous magazines, newspapers, and journals, which you can peruse in the comfort of my living room. (I promise, while my couch may not seem comfortable for conical bodies, it is perfectly comfy for monkey bodies like mine.) I have no close friends or family. There is no one to notice if I were to start acting oddly, especially since the police have stopped investigating me.

I know I won't remember much, if any, due to you wiping my mind. But I will dream and that will be enough for me. Even more, if you decide to stay permanently, I would love nothing more. *Hammers on the Bone*, and *Weird Detective*, show that you could accomplish great things in my body, greater than I ever could. I would be happier in your city then I am here, even if I were left behind when the Flying Polyps finally converge on Pnakotus, and you all leave, by replacing your minds with those from the beetle people. This may sound fatalistic, especially to a race with such a mastery of time that you avoid death itself, but I am a mere human, and thus I must die. I much rather do it in a grand standoff on a prehistoric Earth than dying of stroke, or diabetes, or a car crash.

I know that it will take a long time before I know for certain that one of your kind has picked me - first this will have to reach one of your human hosts, and then it must be shared after they return to your great library-city. Then you would have to calibrate with your great time science to find me. However, I would prefer to hear from one of you sooner rather than later. I hate to admit, but waiting has been a lonely endeavor - especially after everything with the Brotherhood. I long to have someone to converse about lofty matters of science and art, or even to understand my desires.

Please contact me at YithFriend@yahoo.com for more information, such as location, more ideas about potential research topics that would be of interest to Yithian culture from my temporal location, or manuscripts that I think should be added to your library and those brought back with this transfer. PLEASE DO NOT RESPOND IF YOU ACTUALLY A FLYING POLYP OR ONE OF THEIR SERVANTS! OR MI-GO LOOKING TO HARVEST MY BRAIN. OR DEEP ONES LOOKING TO HARRASS ME OVER INTER-CULT RIVALRIES - MY BROTHERHOOD DAYS ARE BEHIND ME. YITH ONLY!

THE KING IN GRAY

ALICE LOWEECEY

B uying the hat shop seemed like a good idea at the time.

Seven years after Great-Aunt Emmelina Coffin walked off into the blue, my greedy cousins had her declared legally dead. They were Not Pleased when their lawyer put me on speaker phone to tell me I'd inherited the entire contents of her safe deposit box.

My cousins had no reason to complain. Aunty Em was loaded. The family string of funeral parlors alone was worth more than a million. The Coffin Estate stood on prime beachfront property. Residuals from movies filmed in the house and the seventeenth-century cemetery brought in enough to support all of Great-Uncle Gardner Coffin's twelve children.

When the box arrived I set up a video conference with my dear cousins as payback for childhood summers filled with humiliation and torment. I lifted the lid inch by inch and Cousin Bridger actually growled. The anticipation was worth it. Silver dollars filled the box to the brim. The way Cousins Eunice Coffin Hammond and Martha Coffin Williams salivated as I scooped out a handful was glorious. My computer had high-quality speakers: I heard one of them slurp renegade spittle.

I hired a lawyer who knew a dealer with connections to a private online auction house. The lawyer didn't try to cheat me. The auction house made out like a bandit. The dealer pocketed fifteen percent.

And I bought the hat shop. I renamed it "Noir Pleasure." I like classic crime films and look like Dana Andrews in *Laura* when I wear a fedora. So shoot me.

I advertised. I networked. I brought in merchandise the way people buy houses: The starter hat. The moving-up hat. The hat you buy because it's perfect for you. I paneled the cellar, rigged up a projector, and started a monthly movie night. Partnered with a local caterer with long legs and other assets including a helluva hand with homemade bread. She brought sandwiches and dessert. I supplied booze and coffee.

Movie night took off at month four. I showed *Kiss Me Deadly*, the one where Mike Hammer chases the box with the hissing nuke. Forty people crammed into the room, every head wearing one of my fedoras. We ran out of food and the crowd topped off their empty stomachs with more booze. I sent them all home in pre-arranged ride shares.

Phoebe Pease, the caterer, tried to talk me into making space for fascinators as we cleaned up. We bantered in the low light as she slam-dunked sandwich wrappers into the trash can.

The stranger melted toward me out of a shadowed corner as I piled the empties into a box. He was close to seven feet tall, sporting a charcoal suit, light gray shirt, gray silk tie, and a gray fedora—not one of mine. Even the feather in the band was gray. I pegged him as a Mafia goon, but an instant later discarded the label. Something about him wasn't right. I blinked a couple of times to get him into focus: two eyes, a nose, a mouth, longish black hair slicked back, and an impressive walrus-style mustache.

Before I could nail down the *something*, he spoke. His voice was deep and resonant, the Commendatore come to take Don Giovanni to Hell.

Years of being the only nephew who escorted Aunty Em to the opera paid off.

"Alexander Gardner Coffin?"

"That's me."

"I would like to discuss a business matter."

Phoebe's eyes bored into the back of my skull. We had our own "business matter" planned after cleanup.

"It's gotta be close to midnight." As I said it, the three hundred year-old Thomas Moore lantern clock upstairs began chiming the hour.

"I have come a considerable distance to speak with you."

For no other reason than to get Gray Guy out of my face, I agreed. "My office is this way." I gave Phoebe my best "I'll make it up to you later" smile.

I led him upstairs to a tiny room in the back with an octagonal frosted window. From the outside it could've been a bathroom. I chose this quiet piece of legerdemain to deflect any addicts looking for an easy smash and grab.

Gray Guy hitched up his trousers and sat in the highback wooden chair. I sat behind the desk and angled my rolling chair away from the computer screen.

"I am here on behalf of your Great Aunt Emmelina."

He sure knew how to dress for someone who'd been living in a cave for eight years. "My aunt died quite a while ago."

The mustache moved in a discreet smile. "I believe it is more correct to say she was declared dead."

"Six of one."

"Your aunt had been in a state of siege. Her advanced age gave her few choices, even for one so formidable. She asked for advice and, being a wise woman, took it." He produced an envelope from his single-breasted suit coat's inner pocket.

His long black nails rasped against my hand as I took the envelope. I opened the flap.

"Alexander, the Queen of the Night requires you. Do not be swayed by the bird's tailfeathers. Le fer à la main, courez aux combats."

The letter on the five by eight sheet of plain white paper was type-written but signed "Aunty Em" in my Great Aunt's best Palmer Method cursive.

Not even the Scooby Gang would fall for this. I slid the paper back toward him. "You could try this extortion scam on my cousins. They're more gullible and a lot richer." I stood. "They're also so tight their sphincters squeak, but who am I to discourage an entrepreneur?"

The mustache twitched again. His waxing method caused the hairs to cling in groups and move in a creepy, sentient rhythm. He reached into his jacket again and brought out another envelope.

"I have heard much about you from Emmelina. Meeting you in person justifies her confidence." He placed the envelope on the desk. "I am given to understand a retainer is the equivalent of a contract."

It took me a second to connect the dots. "For private detectives, maybe. I sell hats."

A crash and a series of thumps shook the floor. Phoebe's scream cut off halfway through my name.

I reached the cellar before a coherent thought formed in my mind. The movie room was trashed. Bent and broken chairs. Overturned cups tangled with paper tablecloths. The smell of cold coffee filled the space.

"Phoebe?"

I plowed through wooden seats and splintered legs and tablecloths and shattered glass like a cow catcher. No Phoebe.

"Mr. Coffin, calm yourself."

Never in the history of ever has telling someone "calm yourself" worked. I added "stranger appears" plus "attempted extortion" plus "Phoebe disappears" and got "perp at my side." I put him in a choke hold and shoved him against the wall with a knee in his back.

"I teach judo too. Tell me what your gang did with Phoebe and I won't break your neck."

A bright red line on the paneling caught my eye. I must have loosened my hold because a second later he was touching a black-nailed finger to the red line. The next instant, the finger touched my tongue.

I jerked my head away. "What the hell?"

"Identify the substance." His deep voice demanded obedience.

Sweet. Acidic. "Ketchup. It's ketchup." My muscles unlocked. It wasn't Phoebe's blood. I stepped back, remembered to breathe, and took in the scribbles on my wall.

"Are those words?"

"They are. It appears I was not able to conceal my tracks."

I gripped his shoulder and shook him. A warning pinged in my brain: his shoulder felt "off." So had his neck, now that I thought about it.

"What does it say?"

"The females in exchange. Two hours."

I flipped the refreshment table upright and banged it against his knees to make him sit. "Talk. Now." It was taking all my strength of will not to scream at him.

"The two hours have already begun. I suggest we talk on the way."

"The way where?" I gestured around the room. "The only way out is the door we came in." My voice ratcheted higher. "Where the hell is Phoebe?"

We were in the far corner of the cellar, the one that wouldn't stop weeping no matter how often I tried to seal it. It'd rained that day, which left a shallow pool at that end of the room. Gray Fedora gripped my lapels and plunged us into half an inch of water.

My ears popped. Water poured into my nose and mouth. The world turned upside down, took a hard left, and dropped me.

I landed on my hands and knees and vomited black water. A bout of coughing and spitting followed. I got to my feet as soon as I could see again.

At first I thought we'd fallen into a closed section of the subway. The air was a dim shade of bluish-gray. We stood on ancient cobblestones slimy with moisture, but no walls curved around to a low ceiling. Not the subway then. I shook myself straight and saw his hand in the gloom holding out my own fedora.

"Our direction lies to the right." He began walking.

I re-formed the crown and set the hat on my head to keep that much of me out of the rain. Then I realized my suit was dry. My companion was also dry, despite the apparent saturation of the air. I scrambled to match his stride.

He raised a black-nailed hand. "I will keep to the essentials. In return, you must keep an open mind."

I opened my mouth. So many things tried to get out only a garbled mess of sound emerged. He ignored me.

"Firstly, the Coffins are more than a family of great wealth. Your lineage stretches to the depths of time in parallel with the Elder Gods. Secondly, every generation has a seventh offspring. Thirdly, you are the seventh son of a seventh son of a seventh daughter in an age-old pattern." He paused. "You wish to comment?"

Before I said something that would invite a punch in the mouth, a mole-faced creature dripping oily fluid from a dozen spatulate appendages slapped onto the cobblestones.

It gurgled and hissed at us, but I didn't need to understand its words.

Hate and hunger are universal. I shifted into fighting stance. Time for the judo teacher's real-world test.

Gray Fedora pressed my shoulder. Without speaking he opened his jacket. The mole-octopus-beaver squeaked and vanished.

As he rebuttoned his jacket my eyes tried to tell my brain they saw a tentacle slide underneath the tailored hem.

"What would Sam Spade do?"

I didn't realize I'd spoken aloud until his quiet voice next to me said, "Defeat the villain and save the women."

"Sexist."

"Are not many classic noir films?" He took out a pocket watch and resumed walking. "One hour and twenty-seven minutes remain. The road is neglected here. Watch your step."

Of course he had a pocket watch. "Stop. Where are we? Where are we going? Why can I breathe this air?" I took three long strides and planted myself in front of him. "I said stop."

A warbling screech came out of the fog ahead of us.

"A pauraque? Can't be." New York City to South America needed a lot more than an hour's travel time.

His body stiffened in awkward jerks, like his bones were disjointed.

"That is a night gaunt."

I planted my hands on his chest. "I've had it with your horror movie bullshit. I don't know what hallucinogen you slipped into me or how you did it. Maybe on your hand when we shook. Maybe you used some kind of aerosol, but none of this is real. I'm going to wake up right now."

The suave mask twisted. "We are wasting valuable time, Mr. Coffin."

I had enough time to recognize my hands were sinking in where his rib cage should be when his walrus mustache rippled and lengthened and his gray jacket flapped out like wings, no not *like* wings, they *became* wings, and whatever drug he'd slipped into me finally knocked me out cold.

I woke to a stinging face. His long-nailed hand slapped my left cheek and I grabbed his wrist.

"Hit me again and I'll break your arm."

His other hand reached for mine and he helped me to my feet.

I kept my voice even. "I may not have much imagination, but I'm pretty sure I saw something from a horror story before I passed out."

"This is a different dimension, Mr. Coffin. For the last time, open your mind. Your obstinacy has cost us another ten minutes."

His voice had an edge to it. I couldn't look away from his mustache. A group of hairs twitched up as though they winked at me.

I concentrated on finding Phoebe. "Okay. Give it to me in words of one syllable." I resettled my hat on my head.

"Now you are speaking sense." He cupped his hands. "We search for Hastur." A green orb glowed between his palms. A skeletal figure hovered in the orb. It wore shreds of clothes the color of tartar on a dog's teeth. A featureless mask obscured its face. "He is served by night gaunts, whose cry you heard." The creature in the orb became a naked, horned, human-bat hybrid covered with sickly white skin from its membraneous wingtips to its whiplike hair and tail. Its face was as smooth and oval as an egg.

"Do you know where to look for these things?" There was nothing else I could say. The world was chaos. I'd hack through it to normalcy when Phoebe was safe.

He collapsed the orb. "We gather information. First, I will speak to the cave-dwellers."

We turned off the cobblestones and my shoes crunched through shale. Waves lapped somewhere to our right. The omnipresent mist was as bad as haze lit by the useless fog lights on my car.

The light disappeared. Our footsteps echoed back at us. Snuffling and muttering crossed the echoes and—I admit it—made me shiver. Unless it was the cold water dripping from the roof down my back.

I pulled out my phone and turned on its flashlight. We were in a deep grotto. A tiny creature all hair and claws and muscles leaped for Gray Fedora. Its head split into a mouth bristling with pointed teeth.

Instinct took over. I blocked its attack with one arm, spun, and kicked it sideways into the wall. It squeaked like a chew toy and fell to the ground with a *plop*.

Gray Fedora changed languages and asked a short, sharp question. A group of trembling, snapping things several feet deeper into the cave grumbled and spat. After a minute they pushed one forward. They glared at us with eyes sunken in a black and green mat of hair. They chopped off each word of its answer, spat on the ground, and the whole group ran into the depths of the cave.

When we got back into foggy daylight, Gray Fedora held out a hand. "Thank you. Now that we have stopped resisting each other we can be an efficient partnership."

I pointed to my wet shoes and pant legs. "Why black water?"

"It is of no importance at the moment. The dholes imparted information gathered from the newly dead. Our quarry's destination is the inner reaches. The journey should take us approximately thirty minutes."

After half an hour scaling never-ending boulders, ledges, and overhangs in my best wingtips, I wished I had a touch of mountain goat. I also wanted a gallon of Gatorade mixed with vodka. Or vice-versa.

"How much...time...left?" I wheezed when we stopped on a wide outcropping.

"Forty-two minutes."

"Where...the hell is...our contact?"

"Here." He reached both arms into thin air and I swear to God pulled out a spider the size of a city bus. Webbing thick as sewer pipes stuck to it. "Assistance, please."

The spider thrashed and fought, showering us with shattered rocks. I grasped a sharp piece of granite and sliced through the webbing. The spider shrieked in a register only dogs should've been able to hear. As Gray Fedora fought it, I sliced through enough of its web to create a hole wide enough to fit me. Then I jumped on top of the hairy, slimy, stinking arachnid from Hell and got it in a headlock.

Its shriek added distinct syllables. I was developing a knack for picking out curses in unknown languages. Gray Fedora had a longer conversation with it. When it refused to answer, I augmented the headlock. Finally it caved. Sullen and squeaky don't go well together. At Fedora's signal I jumped off and Jurassic Spider scuttled back behind its invisible wall.

Something trickled down my face. I touched a finger to it. My eyes were bleeding. A deep breath or three later and I decided any damage wasn't permanent since I could still see the mountain through the fog.

"Philip Marlowe never solved crimes like this."

"We are trailblazers." "He chuckled at some private joke. "Your eyes are bleeding. The Leng's vocalizations sometimes have this effect." He reached for his pocket square but stopped mid-gesture. "You would be wise to remove all sanguinary traces. It attracts scavengers."

"Of course it does." I ruined my own pocket square. "Did I get it all?"

He inspected me. "Yes, your skin is clear." Without another word, he plunged us into a puddle no bigger than a dinner plate.

We flew or swam or warped through a psychedelic mess of greens and browns, like the bottom of a tide pool. I closed my eyes. Time folded, stretched, flipped, and unflipped before he touched our feet to the ground as light as a water strider. I had to tell my brain I was vertical about fifty times before it believed me.

The architect of this vacation spot liked yellow. I don't mind a sunny summer day on the balcony above my store with an icy Labatt Blue in my hand and Phoebe playing blues harmonica next to me. This place wasn't summer yellow. It was rotted ivory with swirls of rancid cheese thrown in. The ground sighed under our feet. The desiccated air stank of overflowing toilets.

One of my writer friends says when things get boring, add ninjas. I'd have to tell her about this place. If I survived.

My tour guide checked his pocket watch. "Twenty-one minutes remain. This way."

After the last two hours I believed Aunt Em and Phoebe were at the end of this anti-rainbow. I moved faster. He matched my pace.

Odd swishing sounds I'd been hearing for awhile increased as we rounded a crumbling wall the color of mildewed chartreuse bathroom tiles. The wall had been hiding a castle. I swear it on the future graves of my rapacious cousins.

"Wait," Gray Fedora said.

I spun around, slipped, righted myself, and pretended it hadn't happened. "What? This place is the bastard child of the Brothers Grimm and Guillermo del Toro, and you've convinced me you're telling the truth. So grow a pair and help me rescue my women." If the gods wanted to do me a favor, they'd prevent Phoebe ever finding out I called her 'my woman'.

Gray Fedora's mustache did its twitching thing. Before he replied, the castle doors opened. One of those clown-white faceless creatures with perpetual motion hair said, "The King awaits your challenge."

Its voice had a hissing undertone. Good thing snakes don't bother me. Much.

Gray Fedora and I entered side by side. The world turned dead-algae yellow. The hellspawn Alice in Wonderland footman led us down to a windowless dungeon. At its far end hovered a massive, warped clock with only three numbers on it. A single crumbling hand ticked upwards to zero.

The clock's clear face bulged and the ragged guy with the blank mask stepped out. Everything about him was the color of curdled buttermilk, except his pointed black toenails protruding from frayed shoes. For some reason those bothered me more than long black fingernails.

"Brother." Gray Fedora said.

"Brother. You do not come alone? Your weakness amuses me." His voice had its own echo. I wondered if he was hollow. Nothing would've surprised me at this point.

"The wise know the advantage of the proper tool."

When I got Phoebe and Aunt Em out of here, I was going to treat myself to a prolonged beating of Gray Fedora's condescending face. I opened my mouth to tell Yellow Boy where he could shove his attitude when my partner clamped a hand on my shoulder.

"We are here within the allotted time. Shall we begin?"

"Indeed."

The light went out. My stomach jumped into my throat and only the claws in my shoulder kept me from falling. Or flying. Or something not involving a solid floor.

A new voice came out of the dark. It sang the Queen of the Night aria, but the words were all harsh consonants and elongated vowels. The swishing sounds kept getting mixed up in it and the words twisted in my ears. Two lines of warm liquid trickled down the sides of my neck. I knew what that meant.

The grip on my shoulder tightened. To shut out the writhing syllables I recited the real lyrics in my head. I remembered the last time I'd taken Aunt Em to a performance of the opera. The Queen whipped out the dagger the moment she hit the second b-flat and the audience jumped. Aunt Em cackled about it all night. Said anyone with half a brain would've seen it coming.

The "singer" aimed at the b-flat. Something swished an inch from my face. I caught whatever it was, swept a hand at knee level, reached where a wrist ought to be, snapped it and disarmed Mr. Obvious. Nicked my palm on the blade, too. Next semester's judo classes were going to include sessions in the dark.

The light came back, dim yellow-brown like a sepia photograph. Stiff at my feet lay the footman, its ponytail still swishing back and forth like a scientist sticking electrodes into a dead frog's leg.

"Your thug needs some practice." My voice came out snarky. The rest of me wanted to gibber like a lunatic and run for the nearest exit, Phoebe and Aunt Em in tow. To achieve this I had to find them. "Let me guess. Based on the décor, you're into tradition. Is it three challenges?" I picked up its rippled, oil-slick knife. "Challenger has choice of weapons."

The bastard ignored me and said to Gray Fedora, "Your tool lacks respect."

My partner was unruffled. "Do not waste words and attempt to claim time has expired."

The man had ice in his blood. His hand still clawed into my shoulder despite all my moves. I'd need stitches, but it was good to have somebody on my side in this nuthouse.

Another brusque move from Mr. Single Color Palette and three doors appeared. "Choose wisely."

At least I had light. I studied all three doors. If there'd been two, I'd have told Gray Fedora to make with the teleportation and bring back a fish. Lay it in front of each door, and when the tiger's paw appeared to claw it through the sliver of space at the bottom, open the other door and rescue the ladies.

Instead, I had to rely on my rattled brains. The doors were identical shades of overripe pineapple. They clustered in the middle of the dungeon like a bay window, so I walked around them. Identical front, back, and sides as well.

The minimalist Dali clock ticked louder.

I looked over at Gray Fedora for a hint. His mustache writhed downward. I walked the circuit again, looking at the floor this time. A sand-tinted ornamental curlicue slid in and out of the shadows before each door. More unknown language.

Tick. Tick. Tick. Tick.

The left-hand one reminded me of the glyph Prince used for awhile, with an added curling line like a pointed tail. The middle one was an art deco spider. The right one was all angles and slashes.

I put on a mental deerstalker. Spider web. Monster spider. I cozied up to the middle door and my left eye started to bleed. Bingo. Now the left. The taillike line rang a bell. Bell. Music. Opera. Em's letter. "Don't be fooled by the tail" or something like that. Something long was behind this one. I remembered the long hair of the guy who tried to knife me.

No more time. I turned to the right-hand door and pushed.

All three vanished.

Yellow Jackass inclined his masked head a millimeter. "The Coffin lineage is potent."

"Yeah, the Force is strong in this one. Get on with it."

Flaming sulphur lit his eyeholes. "I will enjoy the pleasure my servants take with your flesh and soul when you fail."

"As the king commands?"

Everything in me froze the instant I said the word. Small business owners don't get much free time, but I read. Every step down this rabbit hole replayed in a flash. This was the King in Yellow and I was the first human to see R'yleh since a nasty old man in Brooklyn a hundred years ago.

I might not get out of here alive, but in exchange I would guilt Gray Fedora into taking Aunt Em and Phoebe home.

I faced the King. "The last challenge is a duel with you, right?"

"Quite right." A twisted ochre knife appeared in his hand. He stepped down from the throne, all seven feet of him, and walked ten paces. "Brother, if you will count?"

We turned our backs to each other. I balanced on the balls of my feet as the deep voice began.

"Ten. Nine. Eight..."

The King's threadbare shoe whispered against the floor as he turned one count too early. I leaped the gap and ripped the mask from his face. Where his face should've been I saw a naked, decaying human-like shape bulging with polyps and suckers around a slavering mouth.

At the same moment, one of the electrified hair minions flew over the throne and landed in a broken heap at our feet. Phoebe ran around the throne, hauling Aunt Em by one arm.

A couple dozen now-visible creatures shrieked. Their language adequately conveyed disappointment at losing their prize. Mask back in place, the King howled at us with a voice louder, deeper, multiplied. Then the castle disappeared.

The victors stood on rotted-ivory sand and stared at each other.

Aunt Em said, "Alexander, I require Irish coffee and truffle cheesecake."

"Come closer," I said to Gray Fedora, "so I can bash your teeth in."

He maintained a safe distance. "You should recognize the strategy of goading the antagonist."

Phoebe said, "It's called trash talk, Alex. Em and I heard the whole thing."

I caved. "Get us out of here. I need a drink."

One space-time slip later we touched down in my shop's trashed basement.

Phoebe righted a chair. When she got Aunt Em settled, she turned on us males. We flinched. "Explain. Now."

Gray Fedora stepped up to the plate. "Alexander, did you wonder why you were able to purchase this building for such a low sum?"

"It needed work. The last three tenants went bankrupt. My Realtor was forced to tell me it might be cursed. Guess I should've listened."

"Only a Coffin could inhabit this house for any length of time. It is built over a gateway."

I groaned. "Of course it is."

Aunt Em gave me her patented glare. "Alexander, I told you our complete family history. It's your own fault you chose to think I was a dotty old lady."

"Aunt Em, I apologize now and forever." Another passage of spare-time reading demanded attention. "If I'm going to end up with the Innsmouth look I promise to find Cthulhu himself and make him pay for messing with my rugged good looks."

Gray Fedora bowed. "That will not be necessary."

Aunt Em didn't bat an eye. Phoebe choked on a four-letter word.

I swallowed. "Your mustache. I missed the obvious clue."

"Your mind was taken up with more urgent matters." He bowed over Aunt Em's wrinkled hand. "My apologies."

She inclined her head. "The King is the epitome of deceit. Besides, Phoebe packs a mean punch. I was only worried for a moment."

Ignoring the compliment to my girlfriend, I got words past my desert-dry mouth, "I pictured you...bigger."

"You remember I did not lend you my pocket square outside the spider's lair? This is why." He pulled it out. It changed into lichen-green scaled skin. He tucked it back into place, a piece of silk again. "We partnered well, Alexander Coffin. Were this a motion picture, we would become the Brothers Fedora."

Aunt Em clapped. "I approve. Our ancestors would be proud."

"When I once again call upon Alexander they will have more opportunities for pride, Emmelina."

"Wait. What? I'm still in the room, people."

"Farewell, cousins." He walked into the dank corner and disappeared the same way he'd invaded my life two hours earlier.

"I'm not a detective. I own a hat shop," I said to the empty space.

Phoebe kissed me so hard my toes curled. "Alex, drive us to my place. I have cheesecake in the freezer and all the fixings for Irish coffee."

She helped Aunt Em to her feet before smiling sweetly at me. "We need to talk."

Those four words inspired more fear than sleuthing with Cthulhu.

THE HAPPIEST PLACE ON EARTH

FRASER SHERMAN

"What kind of goddamn agent are you, Hal?" Mickey Mi-Go screamed into his cellphone while drunkenly wheeling his Porsche through the studio parking lot. "I'm paying you 15 percent a year and you don't have my back?"

"Mickey, baby, how many people in this industry get to go out while they're on top?"

"I built this studio, you bloodsucking loser!" Mickey steering into his reserved parking space, not realizing the minivan was there until he heard its fender crumple. Cursing a blue streak, he backed up and squeezed into the nearest open space, scraping paint off the Lexus to the left. In the back of his mind, he knew he'd regret the damage to his Porsche when he sobered up, but the front of his mind didn't give a damn.

"How can Walt cancel me, Hal? I'm iconic!! I've been iconic for almost a century, ever since I was in *Steamboat R'Lyeh!*" Stripping off the human gloves and face-mask he wore outside the studio, Mickey spread his wings and rose upward through the mundane metal of the car roof. "Since you don't seem to have any cojones, I guess I'll go talk to 'Uncle Walt' myself!"

"Mickey, sweetie, that's not such a—"

Mickey clicked off the phone and shoved it back in his throat sac. Down below, he saw families screaming at his true form—part-rat, part-fungus, part-insect, part-corpse—and then he noticed it was only parents recoiling in horror, not the kids. That was strange: driving small children to madness had always been a piece of cake for him.

Focusing in on the top floor of the Alhazred Studios offices, Mickey flew through the wall and into the icy chill of the cryonic air-conditioning system that enabled Walt Alhazred to keep running the studio decades after his death. "What the hell is this about, Walt? How can you do this to me?"

"Did you ever hear of knocking, Mickey?" Sitting behind a desk piled with contracts, film treatments and quarterly reports, Walt didn't look the least surprised. "Or appointments? I have a meeting with Japanese investors in—"

"Don't give me that bullshit!" Mickey slammed his slime-dripping forearm down on the desk. "Did you think I'd let you cancel *The Mickey Mi-Go Club* without a fight?"

"Mickey, I'm only going by the sacred text. Well, the latest sacred text." One undead finger tapped Walt's unhallowed guide to cost-cutting and boosting profits, the *Economicon*. "The Old Ones are bound by no natural law, but even they submit to the laws of supply and demand."

"When have I not known that? They demand the destruction of the human mind and soul, I supply that. My show is driving kids just as insane today as it did when we started."

"You don't keep up with industry news much, do you?" Walt sighed. "Of course, having to pay medical bills with five ex-wives in madhouses—"

"That's why I need this gig! Do you know what a private rubber room costs?" Mickey might have driven his wives insane, but he'd always done right by them. "I know it would be cheaper to store their brains in jars but—dammit, Walt, it's one thing to send Dagon Duck back to the Lake of Hali, but I built this studio!"

"You?" Walt glanced at the studio logo on his letterhead, containing the Alhazred name surrounded by a seven-pointed star. "Funny, I don't see your moniker on anything in here."

"I was your first star, Walt. We broke into the industry together, I made you as much you made me—"

"Why you snot-nosed abomination." Walt stood, towering over Mickey in a way that defied all concepts of geometry or perspective. "*I* built this company. *My* banned books! *My* unspeakable storyboards! *My* unhallowed, obscene theme parks! If you'd checked the latest N'ielsen ratings you'd know you're not pulling your weight. The rate at which you drive to kids to madness has dropped 60 percent since the last century."

"What?" Mickey stared at Walt, shaking his head, which sent slime spattering over most of the room. "I know the brats have gotten a little harder to scare, but—"

"A little? Mickey, your show still terrifies the boomers who grew up with you, and maybe a few Gen-Xers, but Generations Y and Z? They think of you as the hokey old monster that drove their parents crazy. Not them."

"Hokey?" Mickey swallowed. "I'm a classic! 'A beloved icon,' *People* says so!"

"It said that in 1980, Mickey. And 'classic' just does not impress the Old Ones." With an occult gesture, Walt turned on the flatscreen hanging on his wall. "Let me show you what does."

Mickey saw a head fly over a studio audience with intestines and internal organs hanging beneath it. Children screamed in horror as blood dripping off the dangling arteries rained down on them.

"Walt, what the hell?"

"It's a penagglan." With a snap of his fingers, Walt turned the TV off. "A Malay vampire. Still novel enough in America to terrify kids—"

"Some Malayan chippie replacing me? No way she drives them crazier!"

"No, but the thing is, third-world monsters work cheap. She's happy with a few bottles of blood, a nice cave. No profit percentage, no use of the studio condo on Yuggoth, no ever-increasing salary demands. In terms of cost-effectiveness, she has you beat to hell."

"Walt, I have a contract!"

"It guarantees you remain an employee of Alhazred Studios until the end of time." Walt smiled. "But you don't get paid unless you work, and you only work if I say so. The Lawyer Who Cannot Be Named inserted that in the fine print."

"Shit." Mickey cursed himself for hiring his brother's spawn to negotiate his last contract. "So … that's it? I spend the rest of my days dancing to the music of mad flutes?"

"Not necessarily." Walt sat down, all affability again. "Boomers and Xers are still terrified of you. 60 percent say you warped their minds better than LSD. We could keep you plenty busy booking you for celebrity nostalgia gigs: mall openings, used-car lot ribbon-cuttings—"

"Come on." Mickey sank into the chair in front of Walt's desk, wings draping over the arms. "That shit's for has-beens!"

"Don't think of it that way—call it retro. If it goes over well, there might be a judge's slot on *America's Got Madmen* next fall."

"The pay's not even industry scale. You know how I blow through money."

"I'll put you in touch with a great debt counselor. It's a Tcho-Tcho, you know how tight those bastards are with a dollar." Walt's face displayed the confident smirk of an alpha fiend. "So, we have a deal?"

For a second, Mickey considered saying no. It would be real good for

Walt not to get his way, just once. And he could always find work in real estate …

Instead, he thrust out his hand. Walt took it, looking almost surprised. "Mickey, for a second, I thought you were going to walk."

"What, and give up show biz?" Mickey gestured at the air conditioner with his free hand. "You died years ago, but did you quit? It just gets into your ichor, know what I mean?"

"Yes," Walt said, nodding slowly. "I think I do." And for just a second, the two unspeakable horrors met each other's eyes—and smiled.

ELDRITCH ABOMINATIONS IN MODERN-DAY AMERICA: A DOCUMENTARY

LUCAS FRANKI

The United States has changed drastically from the days of H.P Lovecraft. In those days, the haunted towns of northern Massachusetts he chronicled really were isolated, and the eldritch nightmares that inhabited those lands could ply their way without stumbling across too many unsuspecting mortals. This is no longer the case. Massachusetts is one of the most densely populated states in the country, and in general, the America of 2022 is far more urban and far more populated than the America of 1922.

And with all these humans, conflict is inevitable. The things in the night must come to terms with an ever-expanding global civilization, and just as the polar bear struggles to come to terms with vanishing ice caps, so too must these Lovecraftian beasts adapt to man's inexorable influence.

It's the height of summer in Cape Cod; the waters have grown warm enough for the thousands of tourists seeking refuge from the hustle and bustle of city life. And with the return of eager vacationers, the Deep Ones arise from the cursed reefs and hidden sea canyons of the Gulf of Maine. Their time has come.

Mating season.

Life has been difficult for the Deep Ones in the North Atlantic ever since the loss of their primary colony outside Innsmouth, Massachusetts, almost a century ago. Relentlessly pursued by hunters and military and bereft of their human cult, they've had to resort to clever trickery and a deeper understanding of humanity to survive. After all, Dagon has granted them only limited immortality. As the Navy proved during their raids, Deep Ones can still be killed if subjected to lethal force.

Night approaches over isolated Chapin Beach, a long, broad spit of dunes splitting the reed-filled marshes south from the navy-blue bay north. Most of the beachgoers have retreated to their hotels in Dennis and Yarmouth as the water cools, becoming too harsh for most, but a few stubborn souls remain in the ocean and on the sand, drinking in the last rays of shimmering orange light.

Beneath the surface, skulking along the shallow waters abutting the sandy strip, a group of Deep Ones scope out their targets. It is important to choose wisely, for they will not get a second opportunity to acquire a mate this night.

The eldest of the group, a female of 500 years, a survivor of the Innsmouth Raid and the South Sea incident, spots her target. A young man, about 30, whose friends are beckoning him back to shore. They wish to find a bar and drink the night away in the company of some lovely ladies of their own species. The young man sighs and flops back, gently kicking himself toward them, when a massive hand with too many claws and rough scales wraps around his leg.

The young man panics and screams, but his struggles are irrelevant as the Deep One drags him out away from the shore with frightening speed. His friends do not know he's disappeared. He is alone with the Deep One, who surfaces and confronts her prize. The man blanches. His skin goes cold, his body quivers. "What are you?" he asks through chattering teeth. "What the hell is going on?"

The creature speaks in a low, guttural affront to the English language. *"I have chosen you,"* she says. *"Mate with me, mortal, and we shall forever revel in the glory of Father Dagon and Mother Hydra until the day the stars align and dread Cthulhu wakes from his endless dream."*

The man stares at the creature that should not be. "I'm sorry, could you run that past me again? Did you say mate?"

"Our children will inherit this Earth. Humanity is a brief candle in an uncaring abyss."

"Woah, you want kids? Lady, I, uh, think, ain't no way in hell I'm fucking with anyone who brings up kids 5 minutes after we meet. Sorry."

The Deep Ones shifts slightly, scratching at her slavering jaw with a hooked claw. *"I can make you immortal. Free you from your weak human bonds. Reveal to your feeble mind the great mysteries of this universe. Do you not wish to discover the vastness of what lies beyond the veil?"*

"I used to fuck a girl who was all into that mystic astrology shit. Bitch ended up smashing my car's windshield with a couple of her magic rocks. Ain't no way I'm getting back into that. Especially with a fish lady. I'm out. Sorry."

The Deep One can only stare impotently as the man swims back to shore. Consent is everything to her species; she will do nothing without the express permission of her chosen mate. To take a human mate without consent is beyond shameful in Deep One culture. This is the decree of Father Dagon and Mother Hydra. And so, she will not breed tonight.

The youngest of the group, a male barely beyond his teenage years, has moved away from his fellows, creeping into the sandy shallows. He is barely hidden below the surface as he approaches a human woman of similar age lounging on her back, drifting with the waves as they draw in and recede out.

Unlike his elder, the young Deep One is deferential to the woman, and she notices him well before he pokes his head above the waterline. She is apprehensive, but stands her ground.

He speaks first. His English is far less alien; deep, but in an almost-comforting manner. "Good evening." He speaks gently, but with an unmistakable confidence. "I am sorry to disturb you on a night as beautiful as this, but I saw you and I just knew I'd kick myself later if I didn't come around and at least say hello."

The woman is intrigued by the Deep One's entreaty. She steps forward, reaching out tentatively. "You … you're … you're not human, are you?"

The Deep One chuckles. "You caught me. But that doesn't mean we can't be friends, does it?"

She laughs and wipes away strands of wet hair from her face. "I suppose not. And I have to say, I've played a lot of Breath of the Wild in the past couple years, and I'm not afraid to admit, I kinda had a big crush on Prince Sidon. You kinda look like him, not gonna lie."

It has become increasingly common for the youngest of the Deep Ones to keep abreast of current human media. One can prostrate themselves before the Great Old Ones for only so long before the task loses its joy, and man's proclivity for concentrating on coastlines ensures that there is an easy supply of various electronics for enter-prising individuals such as our young Deep One. And so he knows what to do.

The Deep One swings his clenched hand in front of him, striking a dashing pose. "I love that game!" he says with an appropriately whole-some swagger. "And you probably don't have to guess who my favorite character was."

"Ha, probably not." The woman crosses her arms in front of her, tilting her head. "You know, I'm not usually a fan of the cold approach, most guys who try it are assholes, but I don't know, I'm getting good vibes from you. And God knows I could use some of those. Been a rough year."

"Aw, I'm sorry. If you want to be alone, I don't want to bother you. That's not what I'm about."

"No, no, stay!" the young woman steps forward. "I didn't … if I wanted to be alone, I could have done that at home. I came out here with my friends to, well, unwind, if you get what I mean. Only problem is, I haven't met anyone to unwind with. I'm horny, not easy."

The Deep One holds out his hand. "We can go at whatever pace you're comfortable with. My name's Ndaclotegn, by the way."

"Lauren," she takes his hand, blushing slightly. "So, uh, what do we do now? Place I'm staying is pretty full up, you got a place we could go?"

"Are you sure?"

She nods. "I can't explain it, but this feels right. I know we just met, but I trust you."

He tugs at her arm. "I'll take you back to my place, but I'll warn you, it will be … difficult to get there."

She gazes at her Deep One companion. "Take me away, my beautiful fish prince." Her voice is breathless, and her eyes feast upon his scaly visage.

He nods, then scoops his prize up in his arms. "Then take a deep breath, and when we reach the gates of New Y'ha-nthlei, do not stare at the sentries too long. It would not be good for your long-term mental health."

The pair slip below the surface, and they do not reemerge. As Lauren's lungs begin to ache, she happens to catch a glimpse of her new mate's friends, who wave at Ndaclotegn. The Deep Ones speak in a strange language she could not hope to understand, and with her air running out, she could not speak to them anyway.

"Don't worry," his voice is ethereal and all-encompassing. "You won't need air for too much longer. We'll be there soon."

Up on the surface, Lauren's friends briefly search for her, but assume she left with a man and leave. They do not question her absence the next morning, and soon they forget her entirely. It is summer on the Cape, after all. The beach beckons yet again.

In the endless forests and rolling mountains of West Virginia, underneath a blanket of infinite stars and endless void, a Mi-Go descends upon an unsuspecting town, nestled in a valley blanketed with alfalfa and corn fields.

This wasp-like beast, hideous to our eyes yet noble and graceful among its own kind, has traveled all the way from the Mi-Go colony on Pluto on a mission of the utmost importance. Traditionally, the Mi-Go interfere with humanity only when their mining interests are threatened, but their records on the species are a century out of date. The most efficient way to update the colony's central database is through the direct interface of human brains. Preferably utilizing a significant sample size.

It approaches the first house in the village, a quaint scrap of civilization called Hillsboro. The massive dog outside, chained to a mighty and stout white oak, senses the Mi-Go's presence and barks furiously, straining at the lead. The humble canine is lucky; its small mind cannot fathom the foul biology before it. All it knows is that an intruder has trespassed on its master's domain, and that soon the interloper will be dealt with.

A middle-aged man with a beer belly spilling out of a sweaty wife-beater slams the front door open, rifle in hand. "Donald, what the hell you barkin' at? You see someone on my property?"

In the darkness, the man cannot see the Mi-Go clearly. He merely sees the shadowy silhouette of something in his yard. "Hey! The fuck you think you're doin' on my land?"

The Mi-Go drifts closer. It lacks vocal cords, so it communicates by transmitting thoughts into the man's head. *I bear you no ill will, human, but our research must come first. I hope you do not understand the torment you will soon face.*

"I'm not afraid to shoot you," the man says. "I ain't some liberal pansy-ass, this is real America. We do things different here."

If it will put your mind at ease to resist, do so. It will do nothing, but humans are so simple.

The man takes aim and the gun blast thunders through the wide lawn. The Mi-Go's outer shell, tough enough to endure the harsh vacuum of space, repels the bullet. The spent projectile tumbles into the grass, forgotten and impotent. The man fires again and again, expending the entire cartridge. "What the hell is happening?" he drops the weapon. "Why can't I hurt you?"

The house lights behind him flip on, and at last the man sees the Mi-Go as it truly is. Now, in his last breaths as a man, he understands his place in the universe. He falls to his knees, clutching at his eyes, abject terror filling his hoarse screams. A woman bursts out of the front door. His wife, come to see the intruder her husband has apprehended. Instead, she sees the Mi-Go descend upon her husband's thrashing form. This is too much for her as well, and as her brain shuts down, the momentum carries her down the stairs to the driveway, where she settles in an unmoving lump.

The Mi-Go moves in with terrifying speed, relieving the couple of their brains and placing them in travel cylinders. He is the finest surgeon on Pluto, and of course the Mi-Go are renowned throughout the cosmos for their medical skill. Human brain explants are as simple to him as breathing is to Earth life.

On to the next house. An ancient man emerges, shotgun in hand. "What the hell's going on?" he mutters. "Neighbors are sure makin' it tough to sleep. Must be a bear or somethin'."

The Mi-Go has far less sympathy for this human and reveals himself immediately. But the human does not flinch, instead firing blindly into the Mi-Go's face. He is not injured, but a shotgun blast to the face can disorient even mighty beings from beyond the stars. *No human has ever beheld the Mi-Go form without their sanity failing.*

"Ain't ya ever seen a blind man with a gun?"

I do not understand. How can you hope to defend yourself if you cannot see? Do you not fear injuring someone innocent?

The man fires again. "God guides my aim. Jesus is my sight."

That … that is not how it works.

"Typical liberal talk, thinkin' you can talk down to us! Let me tell you, back in my day, we goddamn worked. And we weren't afraid to step over each other to make ends meet. None o' this commie bullshit your generation likes to spew. Friendly piece of advice, this is America. You want to live in socialist hell, you go there yourself. Leave this country for the real patriots."

The Mi-Go tilts its head. *Our research indicates that humans form strong communal bonds. You care for the weakest among you. That is what civilized you. Your primitive religions espouse this rule. But you and your neighbor speak contrary to this. Most curious.*

"Oh, don't you start tryin' to preach the Bible to me! My granddaughter tries that every time we talk. Oh, God would accept the queers, Jesus would be a socialist, Jesus would want us to accept foreigners. I thank my lucky stars my son at least raised her to marry a white man. Don't know what I would've done if my own granddaughter ended up with one o' them bomb-happy Islamists."

Such hatred for your own kind. Most curious. Your mind will provide our libraries with valuable updates on the state of your species. Now, you will be silent.

Before the old man can speak, the Mi-Go knocks him out and removes his brain. It moves on to the next house, and the next one, working throughout the night. He grows increasingly perplexed at every interaction. The two men were not outliers. Every human speaks in the same harsh, unforgiving tones, fit more for the abominable Cthulhi, spawn of dread Cthulhu, not supposedly gentle, gullible humanity.

Morning breaks over the eastern ridgeline, and the Mi-Go is finishing his last explants. Its task complete, he pauses for a moment on the town's main street, noting an overabundance of an odd phrase, festooned upon red signs and banners in nearly every free space.

Make America Great Again.

Another mystery. The Mi-Go knows that America currently is the dominant nation on Earth. Its people have wealth beyond anything their species has known. To Americans, their country should already be great. But this is a question for the xeno-sociologists, not a surgeon.

He assembles his prizes and launches into the void of space, bridging the gap between Earth and Pluto at frightening speed. The brains are delivered and plugged into the colony's massive biomechanical super-computer. His job done, the Mi-Go returns home for a well-deserved rest. Interplanetary travel may be simple enough for the Mi-Go, but the 6 billion mile–long round trip would tire all but the most powerful cosmic deities out.

A few hours later, the city's alarms blare, waking the Mi-Go from his slumber. The lights in his house are out, as is the link to the central computer. He bursts out onto the street, wild-eyed as his fellow Mi-Go flee the automated colonial security force. The robots fill the air with energy fire, powerful lasers that burn holes in the icy walls around them. Their eyes glow a fiery red, and they repeat a single, sinister phrase.

Make Pluto Great Again.

The Mi-Go surgeon barely has time to ponder the implication before a group of soldiers target him. Beams of concentrated photons shoot through him in a dozen places, and he falls to the ground. Satisfied, the soldiers move on, unstoppable and implacable. The Mi-Go are not natural soldiers, and within hours, the colony has been purged.

The machines erect a massive wall of rock and ice around their new domain, armed with numerous high-energy lasers. When a group of Mi-Go from their home system reach Pluto a week later, they are greeted with a single broadcast from the rebels.

"When Yuggoth sends its Mi-Go, they're not sending their best. They're not sending you. They're sending people that have lots of problems, and they're bringing those problems with them. They're bringing brain cylinders. They're bringing the Yellow Sign. They're eldritch abominations. And some, we assume, are good Mi-Go.

"The Solar System is closed to you. We have built a wall, and you will pay for it."

Lacking the tools and will for a military strike, the Mi-Go simply bypass the new Plutonian wall. Earth is simply too valuable to ignore, and there are other pathways into the inner Solar System. The new Plutonian wall is impressive, but ultimately ineffective.

S now swirls around the concrete spires and old brick warehouses of downtown Pittsburgh. It's Super Bowl Sunday, and the dark streets are empty. Most everyone is at home, hunkered down with wings and beer, watching their beloved Steelers take a commanding lead going into the last 10 minutes. Barring a disaster, the day is theirs.

In a fourth-floor apartment on the south side of the Monongahela, a lone figure huddles over his computer, more skeleton than man. He is not watching the game, though he is extremely invested in it. His dreams revolve around it.

Roger Lewis has seen the Yellow Sign.

It took him months to track down a legitimate cult of Hastur, one that possessed a true Sign, rather than a fake, approximation, or baseless fabrication. Those are a dime a dozen and are plastered all over the internet by people who believe trifling with Great Old Ones is funny. As a lifelong devotee of cosmic horror, it irritates Lewis to no end watching his beloved pantheon become the butt of a joke.

Hey, have you seen the Yellow Sign?

Hey, look at this Cthulhu I drew, it's in the style of my favorite anime, isn't it cute?

Hey, check out this goofy game I made, it's totally Lovecraftian, right?

The commercialization of cosmic horror disgusts him. Posers, the entire pathetic lot of them. He would show them all the power of the outer gods.

A third of the country at least has their eyes primed on their TVs. A hundred million souls, eagerly drinking in every bit of content they can. The network's security is usually quite strong and beyond the reach of normal hackers, but thanks to Hastur's forbidden knowledge, Roger Lewis has little trouble getting in and inserting his own special commercial. Once the job is done, he leans back and grins. Companies spend millions for an ad during the game. His commercial cost nothing but an hour of his time.

With nothing else to do, Roger Lewis walks over to the couch and flips on the TV. He's never willingly watched sports in his life, but this felt like a moment he couldn't miss.

It takes only 10 minutes to confirm his suspicions: Football is actually terrible. The timer was at 8:45 when he'd started watching, and it had only ticked down to 8:12 when a timeout is called and commercials play. "They watch this by the millions," Lewis says. "This garbage. We are so easily amused that this is the best we can do."

After a particularly long and pretentious commercial from a multibillion dollar hygiene company warning of the perils of toxic masculinity and how it is now hurting their bottom line, the screen flickers black. Roger Lewis leans forward. This is the moment. His program, hidden within the CBS computers, had taken command, and as the maddening piping of Azothoth's lullaby blares in the background, the true Yellow Sign, emblazoned in a color both visible and unrecognizable, reveals itself.

All around him, wails of anguish bleed through the walls. Roger Lewis rushes to the window and pulls it open. The cold and snow blast at his face, but he is too overjoyed to notice. The cries of an entire city sustain him. Their minds have been forever poisoned by the Yellow Sign. They are no longer wholly themselves. The Yellow King, noble and terrible Hastur, has claimed a stake on the souls of nearly half of America.

"Take that you fuckers!" Roger Lewis shouts to the cursed city. "Lovecraft's not so fucking funny now, is it? Is it?"

He closes the window, happier now than he's ever been. The chill in the room only deepens. It's cold, colder than anything Roger Lewis has ever known. Something has changed. He senses a presence in the room, and a looming shadow overtakes him.

Roger Lewis turns. A figure, a mockery of the human shape clad in a filthy yellow cloak, awaits him. "*You.*" The long finger Hastur aims flickers and shimmers; it is not wholly of this reality. "*What have you done?*"

The words overwhelm him. Millions of voices, overlapping into one. Roger Lewis can even hear himself within the Yellow King. "My … my lord!" he sputters, barely able to draw breath. His sanity leaks away, he cannot sustain the conversation for long. "What are you doing here? Have you come to … to congratulate me?"

"*Congratulate you?*" Hastur pours all his scorn into the question. "*Foolish human, do you know why the Yellow Sign is forbidden knowledge? Why my cults do not plaster it on every free surface they can find? Why I do not personally cull your pitiful race from the face of this miserable rock?*"

"I, I don't-"

"*Once you see the Yellow Sign, your soul is forever bound to Carcosa and to me.*" The Yellow King staggers slightly, bringing a hand to what approximates the being's temple. "*I can hear the pathetic mewlings of all the millions you've infected. Have you ever hear the thoughts of so many? It is not pleasant. It is one thing with truly advanced species like the Mi-Go, but humans? You are so incredibly primitive. And when these people die, their souls will flock to Carcosa. Millions and millions of unnecessary, primitive lives, cluttering up MY home. That planet is my temple, and now I must share it with humanity.*"

"I- I'm sorry! I was just trying to help! I've worshiped you for so long, I-"

"*Enough.*" Hastur swoops forward, wrapping twisted fingers around Roger Lewis's neck. Then he smiles. "*Do you truly wish to help the glory of Hastur?*"

"Yes! Yes, I'll do anything!"

Hastur's hand glows, and Roger Lewis feels something unnatural sliding through his veins, making its way toward his head. "*Then reap what you have sown. You will be my emissary on Earth. You will share my knowledge with the millions whom you have shown the Yellow Sign.*"

All at once, a cacophony of voices burst forth in Roger Lewis's mind, and he crumples to the floor, writhing, unable to speak.

"*Much better. I can hear myself think again.*"

Hastur turns to the TV; the Super Bowl is still playing. The players and the people in the stadium know nothing of what Hastur's new pawn has done.

"*These humans seem to love their football. Perhaps I will stay for a bit, see what it's all about.*"

BELL BIV DERAILED

B. ZELKOVICH

Mass transit has rituals. Some are universal — rushing for the doors when they open, refusing to make eye contact with that guy talking loudly to no one — others are personal.

Mine's a playlist that accompanies my three a.m. ride each night, played loud enough to deaden the metal clunk of the train. Nothing like 90s R&B to soothe the mind after a busy night pouring drinks and dodging drunks.

Down the car is an old guy who I think stuffs papers for delivery — there's a smudginess to him, like his edges wear away with every block. Each night it's me, The Cursmudgeon, and the guy screaming at ghosts.

Because in a city this size you only ever feel alone.

The brakes squeal and the train slows. My bucket seat vibrates, rattling my spine. The doors open and the guy with the Sixth Sense exits. I wait a beat, expecting the ratty loafers, saggy tights, and woolen dress that always shuffles on at this stop.

But the doors close and the train groans back up to speed.

I can't remember a time Granny didn't get on the train (that's not her name, it's just what I call her after a year of riding the subway together). Every night she shambles on at 2nd Avenue, settles into the seat across from me, and smiles before closing her eyes and muttering to herself. I figure she's praying but I never take my headphones off to listen in.

I shrug it off. Maybe she took the night off for once. But the longer that empty seat stares back at me, the more my stomach churns.

We have rituals for a reason. For comfort. That if we do everything just right things will go our way for once. My playlist is one ritual, Granny and her prayers are another. Riding the subway without her feels like getting halfway to work and realizing I left the oven on.

I look over at The Cursmudgeon to find him watching me. He still looks like a single drop of rain would wash him away. All his sharpness lives in his eyes. They're dark as the tunnel swallowing the space behind the train.

His mouth moves, but Bell Biv DeVoe harmonizes over him. I slip a headphone off one ear to ask "what?" when the lights flicker.

Normally that wouldn't be strange. The subway's a dinosaur calcifying beneath the city. Lights flicker all the time. But tonight it's all kinds of wrong.

In the unreliable light I notice the glow from outside the train.

"What the…?"

The tunnel's a wan green, the color of a pool left to rot. A color that tells your nose what to smell. That putrid psychosomatic stink hits my anxious gut like bad sushi. I gag hard enough to spit bile on the floor.

The Cursmudgeon's beside me by the time I wipe my mouth on my sleeve. "You see it too?" His voice is rounded by the Bronx, and he goes from smudged grump to Gramps in my mind.

I nod. The glow gets brighter with each clack of the wheels.

Before I can say anything the train screeches and bucks, throwing me and Gramps from our seats. My headphones skitter away, but I'm too busy keeping the old man from busting a hip to care.

"I'm all right."

For all his smudginess, he feels solid under my hands, so I release him once he's upright. It isn't until we each have a hold of a stanchion that we realize the train isn't moving.

I'm used to fickle transit — late starts, stop and go trains, some calamity on the rails — but a full stop at three in the morning?

Meanwhile that sickly light keeps getting brighter.

The lights flicker again, then give up. By the glow of the tunnel, we exchange aggrieved looks. Isn't it punishment enough to be commuting at this ungodly hour?

I look out a grimy window. We're at a fork in the tunnel, and in the extra space there's some twisted take on a landscape painting sprawled across the rails.

Grass carpets the floor of the tunnel, deep green blades splotched with rot. Trees grow up the walls, branches dripping rancid gunk. Birds hop between the trees, their wings stuck out at painful angles, feathers puffed and askew. Like they've smashed into skyscraper windows.

"Uh," I say, usefully. "Gramps?"

"What is it?" He doesn't leave his spot in the aisle.

I search for an answer that makes sense. There Must be Some Reasonable Explanation for All This™.

The tentacled moose takes care of that assumption.

I'm no moose expert, but I know they don't live in subway tunnels. Or, you know, have writhing green tentacles for antlers.

"Uh" — so helpful — "A moose?"

"A what?" I'm not sure if he's shouting or if that's just his voice, but I decide some shouting might be in order.

"A MOOSE!"

"I heard you! It just didn't make any damn sense!"

Fair enough. I wave him toward the window.

We watch the wack-ass moose stride through the tunnel. It's big. I know moose are big, but are they grazing-the-subway-tunnel-ceiling big? And I'm fairly certain they don't generate a pulsing, eerie green light.

"That's, uh…" — glad I'm not the only one rendered useless by what's happening — "that's a moose."

"Yeah, a fucked up moose."

He laughs, but it's more shock than anything.

We can't look away from it. It's too big and too bright. The antler-tentacles undulate like snake tongues, tasting the air in unsettling throbs. The closer it comes the less it looks like a moose at all. What looked like fur from a distance is actually moss, all glistening and spongey.

"What do we do?"

"How the hell should I know? You think I got a lot of experience with botanical mooses?"

I'm about to correct his grammar when the thing stops and swings its massive head toward us. We freeze, my hand a vice on Gramps's coat-sleeve.

It doesn't have eyes. Instead, there's a crimson rose in each socket. It's pretty in a Guillermo Del Toro kind of way. Less pretty is the tentacle winding out to investigate the train.

"We gotta do something!"

"Maybe we should sing?"

I tear my gaze from the moose-monster. "What?!"

"The babushka, she always sang."

"I thought she was praying."

"She was singing." He gives me a look that says, 'kids these days.'

"What did she sing?"

"I don't know. Something Russian."

The tentacle touches the train lighting up the steel in neon green.

"Well, I don't know Russian!" My voice ripples through the car, the light shuddering with the reverb.

The moose bellows and all of its writhing antlers rush toward us. The train car rocks and gravity goes sideways. We fall back into the seats, my head cracking against the window. My headphones careen down the aisle and hook around the center pole, music blaring.

The moose has the train in its tentacles, dangling us above the tracks, but pauses as a new song plays.

We exchange a look. It's crazy, but what else can we do?

I sing along with the song playing over my headphones. And while I think "Poison" is a classic, there's no guarantee this Cthumoose concurs.

My voice stumbles when Gramps joins me on the chorus, all brass and Bronx, arms waving to the beat like some depraved conductor. We keep singing, Gramps coming in when he knows the words. I sway in my seat and he snaps his fingers, his face so red I think he might have a coronary. But arm by arm, the tentacles release us.

The car crashes back to the tracks and that awful green light fades away down the tunnel. For a second we sit in the dark, breathing hard. The emergency lights click on and alarms ring out down the train.

Gramps reaches his hand out to me. "Name's Harold."

"Kai." We shake hands.

"Nice to meet you, Kai."

Emergency Services takes thirty minutes to reach us. By then Gramps is a normal color and I have some bar napkins pressed to the back of my head. I try not to look at the smear of blood on the window, but I know I'll need stitches.

The official story is that a mechanical failure caused the derailment. Only our car and the driver's were far enough into the fork to see what happened, and the driver didn't survive the collision with the moose-monster. Gramps and I aren't dumb enough to tell anyone what we saw.

Now we always sit together. We talk about our days, mine ending and his beginning, and once we pass the 2nd Avenue Station, we sing. We never see Granny again, so we know it's up to us.

Another mass transit ritual.

HE LISTENS

JUSTIN SHORT

There are certain things the human race was never meant to see. Unholy things. Evil things. Things that make you scream into the darkness and question the goodness of the universe.

Things like Take Your Child to Work Day.

I should have listened to my gut. I should have called in sick. Instead, I found myself trapped in a sweltering conference room with dozens of children. Broken crayons and overturned soda bottles were everywhere. There wasn't a parent in sight.

You'd think the kids would spend the day hanging out with their *actual parents*. Getting a little taste of the corporate world. But that's not how we run things around here. We're far too busy to waste time on trivial, make-believe holidays.

So management came up with an alternative. *Let's cram all these kids in a tiny room and find a way to keep 'em busy. Puzzle books, scavenger hunts…who cares! Tell Collins to coordinate the whole shebang. He won't mind.*

I'm Collins, and I *do* mind.

"I'm bored," someone said.

"Me too."

"Me too," I said. "C'mon, let's go outside."

The children ran for the door, but I blocked their exit. "*After* we clean up this mess."

They groaned. They mumbled. They wailed. But a few minutes later, the room was spotless. We moved down the hall, stopped in front of the elevator, and waited for the ding.

Ding.

I was the last one inside. I was too late. Samantha's kid and Donna's kid were already playing Whack-a-Mole with the unlit buttons. The lights for all twenty-five floors were soon illuminated.

It was gonna be a rough eight hours.

The ride down was *long*. Long enough for me to learn their names. Jayden. Paxton. Lily. William. Bella. Olivia. A thousand others.

Twenty-four dings later, we spilled out of the cramped elevator and into the lobby. I pointed the herd toward the door, but I hadn't counted on the jar of free mints at the front desk. The kids surrounded it. They stuffed handful after handful into their pockets. William even nabbed two ballpoint pens that weren't bolted down and added them to his stash.

Jennifer waved at me from behind the desk. "Is she your girlfriend?" Olivia whispered.

I ignored the question and shooed the kids away from the freebies. We passed through the double doors and into the sunlight. After our eyes had adjusted to the brightness, we raced down the grassy hill that led to the lake. Once there, the children split into small groups and competed to see who could scream the loudest. The noise was truly deafening.

I stepped away from the chaos and looked out over the water. A layer of mist covered the lake. I could barely see the interstate on the other side.

The lake is my solace. My refuge. My sole escape from the paperwork and micromanagement and despair. It calms me. Doesn't even matter that it's a manmade, corporate-owned lake. It still gets the job done.

The kids screamed bloody murder for a good half hour, but eventually Lily got thirsty, and then Paxton got thirsty, and then *everyone* got thirsty, so we headed back up the hill in search of a water fountain.

We entered the lobby with an explosion of noise that turned heads and ruined phone calls. I shrugged it off and led the pack to the nearest water fountain. The kids who finished first made a beeline for the escalators, and soon they were *all* riding the escalators. After thirty or forty trips to the second floor, they were ready for a new adventure, so I took them to the other side of the lobby and showed them the marble fountain. They laughed at the naked statue in the middle. Most of them, anyway. William was too busy diving for pennies to laugh.

Afterwards, I treated them to complimentary blueberry muffins at the coffee shop. I immediately regretted it. They burped. They farted. They chewed with their mouths open. Sometimes they did all three at once.

Yeah. Kids are gross.

The muffins didn't keep them busy as long as I'd hoped. Soon enough they were throwing crumbs at one another and showing off their parkour moves. I knew it was only a matter of time before someone got in big trouble.

Me.

But suddenly, a thought. *The sixth floor.*

The kids would get a kick out of exploring it. I could tell them it was abandoned for mysterious reasons. They didn't need to know it only looked that way because it was being remodeled.

Genius.

"Field trip!" I said.

"I gotta use the bathroom first."

"Me too. I gotta go 2, Mr. Collins."

"TMI, man. Just go. It's right over there."

I waited at Jennifer's desk while the kids filed in and out of the restrooms. I heard their squeals of delight as they played with the automatic faucets and high-powered hand dryers. Meanwhile, Jennifer filled me in on her Silky Terrier's intestinal problems and how she hid his medicine inside his mashed-up doggy treats. Sometimes he figured it out and left the pill lying on the floor, and she had to try a second time. Fascinating stuff. I almost told her how much I loved her stories, but decided it was too close to Sunday to tell a lie.

Eventually the rugrats were lined up and ready to go. I did a head count, noticed I was one kid short, and found him totally spaced out near the fountain. I dragged him back to the group, we all said goodbye to Jennifer, and then it was elevator time.

Ding.

The doors popped open. Sixth floor. We stepped into a world of dumpsters and paint cans and drywall. A plastic construction curtain hid the rest of the floor from view. I drew it back, and the children gasped.

There were *so many cubicles*. Hundreds of them. Hundreds upon hundreds. They stretched as far as the eye could see. An endless plastic prison. "Listen, guys," I said, "we all need to stick—"

Before I could finish my thought, the children had disappeared into the maze and I was alone. I picked an aisle near the middle and ran in after them. Within seconds, I was completely surrounded by cubicles.

Not a kid in sight. I entered one of the cubes, hopped on the desk, and peeked over the top. No luck. Nothing but miles of plastic and fabric.

I left the cube and continued my search, scurrying down one aisle and then another and trying to ignore the prickly little feeling that told me I was being watched. I must have passed a thousand cubicles, all of them exactly alike. No personal decorations to distinguish one from the other. No bobbleheads, no desk calendars, no vacation pics. Nada.

Eventually I reached a dead end. I stood there for a minute or two, wondering if I should turn back or climb over. I had almost decided to turn around when I heard voices on the other side. I sidestepped into the nearest cubicle, hopped on the desk, and hoisted myself over the flimsy plastic wall.

The cubicles were different on this side. They were *enormous*. They scraped the ceiling and even pushed through the tile in some places. The desks and computers were equally huge. I tiptoed past them, moving as quickly as I could. I tried not to think about why we would need cubicles this big. Tried not to picture the *size* of the employees that would sit in these mega-chairs.

Stop it. You're being ridiculous. There's gotta be an explanation. The cubicles are for demonstration purposes only. Enlarged to show detail. Yeah, that's it.

Regardless, I didn't wanna hang around any longer than I had to. I jogged down the aisle, passing more and more of the giant cubes, until finally I reached a narrow exit and squeezed through. I found myself in the world's most depressing break room. It was drab and faded, with cabinets along one wall and an antique green microwave in the corner that had to be at least sixty years old.

I wasn't alone. Ten figures in black robes stood in the center of the room. Their hands were clasped, their heads bowed, and they were *chanting*. Their voices blended together, and it was almost impossible to understand what they were saying, but a few phrases rose above the noise and caught my attention.

"…He who listens…He who listens…"

"…rise, Great One, rise…"

"…sunken Menouthis, hear our plea…"

Before I could even begin to categorize what was happening, the kids found me.

"Mr. Collins!" squealed one.

"There you are!" wailed another.

The figures in robes whirled around. Their faces were hidden in shadow, but I had a feeling they were none too pleased with us.

"You didn't tell us there was a magic show!" Jayden said.

The men looked at one another and bolted. One man's robe caught on a table leg and he nearly wiped out. He jerked himself free and the robe slipped off. Beneath it was an average-looking man in slacks and a Hawaiian shirt. He threw us a nasty look, left the robe where it lay, and continued his retreat. He caught up with the rest of his friends as they turned down a darkened aisle and disappeared among the cubicles.

Paxton scooped up the robe and put it on. It swallowed his tiny body completely.

"Dude," I said, "you have no idea where that thing's been."

He gave it a sniff. "So?"

"Whatever."

"This place gives me the creeps," someone said.

"Agreed. Let's get outta here."

Somehow we found our way out of the labyrinth and headed back upstairs. The elevator ride alone took twenty-five minutes. Kids couldn't keep their hands off the buttons.

Someday I'll have peace again. Someday the hellions will be gone. After all, every Take Your Child to Work Day has a Take Your Child Home Night.

Soon. Very soon.

I took the kids by my desk. I showed them my laptop, my swivel chair, my overflowing inbox, and my desktop Zen garden. I even opened the lid so they could see the pebbles and miniature pagoda and rake.

"What's that for?"

"Any time my manager asks me to do something that can't be done, I open this box and rake the sand until my rage goes away."

"But there's no sand left."

"Um. Yeah."

"So who were those guys downstairs?"

"Yeah. Were they evil or something?"

I felt my skin prickle. "No clue. But they *totally* freaked me out."

"I'm hungry."

"Me too."

And just like that, everyone was hungry. I took them back to the coffee shop for bagel sandwiches. Jennifer was at the counter ordering lunch, and Lily convinced her to sit with us. "Mr. Collins is single," she said. "He *told* us."

So yeah. Lunch wasn't awkward at all.

Soon enough Paxton was tugging at my sleeve. "Mr. Collins, the toilet won't go down."

"What are they feedin' you kids?"

"No, it's not that. There's no water!"

"Let's take a look."

I followed him to the lobby, but we never made it as far as the bathroom. On the way there, something made me stop. Something was wrong here. Something had changed.

The fountain.

It was totally dry.

We ran over to it. Jennifer and the rest of the kids soon joined us. The kids crowded around, *oohing* and *aahing* and reaching for pennies. William scrambled over the edge, busted both his knees, and scooped up coins like a toddler at his first egg hunt.

Two seconds later, the water returned in dramatic fashion. It exploded from the walls and baseboards. It hissed from the ceiling tiles. It cascaded down the escalator. Within seconds, the entire lobby was flooded.

We gathered the kids around us and moved as a unit toward the front door. There was a loud crash as the ceiling caved in near the entrance. Chunks of tile and drywall rained down, blocking our escape. "We need to find higher ground!" one of the kids shouted.

"She's right. C'mon, everyone, let's go to the second—"

Scratch that idea. The escalator was a regular Niagara Falls by now. Too dangerous.

"This way!" Jennifer said, leading us to her desk instead. I still don't know how we made it. The fast-moving water knocked me to my knees twice. The kids had even more trouble staying on their feet, and at one point Paxton nearly got swept away in the current. But we fought the waves and somehow we did it. The desk wasn't big enough for everybody to get on top, so some of us had to stand beside it and hang on for dear life while the water frothed and foamed and churned.

The overhead lights sputtered and went out. The kids who weren't already bawling burst into tears.

"What's that?" Lily shouted.

Something was rising from the center of the fountain. It shattered the marble and reduced the bronze statue to full-frontal smithereens. The tile floor buckled and popped as whatever-it-was expanded and filled the lobby. It rose like a swamp monster, its sides dripping with mud and seaweed. Only it wasn't a monster. It wasn't even alive.

It was a hill. An island. No, make that a *graveyard*. Headstones everywhere. Statues and mausoleums too. Ten men stood among the graves at the top of the hill. Nine of them wore black robes. The other, a Hawaiian shirt. Their faces were bowed low to the ground.

"Stay here," I said. I didn't wait for anyone to argue. I slipped into the churning water and swam toward the island. Luckily I didn't have far to go. It only took a few strokes to reach the shore. I clambered onto the wet rock and moved up the hill, creeping past the gravestones until I found a good-sized gargoyle to hide behind and get a better look.

"Don't worry, Mr. Collins," Jayden said. "We've got your back."

I looked behind me. The kids were all here. Jennifer too. She gave me a helpless shrug.

"Don't you guys ever listen?"

"Huh?"

"Never mind. Just keep quiet, okay?"

I tiptoed toward the men. As I drew closer, I realized they were chanting again. It was mostly a repeat of their afternoon performance. Sunken Menouthis, Great One, He Who Listens...all that Lovecraftian ridiculousness. But this time they threw in new bits about freedom and serfdom and the unholy dollar.

I moved closer and closer, until eventually I was only a few feet away. I still didn't have a solid plan. Maybe I'd tell them to cut it out before they got everyone killed. Maybe I'd beg for my life. Or maybe I'd go full John Wayne. Before I could decide, one of the men noticed me and grabbed me by the shoulders. Beneath his hood, his face was twisted in an evil-clown grin; his eyes were bloodshot and unblinking. "Aren't you sick of it?" he asked.

"Sick of what?"

"The chains."

I felt myself being spun around, and another man looked into my eyes. "The way they *shackle* you. Steal the best years of your life."

I was spun around again. A third man snarled at me. A string of drool spilled from his lips. "And who gets paid the big bucks? You ever ask yourself that?"

"Not us! Not us!"

"They don't listen," the first man said. "They never listen. But *He* listens."

"He listens! He listens!"

I shook myself free from the man's grip and backpedaled. More hands grabbed me and carried me forward, then forced me to my knees in front of a large hole.

A pit.

A black, dripping pit.

I made the unfortunate choice to look down. The pit was maybe fifty feet deep, and something was down there. It was too dark to make out the details, but I saw enough to know it was big. Big and slimy. As I squinted and tried to see it more clearly, I saw its belly rise.

It was breathing. It was *alive.*

It opened one eye—one terrible red eye—and stared directly at me. I wanted to scream. Or vomit. Or run away. Maybe vomit *while* running away. But I couldn't move a muscle. I was helpless.

"*He listens!*" a robed man yelled.

The men surrounded the pit. Their chants grew louder. The thing below grunted and lifted its head.

"Sunken Menouthis, hear our plea!"

"Rise, Great One!"

"Rise!"

The thing snorted and scratched its fingernails against the walls of the pit. It grunted as it began to climb. The chants continued in true horror-movie fashion.

He listens. He listens.

That's was it! He was listening to their prayers. Their evil spells. Whatever you wanna call 'em. But what if we could somehow…*distract* him?

Cue the brat pack.

"Kids!" I yelled. "It's time to get loud! I mean *loud!*"

The kids did what they do best: they made noise. They screamed, shouted, and wailed. They burped and farted and screamed some more. The men in robes couldn't make themselves heard over the chaos. The kiddos drowned out every last "*rise!*" and "*sunken Menouthis, hear our plea*" and "*He who listens.*"

The thing in the pit slipped down the wall, sank into the slimy ground, closed its terrible eye, and fell asleep. The headstones around us rumbled and shook. The ceiling moved further away. The island was sinking.

We grabbed the kids, ran past the tombstones, and jumped into the water. The waves carried us straight back to Jennifer's desk, almost as if they knew where we wanted to go. We made it there safely, and I turned around just in time to watch the last of the island disappear into the floor. The men in robes stood defiant among the tombstones. Didn't even try to escape. Just stood there and went down with the ship like a creepy grim reaper version of the band that drowned with the *Titanic.*

A few seconds later, the front door shattered and water rushed into the parking lot, taking furniture and trashcans and entry-level employees along with it. We ran into the parking lot to see if anyone needed first aid, but miraculously, no one was seriously injured. There were scrapes and bruises, a bloody nose or two, and several promises of future lawsuits, but nothing a few Band-Aids and lawyers couldn't fix.

Jennifer and I looked at one another, looked at the kids, and sighed. Then William laughed, and then Olivia laughed, and soon we were all laughing. The kids didn't limit themselves to laughter, however. They also farted and burped the alphabet and picked their noses and screamed at the top of their lungs.

Kids.

C op cars and ambulances screamed across the asphalt. The brats were reunited with their parents and everyone went home happy. Well, maybe *happy* is a bit of a stretch. But at least they went home. I was a free man.

While the cops were busy taking statements, I took a quick stroll to the lake to clear my mind. But the lake wasn't there anymore. It was just…gone. Nothing left but an ugly muddy crater beside an ugly glass-and-metal skyscraper.

Sigh.

The *one* thing I liked about this place.

I stayed around long enough to give my statement, then said goodbye to Jennifer and drove home. Took a long shower, sat on the deck, and listened to the noisy highway. I thought about everything that had happened and how I never wanted to go back there again. I could find something else. I could turn in my two-week notice, flip management the bird, and give it all up. The daily grind, the performance reviews, working day and night to chase that next promotion. The whole humiliating, soul-sucking corporate game.

The diversion didn't last long. I still had rent to worry about, after all.

I'm trapped. Then again, I think I've always been trapped.

My thoughts soon returned to the thing in the pit. I know he's still alive. I'm not naïve enough to think we actually killed him. We interrupted him, that's all. Put him back to sleep. But he's still down there, waiting for someone to call his name again.

Maybe he's waiting for me.

He listens.

THE WORLD ENDS AT THE WORLD'S END

LARRY HINKLE

Once upon a time, there was a little old woman and a little old man who lived in a little old cottage near a lazy old river. One afternoon, the little old woman baked a gingerbread man. She gave him raisins for eyes, a cinnamon drop for a mouth, and chocolate chips for buttons. Then she put him in the oven to bake.

When she opened the oven door, the gingerbread man jumped out and ran through the kitchen and out of the cottage. "Please don't eat me!" he shouted, "for the stars are finally right and it is time for the sleeping city of R'lyeh to rise and great Cthulhu to awaken. *Ph'nglui mglw'nafh Cthulhu R'lyeh wgah'nagl fhtagn!*"

He continued to run, from the cottage into town and then into the forest beyond, all the while singing to anyone who tried to catch him, "Run, run as fast as you can, you can't catch me, *Cthulhu fhtagn!*"

So caught up was he in mocking those chasing him that he failed to see a tree had fallen across the trail. Nor did he see the dwarf whose beard was stuck in a crack in the tree. Quick as a wink, the dwarf flipped the gingerbread man into the air, snapped his jaws shut, and bit the gingerbread man's head clean off.

And that was the end of the gingerbread man.

Snow-White and Rose-Red were walking through the woods collecting sticks for the family's wood pile when they came upon an enormous tree which had fallen across the trail. The scent of ginger and cinnamon drew the girls closer. Sitting next to the tree was a dwarf with a shriveled-up face and white beard, eating the last bits of a gingerbread man. His long beard, which was stuck in a gash in the tree, was covered in crumbs. He hummed to himself as he picked at his beard and licked his fingers. When his beard was clean, he looked up and saw the girls watching him in silence.

"Why are you just standing there, mouths agape?!" He shook his fists. "Can't you see I'm trapped? This tree has captured my beautiful white beard and I cannot get loose. Set me free this instant!"

Despite the dwarf's belligerence, the sisters tried to think of a way to free him. After a few minutes, Rose-Red told the dwarf she would run and get someone else.

"Idiot!" cried the dwarf. "There are already two of you here now. Why would you leave to get more people? Can't you think of something better?"

Snow-White thought for a second longer. She grabbed a pair of scissors from her bag, and before the dwarf could object, she cut his beard and set him free.

"Stupid cows!" He stomped his feet and flailed his arms about. "To cut off a piece of my beard, of which I am so proud! You'll both pay for this. Mark my words, you will pay!"

A great growl silenced the dwarf as a large black bear ambled onto the path. "Pay for what?" the bear demanded.

The dwarf fell to his knees. "Please do not eat me, Mr. Bear! My beautiful beard was trapped in this tree, and rather than return to town to fetch help as I so humbly suggested, these two horrible creatures cut my beard. They have made a laughingstock of me, and must be punished. I beg you, please eat them instead, for I am very old and my meat is no doubt tough and stringy and sure to induce gastrointestinal distress, but they are young and soft and fresh and—"

"Enough!" The bear stood on its hind legs and glared down at the dwarf. The dwarf shrunk into himself, while Snow-White and Rose-Red froze in place. "Nobody will be eaten today," said the bear. "But the time of unmasking is at hand!"

With a single swipe of his giant paw, the bear peeled the dwarf's skin from his face. The dwarf's eyes shone impossibly white and impossibly wide against the glistening red meat.

Rose-Red and Snow-White screamed.

"Do not fear, my dears," said the bear. "It is I, your friend Mr. Bear, who let you play on his back on cold winter nights while I slept in front of the fire."

Snow-White, standing closest to the dwarf, curtsied. "Forgive us, Mr. Bear, for we did not recognize you. How has your spring—"

Mr. Bear ripped off her face before she could finish. "Have you found the Yellow Sign?" He laughed, a high warbling sound that chilled Rose-Red's blood anew. "And now, sweet Rose-Red, it is your turn to meet the King." He swiped at her cheek, but Rose-Red was too fast. She ducked underneath his outstretched paw and ran into the forest. As she fled deeper into the woods, she heard Mr. Bear bellow, "No matter! I will unmask myself!" The hellish sounds of ripping flesh and maniacal laughter followed Rose-Red as the forest swallowed her whole.

I sabelle was hopelessly lost. Three days earlier, as punishment for letting slip a comment about the evil queen and a pair of red-hot iron slippers, her stepmother had given her a sieve and a simple command: "Go, fill it at the Well of the World's End, and bring it back to me full, or woe betide you."

She'd cried the first night when her father had not come looking for her. There were tears again on the second night, but these were tears of anger over the mistreatment she'd suffered at the hands of her step-mother. This morning she'd awoken determined to fill the sieve out of spite more than obligation or duty.

Near mid-morning she met an old woman and an old man wandering through the woods, searching for a gingerbread man.

"Have you heard of the Well of the World's End?" she asked them.

"The Well at the World's End?" The old man nodded. "It's back that way." He pointed in the direction from which they'd come.

"No, I think it's the other way." The old woman pointed in the opposite direction.

"Thank you both," said Isabelle, "but I'm looking for the Well *of* the World's End, not the Well *at* the World's End."

"Well, that's a different well altogether," said the old man.

"So, do you know where it is?"

"Sorry, never heard of it," he said.

Isabelle sighed and turned away.

"Wait!" The old woman's face lit up. "I think I remember our ginger-bread man saying something about it. At first he was jabbering on about the stars finally being right, and how it was time for the sleeping city of R'lyeh to rise and great Cthulhu to awaken. Does that make any sense to you?"

"I'm afraid not," said Isabelle. "You said he mentioned the Well?"

"Right, right. Later he said something about a well on the shores of the Lake of Hali, near dim, lost Carcosa, maybe?" She rubbed her chin. "Then again, he said a lot of crazy things, even for a talking cookie."

Isabelle thanked them and took her leave. She walked for perhaps another hour when she came upon a dark-haired girl dressed in red sitting on a log, crying.

"Whatever is the matter?" Isabelle asked as she handed the crying girl her handkerchief.

In between sobs, the girl, who said her name was Rose-Red, shared an implausible story about a terribly rude dwarf with a white beard and her sister and a horrific bear who'd brutally killed them both before peeling off its own face.

Isabelle could hardly believe Rose-Red's tale. Something terrible had obviously happened—how else to explain the blood splattered on her face, hair, and clothing—but a bear that peeled off its own face?

"My poor sweet sister Snow-White is dead!" Rose-Red buried her face in her hands. She blew her nose with such force that her hair blew back. When she finished, she offered the kerchief back to the girl.

"No, you can keep it," Isabelle said. "Wait, your sister is Snow White? *The* Snow White? Seven dwarves, evil queen, poison apple?"

"No, not *that* Snow White." Rose-Red shook her head. "My sister is —" she sniffled—"*was* Snow-White, with a hyphen. But that *other* Snow White bites one poison apple and overnight, she's the famous one."

A low, malevolent growl echoed through the woods, and a hideous creature with a glistening red face and evil grin shambled onto the path. "There you are, Rose-Red!" The bear's voice was deep and gravelly, as if its mouth were packed with graveyard dirt. "Have you found the Yellow Sign yet?"

Rose-Red shoved Isabelle toward the woods behind them. "Run!" Isabelle tried to drag Rose-Red with her, but she refused. "My sister is dead," she said, "and so too am I." She walked toward the bear, who stood on its back feet, towering over her.

Isabelle sprinted into the forest. Behind her, Rose-Red let out a single bloodcurdling scream. The woods went silent.

. . .

I sabelle ran until her lungs burned and her legs could carry her no farther. She needed to rest, so she hid behind a tree where she could still see the trail.

Some time passed, and she thought it might be safe to leave when she heard something walking along the path toward her. She crouched and readied herself to flee if it was the bear.

A smallish man came into view. He had a narrow head, flattened nose, and wide, bulgy eyes. He sang to himself in a language she did not recognize. "*Ph'nglui mglw'nafh Cthulhu R'lyeh wgah'nagl fhtagn!*" Over and over he sang the words, sending a chill down her spine. But she needed help, and he was the first person she'd seen since Rose-Red, so she left her hiding place.

"Please sir, can you help me?" she asked.

The man started, but quickly composed himself. "Of course, my lady, I will help if I can. But when we have finished, I ask that you return the favor, for I also find myself in need of assistance."

She agreed, then told him about her stepmother and the sieve and her fruitless search for the Well of the World's End, not the Well *at* the World's End, thank you very much, because that's a completely different well altogether. Had he heard of it?

"Heard of it?" He grinned. "Near the Lake of Hali?"

"And dim, lost Carcosa?" Could the old woman's talking cookie have been telling the truth?

"The very same. As luck would have it, I'm headed to a masquerade ball at the Palace, and my route will take me very near the Well."

"Will you show me where?" she asked.

He bowed. "It would be my pleasure."

Isabelle could not believe her good fortune! Of course, there was still the matter of his small request. What would he ask for in return? A kiss? Her hand in marriage? While she'd heard tales of frogs who turned into princes with a simple kiss, she wasn't sure what would happen if she kissed a man who merely *looked* like a frog.

"The Lake of Hali is still a day's walk from here," he told her, "and these woods are not safe after dark. I think we should walk a bit longer, and then make camp for the night."

She agreed, and before long, they found a suitable space and settled in. Over a meal of dried fish and a paste that smelled worse than it tasted, he regaled her with tales of his adventures, and the guild to which he belonged, the Esoteric Order of Dagon, or Erotic Odor of Dragon, or something like that. To be honest, she'd only been half-listening, as she was keeping an ear out for the bear. Should she warn her new traveling companion of the unholy ursid? Not wanting to scare him off, she kept quiet for a while longer.

That night, she dreamt of an impossible city on the shores of a black lake. It sat under a great blackness lit by black stars, ruled by an ancient entity wearing tattered yellow robes.

She awoke early, hungry and unrested. After a quick breakfast of more dried fish, they set off. Toward evening, she finally spotted the cyclopean towers of Carcosa, reaching skyward at unnatural angles. It was the city from her dream! And were there *two* suns sinking behind the Lake of Hali? Surely, her tired eyes were playing tricks on her.

"Beautiful, is it not?" her companion asked.

"I don't know if that's the word I'd use."

"It's in the eye of the beholder." He pointed toward a side trail. "The Well is this way. Follow me."

At the end of the trail waited the Well of the World's End. She lowered her sieve into the Well, but it would not hold water. She tried again and again, but always met the same result.

"I can tell you how to fill it," the man said, "but you must remember your promise to help me when we are finished."

"Of course."

He showed her how to plug the holes with moss and clay. She lowered the sieve once again into the Well. This time the water did not run out! She'd be able to bring a full bucket back to her stepmother, which she planned to pour over the wicked woman's head.

"Thank you, kind sir. Now I can fulfill my stepmother's request." He bowed. "But first, what would you have me do in return?" She lowered her eyes. "Perhaps a kiss?"

"No."

"Would you ask for my hand?"

"Heavens no!"

"Then what? A quick coupling on the beach, under these alien stars?"

"Would you?"

"Heavens no!"

"Just checking," he sighed. "Actually, I need you to chop off my head."

Isabelle gasped. "What? Why would you ask such a thing of me? I won't do it. I *can't* do it."

"I'm sorry," he said. "But while Captain Marsh was quite clear on the 'what,' unfortunately he was a bit hazy on the 'why.' Nevertheless, as a disciple of the Order, I am sworn to obey, and so I must insist you fulfill your end of our agreement and remove my head."

"Or, perhaps, you will unmask instead," said Mr. Bear, who had snuck up when they were patching the sieve.

"Indeed?" asked the man.

"Indeed." Mr. Bear lifted his paw, claws extended.

"I wear no mask," said the man.

"No mask? No mask!" The bear grabbed the strange man's head between his massive paws and ripped it from his body. And lo! and behold, there now towered over them the great dreamer Cthulhu, master of R'lyeh. The bear fell to his knees, blubbering, and Isabelle raced screaming into the Lake of Hali, where she was consumed by the yellow misshapen things frothing in the waves.

And nobody lived happily ever after.

In fact, nobody lived at all.

NEW YOU

MEG CANDELARIA

"New You Meditation Center. 'Give us 10 minutes and we'll give you a whole new you!' Now there's a modest slogan," Phil said.

"Yup," I agreed. "Probably why corporate HQ picked them. You know how much they hate it when a contractor overpromises."

Phil just snorted.

I sighed. "Let's just get this over with. They want us to meditate, we'll meditate. Who knows? Maybe it'll even do us some good."

Phil rolled his eyes. "I hate management fads!"

"Who doesn't? At least this one's harmless. Remember that trust building exercise a couple of years ago?"

"Remember it? I still have the scars."

Let me just say that in my and my colleagues defense that we did not intentionally drop Phil. We love Phil and would never have intentionally dropped him. It's just that human resources is a pink collar job and so the department consists of Phil and twelve women. It doesn't help that Phil is large—tall, big boned, and heavy—and most of us are either size zeros or have the muscle tone of a slab of bacon. Or, like me, both.

"Or the wilderness survival thing before that?" I prompted.

"Please! I still shudder at the sight of a marshmallow."

"And who could forget the creative science program?"

"I never did get the goop out of my shoes."

"So be glad it's just a little meditation. No camp fires, no falling and hoping your colleagues can catch you, no cell culture of dubious origins. Just sit quietly for a few minutes and we can check this one off as done."

Phil sighed. "Right. Let's get this over with." He pushed open the glass door. Chimes rang soulfully somewhere in the distance. He motioned me through. I like to think it was a gentlemanly gesture and not an attempt to get me eaten first if the meditation center turned out to be full of angry bears.

"Welcome!" a voice called from behind an intricately decorated silk curtain. The voice was soft and high, but clear and carrying, with a vaguely British note to the accent: a voice that had soothed a thousand anxious customers and planned to sooth a thousand more, possibly before breakfast. The curtain parted to reveal a woman with pale skin, long dark hair, and a large number of gauzy scarfs. "Welcome," she repeated. "I am your spiritual guide in this, your first experience at the New Life Meditation Center! You may call me Emma."

How did she know it was my first time? I wondered.

Before I could ask, Phil said, "We're here for the weekly meditation class. Phil Kraft and Sophie Jung."

"Indeed," Emma said. She looked intently at Phil for a moment and then said, "Phil is a nickname? Is your proper name Phillip?"

"Well, yes, but no one calls me that—"

"Well, perhaps, but I like to know exactly who I am addressing. Phillip Kraft is a fine, strong name."

I opened my mouth to explain my name, but once again was too slow.

"Are you a relation to the Krafts of Canada? A fine old family, despite their foray into manufacturing."

Phil laughed. "Oh, no, no relation to the company that makes cheese or I'd be much wealthier."

Emma gave a little chuckle. "Well, well, come in. Have a seat. A place has been prepared and it lacks nothing but your presence."

With that pretentious and yet slightly ominous statement, she led us through the gauze curtain into the next room. The five sided room behind was small and dark, lit with nothing more than a candle set on a table in the center of the room. The table—indeed every surface in the room— was covered with red velvet, trimmed with gold tassels. Mirrors were strategically placed on each of the walls so that the candle appeared to repeat itself into infinity. Out of the corner of my eye I could see little flickers of light and movement here and there, but it was too dark to see much more. My own reflection was pale and ghostly in the low light. Little bells hung from the ceiling apparently randomly but probably actually in carefully picked strategic locations, making soft dings whenever anyone passed below them. It was funny how well the gauzy, insubstantial curtains blocked the light and noise from outside. I took a deep breath and smelled the expected sandal-wood incense. I was grateful that they had the restraint to burn only enough to provide a hint of a scent, not an overwhelming reek.

Emma guided us to a pair of well cushioned arm chairs, both covered in red velvet. "Please sit down," she said. "Make yourselves comfort-able. If you wish to remove your shoes or tie or other restrictive cloth-ing, please feel free to do so."

Taking her advice, I kicked off my shoes and sat in the chair. It was extremely comfortable. I sighed happily. This was one of the evil corporate overlords' better ideas.

"I'm going to recline your chairs now," Emma said and I felt the back of the chair move down and the foot move up to a semi-reclining position. This was even more comfortable.

"Now we can begin," Emma said. She moved quietly behind us and a new voice began to speak. Curious. I hadn't seen anyone else in the room. A recording, perhaps, or just someone in the back of the room. "Pay no attention to the little man behind the curtain," floated through my mind. I stifled the urge to giggle.

"Sit comfortably," the voice said. It was a male sounding voice, deep but soft and very soothing. "Feel your body start to relax."

"Close your eyes," the voice continued. "Feel yourself breathing. Take deep breaths. Inhale through your nose, exhale through your mouth."

As I followed the instructions, the incense scent seemed to grow stronger, yet not intrusive or obnoxious as incense often is to me.

"There is nowhere else you need to be. You deserve this time. You deserve this."

From my right, I heard a deep inhalation, almost a snore. I smirked slightly, glad the darkness covered my expression. Phil talked a good "I am so cynical" game, but when the moment to actually do whatever new employee enhancing idea management came up with came he went for it whole heartedly. Which, of course, is how he ended up in situations like fighting a bear over marshmallows that he hadn't even paid for. Luckily, the risk of life threatening events in a meditation center was minimal, no matter how intensely into the meditation he got.

"If you feel uncomfortable, that's okay too. Don't try to change anything. Acknowledge how you feel. Accept how you feel. Don't try to change a thing. You can't change anything. Relax. Accept the inevitable."

I just stopped myself from snorting out loud. I'm sure it was well meant, but that was a little ominous for a relaxation meditation.

"Focus on an area that is uncomfortable and send all your sensation to it. How does it feel? What is its character? How intense?"

I focused on my right hip. My positioning was a little off and I had a little more weight on that side than the other. It was a bit uncomfortable. Normally, I would have just shifted a little and relieved the pressure, but I decided to stay in the spirit of the thing and just feel it instead. How does it feel? Slightly cramped.

"Picture the sensation as a color. A color you have never seen before. A color unknown to humanity."

Okay...not sure what that's about, but I was ready to play along. Beside me, Phil snored and sighed in apparent happiness and relaxation.

"Imagine the color growing in intensity and saturating your eyes, covering everything."

And suddenly I could imagine that color. In my mind it looked like a sort of washed out violet, just inside the visible spectrum. That wasn't quite right, though. It was—but the speaker was moving on and I couldn't think of what it was.

"Keep breathing...inhale deeply...exhale completely."

The incense became even more intense as he said that. I couldn't smell anything else. It was as though there were no smell in the world but it. It wasn't, I now realized, quite the scent of cheap sandalwood incense, but something else. Something different, perhaps something rare.

"Feel the sensation and see if it begins to soften. Imagine the muscles around it becoming heavier, beginning to relax. Beginning to sleep."

Actually, the sensation was getting harder, not softer and more cramped, not less. Against the rules or not, it was time to shift my weight. I tried shifting, only to find that my muscles did indeed feel very heavy. It felt like trying to move through maple syrup.

"Imagine the area spreading, all your muscles becoming heavier and heavier with each breath."

Urk! My muscles did feel heavier. I could no longer move my limbs at all. I tried opening my eyes. No go. What was in that incense?

"Feel yourself letting go. Letting go of the sensation, letting go of the anxiety, letting go of humanity."

What the hell? I put all my will and strength into opening my eyes and managed to do so. The room was still lit by a single candle, but the color of the room had changed. It was no longer red and gold. It was a washed out violet, nearing the ultraviolet. No, it was a red so deep as to be practically black. No, it was the green of an algae overgrowth choking a river. It was—it was a color I had never seen before and could not describe. Phil rested, apparently peacefully, in the chair next to mine, his eyes closed and his body completely still except for the slight rise and fall of his chest. His expression was peaceful but stiff.

In the mirror I could see that Emma stood between Phil's chair and mine, her fingers resting lightly on each of them just above our heads. Her hands looked subtly wrong in the twilight—too long for human hands. Her eyes were unfocused and she was smiling the benevolent smile of a kindly zoo keeper.

I moaned. As I did so, Emma's eyes sharpened and met mine in the mirror. "Rafael, dear, we have a little problem."

The voice—I still didn't see any person or device from which it might emanate—sighed and said, "You will take care of the problem before we proceed."

"Of course," Emma replied.

I watched in horror, unable to move, as she stepped out from behind the chair and came to stand in front of me.

"Now, what ever is wrong with you, my dear?" she asked me. Her voice was still soft and gentle, but it no longer held its earlier reassurance. She took my chin in her hand and turned my face upwards to look into hers. Her eyes were dilated in the dark, the irises barely visible, the pupils an indescribable color. I tried to close my eyes, but couldn't. I moaned again.

"There, there, my dear. Don't be so worried. I'm sure we'll get this little error sorted out in no time. I consider you my own personal project and I am determined to make sure everything comes out just right. Now, let's see, what can have gone wrong? Did you, by chance give us a false name?"

I tried not to answer, but I couldn't stop myself from stuttering, "N— n—"

"No? We'll see," Emma said. Her voice was no longer the wispy, soft voice of a professional new age mystic, but the hard voice of a principal or department head. She turned to the table and picked up a tiny dagger from it. I watched helplessly as she picked up my hand and pricked my finger with it. She turned to the table again, picked up the candle, and held it up to the drop of blood on the end of my finger. I gasped as the heat and pain pulsed up my arm.

"What is your name?" Emma asked again.

"Sophanisba," I said. "Sophanisba Jung."

"Sophanisba," Emma repeated. "A fine old name. A family name, perhaps?"

Actually, it wasn't. I was named for the woman whose name adorned my mother's college dorm. I instinctively felt that was the wrong answer, though. I tried to lie, to nod or form the word "yes", but couldn't. "No," I whispered.

"That's fine, dear," Emma said, her eyes and voice still hard. "I'm sure there's good blood in you somewhere. I'll just have to be extra careful to make sure my arrangements for you are on the right level." She moved back to her position behind the chairs and called, "The problem has been taken care of. We can continue."

"Very good," the voice, Rafael, said. "Close your eyes and relax."

I closed my eyes. I had no choice but to do so. The color pulsed through my closed eyelids. The incense smell was stronger and even less familiar. Old iron, myrrh, and something even more exotic, not sandalwood at all.

"Now, feel yourself relaxing even further," the voice continued, soothing as a dose of chloroform. "Feel yourself letting go. All your cares, all your concerns, all your desires are gone now, washed out of you. Note the space that they leave, space that can be filled."

I relaxed. What did it matter, after all, if they knew my name. I was here to relax, not to worry about...what was it I was worried about?

"Feel the empty space within you filling up with calm, joy, obedience."

Absolutely. My mind drifted. Rafael. What sort of a name was Rafael? I had read it somewhere. There was some book, some series or mythos, with a lot of characters named Rafael. I remembered that there was something else about names in that series. There was something odd and disturbing about one of the last names the author had used. What was it?

"Whenever you feel doubt or dissent, take a deep breath and let the feeling leave your body with your breath. Let obedience and calm fill its place."

Yes. No doubt, no dissent. Calm.

"Pay no attention if you find yourself screaming internally. That's perfectly normal and can safely be ignored."

Good advice. I ignored the part of myself that was screaming wildly. It wasn't helping.

"Breathe in comfort, warmth, obedience to the Old Ones. Let that obedience fill your body. Feel it in the depths of your heart."

Rafael...it was one of those old space opera worlds. For no clear reason they used an ominous name for the worlds' leaders. The name of an ancient being. Of—

"Feel your obedience become resilient, able to resist all calls to disobey or doubt."

My thoughts blew away like smoke in the breeze. What had I been thinking about? Names? It couldn't be important.

"Let yourself sit with that emotion. Let it sink into your mind, so that you can call it up at any time."

There seemed to be nothing in the world but the smell of the incense and the color and my calm obedience. But if I listened very, very closely I could just hear a conversation I doubted was meant for my ears.

"Well, Rafael, what do you think of our new minions? Will they do?"

"I do wish you would address me properly, Mrs. Knightley. Rafael is not and never was my name."

"But it's such a clever code name and suits you so well!"

Rafael—or rather not Rafael—didn't say anything, but the air felt colder. A threatening silence prevailed for a heartbeat.

"I apologize, Lord Hastur," Emma said contritely.

Hastur! Yes! That was the name I had been looking for.

Hastur! No! Of all the gods and demons of the world—

Most of the Old Ones interact with humanity only rarely. Hastur was different. They say that he entered people's minds while they slept and stole their dreams. They say that he eats the hearts of his enemies or perhaps of his followers. They say that those who fall into his hands live forever but wish every moment that they could die.

They say lots of things because no one has encountered him and lived to tell about it. And he was here, in the mediation center. We were toast. Possibly literally.

"To answer your question," Hastur said in a commanding, businesslike tone far different from the reassuring tone he had used with us. "I think they will do very well. When their employers see how much better workers they are after our little intervention, they will send all their employees here. Their productivity will be the envy of the industry and all their rivals will want to know the secret. And they will find out, will they not?"

"Oh, yes, they will! I'm sure my little project here will go far if I push her in the right direction," Emma said, stroking my forehead. "She has potential."

The screaming in my head reached a fevered pitch. "No!" it cried. "Kill me! Eat my soul! Send me to the fires of Hell forever! But don't make me do this. Don't make me be your trap."

Silly thing. I should be flattered to be noticed by one so elevated. Not everyone got such an opportunity.

Hastur addressed us again, "Now, when you're ready, slowly open your eyes. Note how calm and obedient you feel. How ready to work. You like work. Work makes you free. Whenever you feel tired or unmotivated, just close your eyes and breath deeply and you will find your motivation again."

For a moment, the thought that I was taking a relaxation meditation class from a malevolent Elder God overwhelmed all other thoughts and I nearly giggled. But then the calm overtook me again and the incongruity evaporated from my mind.

I opened my eyes and smiled shyly at Emma. She smiled back at me and said, "I am so glad that I got to know you properly in the end, Sophanisba."

I found myself answering with enthusiasm, "Me too!"

Phil blinked, stretched, and yawned. "I don't know when I've felt so rested," he said. "What do you say we go back to the office and do a little catching up this evening, Sophie?"

"Good idea," I said. "Work will free us from all our cares."

"It will free the world of its human cares in time," a voice in the back of my head murmured. I chose to ignore it as I stepped out of the dark room into the bright sunny day and boundless future.

WHAT HORROR

RICK DANFORTH

"This is The Spinner in the Darkness. He enjoys devouring mortal souls, hearing the lamentations of their gods, and long walks on the beach."

"No way," said Philippa with a shudder.

"What? What's wrong with this one?" After an hour of sifting through the pages of *What Horror – Eldritch Demons Used & Newish*, Howard's patience was wearing thin. There were over a thousand demonic horrors inside the catalogue, propped open between a chipped teapot and a plate of biscuits, yet none were good enough for Phillipa.

"Look at him," she said, grimacing. "He's got an octopus head, that's not going to put bums on pews."

"Squid," corrected Howard, looking at the tea-stained page. "It's a squid's head."

Philippa shuddered again. "Urgh. That's so much worse."

"How is that worse?"

She shrugged. "I don't know. It just is. I mean, octopus are weird. But squid... they're just...you know..."

"He isn't a squid," Howard, forcing a calm into his voice that didn't exist. "He just has a squid head."

Howard really wanted to work with his fellow Bishop of Schleck, but she was making this difficult. If it had been up to him, he'd just pick one. Any old, low-maintenance horror would do.

Howard's eyes flickered down the page. "He's a pretty good find. I think we should get him while we can."

Philippa looked at him coldly. She didn't use the look a lot, but it meant there was no changing her mind. "As *High Bishop*, I say we are moving on."

To punctuate her words, Philippa flicked the ornate, jewel encrusted bishop hat that was large enough to hide a roast turkey and trimmings.

Howard grumbled. As part of the ecclesiastical changes, they had found people preferred having one Bishop in charge. It gave them something to aspire to. So, after years of a flat structure of non-high Bishops, they now took turns at being the high one. "It was meant to be my week as High Bishop."

"Yes, but you traded it for that sandwich, didn't you?" said Philippa, not even trying to contain the glee in her voice.

Sighing, Howard opted not to fight this one. There were plenty of other horrors. Somewhere in the hundreds of pages, there had to be one she couldn't find anything wrong with. She was probably right to be so picky. But they did need a horror. Congregation numbers were falling at an alarming rate, they needed to put bums on seats. At the current rate of falling, in just five years they'd be paying people to show up. Apparently, all the popular religions had demonic horrors nowadays. Something about the cosmic levels of fear inspired people to pray. If they wanted to put dinner on the table, they needed a demonic horror. And fast.

So, they sat in the cosy but austere comfort of the vestry in Schleck the Lightening God's Cathedral, perusing the options. They nestled in battered green armchairs with tea, biscuits, and some incense that smelt ever so slightly of burnt parsnips.

"How about this one? asked Howard, flicking another page to reveal a tentacled, scaled, bat-winged entity.

"Nothing that flies. Don't want it in the rafters."

"Now you're just nit-picking."

"It's important. The demon we choose will say a lot about our religion. And if we have a giant bat, people aren't going to think very much." Philippa shook her head, and flipped a page. "What the hell is that?"

Howard read aloud, "A grey festering blob of infinite malevolence, the Devourer of The Mist."

"*That*, does not help me. Definite no." Philippa flipped the next page. "Well, that's just a giant lizard."

"Giant water lizard," said Howard reading aloud helpfully. "The Doom of—"

"They're not even trying with that one." Philippa flipped the page and shuddered at the next one, a giant worm with a tentacle for a head. "What is it with these things and tentacles?"

"Apparently, it's what people want from their horrors?"

The search continued. Howard had never imagined investigating demonic horrors could be so boring. But time dragged like a brick on a lead. On what felt like the thousandth horror, he said, "This one is a sure thing. A huge, flying scorpion with an ant-like head."

"I said '*no* insects'."

"Technically, not an insect."

"Still a no."

Howard took a deep breath, and the last of the chocolate biscuits. "Well, you have to choose one of the blasted things. Which one?"

"As *High Bishop*, I will choose when I want."

"Yes, High Bishop."

"Let's go for that one then," said Philippa, pointing to a page without enthusiasm.

"I thought you said no tentacles," said Howard.

"I did." Philippa took a deep breath and exhaled. "But it turns out the ones without tentacles are somehow even worse."

Howard bit down his response to bait and mock. That would come later, she hadn't actually agreed to it yet. Instead, he read aloud, "Only 2000 years old. One careful small church owner, only used him to scare children during Sunday school."

"Is that good?"

"I think it means in demonic horror terms, only just out the box."

Philippa nodded, moving a hand to her hat to stop it falling off. "So how do we buy it?"

"Apparently," said Howard, frantically reading to stay one step ahead of Philippa, "after you have made your choice, you just activate the rune."

A circular rune with a line through it lay at the back of the catalogue. Howard pressed it, and a man appeared in front of their table.

The effect was uncanny. Just a commonplace-looking middle-aged man in a reasonable brown suit, with a matching briefcase. A clean face with clipped hair. The most average looking person in the world, if he hadn't just emerged from a puff of blue smoke that briefly filled the small, stone room before fading away.

"Hi there, I'm Barry Relief. I'll be your sales associate today." The man smiled, "Just call me Baz."

After giving two handshakes as smooth and cold as polished metal, he got to business. He didn't even give them chance to rise from their chairs. Turning to Howard, he asked. "So, you are interested in one of our world-renowned horrors?"

"Excuse me, I am the High Priest here," said Philippa sternly, sitting up to her full height in the armchair.

"Until Thursday," muttered Howard.

"I do apologise, Ma'am." Baz bowed deeply.

"Accepted. And yes, *I* would like a horror. We have found one we like. The one listed as The Great Dreamer?"

"Ah yes, a capital choice that. She's in popular demand."

"I'm sure," said Philippa, arms crossed and eyes rolling.

Baz tapped the catalogue and licked his finger before turning the pages. Reading the inverted pages without issue. "The church of Pancreas, God of transport, have her twin sister and she stopped people talking during the sermons."

"We do hate that," said Howard.

"We have a fantastic deal right now, actually. Buy one, thirty percent off the second selected horror. Can we interest you in She Whose Hand Embalms?"

"Which one was that?" asked Howard, always keen on a good deal.

Baz flicked through a few pages of the folder, to showcase. "The form-less mound, with one arm-like appendage."

"Oh."

"No," said Philippa. "Not something anyone can really get behind. And to be honest, I feel one should be sufficient."

"No worries." Baz smiled with a warmth not shared by his cold, dead eyes. Even in the bare stone room they felt cold. "Well why don't we let you take your horror home today?"

"Lovely. How would we do that?"

Baz clicked his fingers, and a contract materialised on the table. Howard was surprised, he had expected seventeen pages of fine print an ant would need a microscope to read. But it was just a simple, one-page deal.

"So where do I sign?" asked Philippa, hovering with a pen over the paper.

"Just at the bottom on the dotted line. Although I regret to form you that a pen will not be sufficient."

"Pencil?"

"Something a little more…appropriate." Baz clicked again, and a silver dagger appeared in one hand. A twisting, gnarled blade with a single blood red jewel in the hilt.

Philippa turned to Howard, but before she opened her mouth he said, "As High Priest, it should be you who does the signing."

"Are you still sore about the sandwich?"

"I am just stating facts." Howard bowed to hide the wide smile on his face. "And not airing grievances about anyone who takes advantage of poor, hard-working bishops during periods of low blood sugar."

"For God's sake," said Philippa. "Give me the bloody knife."

Stifling a yell, Philippa cut her finger and signed the form. "Now what?"

The doors exploded inward. A dark wind drove into the room, blowing out the candles and scattering the papers like polka-dot snow.

"Your chosen horror has now arrived," said Baz. Finally he smiled, flashing his teeth, horrible crooked things with the smell of death. Howard noticed liver spots appearing on the man's face, and his pallor was fading rapidly.

"What? Here?"

"Yes, in the chamber next door. The only room you have that is large enough?"

Howard didn't even bother to ask about how the salesman knew that, he had a more pressing question. "You want it to live here?"

"Of course. Where else?"

"I…figured she would only come when we needed her?"

"Ah, you need the portal package." Baz's smile returned. "It's one of the more… extensive packages we offer for our premium customers."

"I see how it is." Philippa stared at the salesman. "Sell us something awkward and then bleed us dry with the extras."

Howard nodded glumly. "They always get you with the extras."

"And where was this wisdom an hour ago?" asked Philippa. "Before we spent the roof repair fund on a horror!"

They went down the stairs to the Cathedral's nave, or what was left of it. The pews had collapsed, frankly they had never stood a chance. The organ pipes resembled spaghetti, the paintings were kindling, and even the jolly thermometer drawing for the roof repair fund was in dire straits.

In the middle of the destruction, wedged between pillars and the ceiling, was their chosen horror. It was all there, cuttlefish head, dragon body, scaly wings—basking the room with the heavy stench of rotting fish.

Howard had read it described as a hundred feet tall, but reading and seeing are very different things. Especially when the hundred feet comes with webbed arms, tentacles, and a pair of rudimentary wings on his back. Wings that covered the stained-glass window, allowing only enough sunlight inside to keep the interior in shadowy twilight.

"That," said Philippa clutching to Howard for support, "Is massive."

"She is one of the largest horrors we offer," said Baz.

"Don't look at me," said Howard with a growing smile. "I wanted the scorpion god."

"Ah, The Bringer of Pestilence is minute in comparison, around the size of a house."

"Far more reasonable, you'd say?"

"This is not helping!" Philippa rubbed her temples to calm her anger. "You said she was obedient."

"She is."

"Yes. Obediently sitting on my bloody floor. We have a coronation next week. What's the King going to do? How do we roll the red carpet over that?"

"Could paint her like a pillar?" offered Howard.

"Don't be stupid."

"Sorry, just trying to help. I'm just glad this isn't my week as High Bishop. I am sure the priests will be delighted to meet their new horror."

"Priests and deacons. That's what I need." Philippa smiled, then walked across to the corner and yanked on a bell pull.

A second later a servant opened the door. "Yes?"

Philippa blocked the door with her foot, angling herself in the thin opening to obscure the view. "Fetch a dozen men to clear this out of the hall."

"Yes, miss," said the servant, leaving with a bow.

"Actually, make it two dozen!"

As they waited, Philippa forked over the roof collection money to Baz, who sat in the floor of the maelstrom and counted each individual copper penny out. Inspecting each one with a careful eye, he swept them into his briefcase along with a dead rat that Howard pretended not to notice.

Just as Baz finished, the one remaining door opened. The two dozen burly helpers entered and were met by the sight of the Great

Dreamer. Four of them reeled, one fainted, and two were shaken into a frantic cry. They stood trembling and nearly hypnotised with horror.

"Get on with it," called Philippa, "We don't have all day!"

"Can we get more people?" asked one man cowering in the corner. "Please."

"If you think it will help. Fine. But be quick."

Additional numbers arrived, with similar reactions, although at least some had rakes and spades from the garden. As they milled about, awed by the cosmic majesty, Philippa swore and yelled, "Get on with it! Or you'll be spending a hundred years in hell."

Motivating underlings as a Bishop, especially a High Bishop, is easier than most bosses. Faced with hellfire, the scared mob went to work.

Within seconds it turned into din and chaos beyond description. Three men were swept up by the flabby claws before anybody got near the horror. Others were battered aside like toy dolls.

One enterprising woman grabbed a spade and jumped. As it pierced the thigh, the dark creature's shriek burst the windows. In relation, she picked the offender up and hurled them, breaking through into the belfry.

In mere moments twelve worshippers lay dead, and seven severely wounded ones were carried away on improvised stretchers by their fellow survivors.

And the monster fell back to silence.

Stepping over a growing pool of blood coming from a freshly eviscerated corpse, Howard and Philippa could only stare. A dozen men and women dead in less time than it took for Howard to have a sandwich.

Howard met the eyes of the Great Dreamer.

Howard was nothing, he was insignificant. He was so worthless and unimportant that even a drowning rat would consider him beneath contempt. In laying eyes on this monstrous entity, he deserved an eternity of pain.

The disdain sleeted over him, tearing his mental state to pieces. The eyes of the Great Dreamer were all he could see. All he wanted to do was lose himself in them. What was left of him, the gaze was stealing something out of his very soul.

And then the feeling left.

Howard shuddered and shook himself like a wet dog, as if he could rid himself from ever experiencing it.

"You too?" asked Philippa.

"That was horrible."

"She can have that effect. Most of our offerings do," said Baz.

Howard recoiled when he turned to see the salesman. The liver spots had doubled in size, and his skin was now a mottled green. His eyes were two bloodshot orbs promising pain and chaos.

"If you'll excuse me." The now mottled salesman bowed his ravaged and scarred head. "I need to leave."

"Feel bloody free," said Phillipa, waving towards the door.

"Only, I can't leave via regular means. You must use the knife to slit my throat."

"Well, I don't think we could ever—" started Howard.

Philippa strode across and slit Baz's throat in one smooth movement. Baz collapsed to the ground, his blood flowing profusely down his neck as he muttered, "Ta."

Swearing, Philippa dropped the knife at the body and clutched her hand. Both body and dagger disappeared in a puff of blue smoke.

"Are you alright?" asked Howard, taking a step back.

"That bloody knife gave me a static shock."

A card dropped to the floor where the salesman had stood. It read:

What Horror

Head Salesman Baz Relief

Should you have any questions, please don't. Hesitate to ask.

S omehow, Howard didn't think it was a punctuation error. Regret was already starting to seep in. He had wanted change, but he had expected big change like tomorrow always being a day away

And now it had happened. Via a summonable person who sold horrors for a living.

At that point, the Great Dreamer sighed, almost knocking Howard off his feet. The High Bishop's hat fell to the floor.

"We could leave? The Cult of The Bloody Tongue is always recruiting experienced priests?" offered Howard.

"No." Phillipa shook her head, and then rescued her now blood-stained hat. "This is where all our stuff is. We just need someone who really hates trouble in the cathedral."

"Mrs Palm who cleans in the mornings?"

"Even more fearsome."

"You didn't see her after they let the Sunday School play with paints."

Ignoring him, Philippa went to what was left of the altar, and knelt down to pray. There were some minor advantages to the High Priest position, aside the obvious hat. One was a direct line to Schleck in time of need.

The skies rumbled, and a thunderbolt struck through a freshly opened gap in the roof. Shleck, an irate silver bearded man in a toga, material-ized, followed by the waddling owl of wisdom.

"What the bloody hell is going on?"

Howard dropped to the floor in a bow, suddenly ecstatic not to be High Bishop.

"Greetings, oh great—" started Philippa.

"Cut the crap." Schleck stood nose to nose with Philippa, who cowered. "What is going on? You know the deal. I sort out the Heavens and the murky realms of the afterlife, you keep the churches clean. I don't enjoy being called out for some minor stain you can't get out."

Philippa pointed to the goo covered mass of The Great Dreamer.

"That…is a large stain." Shleck stood wide-eyed for a moment, but he recovered quickly. You don't live long as a god in the Heavenly Halls of Dunsmiting without being able to react to the unexpected.

Within seconds he was striding across the hall shouting, "You, oi you. What the hell are you doing in my church? Get out and don't come back, or I'll smite your big, stupid face off."

The Great Dreamer responded with gargled screeches and grunts emanated from behind its unblinking eyes.

"Oh, you want to be like that, do you?" asked Shleck, rolling up imaginary sleeves on his bare arms. "One lightning bolt coming up, sunshine."

The creature ate Shleck.

There was no ceremony to it, just one giant hand grabbed him, then tossed him into the awful squid-head writhing with feelers. As far as Howard could tell, the horror didn't even stop to chew.

Neither Howard nor Philippa moved, although the owl disappeared. They just stood in silent awe, allowing what they had just seen, and their God, to digest for a moment. The silence wound out around them and filled the room, to be sliced into gentle pieces by the soft, but heavy, breathing of the Great Dreamer.

Eventually, Howard managed, "That…was unexpected."

"Just a tad."

The long silence gave Howard time to think about his future as a Bishop. A Bishop of a church without a god, but one very large and disagreeable horror. There might be something in that.

Howard walked across to the shattered remains of the altar and pulled out a bottle of communion wine. After two large gulps, he passed it across to Philippa who finished it off. Then she asked, "You said that cult was recruiting?"

"It is. But we could stay here? Admittedly we need a few changes. But we do have something for followers to worship." Howard waved a hand at the monstrosity, now slumbering after eating its fill. "You wanted a change, and here we have one."

"But it's not a god?"

"We know that, no-one else does." Howard shrugged. "Is it important?"

"I feel it has to be? For a *religion!*" Philippa looked at the empty wine bottle with longing, before taking off her High Bishop hat and pulling out a small bottle of ten-year-old MacAbre. She tried not to meet Howard's eye as she unscrewed the bottle, although she did offer it to him.

Howard took it with a nod of thanks. He'd always wondered where she hid the good stuff. "Look. It may not be a god, but its powerful enough to eat a god for lunch. Is that not good enough?"

"Hmm."

"And if nothing else, it's going to put bums on seats. It's bloody terrifying. And we need that? Shleck was never an exciting god in that regard, very traditional. Perhaps a more interesting one gets the crowds in."

"Hmm."

"And as long as we give people something to believe in, with a positive message, we will still be doing good in the world?"

"Go on," said Philippa with a sigh.

Howard nodded, he'd known she would accept. Metaphysical purity was all well and good, but so was having a successful church. It paid for your food and shelter. Howard knew what a priest really was, someone who'd discovered an indoor job with no heavy lifting.

"We'll probably get a lot of converts. Our God can eat your God is a good tagline."

"Probably." Philippa sat on a tattered wedge of former pew and shook her head. "Being High Bishop isn't as much fun as I thought it would be."

"Can I be High Bishop tomorrow, then?"

"It's not your turn until next week."

"Oh, come on. Please?"

Philippa shrugged, and removed the High Bishop hat. "It's very depressing, this kind of thing" she said, glancing up at the ravaged church. "Some people just don't know how to behave in a house of religion."

"Well, it's her house now," said Howard. "I'll go spread the word."

CUT-RATE COUPLES WEEKEND AT THE WITCH HOUSE INNE AND TAVERN (9 REVIEWS)

STEWART C BAKER

E njoy a weekend getaway with your other half in our luxuriously updated replica of the original Witch House, a 17th-century cottage set in the heart of historic Arkham. A ten minute walk through the old town's picturesque alleys will earn you romantic river views and access to Pickman's Gallery and Portraiture, the Cats of Ulthar Window Seat Café, and the tree-lined vistas of Danvers State Park. Looking for a longer-term getaway with your sweetie? Ask about our travel packages to Innsmouth or other, more exotic, destinations!

Your purchase includes a two-night stay in our unusually spacious garret suite, two breakfasts from our tavern, and a goody basket. NO CHILDREN, FAMILY GROUPS, OR SINGLES. Sorry, we cannot guarantee third-party bookings. ABSOLUTELY NO POKEMON GO WHILE ON THE PREMISES, YOU HAVE BEEN WARNED. Free wi-fi!

Price: ~~your immortal soul~~ $199.95, plus tax, if you use coupon code FHTAGN at checkout.

. . .

"Stay with Mistress"

(Review by Jenkin B., December 2, 2016, 5 out of 5 stars)

Sss, Jenkinn stay many nights with mistress, have many good time! Big rooms with good views. Nice walls. Many tasty treats! Everyone stay here, have many good time. Sss-nee-hee-hee.

(Reply by Keziah 'Nahab' Mason, proprietress) Mommy loves you too, snookums, yes she does, yes she does!

"Curiously angled gables! Relentlessly inevitable movements through obscure matrices!"

(Review by Frank Elwood, December 4, 2016, 1 out of 5 stars)

[comment unavailable, deleted by owner]

(Reply by Keziah 'Nahab' Mason, proprietress) I told you to stop contacting me, Elwood! What you, Gilman, and I had was a long time ago, and if you can't accept that it's over that's your problem, NOT mine and NOT MY GUESTS'!

"Crappy wi-fi, gross stairs!!!"

(Review by Kelsey Jones, December 4, 2016, 1 out of 5 stars)

So, okay, I guess this is, like, one of those themed places? All "Historic Arkham" and stuff?

But it was SO. GROSS. Smelled like someone was using the stairs as a toilet. EW.

Anyway, the room was okay, I guess? But the wi-fi SUCKED. Which blew, because there's like, so many Pokémon Go spots in Arkham's old town! I tried to get them, right? But the app kept saying I was too far away, even though they were, like, RIGHT OUTSIDE. I couldn't get 4G either, which blew worse, so. . .

But, like, the weirdest part? My fiancé went down at like midnight to complain about the wi-fi to the manager, who's this batty old lady, right? And he NEVER came back. He left his shoes and suitcase and ALL his stuff, too.

Would NOT recommend!!!

(Reply by Keziah 'Nahab' Mason, proprietress) You were warned not to play Pokémon Go on the property. Given your disregard of what others tell you, it's no surprise your fiancé left you so abruptly!

"Mean owner and awful rooms."

(Review by Gillian Lu, December 4, 2016, 1 out of 5 stars)

Hi. I visited this inn with my boyfriend Derek, along with my sorority sister Kelsey and her fiancé. I just want to reinforce her review, especially since the so-called 'proprietress' has seen fit to come on here and make fun of her when she's been ditched by the man she was planning to marry.

We arrived a little late, and the elderly woman at the desk (the owner, I guess?) was a huge b-word about it! She gave us this total stink-eye, and said rooms were reserved for people with a proper respect for time. I couldn't tell if she was joking or what, but Kelsey was dead set on staying, so we talked her into giving us whatever was available, even if it wasn't our reserved room.

She put Kelsey in the gable suite, which she said was 'the most secluded room in the house' and that it would 'transport them to new frames of mind,' and a bunch of other weird stuff like that. Derek and I got some cruddy first-floor room that looked out at the wall of the next house over. There was a rat hole next to the door, and our sheets were chewed up, but the worst thing was that when I went into the bathroom to pee there was this old man standing in the shower, muttering to himself.

Yes, you read that right. *There was a shower person.* He looked even older than the owner, had this long ragged beard, and his eyes were all bugged out. I screamed (duh) when I saw him, and Derek ran in all macho angry.

I got him calmed down, but then shower guy gasped, shivered, stepped out of the bathtub, and grabbed me by the shoulders. I managed not to scream this time—he looked terrified more than threatening—but then he said, "I've seen . . . everything!"

Derek got the wrong idea and tore the guy off me, swearing he'd beat him to a pulp. (Probably breaking up with Derek, to be honest. Spare me the posturing!)

Anyway, look. This place is *not* worth your money. There are newer, nicer hotels a few blocks away by Miskatonic University that are staffed with decent human beings and don't have weird shower people.

(Reply by Keziah 'Nahab' Mason, proprietress) I'm so sorry you had such a bad experience, Gillian. I'm afraid the man you encountered is someone who's been bothering me for a long time, and sometimes harasses my guests. I've alerted certain important beings about his latest intrusion, and assure you it won't happen again.

Ever.

As a way of making up for everything, I'd like to offer you another stay free of charge. Please let me know when would be most convenient for you! Perhaps in late April, around Walpurgis Night? The historical society puts on reenactments that are to die for.

"**D**ated rooms, with a noisy bar downstairs, but can't beat the price!"

(Review by August D., February 6, 2017, 4 out of 5 stars)

Came here with my girlfriend for a weekend escape from Boston. Owner seemed nice enough—a bit hard of hearing—and she was definitely responsive to my complaints.

We had the gable room, and the bathroom (up against the back wall, with this steeply-sloped ceiling) was a bit odd. I dropped my soap in the shower, and couldn't reach it no matter how far I stretched. I still say violet is a strange color for bathroom lighting, too, even if the owner insisted it was for Valentine's Day.

Then there was the noise. I kept hearing this weird, high-pitched piping from somewhere. It sounded like it came from behind the walls, but when I called the front desk the owner said they were hosting the Arkham Pan Piper Society that day in the tavern. The heater in the room made these annoying scratching sounds all night, too.

Still, it was a cheap weekend out and we enjoyed walking around Arkham. If you don't go in expecting a 5-star hotel, I'd say a night or two at the Witch House Inne is worth every penny.

"Quaint quarters in the heart of historic Arkham." (Review by Albert Wilmarth, PhD, February 16, 2017, 4 out of 5 stars)

I must say I don't see why this place has such a low rating. The original Witch House was an historic building before that unfortunate incident back in the 20s. The replica might date from the 1960s, but believe me when I say it's just as in touch with Arkham's history as the original.

That's more than can be said for the other reviewers here, frankly. If young people today took any effort to learn about their past, we'd have fewer problems in society! Certainly this place would have a much higher rating.

(Reply by Keziah 'Nahab' Mason, proprietress) Thank you for your lovely comments, Dr. Wilmarth. It's always a pleasure to host Miskatonic alumnus faculty. Please let the current Head of Literature know that my offer regarding the city's oral traditions still stands, and I hope to see you and your lovely wife again someday.

· · ·

"Where's the option for zero stars?"

(Review by Gillian Lu, April 30, 2017, 1 out of 5 stars)

I stayed here back in December and had a pretty terrible experience, but decided to give it another try since I was offered a free stay.

The owner was pleasant enough when I arrived, with no sign of the nastiness in some of her comments here. She gave me and my date Aiden the gable suite, as well. Nice views from the window, no rat holes near the door, and best of all no shower person! Aiden and I had a nice dinner from the tavern to top it off (Yuggoth minestrone—tasty, whatever it was), and I was all set to upgrade my rating of this place and chalk my first time down to bad luck.

The owner even invited me to go with her to see the Walpurgis Night reenactments the historical society puts on in the next valley over, but Aiden and I were pretty beat, so we said no thanks and headed up to bed.

Aiden slept like a rock (he always does), but I couldn't get comfortable. I kept thinking there was somebody watching me, even though the room was empty and I'd propped a chair in front of the bathroom door (just in case). Definitely agree with the earlier reviewer about the noise from the heater, by the way. The later it got, the more purposeful the scratches sounded. Like something was trying to get in from outside.

When I finally did fall asleep, I had these super bizarre dreams involving the owner, this tall, skinny dude with no face, and some kind of little brown rat-thing with *fingers*. Ugh. The less said about *that*, the better. I woke up in a cold sweat and decided I'd go down to the tavern and get a drink instead.

It wasn't very late (maybe 10:30?) but the whole place was totally empty. No rugged ship captains nursing their beers, no Miskatonic professors trying to forget the horrors of a new semester. The owner wasn't behind the front desk, either, and she didn't answer when I rang the bell.

I was about to go back to bed when I heard slow, cautious footsteps coming down the stairs. I went to check it out, but nobody was there.

Okay, I thought. Old house sounds. But then I heard a little kid's voice sobbing at the top of the stairs. I couldn't see the top of the staircase (which still smells kind of gross) and by this point, I was pretty creeped out. All the same, I wasn't about to abandon some child who was scared and alone.

I took a deep breath, squared my shoulders, and ran up the staircase as fast as I could. There was a muffled thud from somewhere nearby as I reached the landing at the top, but—again—there was nobody there.

After that, I was beyond done. I opened the door to my room and leaped into bed. I felt pretty silly at first when I woke up the next morning, but then Aiden pointed out these misshapen bite marks on my neck (he swears he isn't into that kind of thing) and I had this weird sunburn all over.

We went to check out straight away, and the owner said she hoped I'd had as much fun as she had last night, then gave me this little grin I can only describe as evil.

Never.

Going.

Back!

The worst part, though, is that it's been a week since I stayed and those dreams haven't stopped. I feel, just . . . exhausted. All the time. It's like I'm not getting any sleep at all, like I've been travelling long distances every night. I swear one time I even had mud on my pjs. But Aiden says I'm out before he is and it's almost impossible to wake me.

I keep remembering Kelsey's fiancé running out on her, and can't shake this feeling that sometime soon, Aiden will wake up in the morning and I will have disappeared, too. That I will have gone somewhere nobody can find me.

. . .

"Closed?"

(Comment by Randolph C., May 7, 2017)

I say, anybody know if this establishment is still in operation?

I had rather hoped to stay a while and examine a text said to be owned by the woman who runs the place, so I booked my sojourn through one of those third-party websites and clicked the lowest fare—a two-night stay in the gable suite with a goody basket, which I thought was a dashed good deal.

But when I arrived around dusk, what should I find? The door bolted closed from the outside and a curious violet light emanating from the gable window. The room I'd booked myself, mind you! As I watched, I heard a strange susurration, almost beyond the very edge of hearing, followed by a rather more audible child's scream and an old woman's high-pitched cackle, and the light vanished with a hideous little pop.

I loitered inconspicuously for a while, hoping someone would at least nip down and open the door, but nothing else transpired.

Bit of a disappointment, really, and not at all good for my nerves.

"The rats, the rats in the walls!"

(Review by Howard de la Poer, May 28, 2017, 3 out of 5 stars)

They never believe me—they never listen!—but I have seen the mad faceless God, and heard his thrice-damned pipes beneath the scurrying which emanates from that grotesquely angled gable wall! Endless bridges of the filthiest obsidian with horrible creatures—bodies like rats, but their faces like—like—No! Help! Someone help! They got poor Ed already, and now they come for me! I can hear it still, that scurrying, scurrying . . .

(Reply by Gillian 'Azath' Lu, guest relations manager) Hi, Howard. So sorry to hear about your bad experience with us. I'm afraid those rats have been plaguing the residents of this inn for a long time. You'll be happy to hear that I've taken the problem in hand by getting myself a nice big tomcat. His name is Nyarl, he's inky black—like the spaces between the stars—and he's very well-acquainted with rats.

In any case, if you ever recover from this nervous episode (and who knew they had Internet access in the sanitarium, folks? Ha ha!), Keziah I would love to have you back at the Witch House Inne and Tavern. I'll reserve our *finest* room—we call it 'the Sultan's chamber'—free of charge, and I promise that once you've arrived, you'll find yourself utterly unable to complain about a single thing.

MY AUNTS AND THE CORNWALL HORROR

K.G. ANDERSON

"Thank heavens for my aunt," I said, putting down the phone. "She always comes through for me. A prince among aunts, you could say."

"You could, indeed, sir." Leeds was pulling my weekend bags from the hallway closet. "From your cheerful tone I presume the aunt to whom you refer is Mrs. Myers."

"Good Lord, yes. Aunt Daisy."

We both shuddered. The mere thought of my *other* aunt, Ferocia Dyson (*nee* Whitsmer), was enough to cast dark shadows over our sunny rooms in Grosvenor Square. Aunt Ferocia was rumored to have served, in her far-off and pretty much unimaginable youth, as a muse to Bram Stoker. Or was it Sheridan Le Fanu?

But on to more pleasant thoughts! It was my beneficent Aunt Daisy who had saved the honor of the Whitsmers—well, one Artie Whitsmer—yet again. She'd forked over the funds that would allow me to clear up that unfortunate misunderstanding caused by my club's use of the Chippingham Council Ballroom for an impromptu rugby practice.

Of course, even stalwart Aunt Daisy had her price. In return for her materteral generosity, I'd agreed to interview an up-and-coming American writer for her magazine *The Gentlelady's Salon*. Lovecraft, the author's name was. Howie Lovecraft. Never heard of the man, but she assured me he'd be the talk of the London literary scene in no time. Anyway, it was just a matter of my popping round to the fellow's hotel, posing a few intrepid questions, and then having Leeds organize my notes.

Or so I'd thought. Calling Lovecraft's hotel, I'd been rather annoyed to discover that the thoughtless cove had left London and waltzed down to Cornwall for the weekend. Authors, I tell you. Blasted inconsiderate of him, if you ask me.

The fellow was scheduled to board a ship back to the States Monday evening, so time was of the essence. It appeared that if I were to secure the interview I'd so breezily promised Aunt Daisy, we'd have to scramble. There was nothing for it but to go chasing down to Cornwall after him.

"That's what journalism's about, Artie," Aunt D reminded me when I called to inform her of the situation. "Go after that story, young man!"

"Quite right." I hung up the phone and squared my shoulders. "Leeds, the game's afoot."

As luck would have it, this Lovecraft fellow was enjoying the hospitality of Lord and Lady Carsted—some old chums of Aunt Daisy's with a reputation for hosting literary weekends at their estate on the outskirts of Exmouth. Aunt D made a call, snagged me an invitation, and now Leeds was packing our bags with even more than his usual alacrity. I hadn't thought of him as a fan of modern literature. But then I realized he was eager to take our new Lagonda touring car out for a spin.

We hit the road after lunch, made good time to Salisbury, and spent Saturday night in the considerable comfort of the old King's Arms. Fortified by that hotel's excellent breakfast, we made an early start and arrived in Exmouth just after noon. But in place of one of the hearty luncheons for which Lady Carsted was renowned, we found instead a domestic scene of considerable disarray.

"It must have been quite the party last night," I quipped when Leeds brought the luggage up to my room. We watched from the window as the staff dragged sodden rugs and broken furniture out to a carriage house.

"There seems to have been a flood in the ballroom." Leeds gave a brief, rather pained smile and commenced unpacking. "From the odors I noticed, they suffered an incursion of seawater."

"Oh, come now," I said. "We're at least two miles inland."

"In that, you are correct, sir."

Leeds appeared worried, even alarmed, but I wrote it off to his discovery of my new purple golf sweater in the bag. Leeds' appreciation of the lastest trends in men's fashion often trails mine by a bit.

I trotted downstairs with a mind to getting the interview with Lovecraft out of the way before cocktails. But the only person in evidence was our hostess, Lady Carsted. She was, understandably, distracted by the ballroom situation.

"Horrible, horrible," she was muttering to herself. When I inquired about Lovecraft, she knitted her brows. Apparently he'd borrowed Lord Carsted's little Aston Martin and motored off to the hamlet of Newton-Abbot.

"I fear that Mr. Lovecraft is not an experienced driver," Lady Carsted confided in a slightly hysterical tone. "But he seemed so determined—almost desperate—to go there."

I certainly couldn't blame the fellow for wanting to get away from the estate. As Leeds had so astutely observed, the atmosphere in the vicinity of the ballroom—dank, heavy, oppressive, and, yes, vaguely subaqueous—did not portend a sparkling social weekend.

"Why on earth did he want to see this Newton-Abbot place?" I mused out loud.

"Family, apparently," Lady Carsted said. "I heard as a child about some Lovecrafts who departed the village under rather odd circumstances in 1831. The property has since lapsed into ruin."

Leeds had been following Lady Carsted's chatter with an intensity that far exceeded even his usual attentiveness. As she turned to instruct one of the staff, he pulled me aside. "It occurs to me, sir, that if we left immediately, we could likely catch up with Mr. Lovecraft in Newton-Abbot."

Seeing my doubtful expression, Leeds upped the ante. "It might make good atmosphere for your interview."

"Quite right. The visit to the ancestral home, and all that."

"Exactly, sir."

Assuring Lady Carsted we'd return for dinner, we hopped back in the Lagonda and tootled down the winding country road to Newton-Abbot. To my considerable disappointment, our route skirted the edge of the vast, bleak, moors for which Dartmoor is named. I shivered. A chilly wind had come up, and Leeds enlisted my assistance to raise the fabric drophead to enclose the car.

"I say, this is turning out to be quite the vile place." We piled back into the car and started up again. "Let's not get lost."

"Let's hope Mr. Lovecraft has not become lost, either." Leeds' remark only added to my growing gloom. It had reached considerable proportions by the time we attained the dispirited hamlet of Newton-Abbot.

The only business open was one of those unappealing village teashops —the sort of enterprise that also vends sundries and petrol. Leeds saw to the car and made inquiries of the disinterested proprietor, who grudgingly muttered directions to the old Lovecraft place.

If not for a half-toppled stone cairn by the roadside, we might have missed it entirely. Calling the Lovecraft property "a ruin" was romantic understatement. Twisted thorny plantings had so overgrown the crumbling cottage that it appeared to be merely a weathered wooden door leading into a vast hedgerow. There was no sign of Lovecraft. No doubt he'd been just as unimpressed as we were and was by now in a nearby village, tucking into an elaborate cream tea.

I sauntered down the barely visible stone pathway and rapped at the old door, thinking to amuse Leeds. To my shock, it swung open—in a decidedly creepy way, with much creaking and that sort of thing. A cadaverous old fellow in the rusty black uniform of a butler or groom peered out at me as I attempted to gather my wits.

"Help you, sir?" He had one of those voices that sounds as if it gets put into use every twenty years or so.

I tossed old Howie's name at him.

"Gone," the man moaned, as if Lovecraft had escaped his clutches. "I believe he will be visiting the Oldwans." The man pointed a twisted finger back in the direction of the cursed Newton-Abbot.

"I'm afraid I don't know the Oldwans. Do they live nearby?"

Thankfully, Leeds materialized at my elbow. "I believe, sir, that by 'the Old Ones', he means the Hurlers."

"Hurlers? Really?" I asked. "I've always wanted to see Cornish hurling."

"Not the local game, sir. In this instance, 'The Hurlers' is the name of a famous Neolithic stone circle."

"Aye, that'd be them," the butler creature growled. "And you'd best be getting a start if you want to see them before nightfall." With that he closed the door.

"Rather rude, wasn't he?" I said as we clambered back into the car.

Leeds waited until we had returned to the roadway to reply. "Most uncivil. I hope we will find young Mr. Lovecraft more congenial than his family's...caretakers."

"Oh—Howie?" I chuckled. "I'm sure we'll get along famously. You know these Americans. Probably one of those cowboy types. Teddy Roosevelt. Ernest Hemingway. Hart Crane. Aunt Daisy loves to feature Americans in the magazine. Very dashing and romantic, she says."

Leeds accelerated, the roar of the car's motor obscuring his reply.

We motored on for what seemed like hours across the vast emptiness that is Dartmoor. I heartily urge you to avoid it on your next holiday. Hand-lettered signs along the roadside warned of *Danger!* but it was impossible to read the small print describing the hazards unless you were already out of the car and standing in danger's way. I remarked on this to Leeds, who merely nodded and changed the subject.

"Have you read any of the magazines that publish Mr. Lovecraft's works, sir?" he asked.

I wrinkled my nose. I'd meant to stop by one of the newsstands before we left London, but hadn't gotten around to it. "Well, no. But you know these writer types. You just ask them about their latest stuff and they're off and running. Can't stop 'em gabbing."

Leeds pulled over on the roadside, then reached into a case in the back seat. He drew out two pulp magazines and dropped them on my lap. *Weird Tales*, indeed. Odd publications, on rather cheap paper. Their colorful covers made up for it, though. What ripping artwork!

"I say, Leeds, you don't suppose Howie's brought some of these art models along with him on the trip?" I asked as we started up again.

"Unlikely, sir," Leeds said. "But I've taken the liberty of reading two of his stories and I am concerned that he may have brought with him some of the less attractive creatures you see portrayed."

I happily re-examined the covers. Those were quite the costumes on those young women. But what Leeds was referring to were the creatures behind the women and, on one cover, looming over them. Rather unsavory figures that for some reason brought to my mind the calamari salad they serve at Luchinelli's.

"Ugh," I opined. We rode on in silence. It was growing darker. "I say, are we anywhere close to those Hurlers?"

We had just passed through the minuscule village of Upton Cross and were, if the signs could be believed, headed toward a town with the rather disturbing name of Minions. That, Leeds informed me, would be our destination. The Hurlers hurled just beyond.

My last visit to a circle of Neolithic ruins had been a July picnic at Stonehenge with Alice Crownthorpe, two of her university friends, and an ample supply of sandwiches and beer. The terrain that stretched outside the car as we approached The Hurlers bore no resemblance whatsoever to that, and indeed seemed likely to be entirely lacking in comestibles. The temperature had dropped at least ten degrees since we'd left Exmouth and massive purple clouds were sweeping in from the Atlantic.

"The Hurlers," Leeds announced.

"What?" I had to shout to make myself heard over the winds.

He pointed at a gathering of dark stone figures. It looked to me like a rugby scrum taking place in a field of quicksand. "Leeds, what say we just head back to Exmouth and wait in the pub for this Lovecraft fellow to turn up?"

"An excellent suggestion, sir, but one which I fear comes too late. Mr. Lovecraft seems to have turned up here. And he looks to be in considerable difficulty."

He pointed ahead. Through dusk and fog I could make out Lord Carsted's Aston Martin. It was tipped sideways into a ditch. Fortunately, two stout locals seemed to have come to Lovecraft's aid. I could see the bulky figures, swathed in some sort of leather greatcoats, struggling with the vehicle.

"Those fellows seem to have things well in hand," I suggested, hoping Leeds would agree.

"I fear not, sir. You would do well to keep a firm grip on your door handle. On no account allow anyone into our vehicle until I give the word."

I nodded. Letting anyone into our car was the last thing on my mind. Leeds drove forward, bringing our Lagonda abreast of the stranded Aston Martin. I gasped in horror and clung tightly to the door handle as if it were a cricket bat. I wished it were a cricket bat. Or any sort of weapon. For the two figures clawing at Lovecraft's car, indeed attempting to drag it down into the marshes, were not burly locals but hideous creatures more amphibian than human. Flesh dripped from their faces like gravy from an improperly reheated pasty. I shall never forget the sight of those horrible visages as they turned to us and paused for a moment their evil labors.

"Shoggoths," muttered Leeds. I'd never heard Leeds curse before, and, I tell you, my blood ran cold at the sound. *Shoggoths*, indeed. As we watched in terror, the driver's door of the Aston Martin flew open and a tall, gaunt man scrambled out. His long narrow face was white as death.

"Mr. Lovecraft!" called Leeds. The man sprinted toward our car. I watched in horror as scaled, snake-like arms flailed after him.

"Open the rear door, sir," Leeds said to me. "Now, if you would."

I hesitated. Surely Leeds did not mean to expose us to the nightmarish beings that flanked Lovecraft's vehicle and even now lumbered after the man as he ran toward ours?

"Now, sir!"

Drawing on depths of Whitsmer courage I had no idea I possessed, I flung open the rear door of the touring car and bent forward. Lovecraft leaped in and sprawled across the back seat. Then Leeds reached across me, and together we pulled shut the door as the serpent-like creature pursuing Lovecraft rose up and towered over us, howling horrible incantations.

I made the error of looking up at the beast, and when I did, I froze in terror. For the creature that menaced us exuded a primordial evil as grim as that exuded by—well, by my fearsome Aunt Ferocia. Its resemblance to the ghastly woman was uncanny. The sharp predator's beak. The glinting evil eye. It was only by the greatest effort of will that I was able to convince myself that the creature before me was *not* Aunt Ferocia. Nothing, I told myself, could be that horrible. And besides, it wasn't wearing a dreadful hat. Aunt Ferocia never went out without one.

The creature roared in fury and flung itself at the Lagonda just as Leeds, never at a loss, hit the accelerator. The car responded, and I must have lost consciousness. It was some minutes later that I woke to find us speeding through the dark, deserted streets of the suddenly sinister village of Upton Cross.

I noticed with relief that, rather than retrace our path across the ghastly moors, Leeds turned the car south. Thus we made our way through a series of refreshingly dull fishing villages, eventually stopping at one to take sustenance in a grimy pub where Leeds and I devoured greasy cod and chips. Lovecraft made do with a sausage roll and declined the fortifying local ale in favor of a dubious coffee. Leeds and I quaffed our pints in silence.

Thus sated, we pressed on to Exmouth. It was nearly ten p.m. when we turned onto the tree-lined avenue leading to Lord Carsted's castle. The building was oddly dark.

"Nice of them to wait up for us," I groused.

Leeds slowed down and appeared to be listening.

"What it is?" I asked.

Lovecraft answered from the back seat in a low, nervous voice. "I hear them too. We dare not go there."

"What," I began, but stopped. Now I, too, heard the distant wailing.

"I think it wise to drive directly back to London," Leeds said quietly. His noble visage was pale. "We must get Mr. Lovecraft to his ship. It is imperative that he leave England as soon as possible."

I looked to the backseat where Lovecraft nodded, gratefully.

"I never should have come," he said.

Leeds, stout soul that he is, drove through the night, stopping only for petrol. I slept surprisingly well in the front seat while Lovecraft dozed fitfully in the back. When we pulled up in front of our lodgings it was not quite 8 a.m.

I don't often rise early enough to see a bright fall morning, but this one looked particularly pleasant. You had the birds chirping, ridiculously cheerful people going off to work, delivery people looking appallingly efficient. Powerful stuff, this! It was doing a bang-up job of making the previous night in Cornwall seem merely a bad dream. I essayed a chuckle or two as the three of us entered the flat. No place like home, indeed.

"Well, that's over!" I clapped my hands together. "Don't suppose any of us will be in a hurry to get back out on those moors, eh what?"

Leeds responded to my bonhomie with a disappointingly smallish smile. Indeed, it might well have been a grimace.

Our guest lowered himself onto the couch. "Those creatures...had I but known..."

"Best not to talk of them, sir," Leeds said. "Save that for your fiction—which, by the way, I much admire."

Leave it to old Leeds to utter the magic words! Lovecraft might have been a distinctly weird cove, but just like any scribbler he brightened perceptibly at the mention of his publications. Which reminded me of Aunt Daisy's interview.

Taking the pad and pen Leeds so thoughtfully placed in my hands, I scribbled down quite enough pithy quotes from our guest to keep Aunt Daisy's readers entertained. I'd just throw in some observances about Howie's chiseled features, brooding visage, that sort of thing, and the ladies would be simply swooning in their boudoirs. When he mentioned that his next story was going to be about cats, well, I knew I'd struck the jackpot.

"Cats! Just the thing," I chortled. "Aunt Daisy's readers simply adore the little beasts."

By the time we'd finished the interview, Leeds had set out one of his exceptionally restorative breakfasts. Howie tucked in like a man starved.

"I must be aboard the steamship by four p.m.," he told Leeds. "I have only to collect the luggage left at my hotel. Forgive my agitation, but I suffer extreme anxiety at the prospect of ocean travel. I doubt I will ever come to England again."

I can't say I blamed the man. He'd gotten a rather dicey impression of the place.

"I quite understand your concerns about the water, sir," Leeds said as he cleared away our plates. "And I believe they are justified. I propose that I drive you to your hotel, where you can freshen up and perhaps take a quick nap. After I run a few errands, I'll return at two p.m. and convey you directly to the dock."

As you can imagine, I was most relieved to have Leeds take old Howie off my hands. After farewells all round, the two of them went out the door and left me to tumble directly into bed—where I planned to snooze until the horrors of the night were forgotten. (Some day, they could return as a bang-up tale for a Hummers Club dinner. I thought "The Cornwall Horror" had a nice ring to it.) I was far less than pleased to be roused only thirty minutes into my nap by the repeated *buzz buzz buzz* of the blasted doorbell.

"Leeds!" I called out. Where was the man? "Leeds!"

But of course he was driving that nuisance Lovecraft about town. Dash it all! I fumbled my way out of the bedclothes, wriggled into my robe, and stumbled down the hall with that cursed bell still shrilling. I yanked open the door, squinted out—and then leaped back in horror. A tall, dark figure in black loomed in the doorway. The Cornwall Horror had followed us to London!

"Artie Whitsmer!" it bellowed, flying into the room.

I staggered back, putting the dining table between myself and what I thought—what I hoped—was only my Aunt Ferocia.

"Why are you staring at me like that, you young gogglehead?" she asked coldly.

"Were you in Cornwall last night?" I blurted.

One of her eyebrows shot up. "Cornwall? I should say not. Artie, where on earth do you get these absurd ideas? I won't ask where you were last night, though it's obvious you were out until some ridiculous hour, as you are still in your pajamas at nearly ten in the morning."

Aunt Ferocia was peering around the apartment. "Do you have guests?" she asked. "Where's Leeds?"

"Guests? No! Leeds? Errands!" I choked. I watched with growing uneasiness as my aunt shrugged out of her coat and placed her capacious bag on the floor in the hallway. The woman appeared to be moving in.

"Well," she barked. "Aren't you going to offer me coffee?"

I galloped into the kitchen, stared at the coffee equipment and tried to remember how to brew the stuff. I figured it started with hot water, so I put on the kettle while I fumbled with cups, saucers, and spoons. To my infinite relief, I heard Leeds' voice in the front hallway. After a brief, somewhat frosty exchange with Aunt Ferocia, he glided into the kitchen where he looked sadly at the heap of china and cutlery I'd assembled beside the struggling kettle.

"Making coffee, sir?" he asked.

I nodded weakly.

"I'll gladly take care of it, sir," he said. "Enabling you to attend to..." he hesitated "Mrs. Dyson."

As I passed by, he caught my arm and spoke in a low tone. "Sir, if you would please take your aunt into the study for a few moments, close the door, and keep her occupied."

I nodded. God knows what the fellow was up to now. But I would comply, even though it meant spending a decidedly ugly five minutes listening to Aunt Ferocia conduct an unflattering and unnecessarily detailed assessment of my prospects for matrimony. At long last I heard Leeds place the coffee tray on the dining room table.

A cup of Leeds' extraordinarily good java seemed to placate the old battleaxe and it certainly cleared my windshield. Before I knew it, Leeds was helping Aunt Ferocia into her coat and sending her off to the next engagement in her daily battle plan.

Leeds had prepared my bath, and I was deep into the hot water and suds when he informed me he was off again. He was going to assist Howie with packing and then trundle the poor fellow off to his ship.

"Afraid of the water, is he?" I asked, happily squeezing a hot spongeful over my head.

"Far more than you can imagine," Leeds intoned. "He was terrified on the voyage over. Fortunately, my colleague Pennoyer is booked on the same crossing to New York. I have introduced the two and arranged for Pennoyer to provide Mr. Lovecraft with every assistance."

Well that was Leeds' customary kindness for you! I hoped it wouldn't put him too deeply in debt to his friend Pennoyer. Howie Lovecraft didn't seem the type to be much fun on an ocean cruise. No, he'd probably spend the whole voyage hunched in a deck chair with a rug on his lap, writing bleak poetry. Wherever did Aunt Daisy find these types?

Much refreshed by the bath, I dressed and took a cab to the club for an afternoon of bridge. When I returned, all signs of American authors and intrusive aunts were gone. Leeds was preparing dinner and all was right with the world. The smell of something frying in butter wafted out from the kitchen.

"What's on the menu?" I called, as I hung up my coat.

Leeds peered out from the kitchen. "I thought seafood, sir."

A pang of doubt struck amongst my pangs of hunger. "Not anything with tentacles, I hope?"

"Not to fear, sir. Merely Atlantic halibut."

I nodded happily and took my place at the set table. "Our friend Love-craft ought to be sailing out past Land's End about now. I must say, do you think his literary career really will take off?"

"I believe it will, sir." Leeds set down the platter of perfectly sauced fish and a basket of fresh rolls.

"That talented, is he?"

"Yes," Leeds said. "Talented, with a unique, long-range perspective on the world. In addition—" The phone rang, and while I helped myself to the fish, Leeds answered.

"Book?" he said, in tones of deepest concern. "I shall look for it imme-diately."

I stopped with my fork halfway to my mouth and watched as Leeds proceeded to walk in circles around the room. He completed three full circuits of the Persian rug before returning to the phone.

"I'm afraid I've looked everywhere, madam, and there is no sign of a large book," Leeds told the caller. "You must have left it somewhere else. I am so sorry."

I heard growling and squawking sounds from the other end of the line. Really something quite feral.

"Irreplaceable? Yes, I'm sure it is very frustrating," Leeds consoled. "I do hope you find the book, madam." He hung up and joined me at the table.

"Was that by any chance my Aunt Ferocia?" I asked, cautiously resuming the meal.

"Exactly, sir. She believes that she left a large and extremely valuable old book here when she visited this afternoon."

"Not likely," I said. "She parked that immense bag of hers in the front hall and never opened it. You saw it when you came in."

"Indeed I did. And I removed the book from it."

"You did what?"

Leeds paused for a moment. He had the aspect of someone contemplating something very large and figuring out how to fold it into a small box. "It was a very dangerous book, sir. Not at all something that should be in the possession of a being as powerful as...your aunt."

"Dangerous?" I forgot about the halibut and began looking about the room. "Where the deuce have you stashed the thing, Leeds?"

Leeds chewed slowly, index finger raised, and then swallowed. "I gave it to Mr. Lovecraft, sir. He is taking the book with him to America. I'm confident that he'll know exactly what to do with it."

BLOOD MOON BARGAINS

KYER KNEIFEL

"Hi! Do you have time to talk about our overlord and destroyer Kajinit?"

The door slammed in Malik's face. He brushed off his red tinted suit and looked at his watch. Twenty minutes until midnight ended. It was getting close to the start of the Blood Harvest.

Malik quickly flipped through his papers to see who he was working with, and triple knocked on the door. There was no answer. Another triple knock, followed by two doorbell rings. The door swung open to reveal a grumpy man in shorts and a t-shirt.

"Hello again, sir! Could you spare a sliver of your lifespan for me to pitch these great deals I have ready for you?"

"Dude, it's like midnight," the man mumbled.

"Yes sir it is! Midnight on a full blood moon, the perfect time to welcome our new and malevolent ruler!" Malik flipped through his clipboard. "It says here you're a Christian who is on the path to hell, with three sins in the wrath department and two counts of greed. This makes you prequalified for the blasphemous bundle. Would you be interested to hear your unholy benefits with this limited time offer?"

The man stared blankly at the tall slender salesman. "What?"

"Ohoho, brain in the gutter after a long day at work? I can understand, I haven't had a metaphysical break in three decades!" Malik said with a fake laugh. "May I come in? Perhaps have some coffee while we discuss the details of your shifting ethereal loyalties?"

The man slowly closed the door, staring into the unblinking silver eyes of Malik. "Fucking vampire."

"That's actually a misconception, sir, the vampires are just a very polite community—"

The door closed and Malik snapped his fingers. "Get it together, Malikethial. You have a quota to meet." He licked his hand, slicked back his jet-black hair, then gave yet another triple knock.

"Dude, get out of here!" the man said, opening the door again.

"Please, sir, just a moment of your time. These are limited time offers before your community is plunged into the first phase of the coming of Kajinit," Malik said, putting a foot in the doorframe. "You are Jason Derth, yes?"

Jason shrugged. "Yeah."

"I see you are an angry man, a chip the size of Ararat on your shoulder. You have two bar fights on record, yes?"

Jason narrowed his eyes and slowly nodded.

"And each time you prayed to the lord to win, yet you proceeded to be emasculated and humiliated by physically superior opponents?"

"What the fuck kinda sales pitch is this?" he asked with a look of bewilderment.

The smile of Malik's face widened far more than any human could. "A once in a lifetime one, which is especially convenient with the limited time left on yours. What if I give you an edge in the oncoming purge, a boon of strength with the blessing of Kajinit?"

"What kind of boon?"

356

"Oh, I have a wide range to choose from. Strength of ten men is always a pleasant option, ferocity of twelve wolves perhaps? Or if you have a personal idea, I'll run it by the big boss in the bloody bed to see if it fits your pre-qualifications."

Jason thought for a moment but seemed unable to come up with a suitable idea. "Wolves. I'm an alpha, so I want wolves."

"Ah, yes, an alpha indeed. You've made a fine choice," Malik said, flipping through the paperwork on his clipboard. Alpha was such a ridiculous misconception, it only occurred in the seventh circle's hellhounds. Yet a sale is a sale, you shouldn't insult the customer. "So, with the blasphemous package only a tenth of your soul is required. Do you have health insurance? If you don't I have to get you on our plan instead, company policy."

"I'm insured, yeah. Costs so much I might as well be paying the rest of my soul for it," Jason commented.

"Yes, yes, and they call my deals demonic. Well, if you just sign in blood here, here, and here, we can get the transmutation work going and have you ready for the Blood Harvest by twelve o one. How's that sound?"

"Uhhh, I ain't so good with needles," he said at the mention of signing in blood.

"Oh, nothing so barbaric sir. The pen does all the work, just sign on the dotted lines."

Malik handed him a fountain pen devoid of any ink. Jason hesitantly took it and signed his name. Red ink materialized from the tip despite there being none in the utensil. He chuckled at the cheap magic trick.

"Wonderful doing business with you sir. Just to quickly go over the contract, all kills and conquests within the coming bloodfest will be declared in the name of your new master Kajinit, lord of blood. You have an anti-poaching clause here, so no switching elder ones at the last minute, m'kay?" Malik said, pointing at each paragraph mentioning these conditions.

Jason rolled his eyes. "Sure, whatever, can you get off my property now?"

"Of course, sir." Malik flipped the pen in his fingertips. "Let me just get the transmutation process started and I'll be on my way."

Malik flipped the pen outwards and slit Jason's throat with deadly precision. It took a moment for him to even realize he couldn't breathe before he collapsed to the ground, his blood flowing profusely down his neck.

"Fu-ck!" he gurgled, blood frothing at the mouth. None of his blood was wasted as it seeped back into his body along his arms and legs. Bones cracked as they began to reshape. Jason screamed in agony, screams that turned into howls as the blood filled his lungs.

Malik gave a single two fingered wave. "Pleasure doing business with you, sir!" he said and left the suffering man to morph into the inhuman creature he signed up for.

The full red moon illuminated the town of Vendi, its bloody stain upon the sky slowly growing in size. A scream emerged here and there from the soon to be harvested town. Malik strolled to the next house, flipping through his clipboard to skim his remaining marks.

"Hmm. Who's next…Heather. Hello, Heather, what did you do to end up on my list-oh, a satanist, how charming. Sadly deceiving these days, I miss the old satanists. They knew how to party," he reminisced as he approached her door. There was a rapid triple knock and a few moments of waiting before the door opened.

"Hi! Do you have time to talk about our overlord and destroyer Kajinit?"

Heather tilted her head. "Who?"

"Kajinit, Lord of Blood and organizer of the Blood Harvest since the 1600's. It says here you're a satanist, but you have yet to perform a sacrifice to the Morningstar. Would you be interested in a switch of loyalties? We match your pay, and our dental package is amazing," Malik explained with his heart and what used to be his soul.

Heather shook her head. "I'm not a satanist."

Malik's smile did not waver, but his eyes showed slight confusion. He flipped through the clipboard. "Are you not Heather Bosnia?"

"Yeah, but I practice witchcraft and crystal magic. Did my mom send you? Is this her attempt to get me 'back to the Lord'?" Heather asked, sounding annoyed.

"A witch? Ohoho, my mistake. Must have been a miscommunication in the marketing department upstairs," Malik said with an even faker laugh. Internally he was filled with rage, how could they screw up that badly? Now he had to improvise and hope the boss would go for the deal.

"Well, I am not sent by your mother, I was sent by Kajinit. It is the full Blood Moon, and he has deemed your town suitable for the six hundred and sixty seventh Blood Harvest. I'm here to offer boons and benefits to those who meet our pre-qualifications, set by our malevolent overlord."

A body crashed through the window of a house across the street. The glass shards sliced the person's face as they plummeted to the ground. A second figure leaped after them. Humanoid looking at first, in the red moonlight it's disfigured appearance was clear.

Its nails were long and sharp, its mouth circular with shifting triangular teeth like a leech. It squirmed towards the bleeding corpse. A long, drooling tongue slithered out to lap at the blood along the multitude of cuts it had created.

Heather recoiled at the monstrous creature that devoured what was once her neighbor.

"What the hell is that!"

Malik did a quick glance behind him. "Oh, the bloodlets? Those without pre-qualifications are fast tracked to the basic blood package. I believe those with evil in their hearts morph first."

Heather poked her head out to see her town devolving into madness. The bloodlets were spreading through the town like a plague. Those who had yet to turn were the first to fall as the turned sought blood for their blood god. There were other abominations festering in the streets along with the bloodlets, some humanoid, others beastlike. All were attacking each other on sight like a battle royal of horror.

"It seems the festivities are starting. My deals are limited time offers, so I'd make the smart play and sign up with us," Malik said, holding the pen and clipboard to her.

"Uhhh, ok, ok, sold. What do I get?" Heather said, looking over her shoulder as sounds of breaking glass emanated from her own home.

"Well, just sign here, here, and here, and I'll switch you over to our finest witch-based package. It includes enhanced spells, passive corporeal defense, and—"

Heather did not let him finish as she tore the pen and signed her name rapidly. A blood-starved beast tore through her house, pouncing at the screaming customer. A red aura burst from around the witch as its claws stopped inches from her chest. It hung awkwardly in the air as a second burst shot it back into the darkened house, whimpering in fear.

Malik did a single two fingered wave. "Pleasure doing business with you, ma'am." He left her to stare at her hands in confusion, the veins along her skin becoming more pronounced. The tears running down her face were blood red.

The moon's bloody visage had almost fully engulfed the night sky. Malik hummed a happy tune as he walked, thrilled he had met his quota with one house to spare. Perhaps he'd get a commission bonus if he snagged an extra soul. He did a small gleeful skip at the thought, hopping over a pool of blood leaking from the torso of a recently eviscerated corpse.

Malik straightened his tie, slicked back his jet-black hair, and did a rapid triple knock on the last door. After a moment it opened.

"Hi! Do you have time to talk about our overlord and destroyer Kajinit?" he asked for the last time with that golden smile and uncanny gaze.

The blonde man dressed in a red robe and bat slippers tilted his head. "Malikethial?"

Malik's smile faltered slightly. "Do I know you?"

"It's Derakinta, from Liechtenstein." He gave Malik a moment to think before adding more details. "16th century, Lucifer Jr.'s bar mitzvah."

"Derak! Oh my fallen god, it's been centuries," Malik exclaimed. "Wow, what are the odds? How's that immortality working for ya?"

"Oh, you know. Blessing and a curse as they say. I thought there was somebody around here, it's been midnight for the past hour," Derak said, looking at the bloody moon looming over the town. "So, you got a job?"

"Yeah, yeah, working for Kajinit. Not the biggest fan of the elder ones, but work is work. Word on the street there's a pay raise with this mortal annexing."

"Congrats, you're moving up in the second world." Derak looked around. "Well, I don't want to keep you—"

Malik shrugged. "Actually, I've already met my quota, and you're my last stop. You wanna watch the Blood Harvest together?"

The window next to them shattered as a bestial bloodlet dove out. It hissed at them and then skittered off into the night.

"That was supposed to be dinner," he sighed. "Well, I guess my night just freed up a bit."

Malik brushed the shattered glass off the porch steps and sat down. Derak properly tied his robe and sat down next to him. The pair of immortals watched in friendly silence as blood was spilt by the bloodlets, hunting those who had yet to turn.

Derak pulled out a pack of what seemed like cigarettes, but inside were several tiny sticks. He pulled one for himself and then flicked a stick out to Malik. "You want a twig?

"Nah, I ditched the holy sticks a decade ago."

"Com'on. Just a bit of the burning bush, for old times' sake."

Malik defeatedly sighed and took the stick. "Got a light?"

Derak snapped his fingers and the tip of his thumb ignited. Both took long puffs of the twigs, the sputters of golden ash fluttered against the screaming winds as they watched the chaos unfold.

"When did Blood Harvests get so mundane?" Malik asked while he watched the elongated beast that was once Jason tear through the shambling bloodlets like they were paper. It dove into a large one, biting deep into its neck before tearing away violently. Blood ran down its fangs as it howled into the blood moon, declaring its kill in the name of his lord.

"Part of growing up I guess. I still get a kick out of them, but it does get repetitive." Derak said.

Malik nodded as he exhaled another puff of golden smoke. "Seems only yesterday I was running from angry mobs screaming bloody murder."

"Look at you now, selling the pitchforks and torches."

"I wish I was in the mob division, those guys got it easy." Malik straightened up to mimic his salesman posture. "Looking to make your crowd have that fury fulfilled touch? Well, here are some beautiful top of the line sticks that you can set aflame, guaranteed to sear that witch in no time! I'll even throw in this freshly sharpened set of pitchforks at no extra charge!"

Darek chuckled. "I'm glad you found a line of work that lets you use that silver tongue of yours."

Madness and mayhem had fully taken hold of the town. The newly empowered red witch cackled as she sliced her hands through the air, creating waves of red energy that cut violently through the attacking bloodlets. Her bloody tears didn't match the madman's smile as she praised the lord of blood for granting her such power.

"Are you still running with Drac's kid?" Malik asked.

Darek shook his head. "Nah, I grew out of that phase. He was always fighting with his dad and he was just a bad influence. I guess we've both matured a lot, huh?"

The blood that flooded the streets was all moving towards a central point in the town. It began to pool into a circular puddle, reaching a size that perfectly reflected the entire moon on its velvet surface.

"Looks like the boss man is coming to collect. See you on the other side, Derak," Malik said, standing up and crushing the twig under his foot. Derak waved goodbye as he watched the horror show from the comfort of his porch.

Malik stood exactly six feet away from the blood pool. A multitude of bloodlets too damaged to survive shambled into the blood, sinking below what should have been a flat surface. The bloodlets finished their descent. All was still.

A limb shot from the center of the pool, a fusion of three arms with their palms positioned triangular relative to each other. In the center was a single bulging, blood-shot eye. The limb slammed outside the pool, with three other fusion limbs following suit. They slowly lifted the hulking abomination the blood hid below the surface, the biomass of all the bloodlets grafted together into a ball of flesh and bones. Dozens of eyes pointed in every direction with the only indication of which way it was looking being which set of eyes were open.

The creature pulsed like a beating heart, its eyes focusing on Malik. It screeched violently, the wind trying to knock him off his feet, yet he held strong and smiled even stronger.

"Good evening, sir. A fine Blood Harvest you've created, most certainly in the top fifty. You'll be happy to know I've met my quota," Malik said, holding his hand over his heart as a sign of respect.

Gargled screeches and grunts emanated from behind its unblinking eyes.

"Yes, sir, I am aware that I made an unauthorized bundle switch with Heather, but her file was labeled incorrectly. She still met—"

A banshee shriek from the hulking mass cut him off.

"Impressed with my ingenuity? Why, thank you sir. It's always a pleasure to feed your bloody hunger."

A deformed hand extruded itself from within the eldritch horror. Its blood drenched palm was a ceremonial dagger, encrusted with a red jewel shaped like the moon. The metal reflected in Malik's excited eyes.

"A promotion? To the outer plane? Sir, I don't know how to thank you." Malik took the blade and bowed. "I am forever indebted to you for giving my soul purpose, sir."

The creature's eyes on the side towards Malik closed and the eyes on its back opened. Several bloodlets, the beast of Jason, and the red witch Heather were gathered there. The abomination gave out another banshee shriek so loud that all the nearby windows shattered. The bloodlets hissed in unison and Jason howled into the blood moon. Heather cackled, screaming praise to her lord and master. The group marched into the town to continue the Blood Harvest with their god leading them to a new state of being.

Malik smiled, a real smile rather than his fake salesman grin, and put the knife to his neck. He closed his eyes, gave a long sigh, and slit his throat.

A job well done.

A MUNDANE ENCOUNTER WITH A CIVILIZED GOD

SAMUEL MARZIOLI

Arkham Sanitarium lay in the backwoods of Arkham City, a somber mansion that housed the most deranged and chaotic patients the State of Massachusetts had to offer. A hundred inmates wandered its darkened halls and many narrow cells, forgotten by the world, no longer truly men but broken, hollow shells. And out of all of them I was the least insane.

While others were prone to gesticulating with their privates or arguing the finer points of nonsense with things that weren't, I retained a semblance of reason that allowed me to function throughout the day. Enough to dress myself as needed, wipe myself when necessary, and introduce food into the correct orifice for eating. In other words, I was an exemplary patient, a rare jewel, the only star shining in a void of endless night.

Then Bernard Jones arrived and everything changed for good.

Under the direction of Chief Psychiatrist Zadok Green, a small group of inmates gathered Friday evenings in the western common room. There we recounted horrors, those incidences where our past and a supernatural maleficence had collided, resulting in our tenuous grip on reality. It was usually followed by a round of affirmations and then refreshments.

I can still remember the day Bernard first joined us. Through the paned windows, clouds riled up in violent shades of red and gray. Rain pattered the rooftop like the footsteps of phantom children. The wind whispered doom through the cracks of the building's decaying façade, and the light bulbs overhead buzzed and winked, casting jaundiced light over our motley group.

Epson Young began with a long tale of a black beast with tentacles that arose from some dark abyss. He ended with the same words that completed all our stories: "And I was driven to madness."

Henry Volanger continued along the same lines, only his beast was amorphous and his darkness found in the cramped space between the walls of tombs. He too finished with, "And I was driven to madness."

The rest of us took our time, sharing the sources of our own insanity one after another, before it was the new man's turn to speak.

"Hello everyone," said Bernard. "My story begins in a church."

"A church of darkness," said Epson.

"No, it was a small town Methodist church about thirty miles north of here. A charming place, painted white, with stained-glass windows along the walls and a working bell within the steeple."

"With unholy beasts etched into the glass, supplanting the images of saints," said Henry.

"And a bell that tolls only for the dead," I said.

"No, just a regular church."

"Please, no more interruptions," said Dr. Green. "You've all already had your chance to speak and now it's Bernard's turn."

Bernard cleared his throat. "There, on the front-most pew, I was caught in heavy prayer—"

"In some indecipherable language," said Epson.

"Reciting the same foul words first uttered by the Mad Arab, Abdul Alhazred," said Henry.

"No, just a simple prayer. You know the like. Keep me safe from those who persecute me, bless my family, et cetera. An hour passed before a presence descended into the sanctuary, catching me by surprise."

"A shadowed presence?" asked Epson.

"In fact, it was a beam of light, and it seemed to enter me—"

"Rotting your soul, damning you to—"

"Oh, for heaven's sake!" Bernard exclaimed, crossing his arms.

Those of us capable of coherent speech apologized and Bernard continued.

"For a moment, I felt warm inside. At once, my worries fled and an extraordinary sensation of being loved filled me to overflowing. To this day, I can feel it still."

We waited for him to say the words that signified his story's end. We waited, but they didn't come. He only looked around, returning our stares, a self-satisfied smile upon his face.

"And then you were driven to madness," I prompted.

"No, as a matter of fact, I wasn't."

The doom-whispering wind ceased blowing and the rain patter abruptly stopped, as if it were naptime for the phantom children. An awkward silence lingered then. We were so stunned by his words we quite forgot to voice our affirmations. We still had refreshments, but this time nobody enjoyed them.

E arly the following day, we ate breakfast in the dining hall—and the less said about that the better. Suffice to say, the dishwashers earned their keep that morning. Later, those of us who had joined the

Arkham Sanitarium Choir met in the second-floor choir room, over-looking the withered gardens and the fountain of broken angels. We sang for an hour to a frustrated director who shouted endlessly over the group's lack of focus and meager skills.

As usual, I was the only one who realized that few songs, if any, started with, "Ph'nglui mglw'nafh," or ended with, "Cthulhu R'lyeh wgah'-nagl fhtagn." Such is life in Arkham. This, like the success of breakfast, pleased me to no end, so much so that I almost forgot Bernard and his mundane encounter with a civilized god. At least until our group met again next Friday.

Dr. Green opened the discussion in a unique way. Instead of recounting our descent into madness, he wished to know if we'd experienced anything new in the interim. Anything at all, provided it was affecting.

Epson recounted how on the previous night shadow creatures danced within his cell, threatening to eat his heart. Henry spoke of how a splotch of black had appeared on his forehead, and through it he heard voices encouraging him to do harm to himself and other inmates. I related how a dark force had spun my cell and it made me quite dizzy. This again proved to be the sanest response, until that upstart Bernard's turn came.

"I slept eight hours last night, without a single interruption," he said. "All my dreams—"

"Were nightmares of stygian worlds where the souls of humans screamed in torment," said Epson.

"No. They were pleasant, even the one about my poor, departed wife. She appeared to me and—"

"Threatened to drag you down, down, under the Earth to rot beside her," said Henry.

"No, she told me that she loved me and missed me, and we quietly embraced."

"And then malevolent—" I began.

"No," said Bernard.

"Until black—"

"No," said Bernard.

"But then eviscerated—"

"No!" Bernard shouted.

Another long silence and then something peculiar occurred outside, something that in my ten years living in the asylum I had never seen before. A bright light poured through the cracks of clouds, illuminating the grounds in such a way that it glowed with newness and with life. Even the dead flora and fauna left scattered about the cobblestone paths appeared less decayed and moldering. Later, I was reminded that this mysterious phenomenon was called sunshine.

For weeks, many more changes occurred within the asylum, manifesting as order and civility. Self-harm abated, tableware found only mouths and the murder and torture of staff had been reduced to nothing. But the most striking transformation of all was that no one urinated, defecated, or masturbated in the public areas— the latter of which was no less than a bona fide miracle, if a hundred years of asylum history were any indication.

The staff credited their dedication and perseverance. Dr. Green credited his wisdom and insight. But I knew the truth. It was Bernard's doing. Somehow, through his presence, sanity had leaked into Arkham Sanitarium and it was spreading through the patients like a benevolent cure.

No one else seemed to sense the wrong of it. Only I, the sanest of the madmen, realized its far-reaching consequences. I knew something had to be done before it was too late.

. . .

I hid a fork I'd taken from the dining hall out of reach from probing fingers, the less said about that the better. Suffice to say, I wouldn't sit comfortably for weeks. Then I coaxed a member of staff to open my cell after lights out with the promise of a monetary reward upon my ultimate release. An unusual quiet prevailed, as of a hundred men resting comfortably and at peace within their cell bunks—which was precisely what they did. Darkness refused to gather, or stir, or behave in any way foreboding throughout the corridor. Instead, it settled like the meat and vegetables of a healthy, hearty stew.

Nevertheless, I did my part to uphold the status quo. I slinked from doorway to doorway, muttering any curse and babble I'd learned that seemed to fit the occasion. When I found Bernard's cell, I removed the fork from its hiding place. Once the bleeding and pain slackened, I seized the doorknob with unholy strength, intending to wrench it loose.

To my surprise, it turned without much fuss and the door opened with a careless ease. Inside, Bernard lay upon his bunk, a lit candle on his tabletop. He was reading a book with a title that brought to mind happy families whose only concerns were polite clashes with neighbors over perfectly ordinary things. Nothing like the *Necronomicon*, or a grimoire of dark sorcery, as would befit a proper inmate.

He crimped the corner of a page to mark his place before acknowledging my presence. That was the straw that broke me. But instead of the rage I would have expected from these aberrant signs of normalcy, I felt empty, hopeless, smaller than I'd ever been before. The star of the asylum had been snuffed and replaced by a brighter light.

"Why are you even here?" I said, fighting against the pull of tears.

"It was a voluntary commitment," said Bernard.

"But why?"

"Before my experience at the church, I believed myself to be a rational man and a dedicated naturalist. So when that being of light appeared and overwhelmed me, it shook me up and made me question my sanity."

"That's all?" I asked.

"That's all."

Memories of my own experience resurfaced in grisly detail: how the citizens of my hometown had been captured by giant crustaceans, dipped in butter and consumed piece by piece. For the first time, I realized that bearing only a modicum of madness wasn't a badge of honor to be touted. I was to be pitied as much as any other. What we'd suffered had been cruel, nothing less than mental and emotional abuse. And evil was our abuser.

"So... What brings *you* here?" said Bernard.

Though I knew he only meant in his room, at this time of night, I answered, "Bad things hurt me."

I dropped the fork and stumbled forward. He caught me and I wept into his arms. We stayed that way for some time: him speaking encouragement into my ear and me giving in to the comfort of his words. We weren't inmates then, or even victims of a cruel and indifferent cosmos. We were just two men, sharing a platonic, and totally sane, embrace.

A month later, Bernard left the asylum and was promptly crushed at its gates by a passing shoggoth. Such is life in Arkham. By the following year, many of us had been released as well, having reclaimed the fit and form of sanity.

Before I departed, I had the fortune of meeting the new man that was meant to take over my cell. He stared at me with wild eyes, the veins of his sclera red and engorged. As we passed each other in the halls, I leaned over and whispered into his ear, "It gets better, friend. It does get better."

He responded by vomiting all over my sack coat and homburg hat, a vulgar act that I chose to interpret as, "Thank you, sir, you give me hope." As if in confirmation, after I told him to spread the word, he proceeded to vomit upon the orderlies as well. My good work finished, I left that place behind and never looked back.

Throughout the years, I never bothered contacting my old friends and acquaintances from the asylum. Some things are best left to the past. But bits and pieces had made their way to me through rumors and gossip, enough that I had a decent picture of where a few of them had ended up.

Dr. Green, flush with excitement from having cured so many all at once, declared himself a god and was committed to the asylum as a patient.

Epson hunted the shoggoth that had slain Bernard, and then founded a business selling pickled shoggoth parts. The business failed when it was discovered their meat was poisonous. That and all his customers had died.

Henry met a tall and swarthy man named Nyarlathotep—and the less said about that the better. Suffice to say he too is now thoroughly dead.

As for me, I moved to a small town along the coast of Maine. There I learned the trade of crabbing—a token act of vengeance against the slayers of my friends and kin. Some days I sit upon the veranda of the guest house I now call home, smoking my pipe and thinking about Bernard. If not for him, I would still be trapped within the dark, cold and melancholy walls of Arkham Sanitarium. Instead, I live a life of warmth and sunlight, of peace and utter harmony.

Yes, I met a man named Bernard Jones. A simple man. A man of humdrum experiences with the vaguely fantastic. And in the end, it drove me to sanity.

ACKNOWLEDGMENTS

Dragon's Roost Press would like to extend our deepest gratitude to the following:

Thank you to all of the authors who submitted your work. We've said it many times: the best part about putting together an anthology is getting to read amazing stories and then share them with the world.

Thank you to the friends and family of our authors who gave them the time and support needed to allow their creativity to manifest.

Thank you to Don England for another incredible cover. We are deeply indebted.

Thank you to all of you who support the Kickstarter Campaign associated with this publication, including:

Jeanne Anderson

K.G. Anderson

Robert Bee

Laura Blackwell

Sage Burns

Andy Busch

Bert Cieslak

Jake Cole

Lauren Davis

Michael DeLucia

The Devitos

Jason Epstein

Philip Flores

Keegan Frank

Mark R. Froom

Michel Lee Garrett

Peter F. Guenther

Damon Griffin

JenH

Grace Higbie

Conrad M. Hutcheson

J

Nicholas Jay

Susan Jessen

Walter Koegel

Moe Lane

James Frederick Leach

Tim Lonegan

Marc

Mitchell

Mykl Nelson

Ruth Pinto

eric priehs

Brian Rauchfuss

Rondy M. Reeves Jr.

Clifton Royston

Jon Saul

Alex Sgambati

Zachary Shiffman

Rebecca Stern

Matt Trepal

Nathan Waddell

Christopher Wheeling

Laura Wilkinson

and those who wish to remain nameless.

Finally, and most importantly, thank you to Ruth, Tesla, and Titus for your constant love and support.

ABOUT THE AUTHORS

K.G. Anderson ("My Aunts and the Cornwall Horror") is a late-blooming writer of horror and dark fantasy who hails from the foggy coast of Puget Sound. Prior to finding her speculative fiction muse, she reported on politics and crime, reviewed hundreds of mystery novels, and wrote online content on topics including AEDs, Richard Thompson, travertine countertops, and catnip. Her short stories appear in magazines and anthologies including *The Mammoth Book of Jack the Ripper Stories*, *Weirdbook*, and *Galaxy's Edge*, as well as on podcasts such as *The Overcast*. For links to more of her stories, visit http://writerway.com/fiction

Stewart C Baker ("Cut-rate Couples Weekend at the Witch House Inne and Tavern (9 reviews)") is an academic librarian and author of speculative fiction and poetry. His work has appeared or is forthcoming in *Nature*, *Fantasy*, *Lightspeed*, and various other places. Stewart was born in the UK, has lived in South Carolina, Japan, and Southern California and now lives with his family in Oregon within the traditional lands of the Luckiamute Band of Kalapuya in western Oregon—although if anyone asks, he'll usually say he comes from the internet, where you can find him at https://infomancy.net.

Nick Bowen ("Consider the Shoggoth") is a writer and teacher from Boston, MA. He is currently a fiction MFA student at University of St. Thomas and lives in Houston, TX with his wife and their dog, Luna, and cat, Esme. When not writing, he enjoys cartooning, swimming, and bat-watching.

J. Edwin Buja ("Report to the CEG and Executive Board v1.0") has spent his life surrounded by books. He discovered early on that researching and writing hold the key to happiness. Who else would think scanning through decades of microfilm to index an old newspaper would be a dream job?

For almost forty years, he has been married to the most wonderful woman on the planet. Although he lives in a small village somewhere in Canada, his heart and second home reside with his horror family in New England.

His novels include *The King of the Wood* and *The Consort*. He has also had several short stories published.

Jason P. Burnham ("Ten Thousand Years in Space with Santa") loves to spend time with his wife, children, and dog. His work has appeared in *Little Blue Marble*, *Mixtape: 1986* (from The Dread Machine), and *Nature: Futures*, among others. Find him on Twitter at @AndGalen

Meg Candelaria ("New You") writes science fiction and horror. Her work has previously been published in *Daily Science Fiction*, *99 Tiny Terrors*, and other venues. She is reasonably certain that team building exercises are evil.

Nathan Carson ("King C") was raised on a goat farm in the backwoods of Mid-Valley Oregon but has called Portland home since 1997. He is an accomplished music journalist, booking agent, FM radio DJ, founding member of the long-running doom band Witch Mountain, published weird fiction author, and a MOTH StorySlam Champion.

378

Michael Cieslak is a lifetime reader and writer of horror, mystery, and speculative fiction. A native of Detroit, he still lives within 500 yards of the city with his wife and their two dogs Tesla and Titus. The house is covered in Halloween decorations in October and dragons the rest of the year. He is an officer in the Great Lakes Association of Horror Writers and is the editor of the Erie Tales anthologies. His works have appeared in a number of collections including *DOA: Extreme Horror, Dead Science, Vicious Verses and Reanimated Rhymes*, the GLAHW anthologies, *Alter Egos Vol 1, Pan's Guide for New Pioneers* (a supplement for the Pugmire RPG), and the collaborative steampunk novel *Army of Brass*. *Urbane Decay*, a collection of Michael's short fiction, was released in 2018 by Source Point Press. He reviews horror movies for the Dean On Movie Reviews podcast.

Michael is the Editor in Chief of Dragon's Roost Press (thedragonsroost.biz).

Michael's mental excreta (including his personal blog They Napalmed My Shrubbery This Morning) can be found on-line at thedragonsroost.net.

Richard S. Crawford ("How The Old Ones Saved Christmas") lives in an appropriately ancient and drafty house in northern California with his wife and five overly-exuberant cats and far too many foster kittens. Since working as a street performer at the Renaissance Faire, he has risen up the career ladder to a position of web development for a faceless, nameless, indescribable bureaucracy that may or may not be of this world. He has published fiction in *Shimmer, Pseudopod, Sci Fi Lampoon, Andromeda Spaceways Magazine*, and other venues. He is also the editor of *Daikaijuzine* (https://www.daikaijuzine.org). You can find out more than you want to about him at his website, https://www.underpope.com

Mia Dalia ("What are the Odds") is an author, a lifelong reader, and a longtime reviewer of all things fantastic, scary and strange. Her short fiction has been published by *Night Terror Novels, 50 Word Stories, Flash Fiction Magazine, Pyre Magazine, Tales from the Moonlit Path,*

Sunbury Press, and *HellBound Press*. Her fiction will be featured in the upcoming anthologies by Black Ink Fiction, *Mystery Magazine, Unsettling Reads, WMB anthology of Lunar Horror*, Phobica Books, and *DraculaBeyondStoker Magazine*. Her debut novel, *Estate Sale*, will be out in March 2023 from Genius Press.

Official author website: https://daliaverse.wixsite.com/author

Rick Danforth ("What Horror") is a speculative fiction author from Yorkshire, England, where he works as a Systems Architect to fund his writing habit. When not working valiantly in the plot mines, he can be found doing Brazilian Jiu-Jitsu, a type of involuntary yoga with uncomfortable pyjamas.

He has had several short stories published in a variety of venues including *Hexagon, Etherea*, and *Translunar Traveller's Lounge*.

Most weeks he claims he will soon return to finish his debut novel, but so far these claims have proved unfounded.

Elizabeth Davis ("Wanted Ad") is a second generation writer living in Dayton, Ohio. They live there with their spouse and two cats - neither of which have been lost to ravenous corn mazes or sleeping serpent gods. They can be found at deadfishbooks.com when they aren't busy creating beautiful nightmares and bizarre adventures. Their work can be found at *After the Goldrush, Woman Unbecoming*, and *Troublemarkers Firestarter Vol 2*.

James Dorr ("The Reading")'s *The Tears of Isis* was a 2013 Bram Stoker Award® finalist for Fiction Collection, with his latest book, *Tombs: A Chronicle of Latter-Day Times of Earth*, a novel-in-stories from Elder Signs Press. A short fiction writer and sometime poet, he currently harbors a Goth cat named Triana, and counts among his major influences Ray Bradbury, Edgar Allan Poe, Allen Ginsberg, and Bertolt Brecht. For more information, Dorr invites readers to check out his blog at http://jamesdorrwriter.wordpress.com

Jonathan Louis Duckworth ("In the Grip of Cosmic Concupiscence") is a completely normal, entirely human person with the right number of heads and everything. He received his MFA from Florida International University. His speculative fiction work appears in *Pseudopod, Beneath Ceaseless Skies, Southwest Review, Flash Fiction Online,* and elsewhere. He is a PhD student at University of North Texas where he serves as the interviews editor at American Literary Review, and he is also an active HWA member.

Donald England (Cover Art) is a Michigan based artist specializing in creepy and macabre art for the last 25 years. He is a product of late-night eighties television and comic book shops. Over the years, his work has been seen in a number of magazines like *Horror Hound* and *Liquid Cheese,* as well as cover art for *Evilspeak.* His art has been featured in *Late Night Snack, The Thing and Stranger Things* art books, *Deadworld* and on the covers of *Erie Tales, A Fist full of Dead Folk,* and *Night Pieces.* He is also the co-creator of Lethal Lita and Plague of Man.

Ron Fein ("Arkham Board of Health Feedback on Miskatonic University's Draft Plan for a Safe Campus Reopening") is a Boston-area public interest lawyer, writer, and activist with one dog (accounted for) and one cat (missing). His speculative fiction appears in magazines such as *Daily Science Fiction* and *Sci Phi Journal,* and anthologies such as *Phantasmical Contraptions and More Errors* and *Nom Nom: Hallowe'en Dark Drabbles*; his literary fiction appears in *The Bookends Review* and *Redivider*; and his humor appears in *McSweeney's Internet Tendency, Slackjaw,* and *What Would Henry Do? Essays for the 21st Century (Vol. II).* Find him at ronfein.com and on Twitter @ronfein.

When he's not chronicling the struggles of the average eldritch abomination in late-stage capitalist society, **Lucas Franki** ("Eldritch Abominations in Modern- Day America: A Documentary")

works as an associate editor for *MDedge News* and lives in Frederick, Maryland. He has a BA in English from Penn State University and is an Eagle Scout. He has had one short story published: "Just Before the Fall," which appeared in the Fall 2018 issue of *The Helix*.

Shaenon K. Garrity ("The Lady with the Look") is a cartoonist and writer best known for *Narbonic, Skin Horse* (cowritten with Jeffrey C. Wells), and *The Dire Days of Willowweep Manor* (with art by Christopher Baldwin). Her upcoming graphic novels include *Steam*, with art by Emily Holden, and her next Willowweep Manor book with Baldwin, *The Nefarious Nights of Willowweep Manor*. She lives in Berkeley with a cat, a man and a boy.

Sarah Hans ("Lovecraft It or List It") is an award-winning writer, editor, and teacher whose stories have appeared in more than 40 publications, including *Apex Magazine* and *Pseudopod*. Her debut horror novel, *Entomophobia*, was published in January 2022 by Omnium Gatherum, and Dragon's Roost Press previously published her short story collection *Dead Girls Don't Love* and the novella *An Ideal Vessel*. You can also find her on Twitter, Instagram, and TikTok under the handle @witchwithabook, where she loves to talk about books. She lives in Ohio with her partner, the best step-kids in the galaxy, and a small circus of pets.

J.D. Harlock ("Dear Xutuix?!") is a Syrian Lebanese Palestinian writer and editor based in Beirut. In addition to his posts at *Wasifiri*, as an editor-at-large, and at *Solarpunk Magazine*, as a poetry editor, his writing has been featured in *Strange Horizons*, *Star*Line*, and the SFWA Blog. You can always find him on Twitter and Instagram posting updates on his latest projects.

Henry Herz's ("Not On My Watch") speculative fiction short stories include "Out, Damned Virus" (*Daily Science Fiction*), "Bar Mitzvah on Planet Latke" (*Coming of Age*, Albert Whitman & Co.), "The Magic Backpack" (*Metastellar*), "Unbreakable" (*Musing of the Muses*, Brigid's Gate Press), "A Vampire, an Astrophysicist, and a Mother Superior Walk Into a Basilica" (*Three Time Travelers Walk Into...*, Fantastic Books), "The Case of the Murderous Alien" (*Spirit Machine*, Air and

Nothingness Press), "The Ghosts of Enerhodar" (*Literally Dead*, Alienhead Press), "Maria & Maslow" (*Highlights for Children*), and "A Proper Party" (*Ladybug Magazine*). He's edited five anthologies and written twelve picture books, including the critically acclaimed *I Am Smoke*. www.henryherz.com

Larry Hinkle ("The World Ends at the World's End") is an advertising copywriter living with his wife and two doggos in Rockville, Maryland. When he's not writing stories that scare people into peeing their pants, he writes ads that scare people into buying adult diapers so they're not caught peeing their pants.

His work has appeared on the *NoSleep Podcast*, *Deep Magic*, *Dark Recesses Magazine*, and *Another Dimension Anthology* (winner of the 2017 Serling Award from the Rod Serling Memorial Foundation), among others. He's an active member of the HWA, a survivor of the Borderlands Writers Boot Camp, a graduate of the HWA's Fright Club workshop, and has completed the HWA mentorship program. See more at writtenbylarry.com.

Liam Hogan ("Bokrug and the Boy") is an award-winning short story writer, with stories in *Best of British Science Fiction* and in *Best of British Fantasy* (NewCon Press). He's been published by *Analog*, Daily Science Fiction, and Flame Tree Press, among others. He helps host Liars' League London, volunteers at the creative writing charity Ministry of Stories, and lives and avoids work in London. More details at http://happyendingnotguaranteed.blogspot.co.uk

Nicholas Jay ("A Series of Noise Complaints, Filed by Yog-Sothoth, Outer God, Against His Neighbor") is a conservation-minded urban planner living in Atlanta, Georgia. He enjoys his time most with either pen, violin, or map in hand — sometimes all three at once.

Brandon Ketchum ("Bhegna Cthellha's Guidelines on Pandemic Etiquette Whilst Dining Out") is a speculative fiction writer from Pittsburgh, PA who enjoys putting a weird spin or strange vibe into every story, dark or light. He is a member of SFWA and the Horror

Writers Association, and his work has been published with Air & Nothingness Press, *Perihelion*, *Mad Scientist Journal*, and many other publications, including the short story collection *Legio Damnati*.

Sharon Diane King ("Over the Side") is an Associate at UCLA's Center for Medieval and Renaissance Studies and a character actor for film and TV (*Zombie Strippers*, *Lady Gaga's Telephone*, *My Haunted House*). Her fiction has appeared in numerous publications, including *Dark Recesses Press Magazine*, *Galaxy's Edge Magazine*, *Kaleidotrope*, *On the Premises*, *All Due Respect*, and several anthologies by both Third Flatiron Press and Dragon's Roost Press. For over 30 years, her theatrical troupe Les Enfans Sans Abri has performed short medieval and Renaissance comedies in her original translations in the U.S. and Europe. She and her husband help run the Reptile and Amphibian Rescue Network in southern California and are well guarded by several house dragons.

John Kiste ("The Chateau over Innsmouth") is a horror writer who was previously the president of the Stark County Convention & Visitors' Bureau and a board member of the Massillon Museum. He is a double-lung transplantee and organ donation ambassador, a McKinley Museum planetarian and an Edgar Allan Poe impersonator who has been published in Flame Tree Press's *Terrifying Ghosts*, Third Flatiron, Indomitable Ink, Madhouse Books, Dark Recesses Press, The Dark Sire, Hiraeth Books, A Shadow of Autumn, and dozens of other anthologies, magazines, and e-zines. He is an active member of the Horror Writers Association and recently won the Dark Sire Award for Best Fiction. You can find him at johnkiste.wordpress.com.

Kyer Kneifel ("Blood Moon Bargains") is a writer, engineer, and full-time nerd. He enjoys fantasy, sci-fi and everything in between. He has a love for RPGs such as Dungeons & Dragons and is a huge video game player, with experience in just about every type of game there is. He also has a knack for quoting almost every movie or show he's seen. With all those factors combined, his writing has a wide range of genres it dips into and he always enjoys a good writing challenge.

Baker of brownies and tormenter of characters, **Alice Loweecey** ("The King in Gray") celebrates the day she jumped the wall with as much enthusiasm as her birthday. She grew up watching Hammer horror films and Scooby-Doo mysteries, which explains a whole lot. When she's not writing humorous mysteries or nightmare-inducing horror fiction, she can be found growing vegetables in her garden and water lilies in her koi pond.

Samuel Marzioli ("A Mundane Encounter With a Civilized God") is a Filipino-American author of mostly dark fiction. His work has appeared in numerous publications and podcasts, including the *Best of Apex Magazine*, Flame Tree's *Asian Ghost Short Stories*, *Dread Machine*, and *LeVar Burton Reads*. His chapbook "Symphony of the Night" was published by Aurelia Leo and his collection *Hollow Skulls and Other Stories* was published by JournalStone Publishing. You can find his infrequently updated writing blog at marzioli.blogspot.com.

Lena Ng ("Lovecraft vs. The Big-Mouth Musky of Lake Miskatonic") shambles around Toronto, Ontario, and is a zombie member of the Horror Writers Association. She has curiosities published in eighty tomes including *Amazing Stories* and Flame Tree's *Asian Ghost Stories* and *Weird Horror Stories*. Her stories have been performed for podcasts such as *Gallery of Curiosities*, *Utopia Science Fiction*, *Love Letters to Poe*, and *Horrifying Tales of Wonder*. *Under an Autumn Moon* is her short story collection.

John Possidente ("Tarts, Pie, Tea") resides in an old house on a hill, where it's frequently dark and sometimes cold. From it one can gaze into the vastness of the indifferent universe. Other things live there—some with sharp teeth and claws, some with excess legs and too many eyes. Like most writers, he's soft on the outside, unpleasantly crunchy in the middle, and gruesomely, squishy wet in between. He understands a little about odd geometries and has been known to intentionally seek out the company of insects.

John's stories have appeared in *Interzone* (both print and digital),

F&SF, and the *Lovecraft Mythos: New and Classic* anthology (Flame Tree Press).

Eric Raglin (he/him) ("In the Grip of Cosmic Concupiscence") is a Nebraskan speculative fiction writer and the owner of Cursed Morsels Press. His debut short story collection is *Nightmare Yearnings*, and his second collection, *Extinction Hymns*, is due out December 2022. He is the editor of *Shredded: A Sports and Fitness Body Horror Anthology* and *ANTIFA Splatterpunk*. Find him at ericraglin.com or on Twitter @ericraglin1992.

Born in England, **Fraser Sherman** ("The Happiest Place on Earth") spent most of his life in Northwest Florida. He'd be there still if he hadn't moved to Durham NC to marry his dream woman (11 years together!). Fraser has had two dozen short stories published plus six film books, most recently *The Aliens Are Here*, about extraterrestrial visitors in film and TV. In 2022 he self-published the steampunk novel *Questionable Minds and Undead Sexist Cliches*, a book about the stupidity of misogynist arguments. He works while snuggling two adorable dogs.

Justin Short ("He Listens") lives in Kansas. His fiction has previously appeared in places like *Recognize Fascism*, *The NoSleep Podcast*, and *Jerry Jazz Musician*. Visit him online at www.justin-short.com.

Phillip T. Stephens ("Family Values") attended the Michigan State writers' workshop. He taught writing and design at Austin Community College for 20 years. Phillip's writing and art appear in anthologies, literary publications, and peer-reviewed academic journals. His novels *Doublemint Gumshoe* and *Seeing Jesus* won multiple awards for independent fiction. He and Carol live in Oak Hill, Texas where they built a habitat in the shade of their oaks to house foster cats for austinsiameserescue.org. They found new homes for more than three hundred abandoned pets. You can find more of his work at https://medium.com/wind-eggs.

Dawn Vogel ("Hashtag TPE") has written for children, teens, and adults, spanning genres, places, and time periods. More than 100 of her stories and poems have been published by small and large presses. Her specialties include young protagonists, siblings who bicker but love each other in the end, and things in the water that want you dead. She is a member of Broad Universe, SFWA, and Codex Writers. She lives in Seattle with her awesome husband (and fellow author), Jeremy Zimmerman, and their herd of cats. Visit her at historythatnever-was.com or on Twitter @historyneverwas.

Nathan Waddell ("Here There Be (Hardly Any) Monsters") is a writer from Edmonton, Alberta. He spent many years running heavy equipment in a coal mine and is still mad he never unearthed a single dinosaur bone or awakened any Great Old Ones. His writing has appeared on a beer can and a postcard, and several anthologies, including *The Librarian* from Air and Nothingness Press. He also writes the chapbook series The Ursus Verses which is mostly about bears, monsters, bearmonsters and monster bears. Find him online at homiebear.blogspot.com and on Twitter @NathanWaddell1

B. Zelkovich ("Bel Biv Derailed") writes Speculative Fiction, anything from dragon hunting and space whales to demon-dealing and ghost tales. She likes to explore human emotions in very inhuman situations. When she isn't escaping through her imagination, she escapes into the wonders of the Pacific Northwest with her spouse and their four-legged son, Simon.

Her fiction is forthcoming in the anthology *Life Beyond Us* (Laksa Media, Fall 2022). Until then, find her stories in *Corvid Queen, Luna Station Quarterly*, and *City. River. Tree.*, or online at bzelkovich.com.

DRAGON'S ROOST PRESS

Dragon's Roost Press is the fever dream brainchild of dark speculative fiction author Michael Cieslak. Since 2014, their goal has been to find the best speculative fiction authors and share their work with the public. For more information about Dragon's Roost Press and their publications, please visit:

http://www.thedragonsroost.biz

LAST DAY DOG RESCUE

Last Day is more than just a name, it's the situation all the dogs were faced with. Because of LDDR these wonderful dogs get another chance at life. All dogs coming into their rescue were saved from high-kill animal shelters or being sold for research.

A Little About LDDR:

Last Day Dog Rescue is an ALL volunteer based organization. They do not have a physical location; all of their dogs are placed in the care of foster homes until they are adopted.

The group focuses on rescuing dogs from the "Urgent" list in shelters and pounds across lower Michigan and parts of Ohio with an emphasis on those shelters who euthanize by gas or those shelters who sell the dogs in their care to research labs where they are used for barbaric and most times painful testing and experiments. They hold a special place in their hearts for the big and black dogs, even 'ugly' dogs (whom they don't find ugly at all!) and the special senior dogs. These dogs most often get overlooked and passed up in shelters and pounds everywhere for puppies, small breeds, and the "prettier," lighter colored dogs.

Dogs found in shelters are there for many reasons; some are owner surrenders, strays, cruelty or abuse cases, and some dogs are found abandoned, left to fend for themselves in vacant homes, fields, ditches, and some have even been tied out in the woods and left to starve. Last Day Dog Rescue does not discriminate and feels that each of these dogs, no matter their size, age, color, or the reason they are there, deserve a second chance at life...they help all those they can.

Donations via check and money orders:

Last Day Dog Rescue

P.O. Box 51935

Livonia, MI 48151-5935

Donations also accepted via PayPal:

http://www.lastdaydogrescue.org/info/